Iain McDowall was born in Scotland but now lives in the English Midlands where he sets his crime novels. *Envy the Dead* is the sixth book in his highly regarded Crowby series. He has also written *A Study in Death, Making A Killing, Perfectly Dead, Killing For England* and *Cut Her Dead*.

ENVY THE DEAD

The 1980s. The Falklands War. The IRA. The Miners' Strike. Cruise Missiles. Anti-Nuclear Protests ... And in the thick of it all, beautiful Claire Oldham, the revolution's poster girl — until the day she turns up brutally murdered. A young, troubled drifter, Martin Grove, is swiftly prosecuted and jailed for the crime. Fast forward twenty years: Martin Grove walks free, cleared by advances in forensic science, seemingly the victim of a miscarriage of justice. Fast forward a few more years, come right up to date: Martin Grove is shot dead in his reclusive home, 'executed' at close range. DCI Jacobson and his team are on the case. But which case? And do the answers lie in the dangerous past or in the even more terrifying present?

Books by Iain McDowall
Published by The House of Ulverscroft:

A STUDY IN DEATH
PERFECTLY DEAD
MAKING A KILLING
KILLING FOR ENGLAND
CUT HER DEAD

IAIN McDOWALL

ENVY THE DEAD

Complete and Unabridged

CHARNWOOD
Leicester

First published in Great Britain in 2009 by
Piatkus
An imprint of Little, Brown Book Group, London

First Charnwood Edition
published 2010
by arrangement with Little, Brown Book Group
An Hachette UK Company, London

British Library CIP Data

McDowall, Iain.
   Envy the dead.
   1. Jacobson, Frank (Fictitious character)- -Fiction.
   2. Kerr, Ian (Fictitious character)- -Fiction.
   3. Police- -England- -Fiction. 4. Ex-convicts- -Death
   - -Fiction. 5. Detective and mystery stories.
   6. Large type books.
   I. Title
   823.9′2–dc22

   ISBN 978–1–84782–960–3

Published by
F. A. Thorpe (Publishing)
Anstey, Leicestershire

Set by Words & Graphics Ltd.
Anstey, Leicestershire
Printed and bound in Great Britain by
T. J. International Ltd., Padstow, Cornwall

This book is printed on acid-free paper

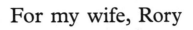

For my wife, Rory

The survivors will envy the dead
— CND banner,
Hyde Park, London,
Saturday 22nd October, 1983

Tuesday

1

At first glance, there was nothing remarkable about the corpse. An execution-style killing: a single bullet to the head, fired at close range. Martin Grove had fallen where he'd stood, had crumpled face down into a dead heap on the floor, dead blood seeping onto the Italian floor tiles from the two holes in his skull. It was only when the pathologist, Robinson, turned up and took a closer look that Grove's bodily remains revealed their Unique Selling Point: a good half of his tongue had been cut out of his head, had maybe even been ripped out. Ten minutes later, two of the Scene of Crime officers found the severed slice, plumper than you'd expect, dumped into one of the rubbish bins at the rear of the property: still pink, still bloody — and thrust inside an otherwise-empty Sainsbury's orange carrier bag.

'Before or after?' Jacobson was asking now.

Jacobson, Kerr and Robinson were standing in the lounge, careful not to stray from the stepping boards. The killing had taken place in the kitchen and the SOCOs were concentrating their initial detailed efforts there, would deal with the rest of the house later, moving out methodically from ground zero.

Robinson scratched the side of his nose with the pen he'd been using to scribble notes onto his clipboard before he answered.

'Impossible to say right now, Frank. Maybe at the post mortem. Let's hope for his sake it was after.'

'Amen to that, old son,' Jacobson replied.

Robinson was evidently ready to sign-off from the crime scene. Jacobson and Kerr followed him out through the hall towards the porch and then out into the front garden. It was a Tuesday morning in June. It was already warm even this early in the day, the sky global-warming blue and nearly cloudless. Robinson rapidly discarded his protective clothing, ditching the slip-on shoe covers before pulling off the body suit, trouser legs first. He'd done everything his job required him to do in situ. The next time he'd see the body would be later in the day up on the mortuary slab. He promised to phone Jacobson — or to get someone to phone him anyway — as soon as he'd fixed up a definite time slot for the PM.

Jacobson waved his thanks, watched him head off towards his car, came as close as Jacobson ever did to smiling. The idea of Robinson delegating a mundane task to a minion was still a novelty. So was the boy wonder's new transport. Robinson had finally ditched his battered, student-image Volkswagen beetle for some kind of gleaming, powerful-looking Saab. He'd pretty much ditched his keen, awkward postgrad manner too — in favour of a suit and a tie and an air of calm, professional competence. But at least his tall, bookish stoop had survived the makeover. So had his willingness to talk to CID in plain, helpful English — in total, heretical

4

contrast to Merchant, his deceased predecessor (and former boss). Merchant's smug, supercilious bones must have been rotting for more than two years by now, Jacobson thought. Late and very unlamented.

There were still half a dozen vehicles drawn up in an unneat line down the tarmac driveway after Robinson drove off. Marked and unmarked. SOCOs, uniformeds, the first few CID. Jacobson had requisitioned the MIU — the mobile incident unit — as soon as he'd arrived but he'd been told it would take the best part of an hour to reach him. There were the roadworks on the Wynarth Road for one thing, the control room had pleaded, and after Wynarth, the route would be along twisting B roads all the way. He checked his watch again. Eight twenty-two AM. Which meant at least another thirty minutes before the MIU showed up, if the control room estimate was remotely accurate, and another ten minutes after that before there was any possibility of getting the drinks dispenser properly operational. He was parched for coffee. Even coffee that came in a Klix plastic cup. Not to mention a cigarette. But while coffee was possible, if infuriatingly delayed, cigarettes, in theory at least, were irrevocably a thing of his past. Two months now they'd lasted out, himself and Alison Taylor, both pledged not to backslide. Alison was using patches but Jacobson had hated them from day one, couldn't get on with them. Smoking was a psychological habit more than a physical addiction, he'd always thought anyway. Since day two, he'd just gone total cold turkey, had just said no and had just carried on saying it. As a very poor substitute for the burnt-sweet taste his mind could still conjure in every detail, he stuck the edge of his right thumbnail in the corner of his mouth and ran it against his bottom teeth for an idle second or two.

The house was modest for its location. A bungalow in all but name, dismally modern. But isolated, secluded, set in its own acre of land. The local legend, down at the Crowcross Arms, was that you could see Grove most days, and at all hours, wandering the area's fields and hedgerows, daypack on his back, trousers tucked into walking socks, walking socks tucked into walking boots. And always on his own, despite the woman. No one ever saw the woman, the locals claimed, they just knew she was there. All this data had come from the area plod, sex-bomb Helen Dawson. Dawson shared the North of Wynarth rural beat with one other patrol officer, alternating day shifts and back shifts between themselves. Both of them had been tasked with keeping a discreet eye on Grove's place, though the job was well down their strategic list of priorities. Both of them claimed that they had. Dawson maintained that as a matter of fact she'd driven past the road-end last night, elevenish or thereabouts. The porch light had been on and there'd been lights on in the lounge as well; everything had looked normal.

Jacobson hadn't pressed her about it yet, there would be time enough for that later. His immediate priority was to talk to the woman. Before someone had air-vented his cranium,

Grove had erected a cream-coloured gazebo in a shady corner of the front garden, presumably in response to the spell of hot weather. Inside there was a big green garden table and a set of matching garden chairs. The woman was still sitting in there, had been sitting in there all the time that Jacobson and Kerr had been gawping at Grove's bullet-holed head. PC Dawson was with her, instructed to keep her out of the house, trying to keep her calm. Not an easy job when, if she was telling the truth, she'd come home to find bits of her lover's brain dribbling down the front of the tumble dryer. The woman was the only one on the premises with a drink — brandy from the bottle that Dawson always carried, not exactly officially, as part of the emergency kit in the boot of her patrol car.

Jacobson recalled Helen Dawson from last year, the video gang case. And not just, not even mainly, because of how she looked. She'd impressed him then as capable, resourceful. In any case, at Jacobson's instigation, Kerr had discreetly slipped his new mobile phone into Dawson's hand when Jacobson had assigned her to babysitting duties. Switched off for calls but switched on to the voice recorder. If the woman inadvertently told Dawson anything worth knowing, Kerr's phone would record every word for later illicit, non-ethical playback. The phone would record the rest too. Every cry and moan. Every muted little sob.

2

Jacobson's own mobile rang as they were crossing the lawn towards the gazebo: DC Mick Hume back at the Divisional building. The MIU, when it got there, would mainly function for the benefit of Jim Webster's Scene of Crime team. Somewhere safe for them to store and protect potential scientific evidence during the crucial first hours of the investigation. As far as CID was concerned, the nerve centre of the operation would be the dedicated incident room back at the Divi. Hume was phoning from there right now, already had Ray Williams and Emma Smith with him for company, plus a handful of the non-specialist DCs that Jacobson had drafted in from the duty shift roster to make up the numbers and to do the idiot work. Hume had fast-searched Crowby's localised intelligence database as well as the PNC, was reading out the small print in relation to Martin Grove. His exact date of birth, his exact prison release date, half-a-dozen other official markers and data items. The surprise, although not a total surprise, was the woman. Present not just as a known associate of Grove but in her own right and with her own PNC reference number. Minor convictions for petty Class A dealing, ditto for soliciting. Nothing very recent though. And nothing doing at all in the last three years.

Jacobson nodded to himself as he listened.

8

Maureen Bright (at least she was who she'd said she was — probably). No middle name, unmarried, no kids, thirty-two on her last birthday. Three years: Jacobson's mind homed in on that one detail. Three years was how long she'd told Dawson earlier that she'd known Grove, how long she'd said she'd been living out this way with him.

'All the systems up and running then?' he asked Hume after a moment.

'Near enough, guv. One of the computer's giving problems, but it's been logged with technical support. Otherwise we're A-OK.'

Hume added that he was ready to head over to the crime scene just as soon as Jacobson wanted him there. DC Williams also. Emma Smith had volunteered to stay on at the incident room, according to Hume, until all the inquiry systems were fully operational and officially tick-boxed. Volunteered or outnumbered, Jacobson wondered, but let it go. It was pretty much the division of labour he was in favour of anyway. Smith was the smartest of the threesome, would do the best job back at base. Meantime, Hume and Williams could concentrate on organising the initial door-to-door effort. Jacobson had decided on a two-mile radius for starters, everything from here back to Crowcross village.

'OK,' Jacobson told him, ending the call, 'but let Ray drive.'

Hume was old school. A solid, reliable detective. But his *Boy's Own* driving style probably suited the Lisbon to Dakar rally better than it suited the narrow back roads north of Wynarth.

9

Maureen Bright barely seemed to notice Jacobson and Kerr pulling up a chair each on the opposite side of the table and sitting down. Helen Dawson refilled her brandy glass for her. Brandy Starbuck's paper cup to be more exact and precise. Everything inside the house was out of bounds until the Scene of Crime team had completed their first sweep, glassware included. Dawson had found the takeaway cup in her glove compartment, had rinsed it out as best she could with the remains of a similarly located bottle of Evian water.

'Can I see him? I need to see him again,' Grove's woman said eventually, looking at Jacobson but seeming to speak to no one in particular.

She was wearing a loose, blue jog suit that had come from one of the Scene of Crime vans. She'd embraced him, cuddled him, held him close to her — all her words — before she'd accepted he was dead, before she'd made her garbled, semi-hysterical 999 call. The clothes she'd been wearing at the time, blood-stained even to the naked eye, had been bagged and sealed for subsequent forensic analysis.

'Sorry, Maureen,' Jacobson answered. 'There's a lot to do here before that can happen. But there'll be all the time you need later. As much time as you want.'

Always go for the first name, he was thinking, use it just as soon as you can.

She bit her lip, slugged some brandy, coughed. She was a definite looker, Jacobson noticed — or would be on a day when the murder squad

10

hadn't just called by.

'Maureen still doesn't want a doctor near her,' Dawson commented, giving Jacobson a cue, another approach, another possible way *in*.

'You're sure about that, Maureen?' he asked her. 'Something like this — it's a shock all right. Maybe a sedative would — '

She cut him off, sharp-minded despite her wet, blank eyes.

'I can't touch sedatives. I shouldn't really touch this,' she said, indicating the brandy. She had a Dunhill on the go in her other hand. Jacobson watched the tip flare up fire-red when she took a puff, sniffed the air around the table enviously.

He reminded her of the main points of her earlier story — or at least the version of it he'd gleaned from Dawson, who'd been the first police officer to reach the scene. He mentioned that he'd need a formal version — a statement — as soon as she felt able to give it. Bright had told Dawson she'd driven onto the property just before seven AM. She hadn't noticed anything odd or unusual until she'd walked into the kitchen and found Grove's body on the floor. She'd had to use her key at the front door, just the way she always did. She hadn't seen any kind of sign of any kind of break-in. She'd freaked-out, panicked, when she'd found him. She wasn't sure how long for. Then she'd come to, dialled 999.

'I know what a statement is. I'm not from Mars,' she said when he was done. 'Sounds like you know it all already. Why don't you write it up

11

yourself, get it just the way you want it?'

A rhetorical slap in the face, Jacobson thought. Just so they'd know that she was capable of attack, that they shouldn't assume they could kick her because she was down.

'I'm sorry, Maureen,' he said, 'that's not how it works now. It's not how *I've* ever worked, if you're interested to know.'

She shook her head and looked at him. Really looked at him. Two thirds contempt, one third total, absolute disbelief.

He'd got the first name in again anyway, he thought, even a corporate apology. He took out his notebook. Far too early to have anything in there yet — but he wanted to give her the impression he was reading from it all the same.

'You weren't here overnight, you've said? You were visiting your friend in Crowby. Jane Ebdon.'

Her eyes were blank again, staring down at the rim of the paper cup.

'Why was that, Maureen? Are you often away from here nights?' Jacobson persisted.

She'd told Dawson that her friend, Jane, wasn't too well 'in herself', she'd had a few problems recently and she'd just wanted to help, 'to be there for her'.

Another slug of brandy. Then:

'I've been spending the night at Jane's a few times recently. She's been having a rough time of it one way and another.'

'What kind of ways?'

'Is that relevant? Marty's dead and you want to know about Jane, who's never even met him.'

He watched her take another draw. This time, disappointingly, she held the cigarette away from the table afterwards, keeping the smoke trails at a distance. It was the way most smokers smoked in company nowadays, adapting to survive in a hostile world.

'We need to check your story, Maureen. You know that. Same way we need to check the clothes you were wearing. So we can — '

'*Eliminate me*. Yeah, yeah. That's hardly a new line either.'

Jacobson didn't reply, just waited.

'Breast cancer, *all right*?' she said finally. 'She's been told she might have fucking breast cancer. That's why I've been stopping over there. Doing what I can. Mainly just sitting up late, mainly just *listening*.'

'You left to come back here early though?'

'I can't be in two places at once, can I? Marty needs me too. He likes me around here in the mornings, doesn't like to wake up on his own. He always says — '

The use of the wrong tense stuck in her throat and she fell silent. She put down the drink and the cigarette and hugged herself violently against some cold, unseen Arctic gale. Jacobson decided just to leave her be for the moment. He needed to know everything she knew about what had happened here this morning, needed to know everything she knew about Martin Grove. But you couldn't push grief any more than you could push a river — and he'd already mentally excluded her as a serious candidate for pulling the trigger. Jacobson's instant snap was that she

13

was probably the last person in the world who'd want to see Grove dead. Grove had brought her here to live with him, had got her out of her no-life life. That was why, paradoxically, he was insisting on a thorough forensic examination of her clothes and why he'd already dispatched half-a-dozen uniforms on a weapons search of Grove's acre of the English countryside. He expected the outcome would be futile but this was a case that came with serious baggage: police incompetence, prosecution errors — and worse. Jacobson intended to dot every *i* and cross every *t*, had no intention of contributing a new chapter of his own to the sorry history of Martin Grove's encounters with British justice. Plus, in the corner of his eye, he could see a figure that could very well be Jim Webster, the Crime Scene Manager, emerging at last from the front porch onto the lawn. Which might mean that Jacobson and Kerr could finally take *chez* Grove's grand interior tour.

Or a sneak preview at any rate. Webster's team still needed several hours, Webster told them, to complete their initial work and before Jacobson and Kerr could conduct the kind of hard-core snooping they were known to favour — pulling out drawers, pulling up carpets, even lifting floorboards and de-constructing cavity walls if they were really in the mood. Instead Webster led them carefully to the one place he suggested (uncharacteristically) that they might want to see straightaway: Grove's third bedroom, the one he appeared to have kitted out as a study. The room was small and standing-space was limited. The three of them squeezed in where they could. Three of the four walls were ceiling-high in book shelves, most of them crammed, some of them overflowing. A couple of shelves near the door held the books which might have been there for Grove's everyday personal interest. Travel guides, some books on philosophy and (mainly) Eastern religion, a few crime novels, a well-thumbed collection (in the old, superior Constance Garnett translations, Jacobson noticed) of Dostoevsky, some other European classics (nothing English). But that section apart, the volumes on the shelves emanated Grove's focus on an all-consuming *task*. Sociology, criminology, legal textbooks, and all the standard works on miscarriages of justice: the Birmingham Six, the Guildford Four, Stephen Downing, Winston Silcott, a score of less well-known cases that Jacobson was not as familiar with. There were two big, grey filing cabinets near the desk, which, surprisingly, Webster allowed them to peer into. Correspondence and legal papers relating to Grove's case made up about seventy per cent of the well-ordered, impeccably catalogued contents. The other thirty per cent were press cuttings: Grove's arrest, his trial, his lengthy series of appeals. There were yellowing, fading pages that had obviously been snipped out on the day of publication plus recent photocopies and facsimiles which were still pristinely white and readily legible. Everything to do with the case had been organised chronologically — all two and a half decades' worth of it.

Grove had been using a Georgian-style walnut table as a work desk. Repro probably but skilfully done. The whole interior likewise, from what they'd seen so far. Despite the uninspiring exterior, there was nothing inside the house to seriously offend a *Homes and Gardens* reader. Jacobson had started to notice that kind of thing again recently — interior design, what went with what — things he'd barely considered in the post-Janice, pre-Alison decade. Admittedly, the modern executive chair, in deepest black leather, didn't really match the table — but it had the latest orthopaedic design, might have been chosen for over-riding health and posture reasons. The chair and the table were positioned side-on to a window which looked out over the rear lawn towards the well-tended vegetable garden. There were a couple of framed pictures placed on the table — one of them was Maureen Bright, the other one was of a sullen, elderly grey-haired woman. Jacobson's best guess: Grove's mother, Evelyn, who'd died of a heart attack the day after Grove's third unsuccessful appeal to the High Court.

'Fascinating, Jim,' Kerr was saying, 'but what's so special about this room in particular? Looks like he's used it as his study. So what?'

The three of them were still wearing their protective suits and still hooded up. But at least in here, well away from the carnage in the kitchen, they were able to work without face and mouth protection.

Webster looked pleased with himself, looked set to utter a patronising reply, but Jacobson had already grasped the point, and beat him to it. He rested one hand on Kerr's shoulder, pointed his other hand at the surface of the table, intoned a list of what they could see.

'Pictures of his mother and his girlfriend. A meditating Buddha. A desk lamp. An Epson printer. A couple of *unconnected* power cables — '

Kerr nearly blushed: 'Oh right. I see what you mean.'

'I assume you've had a good look in the other rooms, Jim?' Jacobson asked.

'Not exhaustively, not yet — but yeah, we've had a pretty good look for it,' Webster replied.

'And no sign anywhere?' Kerr asked, trying to recover his diminished credibility.

Webster shook his head.

Jacobson yawned, still needing coffee, before he summarised the possible scenario.

'Put a bullet in his head. Remove his laptop or his pc or whatever from the premises. And just in case the message still isn't loud and clear enough — cut the poor bastard's tongue right out of his mouth.'

3

Martin Grove.doc

Where to begin? On the day the judge told me I was evil, wicked, dangerous, a menace to society? Or on the night I couldn't stand the pressure anymore and signed my 'confession' on the dotted line, signed my whole life away just so they'd stop it, stop it, stop it, just so they'd leave me alone?

Or earlier, much earlier? The very earliest thing I remember, funnily enough, is my dad. My dad sponging my face with warm soapy water and telling me I was a good boy. I say funnily enough because I only have a handful of memories of him altogether. He wasn't around when I was growing up, wasn't there to pull me up when I blagged off school or anything like that, never there to say well done the few times I did something that was worth doing, like when I saved that little kid from drowning, really saved him.

No, hang on, all of that — my troubled, traumatic childhood — should come later, shouldn't it? That's not what you want to hear about first, is it? Nobody wants a linear narrative these days. Everything's got to be cut up, flash-backed, fast-forwarded, sampled, re-mixed. Everything has to be made to seem more complicated than it really is. Who's going to take a story seriously otherwise? And I want you to take my story seriously. Oh yes, I really do want that.

But, still, all the same, my dad. My dad who never lifted a finger to help me. My dad who only turned up once at the trial. On the last day, the day of the verdict. Sat there stony faced in the upstairs gallery. Right in the front row. He came to see me in prison right after too. Just that one time. While I was still at Winson Green, still waiting for allocation. *I can't believe they don't have hanging anymore for scum like you. I'd string you up myself if they'd let me. String you up high and let you dangle. You are no son of mine, understand? You're not even human, you piece of filth.* It all came out pat, as if he'd rehearsed it. He left as soon as he'd delivered his supportive little speech, just stood up and left, and I never saw him again, never heard from him again. He died when I'd done ten years. A sudden heart attack — just like Mum did later. They let me out for his funeral. I didn't care less about him by then. But I wanted out for the day. Holy Christ yes, I wanted out for the day. Fresh air. Sky. The big, shady lime trees in the churchyard. Everything normal: cars, shops, houses, normal people walking in the normal streets.

Then again maybe you just don't want to hear about any of that at all. Who I am. Where I came from. Maybe there's only one thing you really want to hear about — and maybe you still don't believe me about it, maybe you believe instead that there's no smoke without fire. *If Martin Grove didn't do it, then who did?* Who

19

murdered that young, beautiful, clever woman? But I'm coming to that. Oh yes, I'm coming to that. You'll get your money's worth all right. You'll get full value for your money. No worries. But I can't start there — with the murder, with what really happened — that way you'll learn nothing, understand nothing. And I need you to learn, need you to understand. You need to know about her first, don't you see? You need to know about them. How I met them. How I got involved. How I got involved and lost everything. Absolutely everything.

I was different then of course. Not like now. Not 'educated'. Prison gave me that, although it gave it grudgingly, stingily, resentfully. Degrees. Education. The Means of Expression. But I didn't have that then. Not a scrap of it. Not much more beyond read the *Sun*. Not much more beyond write your name and add up. Not much more beyond place a bet or check your football pools coupon. That was what we did back then by the way. The football pools, not the lottery. My life ended when I was nineteen, ended before it got started. So long ago that it was *before* the lottery, just like it was before mobile phones, before the internet, before DNA analysis and tape-recorded police interviews. Quite possibly, my friend, before you were even born.

4

Jacobson decided not to wait for the MIU and its drinks dispenser. There wasn't much else to do out here until the SOCOs were finished. He took Helen Dawson to one side before they left the property, asked her to get Jane Ebdon's details from Maureen Bright and to phone them through to the incident room ASAP. Surreptitiously, Dawson snuck DS Kerr's mobile into Jacobson's jacket pocket before she rejoined Maureen Bright inside the gazebo.

After a technophobic panic or two, Jacobson managed to set Kerr's mobile's voice recorder onto broadcast replay while Kerr drove them back in the direction of Wynarth and Crowby. Result: nothing — or nothing that added to the existing picture anyway. Mainly just Maureen Bright sobbing and crying — and using the same dozen words over and over: *He was a good man, people don't realise that, a good man.*

Nothing new came in on Jacobson's own phone. He asked Kerr to pull into the Texaco garage at the Crowby end of the Wynarth Road when they reached it, recalling that it had a decent-enough coffee machine next to the over-priced paninis and shrink-wrapped cheese sandwiches. Kerr parked up in a quiet corner of the forecourt, went and fetched the drinks. The garage wasn't far from the entrance to the Bovis estate, and just along a bend or two from the

21

uncared-for house, with the forlorn For-Sale sign in its driveway, that still belonged to the 'patriotic' Stuart brothers.

Jacobson leant on the blue bonnet of Kerr's car and devoured an extra-large double espresso. John and Phil Stuart, along with their self-styled 'fuehrer', Rick Cole, were serving two non-concurrent life sentences each for race-hate murders (although the racist motives for their crimes had been suppressed from their trial), wouldn't be needing their place, wouldn't be needing any kind of private accommodation, for a while. A while as in two or three decades. The wages of sin were death according to the Bible. But before God judged you — if God judged you — what the courts dished out was a bill to be paid with your time: minutes, hours, days, weeks, months, years. The Stuarts had gone in young, wouldn't get out until they were middle-aged or old. The difference, of course, Jacobson thought, was that the Stuarts were guilty as hell.

'Poor Martin Grove. Wouldn't you say, Ian?' he asked Kerr.

Kerr nodded across the bonnet.

'I'd say so all right. Aged nineteen or thereabouts when they fitted him up for Claire Oldham. Then banged up for another nineteen, wasn't it?'

'Twenty years altogether by the time he was finally cleared.'

Kerr sipped his tea and scowled at the thought.

'Not much of a life, eh?'

'Not much of a death either, old son.'

Jacobson finished his coffee, binned it, clambered back into the passenger seat. Kerr was driving a Honda now, had sold off his accustomed Peugeot the way a lot of Midlanders had done since the company had closed their local factory and put their local workers on the dole.

Jacobson called Emma Smith in the incident room. As soon as everything was settled there, he told her, she should pay a call on Jane Ebdon, find out whether she was backing up Maureen Bright's story about last night and early this morning or not. DC Smith sounded relieved at the prospect. By now, Jacobson was thinking, the authorised civilian incident room manager, Brian Phelps, would have clocked on. Phelps was efficient enough and understood all the approved procedures. But he had an officious side to him that could all too easily wind up front-line DCs. Phelps only had his computers, his photocopiers and his paper clips to worry about; they had to deal with the real, messy world outside the Divisional building, never knew what was coming at them next: a friendly soul offering a cup of tea or a nutter waving a meat cleaver.

Coffee stop and roadworks included, it took Kerr forty minutes to reach the Divi car park.

'What's next then, Frank?' he asked Jacobson, cutting the engine.

Other than staying informed and available, the details of the operation didn't really concern either of them for the next couple of hours. Jim Webster's SOCOs would forensicate Grove's property. The uniformeds would extend the weapons search into the surrounding country-side. The traffic cops would monitor the rural road network and quiz early-morning drivers as potential witnesses to anything unusual. Duty CID, supervised by Hume and Williams, would conduct door-to-door inquiries in the Crowcross area and, via the incident room, collate any relevant CCTV sources. All of which — theoretically — left Jacobson and Kerr free to take a broader, strategic view.

'Well, if we're lucky, Grove pissed off a neighbour in a major way is all — there's a lot of weaponry out in the rustic hinterlands don't forget — and something will turn up from the door-to-door operation.'

'And if we're unlucky?'

'Then life gets more difficult — but also more interesting. Two things, Ian. One is that you need to start speaking to the prison service,' Jacobson answered. 'We could do with knowing about every jail that Grove spent time in, who he was banged up with, who's still inside, who's outside.'

'You're thinking this is *prison*-related in some way?'

'Grove had an enemy — or enemies, that's looking pretty clear. Plus he spent most of his adult life behind bars — so, if it isn't something local, where else has he acquired them? It's certainly a fundamental line of inquiry at this stage.'

'And the second thing?'

'That's the angle I'm going to cover. The court of appeal finally accepted that Grove was

24

innocent — that he could be scientifically excluded as a suspect. But the fact remains that somebody did the crime. Somebody who by now has probably got very used to the idea of getting away with it.'

'You mean that Grove might have actually discovered the real murderer?'

Jacobson pulled himself out of Kerr's passenger seat. The day wasn't getting any cooler — and the sun was still a long, long way from its zenith.

'It's what he promised to do when he won his appeal, remember? It was all over the front pages at the time. *If the police wouldn't do it, he would* — and so on.'

'But that was just bluster surely, Frank?'

'Maybe, old son. But it's a possibility we certainly can't exclude *a priori*. You saw his study for yourself — all that obsessive detail about his case. That's why I'm going to pay an urgent visit to Alan Slingsby.'

Kerr ignored the detour into Latin, hoped it wasn't important.

'Alan Slingsby?'

'He stuck with Grove through thick and thin, don't forget. If anybody knows exactly what Grove's been up to recently, Slingsby could very well be the man.'

Kerr fob-locked his car after he climbed out.

'No, you've got that wrong, Frank. Slingsby could very well be the smug, up-his-own-arse dung beetle.'

'So everybody keeps telling me. But, man or insect, I'm still going to speak to him,' Jacobson replied, loosening his shirt-collar and the knot in his tie.

He was already feeling the need for his next coffee, already trying not to remember what a fresh, new cigarette tasted like on a warm sunny morning.

5

Jacobson cut across the pedestrianised precinct and headed towards Silver Street, where Slingsby and Associates were located in a Grade 2 listed building that had somehow managed to survive the previous century's planning vandals: late Victorian, Midlands red brick, the home of three generations of a family firm of solicitors until the Second World War killed off the last of them. After the war it had been a doctor's surgery, then insurance company offices and, latterly, an estate agents. One of Alan Slingsby's pleasures in acquiring the property had been in returning it to its original purpose and function — or something close to. The exterior had been carefully repaired and restored and the interior had been gutted — the technical term was adapted — to yield a harmonious blend of old-fashioned solidity and bright, modern convenience. Slingsby's empire had grown over the years — to six other branch offices region-wide — but Crowby remained his favoured personal base of operations.

They'd both been young men when they'd first crossed swords. Slingsby, the radical firebrand, straight out of university, intent on using the capitalist state's own laws against it, eager to hasten its overdue demise. And Jacobson, wet behind the ears, the youngest, newest officer in CID, still conventional, still

27

light-years away from *thinking* about policing, still less thinking about it critically. Both of them had changed. Slingbsy's *firm* (the experiment with the Crowby Radical Law Collective hadn't lasted more than a few years) had prospered, funded by the profitable combination of endless routine legal aid cases and expensive, complex defence work in some of the region's highest-profile trials. I *want somebody from Slingsby* was the daily cry in custody suites from Crowby to Coventry via Birmingham and Derby and back again. Unsurprisingly, mediocre, lazy-arsed coppers, whether CID or uniformed, loathed Alan Slingsby and all his works as a deep article of faith. They hated the way his lawyers made them look moronic in court when (as frequently happened) they couldn't find their botched-up notes or when one lazy-arsed piece of police testimony contradicted the previous lazy-arsed piece, hated the way his clients always pleaded not guilty, always opted for jury trials if they could. But prejudices spread, and even competent, decent officers like DS Kerr had come to believe that Slingsby was the Great Satan, the Divisional building's public enemy number one.

Jacobson, contrarian as ever, almost liked him.

They'd be talking in Slingsby's personal suite of offices, up on the fourth floor. If you looked out of the wide bay windows up there, as Slingsby probably often did, you could make out the back roofs and skylights of the court buildings, around the corner in Clarence Square. Jacobson took the discreet lift in preference to the broad, marbled Victorian staircase. He hadn't told the effortlessly polite receptionist why he needed to speak to Slingsby, knew that Slingsby would know he'd never call here on a whim, that there would be a very good, very serious reason for the visit. The receptionist hadn't asked anyway, had just said that 'Alan' would be pleased to see him, even though 'Alan' had to attend a case conference in Wolverhampton this morning, even though 'Alan' was already booked on to the ten thirty-five train.

He let Slingsby request coffees, let both of them settle down into excessively comfortable chairs before he broke the bad news. Slingsby had a face that was best described as professionally bland, that was singularly difficult to read for signs of inner thought and emotion. But not today. Jacobson watched the colour drain out of it, even worried that Slingsby might be about to faint.

'You're sure, Frank? Well, of course you are,' Slingsby said quietly after a long moment.

Not any kind of question really, just something to say, just something to get his mind working again. He stood up after that, found a twelve-year old Glenmorangie in a mahogany cabinet, poured himself a stiff one, waved the bottle at Jacobson.

'No thanks,' Jacobson replied, 'I'll stick with the coffee when it comes.'

Slingsby drank deep, topped up his glass to the brim again before he sat back down.

Jacobson had kept to the basic facts, slightly edited: an execution-style shooting, the body discovered by Grove's live-in girlfriend. It was

29

too early, he decided, to burden Slingsby with the indelicate details concerning Grove's severed tongue.

'I don't suppose you've got a cigarette? I don't anymore. Not usually. But — '

Jacobson told him no, he didn't either, not for a couple of months now.

'Too bad. Bloody health fascists, getting to us all in the end, picking us off one by one,' Slingsby said, chasing after his normal self.

'You kept in touch then?' Jacobson asked.

There was a period grandfather clock ticking steadily in the corner. Roman numerals. The manufacturer's name in an ornate script. *Knight and Gibbins, London.* Jacobson translated the time: nine fifty-nine AM.

Slingsby took another drink before he spoke again.

'Yes I did. To an extent. It's not what I usually do, not at all. But Martin was hardly a usual client for me.'

'To an extent?'

'Hardly a usual kind of guy either. Not easy to talk to, not easy to spend time with. Intense, Frank, *intense.*'

Slingsby's personal secretary brought in a pot of newly-brewed coffee, offered to pour. Slingsby declined but Jacobson didn't, took it with a slither of cream this time. He waited until the secretary had gone.

'So how often did — '

'I don't know offhand, although I can check my diary easily enough. But let's say half a dozen times in the years since he's been released.

That's not counting when he first got out.'

'When you had him stay out at your place?' Jacobson asked, suddenly recalling the forgotten fact.

Slingsby nodded.

'There was nowhere for him on the outside after his mother died. Only that crazy woman who wanted to marry him.'

'Who *did* marry him surely?'

The Martin Grove saga was coming back to Jacobson piece by piece. But not every single detail, and — without further checking — not necessarily accurately.

'No she didn't. Martin had the good sense not to go through with it in the end. Anyway, *we* took him in for the first month or so. Jill, my partner, couldn't stand it after that, put her foot down. We had the press all over the place, long lenses, infra red cameras, the fucking lot. It got so they'd follow us down to bloody Waitrose. Martin didn't really help much either. He'd take a cab into Crowby, hit the night spots, come back rat-arsed or worse.'

Slingsby lifted his whisky glass, raised it near to his lips, but didn't follow through and drink it.

'It was just a phase. Getting it out of his system. But it was a relief for us anyway when he found himself a bedsit. That was before his money was sorted out of course, before he bought his own place.'

Jacobson already knew the answer to his next question, or thought he did anyway.

'But you'd done your job, Alan. Stuck with

him, eventually got him released. Why the guilt trip? Why put yourself out? I mean he can't be the only client your firm's defended who's gone down for something they didn't do.'

Slingsby managed something very like his usual, bland smile.

'The jails are full of innocent sods, Frank. You know that as well as I do. And I've had my fair share of failures. It goes with the job. But Martin was the first — or the first big one anyway. Plus you know my background, where I was coming from back then — in the early years, I took a lot of the conspiracy theories seriously. I thought that his case would lead somewhere *politically*.'

'You mean that Claire Oldham had been assassinated by the Secret State and all that?'

'Exactly. I thought I was going to do a number on MI5, stick one on the spooks and the government. As if, Frank. As fucking if.'

Slingsby took his swig finally. Then:

'The case just got under my skin over the years, I guess. I felt an *obligation* really. That's probably the best word for it.'

'When you say you kept in touch, how do you mean exactly? Socially?'

'I'm not sure social's the right word where Martin's concerned. But, yes, he invited me over to his place now and then. Maureen Bright's a pretty good cook as it happens. How's she taking this by the way?'

'Badly, in a word. A funny old dinner engagement for you surely? Crowby's leading solicitor, an ex-lifer and an ex-call girl.'

Slingsby's face was giving nothing away again,

or only what Slingsby wanted it to.

'I'm sure that's how your less-intelligent colleagues would see it, Frank. But I'd expect more from you. On one level, most of Martin Grove's life's been — was — a catalogue of shit, a total nightmare. On another level, he'd learned from it, gained real insights. I couldn't take him in more than small, irregular doses — but he was an interesting man, reflective, worth spending time with.'

Jacobson mentioned Grove's study, the suspicion that his computer had been removed by the killer or killers.

'It looked like whatever he was up to in there was still connected to his case.'

'I know it for a fact, Frank. He was writing his autobiography, has been for the last three years or thereabouts. When he was getting started on it, I had my clerks set him up with copies of our complete files on the case. Every single document we hold.'

Jacobson drank Slingsby's predictably excellent coffee, tried to picture Slingsby dining *chez* Grove, couldn't quite manage it.

'To what purpose though, old son? I can see why he'd need your files just to tell the story of the trial and the appeals. But what I'm getting at is whether he had any grander ideas about looking again at Claire Oldham's murder itself — as in if Grove didn't do it, then who the hell did? It's what he promised to do when he won his appeal after all.'

'I wondered that too, Frank, and I advised him against it, strongly advised him. *All kinds of* investigators have had a go over the years, raked over the coals, got nowhere. I thought telling his story in general was a good idea. He could put it behind him, lay it to rest, probably make a tidy sum into the bargain — *but leave solving the murder alone* — those were probably my exact words. I could just see him getting obsessed by it, going round in circles, losing another couple of decades of his life to it.'

Jacobson drained his coffee down to the dregs, wondered if he had time for a second cup. Probably not, he thought, not if Slingsby had a train to catch.

'You think that's why he came back to the Crowby area in the first place then? Or why he stayed after he got his compensation and damages payments? That he really did have some idea about *solving* the case?'

'Not in the first place. I don't think so. Or not seriously anyway at that stage.'

Slingsby stood up, refilled his whisky glass. Jacobson wondered if he'd actually forgotten about his booked train seat to Wolverhampton.

'The thing that really pissed him off once he was out, Frank, was when the force — *you* — declined to re-open the original investigation. He took it as a non-vindication, as a sign that he was still the guilty man as far as the police were concerned — and whatever the science said to the contrary. The tabloid press took much the same line.'

Jacobson held two hands up wide.

'Not so much of the *you*, old son. I was never asked for my opinion. I don't even think that

34

Smoothie Greg was consulted. The decision was taken at the Chief Constable's level, way above the heads of CID.'

Slingsby replaced his vintage bottle in his vintage cabinet.

'And it would have been *so* different if Greg Salter had been calling the shots, Frank.'

The edges of Jacobson's mouth conceded a near-smile. He couldn't stand his boss, DCS Salter, Crowby's official chief of detectives, as Slingsby well knew.

'So Grove stuck to his idea of finding out who the real killer was — and didn't take your advice to leave well enough alone?' he asked, when his face was straight again.

'I think it's possible. I know he pestered Michael Mott more than once.'

'Mott?'

The name rang a dim bell.

'Mott Legal Investigations. Over in Birmingham. I hired them back in the nineties, when Martin was losing appeal after appeal. That was the brief I gave them: find the real killer.'

Jacobson stood up too, walked over to Slingsby's bay windows, wanting to see the rooftop view before he left the premises. Slingsby walked over and joined him.

From this height, you could also see behind the security barriers and into the narrow alley where the white Reliance vans picked up and delivered prisoners to and from the courts.

'Mott never turned up anything, of course, or not anything substantial anyway.'

'But did Grove know that?'

'Yes he knew it all right, Frank. I never kept anything back from him. But Martin was an *expert* in clutching at straws, clinging to the last shred of hope. He was a fucking doctoral candidate in that regard. You'd have to be, wouldn't you? An innocent dupe doing twenty-plus years for aggravated rape and murder.'

6

Martin Grove.doc

Halloween. It was Halloween of all nights when I first set eyes on them, first set eyes on Claire. I was roughing it that year, hitching around, casual job to casual job. Well, I'd been roughing it for a couple of years by then in fact; ever since I'd packed in school, packed in life at home, packed in life as my mother's son. I was pretty much rootless, pretty much up for anything going. I'd had a job down on the south coast for a while, not far from Brighton, cash-in-hand on a building site, making tea for the navvies, shovelling the shit that nobody else was prepared to shovel. But then there was some problem with the developer's budget projections or something. Everybody non-essential got laid off and Yours Truly was at the front of the queue. I tried London for a time, but it was no place to sleep rough, no place to be without a decent set of threads and half a dozen credit cards, not even back then. London gobbled up my building-site money like a hungry horse and made sure it kept the change. So I decided to head out, try my luck somewhere up north again. That's one of the stupid things about it. I'd no intention of coming back to Crowby, not the slightest intention. It was just the luck of the road that brought me back, that was all. Bad luck, as it turned out. The baddest of bad luck. I'd got out

37

of London easily enough as well, got off to a good start. A trucker brought me right up the M1 as far as the Newport Pagnell services and then this sales guy offered me a lift, said he was going as far as Birmingham on the M6. The only problem was that later on he turned out to be gay, turned out to be cruising, even offered me a tempting amount of pound notes. When I said no, he threw a fit, turfed me out onto the hard shoulder just before the North Crowby junction. It was near enough sunset by then, evening turning into night, the traffic speeding past like I was invisible. I was starting to think fuck it, I'd walk off the motorway, walk all the way back to my mum's place, maybe doss down there for a couple of days, rest up, let her make a fuss, put up with her pleading for me to stop on. Except that's when pointy-hatted Claire pulled up in her little green sports car. The MG. Smiling at me, blonde and blue-eyed, almost ridiculously beautiful. I was barely nineteen right? Barely knew how to tie my shoelaces, barely had ten quid left in my pocket. And here was Claire, dressed up like a stripogram witch in her long spangly cloak and her short black dress, offering me a lift, asking me if I'm cold or hungry, telling me there's a party at her place, that I could stay the night there if I wanted to, have a drink, something to eat, plus they could easily find a bed for me, easily cook me breakfast. She's got Bowie on the radio too, 'Let's Dance'. The thin white duke.

Claire's place was — well, you probably know where Claire's place was, what Claire's place looked like. The tabloids weren't content with straightforward photographs after all. Not then, not later, not now. Along with the lies and the exaggerations, they always like to publish plans, diagrams, artist's impressions, aerial views. Claire was in a good mood that night. She could be up or down, superficial or serious, as I'd find out later. But that night she was all up. I think there'd probably been some temporarily good news about the campaign, that all of them were in the party spirit. As for me, I'd never seen anything like it, never met anybody like any of them.

The cottage isn't all that far from where I live now. I walk a lot these days, living out in the country the way I do. Fresh air, exercise, freedom to roam. All of that means a lot to you when you've spent the best years of your life inside like I have. So I walk past the cottage sometimes, even occasionally take a closer look around. It's been derelict for years now of course. At first nobody wanted to buy it because of what happened there and because of all the publicity. And now it would cost a small fortune to do it up to anything like modern standards. So I guess it'll just stay the way it is, slowly rotting and crumbling into the ground. Not long after I won my appeal, one of the papers said I was going to buy it, going to move in and live there. I've no idea where they got that one from, probably just made it up themselves. Believe me, I couldn't live there again, not for so much as a single day.

Back then, of course, it was a different story.

The place was crowded, packed, *alive*. There were maybe twenty or thirty people living there at the peak of it all. Christ knows how they all fitted in, how they all found bed space or floor space. I mean the place wasn't exactly large. There were a couple of tipis out in the garden of course. And any number of vans and old cars in the lane that mainly belonged to the itinerant supporters, the non-hard-core, who came and went as the mood suited them, contributing something useful in some cases, sponging off the community in others. Plus the in-betweens who did a bit of both. Contrary to popular belief, nobody lived in the famous 'freedom field' on a permanent basis. The field was home solely to the most temporary of the protestors, day-trippers and weekenders who might turn out for one of the special mass actions that the campaign organised from time to time.

I've thought about it often. What exactly Claire said to me in the car that night when she was driving me over there for the first time. But I spent as much time looking at her as listening to her and all I've got in my head are fragments. I'd no idea at the time how important, how significant, meeting her would turn out to be. If I could have seen what was coming, I'd never have got in, just kept right on walking. Or thumbed for another lift, any other lift. Even stayed with the sales guy, let him have his sodding blow-job.

I guess though that she didn't actually say all that much. Not about what they were really up to anyway. They were careful like that, careful not to frighten newcomers off. She mentioned the party again, mentioned something about the real significance of Halloween and Beltane, all that Celtic heritage stuff. That's what I thought they were at first probably — hippies, a harmless bunch of New Agers. And some of the hangers-on were just that. But not the hard-core. Not the committed. Not the *politicos*. If I'd been more clued in, I might have guessed that straightaway — when Claire turned off the radio, killed Bowie, shoved the Crass onto her tape deck instead, 'Bloody Revolutions', told me they were her favourite band. Maybe you don't remember them? Maybe you've never heard of them? I wouldn't worry about it if I were you — just count yourself as one of the lucky ones.

The sun had completely gone by the time we got there and the party was already in full swing. I helped her up to the cottage from the car with the crates of cheap plonk she'd been picking up in Crowby in case they ran out of booze. And that was when I first met Nigel. Nigel with his face painted red, green and yellow for the party. Nigel heading out into the yard to chop some more wood for the bonfire. Nigel waving his shiny axe-blade at me with an over-friendly grin.

7

DC Emma Smith checked out Jane Ebdon's electronic footprint before she left the incident room. No known convictions, or nothing that had found its way onto the PNC anyway. But there was something connected to her inside Crowby Division's own local systems: a terse entry on the Vice Squad's intelligence database. Name, Latest Known Address, DOB, a couple of sentences under Comments to the effect that Ebdon was believed to be working as an independent escort, finding clients via the internet. Not strictly illegal but the vice team saw it as part of their mission statement to store as much data as came their way about local sex workers, those working off the streets included. Usefully, the entry included her web address. DC Smith copied it into a browser window, took a look at the site itself. *Mandy Rivers Welcomes You*. The usual, unconvincing pseudonym, the usual mauve and purple backgrounds and cheesy, over-elaborate fonts, the usual attempt to kid the punters that they were buying into something classy, something sophisticated, something that shouldn't be remotely confused with renting a stranger's body for an hour or two, cash upfront. On the 'Latest News' page there was an unusual entry: *Mandy regrets that she is unable to accept new bookings until further notice.*

She drove out to the place via the ring road. A small, newish estate not far from the Waitrose complex. (Narrowly) detached houses with car ports and hastily turfed lawns arranged into a bland labyrinth of drives, closes and courts. Jane Ebdon's front lawn was distinguished by a water feature: a Greek maiden filling a water jug from a fountain. There was an Audi convertible on the driveway. Nice-looking enough but not particularly new. This early in the day, she guessed it was Ebdon's own car, although in any case her type of escort mainly worked the business hotel circuit, rarely brought clients home, rarely upset the neighbours. She memorised the registration number in case she found a use for the information later. It wasn't something she could go for herself, opening her legs to all and sundry (since the Ray Williams fiasco, she wasn't sure about opening them again in any circumstances), but, like most police, she wasn't judgemental about it. Paying for sex and earning from sex were things that people had always done, always would do, whatever laws came and went. Ditto for drug-use. The sooner both were properly legalised, the sooner the force could get on with its real work: catching bad people and keeping good people safe.

There was a home CCTV camera focused on the mat outside the front door — and an intercom and buzzer instead of a doorbell. Jane Ebdon answered the buzzer quickly but kept her visitor waiting before she finally undid several locks and peered out.

'I've the kettle on in the kitchen,' she said,

pleasantly enough, ushering her inside.

You could see she was definitely the woman on the website. Early thirties, tall, busty. Smith reckoned she looked more attractive without the make-up and the clichéd black leather basque — but then she wasn't in the market for what Jane Ebdon sold, or had been selling until very recently.

She followed her through. All she'd told her so far was that she might be able to help them with a serious inquiry but that it didn't involve her directly, that she wasn't in any trouble herself. If the plod out at the crime scene was doing her job properly, Maureen Bright wouldn't have been in touch with her yet, wouldn't have told her what had happened to Martin Grove.

She waited until Jane aka Mandy had fixed two herbal teas — one camomile, one peppermint — before she asked her when she'd last seen Maureen Bright.

'What's Maureen supposed to have done?'

'She's not supposed to have done anything, not if she's been telling us the truth.'

Jane Ebdon hesitated, fussed over a sheer-black cat who'd slunk into the kitchen from elsewhere in the house.

'If I said she was here last night, that she stopped over, would that — '

Smith tried to keep her voice in neutral, tried to give no clues, no cues.

'*Is* that what you're saying, Jane?'

Jane/Mandy found a carton of milk inside the hidden depths of a big, American-style fridge, poured some into a pale-blue saucer, put the saucer down in front of the meowing cat. Amy Winehouse was on a CD player at low volume. She turned the volume down further, then turned the player off altogether.

'Yes that's what I'm saying,' she answered finally. 'I asked her to come. I've asked her a few times recently. She drove over from Crowcross, got here nineish — or not much after. We sat up talking late, maybe as late as two thirty, three. I've a spare bedroom, she slept in there for a bit after that. She usually leaves early though. Half-six or thereabouts. Her bloke doesn't like to wake up on his own.'

Smith asked her if she was sure about the times — she said that she was — and then told her a minimalist version of what had happened to Martin Grove.

She sat down slowly at her kitchen table.

'Jesus, poor Maureen,' she said after a long moment. 'He's been everything to her in the last couple of years. I've never met him though, never been out there. I don't think Maureen likes to rub his nose too much in — you know — how she used to earn.'

'That's how you know her then? The escort business?'

A statement of the obvious, a prompt more than a question.

'We worked together sometimes, when I was still using an agency. I liked her and we got on well — before Maureen lost it anyway.'

Smith thought about Maureen Bright's PNC data.

'Lost it? You mean when she got into a spot of

45

dealing on the side?'

'I mean when she got into using — that's *why* she was dealing. The agency dropped her like a hot potato. She was doing business on the streets by the end of it. A junkie whore basically.'

'But you stuck by her?'

'I did what I could. Which didn't amount to much. A safe bed for the night now and then, cash sometimes if I thought she really needed it.'

'And then Martin Grove rode into the rescue?'

Jane Ebdon shook her head slightly, maybe unconsciously.

'I think it worked both ways. He got her off the streets OK, paid for her rehab. But Maureen's been good for him too, got close to him in a way nobody else could, calmed him right down. That's the impression I've got from Maureen anyway.'

Smith tried the peppermint tea — still too hot.

'He met her when she was still working?'

'Grove went wild when he got out of prison. Who wouldn't in his shoes? Maureen told me he was getting through dozens of street whores at the peak of it. She was one of them. More or less the last one as it turned out.'

Smith knew she would need to take a formal, signed statement, would need to insist on removing the CCTV tape from the premises (to help prove when Maureen Bright arrived and when she left). It was the textbook moment for an unofficial interlude.

'Your website says you're closed for business until further notice. Is that because of — '

'The cancer? Yes, it is. I can't face working

right now. Though it still might be nothing. The tests are inconclusive so far. I'm under the knife again tomorrow. Another biopsy. Another night of not sleeping.'

'But nowadays, if they catch it early enough — '

'Yeah, yeah. There's old dears have made it to ninety with just the one tit. It's just I'd sooner not be one of them, you know?'

DC Smith nodded. Like every other woman, she knew all right.

* * *

Jacobson paid a visit to the Central Records Office on the second floor when he got back to the Divisional building. There was no chance that anything from the original Claire Oldham murder investigation had found its way onto the force's computer system so the clerks would have to trawl through the dusty shelves of ageing paper records to retrieve whatever they could. Jacobson's instinct was that he might need everything they could find there so the sooner they got started on the hunt the better. There was a major IT project underway to make electronic copies of the force's paper-based archives. But the work still had a long way to go until it was completed and, in any case, the project's cut-off date had been set at 1990. Anything before then, the Claire Oldham case files included, were automatically excluded as being too far back in the past. Ancient history as far as the force's modern hierarchy were

47

concerned. Dead dogs which had been designated for quiet, undisturbed rotting.

The young woman behind the service desk hid her lack of enthusiasm for the task reasonably well but she claimed that the search would need to be approved by her supervisor. Jacobson, entirely unfazed, said he'd wait. Five minutes later, her boss finally put in an appearance beside her. The boss in question, an old trout by the name of Mary Brampton, laboured under the delusion that the boxes of documents gathering dust in the Records Office storerooms were her personal private possessions. She'd been the head records clerk in times past but now, nearing retirement, she'd been re-badged and re-labelled as the Archival Resources and Information Manager. Jacobson knew from experience that it was no good emailing her or leaving a message on her telephone extension. Only a promise extracted from her verbally — and in front of least one witness — was guaranteed to produce results. She flannelled him as usual about insufferable workloads, staff shortages, sicknesses and absenteeism. But Jacobson stuck to his guns: he was running a murder inquiry and he wanted everything — *everything* — on the Claire Oldham case delivered to the incident room before the day was out. Mary Brampton finally conceded defeat with a show of grace. Jacobson, although Jacobson didn't know it, was one of the few senior officers that she had any time for.

He took the lift up to his own office on the fifth floor. Before he checked (reluctantly) into the incident room he wanted to find out what he

48

could about Mott Legal Investigations from his best contact over in the City of Birmingham force — DS Barber, who'd been DC Barber, when he'd worked on Jacobson's team in Crowby. It was unlikely, in his view, that a team of private snoops had uncovered something that had escaped the original police investigation. But, if Grove had been speaking to them recently, as Alan Slingsby had claimed, they might know something in more detail about Grove's own digging into the case. He was scrolling through his mobile, looking for Barber's number, when his desk phone rang: DS Kerr on his internal extension.

'The prison service bureaucrats are hopeless, Frank. It's going to be days before they can give us a proper list of all the prisons Grove served time in. You'd think they'd have basic stuff like that on a database by now wouldn't you?'

'You would, old son — if you were a naïve idiot. This is the shower who mixes prisoners' records up, lets some of them out early by *mistake*.'

'Anyway, the one thing they were able to tell me straight off is that Grove spent the last stretch of his sentence at Boland' — Kerr paused to emphasise the name — 'and bear in mind he's been out of jail for near enough five years by now.'

'*Boland*. You mean he was there at the time of the riots?'

'Yes, he was — and there's more. I've just been speaking to one of the assistant governors down there. According to him, Grove never took any part in the disturbances, mainly barricaded himself in his cell for the duration. After it was sorted, he gave evidence against the ringleaders. Apparently he was one of the star witnesses.'

'That must have made him popular. Some of those sods must have had years added to their sentences.'

'Exactly. Most of them are still banged up.'

Jacobson strolled over to his window, cradling the handset, thinking through the implications. The Boland riots had been amongst the worst ever seen in a British prison. Two prisoners — sex offenders — had ended up dead. And so had one prison officer. Prisoners who'd testified against the rioters had — controversially — been given anonymity by the courts.

'But not all of them, Ian, is that it?'

'He's going to send me a list — from his own records fortunately, so he reckons he might get it to me today.'

There was another caller on the line the second Kerr rang off: Mick Hume again.

'There's been a development, guv. A big development. There's a second dead body out here. Fresh, according to Webster.'

'Another one?'

'In Crowcross Wood. Same MO as Martin Grove, it looks like — shot through the head anyway — and, eh, the tongue could be missing. We can't check too closely until the path gets here. A woman this time, maybe in her late twenties? Sod all in the way of ID though.'

'Jesus, Mick,' Jacobson exclaimed. 'This is getting worse than a quiet day in Basra. How was she found?'

'By the uniformeds on the weapons search, guv.'

Hume read out the precise coordinates and Jacobson scribbled them down on a yellow post-it note. He told Hume he was on his way, ended the call and dialled through to the control room: he needed a patrol car to take him back out to Crowcross, needed it straightaway. He returned Kerr's call after that, told him to follow on as soon as he could. The patrol car would get him out there in short order, lights flashing all the way, but hc might need access to Kerr's less indiscreet vehicle afterwards.

He stuck his unused mobile back in his pocket (he'd phone Barber en route, he decided now), realised that he hadn't even had the time to take his jacket off. But at least there was the minor consolation that he'd be able to avoid the dozen or so check-lists, requisition sheets and pro formas that Brian Phelps would want him to sign down in the incident room for a little bit longer. And even if it meant gaping at another corpse (and another pair of dead, unseeing eyes), at least he'd be back out in the sunshine while Mary Brampton's clerks toiled indoors for him, unearthing the dusty, fading files on the Claire Oldham case.

★ ★ ★

Nigel Copeland walked out of the foyer of the Crowby Riverside Hotel and sank into the backseat of his Lexus, pausing only for the porter to open the door wide for him.

Once ensconced, he checked that his driver knew exactly where he was going and then buried his head in the *FT* for the duration of the journey. Or he tried to anyway. But every now and then he found his gaze pulled away from the lead story — new problems in the sub-prime market again — and outside towards familiar streets and buildings. Crowby, he thought — Crowby again, after all these years. A lot had changed, but a lot hadn't too. He'd taken a walk through the town centre last night, hadn't been able to resist the impulse. The old Town Hall had still been there and so had the cop shop opposite, not to mention the dreary concrete mess of the shopping centre. The Town Hall especially had felt like an enemy citadel back in those days, a fortress to be stormed and taken. And now it just looked old, solid — and oddly comforting. All these years, all the places he'd travelled to, the things he'd seen and done, the changes he'd been through — and all that time, Crowby had still been here, the clock on the Town Hall's white Art Deco tower still tick-tocking away, ringing out the passing of the hours and the days.

They were out on the North Crowby by-pass now, the Science and Business Park already signposted on the direction markers. He checked his watch. Eleven fifteen. They'd arranged their meeting for eleven AM, would all be sitting anxiously in their boardroom by now, fidgeting, tapping their fingers, fretting that maybe he'd decided to pull out at the last minute. The thought of that made him smile, the idea — the

52

certainty — that they needed him a lot more than he needed them.

He needn't have come in person really. It was a trivial enough acquisition, a sitting duck. Any of his executive directors could have thrashed out a satisfactory deal with ease. But he'd had his own reasons to be in the area, however briefly. And it was no bad thing for him to get his hands dirty with bread-and-butter negotiations occasionally, to keep himself streetwise, clued-in, fully up-to-speed. He folded the newspaper away when the Lexus cruised into the business park. Like so many of these Godforsaken places, the layout had been designed as a simple, childish oval — all you did to find wherever you wanted to go was to follow the single main road around until you got there. Sameness everywhere, that was the modern world. Sometimes, and especially on a hot day like this one, you had to blink and wonder to yourself which country you were in, even which time zone.

He checked his PDA before he got out of the car. Nothing, no urgent texts or calls — or nothing that couldn't wait anyway. The current Managing Director was waiting outside the main entranceway to greet him in person, had maybe dispatched himself down from the boardroom for just that purpose. He had a standard-issue PR woman with him, all blonde smiles, phoney confidence and enough leg showing to keep the moment interesting. Not that anything they could do would alter the outcome one iota. Their company was fucked, completely washed up, unless Copeland Insight PLC decided to bail them out — on virtually any terms he decided to put on the table. He returned the woman's smile glibly, shook the MD's weak, cagey hand as an afterthought, wondered idly just how ridiculously far he could push them.

8

Martin Grove.doc

They lit the bonfire at midnight. Everybody counting down — FIVE, FOUR, THREE, TWO, ONE — and Claire herself lighting the taper that set the blaze going. Before that the larger-than-life-size effigies had been carefully — ceremoniously — placed on top. Margaret Thatcher and Ronald Reagan. I've always remembered the Thatcher as being a more convincing likeness than the Reagan. Something hawk-like about the expression: a cold, severe mouth, eyes like calculators. They all went wild when the leaders of the free world went up in flames. Feet stomping, hands clapping, cheering, chanting. *Maggie, Maggie, Maggie — burn, burn, burn*. A girl, Christine — I never caught her second name properly — had taken an interest in me by then. Claire had looked after me the first half-hour or so I was there, showed me where I could stow my rucksack, sorted me out a plate of food. But then she was swept up in the party, left me to my own devices. I guess I looked a bit lost, not knowing anybody, not really having met anybody of their kind before — students, 'intellectuals', middle-class drop-outs, radicals. Christine was nice. That's all. Just nice. She shared her sleeping bag with me later in the tiny tent she'd pitched in the far corner of the freedom field. But she left the next day and I never saw her again. She was a student at

Birmingham or Nottingham or somewhere like that, only visiting the protest for that one weekend. She made a shy hint the next morning that I could hitch back with her, maybe kip down in her Halls of Residence for a while. But I didn't fancy the idea — or not enough anyway. Already, all night, I'd been watching Claire whenever I could get a glimpse of her. Already, I was thinking I might try and hang on around there, keep her in my sights for a while. I've no idea why I thought I'd a chance with her. But I did anyway, right from that first evening. Even though I was no kind of Romeo. Even though, up till then, I'd failed with women more often than I'd succeeded. As for Christine, years later I'd think about her in my cell sometimes, obsess about her if I'm honest with you. About how different my life would have been if only I'd had the common sense to take her up on her offer, to get the hell out of there while the going was good.

It was a fun night though, that first Myrtle Cottage night. Some kind of reggae band, who'd had a Halloween gig in Crowby, turned up around one in the morning, managed to get power to a couple of their amps somehow, got everybody up and dancing out in the garden. Someone had put a big bowl of 'shrooms in the front room near the buffet. A case of help yourself. You could forage for them easily enough in Crowcross Wood, I found out later. I only took a couple, just enough to get a bit of trippiness going. But it certainly helped to put me in the party mood. That and the strong cider. That and

Christine. I remember the two of us standing outside her little tent in the middle of the night, swaying really. Both high, both loved up, both staring at the stars. It was a cloudless night, bright with a full moon, and I was a young man standing on God's earth, *free*, with a sweet girl in my arms. It's a moment I've clung on to, I don't mind telling you. Inside your head, don't you see? If you can stay right in your head, nothing else matters.

After the murder of course, the tabloids had a field day about the 'lifestyle' out at the cottage. According to the *Sun*, the *Mirror* and the rest, it was all group sex orgies, group drug orgies — even group devil-worship and witchcraft. Crap of course. Complete and utter crap. Yeah, there was sex, why wouldn't there be? Most of the people there were under thirty, a lot of them slept with each other, changing partners now and then, falling in and out of love or lust. And, sure, there were a few pagans around, convinced that a little dollop of white magick would aid and abet the demise of the Great Evil Beast. But their ceremonies were totally benign as far as I could see — and beautiful to watch, joyful to behold. As for 'drugs', what exactly does the term mean? An aspirin is a drug, isn't it? And a cup of coffee or a glass of whisky can change your mood. Since when did the Oppressive Capitalist State have the moral right to get inside your brain, Dear Reader, dictate to you which modes of perception are legal and which are illicit? The concept of 'drugs' is state-sponsored bullshit — and, in any case, I saw more drugs the first week I was in prison than in the entire time I lived at Myrtle Cottage. It was a side-issue, an interest for the hangers-on mainly. Claire, Nigel and company, the real, true hardcore, rarely touched them. If ever. To them, drugs were a distraction — and the fact that they weren't legal made them dangerous from their point of view; drugs provided the agents of the state with a nice, convenient reason to give anybody the once-over any time they chose. As I learned eventually, Claire lived in constant fear of being busted, of the OCS sifting through everything she owned with a fine-tooth comb. And it did as well, ironically enough. But only — as you already know — after Claire had been raped, butchered and left to die.

I guess the expectation was that I'd move on after the party. But move on to where? I was in no particular hurry to find another crap job in another crap town, one that might just, if I was lucky, pay enough money to rent a crap, smelly bedsit to go with it. This was the Eighties, don't forget: millions on the dole, whole industries falling apart and Maggie bashing the unions from Land's End to John O'Groats. When Christine had packed up her tent and gone, I went back to the cottage. Everything was a serious mess after the party so I mucked in with the big clean-up effort. Nobody seemed to object. Nigel in particular was friendly towards me that first day, wanting to know where I came from, what I'd been doing, what I thought about this, that and the other topic. Politics mainly (naturally): the recent war in the Falklands, various strikes and layoffs, the nuclear missile threat. He obviously liked the idea that I was a local, born and bred on a Crowby council estate, a true son of toil. Later on, of course, I realised that the hardcore were obsessed with 'reaching out' to the proletariat, winning them over to the revolutionary cause. Mid-afternoon, I helped him — and an uncommunicative guy called Oliver — load up a van with accumulated party trash. Nigel drove us over to the municipal tip — which had just begun a rudimentary recycling service — and we off-loaded our cans, bottles and paper plates. Myrtle Cottage was hot on ecology, years before the government and big business got in on the act. Another aspect of the story that the papers didn't cover.

Somebody suggested I stay on for the communal evening meal when we got back and I didn't argue, realising that if I could hang on for that long, I could probably easily kip there for another night at least. Oh yes and we really did have a lentil bake, my friend, washed down with a few glasses of the potent rice wine that Andy (see later) was apparently home-brewing in large quantities down in the basement. All of which explains how I ended up attending my first Monday Evening Planning Meeting of the Myrtle Cottage Anti-Airbase Alliance, although in fact it was already Tuesday by then. Halloween had fallen on a Monday that year and the weekly-without-fail meeting had been moved a day because of the party.

The main lounge was the only room big enough to accommodate everybody who wanted to be there and even then it was a tight squeeze.

Apart from anyone currently resident in the cottage or its environs, the meetings attracted regular visitors from Crowby and Wynarth as well. Students and lecturers from Crowby Polytechnic, a few long-in-the-tooth CND types whose memories of protest stretched all the way back to the Sixties, and, in pride of place that particular evening, a couple of women from the Greenham Common Peace Camp who'd hitched up for the party and who'd agreed to give an update on the latest state of play at the Yellow Gate. Nigel and Claire were in the thick of it. The leaders of the protest in all but name. Claire wasn't witchy anymore, was wearing everyday jeans and a plain blue sweater. It hardly mattered: she was one of those women who looked good regardless of what she was wearing — or wasn't wearing. Nigel looked different too without his Halloween face colours. But he was still tall and broad-shouldered, the restless kind of big guy who always looks vaguely trapped inside a house — any house. Somebody told me once that he'd been a keen rugby player before he'd discovered revolutionary politics and decided that sport was 'bourgeois', a reactionary diversion, a part of what he and Claire used to call 'the society of the spectacle'.

God knows what they all talked about that night. In detail I mean. There were always interminable details that always needed sorting, that were always treated as being far more complicated and far more pressing than they really were. But at least I started to get an idea of what kind of thing was going on — about who they all were and why they were there. The fundamental issue was the disused RAF airfield near Crowcross Wood. 'Disused' wasn't strictly accurate — it had been built as an auxiliary fighter base during the Second World War but had never been used for the purpose. The war had ended before it was properly ready for active service. Afterwards, it had been left abandoned, weeds and wild flowers sprouting along the edges of the runways, the hangars lying empty. It's still there actually, still rotting away. Maureen (more about her later too) says there used be some big raves there on occasional weekends back in the Nineties. I take her word for it (like I do for most things that happened in that decade). I wouldn't know obviously. The Nineties were just something I saw on television — nothing at all to do with me in my narrow little prison hell world.

But back to the Eighties. The word was that the site had been leased to the Americans under a secret MOD deal (secret until some journalist from the *Guardian* had splashed the details all over the front page anyway). The buildings would be refitted, the runways repaired and expanded and, as soon as the work was complete, it was to be used as a USAF 'facility' — one with 'nuclear delivery' capabilities. In the event of the cold war going into meltdown — and in the event of the ground-based weapons down at Greenham and Molesworth failing to do the business — the plan was for the bombers at USAF Crowcross to take up some of the slack.

Which was where the property of Myrtle Cottage — and its solitary, accompanying field

— fitted in. The government had neither confirmed nor denied the leaked plan but the protestors believed utterly in its existence. They also believed that the MOD was about to compulsorily purchase large chunks of the surrounding countryside to make the airfield expansion possible since the original WW2-sized runways wouldn't be adequate for use by the latest US warplanes. So the protestors had come to Myrtle Cottage with the express purpose of making a stand, of defying the anticipated order to give up the land. NO TO THE AIRBASE, NO TO THE BOMBERS — as the banners on the cottage roof proclaimed to any spy satellite remotely interested in what was going on in the vicinity.

I didn't take all this in immediately that night of course. Not even in the next few days and weeks. I was still a kid from the streets then, don't forget. The only 'politics' I had up to that point was the view that the system sucked — and if you could rip it off or lift up two fingers to it then you should. Some of it I didn't really understand until years later, until after I'd got degrees to my name — and until after I'd endured endless days with nothing else to think about except the past; the past in every microscopic detail I could remember. All I knew that evening was that the party had been ace and that the cottage was an interesting place, probably worth hanging around for a while longer. Most of all, watching her speak, watching her hold the meeting in the palm of her hand, I knew that I wanted to get closer to Claire if I could. As close as I'd be able to, as close as she'd let me.

9

The geography of the area was simple enough. A B road detour from Wynarth brought you to Crowcross itself, a hamlet more than a village, located on an obscure stretch of the River Crow. Less than a dozen well-preserved, ivy coated houses, a long-deconsecrated church, a shop/petrol station and a single functioning pub, the Crowcross Arms. Carry on the same B road for a further mile or so and you came to Crowcross Wood, a Forestry Commission woodland (like several others in the rural hinterlands) and a popular spot for birdwatchers and ramblers who'd drive out from Crowby on weekends and summer evenings. There were a couple of farms over there too and a few even more isolated cottages and bungalows like the place Martin Grove had sunk his compensation payments into. Beyond the wood was the abandoned RAF airfield and, beyond that, Jacobson was recalling now, was the cottage where Claire Oldham had been living at the time of her murder.

His mobile rang as the patrol car sped past the Crowcross Arms: Robinson, the pathologist, confirming that he'd got the message from the control room and that he'd meet them at the wood as soon as he could. Jacobson gazed out at the pub car park, still quiet this early in the day. He didn't really care for country pubs too much, didn't really care for the countryside full stop.

Not in England anyway. He didn't like the way nature had been tamed and neutered, fenced off, hemmed in, parcelled out neatly as estates and over-priced property. In the countryside he always seemed to pick up too many echoes of England's dismal, shoddy history, always seemed to sense the ghosts of too many braying toffs, too many cap-doffing toadies and too many starving urchins. Unfortunately, Alison took a different view, was always keen to sample the menu at some rural gastropub or other on one of their rare, shared days off. The Bideford Arms, one of her favourites, wasn't more than a couple of miles away, but he couldn't recall them visiting this one. Maybe the place lacked a known chef, which seemed to be foodie Alison's chief selection criterion. So far, Jacobson had gone along, uncomplaining, for the ride. It was a harmless enough diversion and, more importantly, it was something Alison obviously really enjoyed. That was the key thing. He'd known her for a couple of years now but he was still a long, long way from complacently taking her for granted. He still couldn't believe his luck basically, was still taking pains not to self-destruct another relationship.

He made a mental note to call into the pub later. It was on the door-to-door list in any case, but Jacobson was still too hands-on to leave the best source of local gossip entirely to the inquiry's foot-soldiers. Property out this way *cost*, belonged mainly to the second homes and weekend bolt-holes brigade or to well-heeled incomers who commuted to profitable occupations elsewhere. None of them, he was prepared to bet, would have been overjoyed at Martin Grove's arrival in the neighbourhood, might well have kept a suspicious eye on his comings and goings, might just have seen something worth seeing. Last year's video gang case had brought Jacobson out this way too (although in the opposite direction to where they were heading now) but only in the final, bloody stages — and there'd been no need to bother the locals.

Jim Webster, the Crime Scene Manager, was waiting for him in person by the roadside when the patrol car reached Hume's coordinates. Behind him, a Scene of Crime van and a few other police vehicles had parked up, squeezing onto the grass verge as far off the narrow road as they could. Webster told him he'd divided his team's efforts for the time being: fifty per cent back at Grove's house, fifty per cent over here. Jacobson suited up again and followed Webster into the woodland. They didn't have to walk too far. Twenty or so yards from the roadside they reached the body. One of Webster's SOCOs had made a non-thorough (and unsuccessful) search for ID but otherwise the corpse had been left as undisturbed as possible — and would remain that way until all the in situ procedures had been completed and, crucially, until Robinson had made his initial examination.

Jacobson bent down with Webster to take a look. Hume had been right about her age, he thought. Twenty-seven, say, or twenty-eight. Something in that general area anyway. Jacobson thought her clothes looked expensive although he was no great judge. Well-cut jeans, a silky top, sleeveless and bare at the belly. The kind of thing a young woman might wear on a night out at this time of year. She'd been a redhead and she'd had a good figure. Hume had been right about the MO too — or the shooting part of it anyway, the rest would have to wait for Robinson's examination when he got here. The mouth didn't look, well, *right*. But Jacobson was more than content to leave it to Robinson to investigate further. The skin around the entrance wound was lacerated and sooty, characteristic of a direct hit from a gun pressed close against the head, as far as Jacobson understood anyway. Ditto for Martin Grove. But neither Mick Hume nor Jacobson were ballistics experts — and Jacobson knew that only a full scientific assessment would establish for a fact that the method in both killings had been identical.

He stood up and moved out of the way to let the SOCO with the digicam carry on filming the scene. Hume and DC Williams were standing over at a nearby willow tree, keeping well out the way now that the SOCOs were doing their thing. There were a couple of young PCs with them, the uniformeds who'd discovered the body. One of them looked white as a sheet, looked precisely the way Jacobson had done himself when, in the primordial, pre-historic past, he'd encountered a murder victim himself for the very first time.

He took out his mobile and made a succession of necessary calls. The case had been high priority all morning but now it had become top priority. In Los Angeles or London — maybe even in Crowby — you couldn't just assume that two killings overnight within a mile or so of each other were definitely related. Out here, Jacobson felt sure, it was a different matter. The upshot was he needed more of everything. More SOCOs. More CID. More uniformed searchers. He also needed — reluctantly — to speak to his boss, Greg Salter. Salter would want to set up a 'media strategy' (if only to get himself on TV again) and Jacobson knew from experience that it was far better to exert some influence of his own on what got reported and what didn't than to leave the decision solely to Smoothie Greg's publicity-seeking instincts.

The calls kept him busy for ten minutes. And then DS Kerr and the pathologist, Robinson, turned up more or less simultaneously. Robinson's in situ examination was professional, careful — and slow. So that Jacobson spent a full hour in Crowcross Wood before he realised precisely where the hell he was. Shaken, he walked over to the old willow where Hume and Williams had been standing earlier with the two young coppers. *HG + HS 1903*: the initials and the ancient date were still there and so was the carved heart which contained them. He wanted to take off his crime scene gloves, wanted to touch the cool bark with his fingers. A fragment of the past, etched by Edwardian lovers. A courting couple, maybe, cycling out to the countryside on a Sunday afternoon. The odd kind of little detail you could carry around, unknowing, in your head for years and years until it suddenly became relevant again. She hadn't been the first murder victim Jacobson had ever seen. More like the fifth or sixth. Yet for some reason, her corpse had been the one that had made him physically sick, sick to his gills.

It was a rite of passage, something that happened to every police officer sooner or later. Claire Oldham had done it for Jacobson, had made him retch up his breakfast, his lunch and his dinner. He'd been peripheral to the case, had been Crowby CID's rawest, greenest recruit at the time, barely a month out of uniform. But all the same, he'd been DCI Hunter's driver that night, had driven Hunter and his sergeant out to the crime scene when the body had been found. He'd carried one of the torches as they'd made their way through the woodland. He remembered it now, wondered why he hadn't remembered it instantly. They'd made their way here. Claire Oldham had been left for dead here. Claire Oldham had died at the foot of this tree.

* * *

Nigel Copeland condescended to be wined and dined by the Planet Avionics board after the meeting ended with the co-signing of the draft agreement that he knew — and they knew — they had no real choice about: a rescue package that would save their sorry arses but only in return for a massive equity give-away in the direction of Copeland Insight PLC. The food was edible at least (courtesy of outside caterers) and somebody had forked out for some more-or-less drinkable Chablis to accompany the fish course. He'd resigned himself, affably enough, to an hour or so of mild tedium before he could escape the place. They'd better make the most of him, he thought, as they'd probably never see him again in person. The Planet Avionics re-launch would be distinctly a junior-league gig. He'd probably give it to one of his medium-talented keen young men (or women), see how they got on with it. It certainly wasn't a big enough deal to merit the talents of one of his potential high-flyers. He'd leave after the puddings and the cheese board but before they got so far as the coffee and liqueurs, he'd decided, and would abandon Crowby to its own devices for another couple of decades — or, much more likely, for ever.

The leggy PR woman had been placed next to him with the current MD on his other side. The MD — with a couple of drinks onboard — was under the false impression that he was a humorist, was mid-way through another one of the non-original jokes that he'd probably downloaded from the internet. Question: what do you call a lawyer who's taken Viagra? Answer: an even bigger prick than usual. And so on. Nigel politely ignored him and concentrated on letting the PR blondie think she was getting somewhere with her amateur-hour flirting. Nigel made her thirty, career-obsessed, read her in a dead-in-bed marriage to a boyfriend she'd met in college and had probably long since grown tired of. She was a prospect that intrigued him about as much as a long weekend on Saturn. All the same, he smiled encouragingly while she told him about her plans to move out of PR and into Human Resources.

The only man in the room that he might have enjoyed talking to — Dyson, the company solicitor — was out of immediate conversational reach. Dyson had been on the scene when disaster had struck, was probably good for a few amusing war stories about the whole debacle.

'You weren't here at the time of Gus Mortimer, then?' he asked the PR woman out of the blue, just to see how she'd deal with the question, maybe catch her on the hop.

'No,' she told him, quick as a flash, had obviously rehearsed for the possibility, 'ninety per cent of the board is, eh, post-Mortimer. There are one or two of us, Bill Dyson for instance, who've stayed on from those days to provide continuity. But only those with clean hands — completely clean hands.'

Nigel sank the remains of another glass of Chablis, waited until one of the hovering waiters re-charged his glass.

'Clean hands are good — in most circumstances,' he answered her, still making her work for her money.

She smiled for a reply, leaned closer towards him, took a lip-glossed, mouthy sip from her own glass.

Planet Avionics had been a moderately successful company until, five years or so ago, they'd appointed a hotshot new MD who'd promised to massively expand the sales profile of their product lines (tachometers, altimeters and other guidance system components for the aircraft industry). Instead Gus Mortimer had embroiled the company in the thick of an illegal

Euro-scam to sell military kit to various banned rogue states and dictatorships. Worse still, the scam had failed and had been publicly exposed. Since when the company had struggled to keep its head above water. It was a small miracle really, Nigel thought, that they'd managed to keep going this long, even at the expense of lay-offs, redundancies and all-round cost cutting and penny pinching. Which was where Copeland Insight PLC came in — with the pledge of a significant cash injection plus a full company restructuring and a major market re-brand.

The MD, the third to hold the post since the Gus Mortimer period, started making heavy weather of another gag (about politicians this time). Nigel polished off his sea-bass, resisted the temptation to cut in with the ancient punch-line, amused himself instead with the knowledge that the MD was a virtual certainty for redundancy when Nigel's consultants got to grips with 're-configuring' Planet Avionics' senior management layer.

'Children at home?' he asked blondie, wondering if the theme of domesticity would dampen her over-enthusiasm to any extent.

It didn't. *No,* she told him, *not yet — it can be fun trying though.*

Back when he'd started to play capitalism at its own game, you rarely got women in the boardroom. Then you got the generation (his own generation) of the fierce, angry feminists, smashing through the glass ceiling, daring you to even think about holding a door open for them. Nowadays you got types like blondie here.

71

Would-be soft touches on the outside, would-be armour-plated inside: the *sex sells* contingent — the latest division from the regiment of ambitious women.

Just for the hell of it, still just playing, Nigel let her see the faintest hint of his expensively-achieved, perfectly-white smile again: *Yeah*, he answered her, *I'd heard that*.

★ ★ ★

It was certain now that there'd been no ID on the corpse, no ID anywhere in the immediate vicinity. Something could still turn up of course. In the half-hour since Robinson had done his work, several van loads of uniformed constables had been drafted in. Apart from the out-of-bounds inner cordon (where the SOCO team was still at work), Crowcross Wood was getting the finger-tip search treatment, inch by solid inch. Not just for anything relevant to the second body but also in relation to the weapon that had killed Martin Grove. The best time-of-death estimates for both the woman and Grove remained pending until Robinson's full post mortem examinations. But already he'd indicated — based on rectal temperature readings — that Grove had probably died first. Ergo, there was always the possibility that the killer's gun had been discarded out here somewhere. Jacobson seriously doubted it. Both killings looked professional — and professionals didn't usually make life easy for the police by leaving their weapons behind at or near the crime scene.

But the searching still had to go on, couldn't be shirked. You plodded on — it was what the term *meant* — you covered all the bases, the seemingly hopeless as well as the hopeful.

Jacobson followed Kerr out through the trees to where the police vehicles were parked up on the verge of the B road. He was speaking to Emma Smith on his mobile. Back in the incident room, Smith was trawling through every *misper* — missing person — report that had come in during the last twenty-four hours: there was nothing so far that remotely matched either the general age profile of the dead woman in the wood or the specific photos of her corpse which the SOCOs had emailed to her.

'OK, lass,' Jacobson told her, 'keep going — and take it back over the last couple of weeks if necessary. The body's recent — but she wouldn't be the first to disappear for a while and then turn up dead later on.'

Kerr drove them over to Martin Grove's place. PC Helen Dawson was still baby-sitting Maureen Bright. She'd been allowed back into the house to collect some clothes and over-night items. The plan was for Dawson to drive her to Jane Ebdon's (the brandies she'd drunk, if nothing else, precluded her from driving herself) where she could spend this afternoon and probably tonight as well without being on her own. It would be at least a day, maybe even a couple of days, before everything that the police teams needed to do at the crime scene would be finally completed. She'd be able to move back in after that — always assuming that she'd want to.

In the meantime, there would be a police guard maintained on the property around the clock.

The two women were coming out of the front door just as Kerr's car drew up on the tarmac drive. Maureen Bright was carrying a hold-all.

Jacobson attempted to prepare the way. He suggested that she might want to sit down in the gazebo again for a minute or two: there was something new, something important, he had to ask her about.

'Marty's dead,' she said, 'I've told you everything I know about it.'

'This isn't about Martin, Maureen — or not directly anyway,' Jacobson replied, trying to sound gentle, nonthreatening. 'I really need your help with this.'

Kerr had stored a series of close-ups of the unknown victim's face on his phone. Hardly pleasant to look at, but enough of her features had survived intact to make them recognisable to anyone who'd known her. As soon as it could be arranged, the civilian computer officer, Steve Horton, would run the imaging software which would reconstruct the way she'd looked before someone had discharged a handgun (the instant, informal theory was a Walther PPK) into her skull. But for now the camera-phone jpegs were all they had to work with outside of the incident room.

She dropped her bag at her feet, didn't budge from the spot.

'Whatever it is, let's just get on with it,' she said.

Jacobson decided not to argue the point. He

knew that he was just police to her, the lowest of the low, a bastard copper. Somebody you couldn't trust, somebody who was only ever bad news. He nodded to Kerr: *go ahead*.

Kerr showed her the close-ups on the tiny screen one by one. Her whole body winced. She looked like she might be set to scream — but nothing came out. She looked unsteady on her feet — but she didn't fall, didn't faint.

'I don't know her,' she said after a moment, turning her gaze slowly from Jacobson to Kerr and back again. 'I don't know her and I never saw her before.'

Her voice was calm. Her eyes didn't flinch.

'You're sure about that, Maureen?' Jacobson asked.

She ignored his question, asked her own.

'Is that it?' She leant down, picked up her bags. 'Can I go now? I want to go to Jane's now, please.'

10

Martin Grove.doc

Andy I didn't meet until a few days later. He'd been down in London at the big CND demo the previous weekend and had stopped on — although he never really said too much about what he'd been doing there, as far as I could ever recall. Virtually everybody from Myrtle Cottage had gone down to the demonstration of course: nearly a million people on the capital's streets against the arrival of Cruise and Pershing missiles in Europe according to the organisers, upwards of 250,000 according to the BBC, no more than half a dozen old age pensioners and a small, lame dog according to the Metropolitan Police. I'd been in London that weekend too but I'd been nowhere near the action. I'd spent most of Saturday in a cheap Irish boozer in Kilburn, guzzling cider and trying not to get into any arguments about Ulster or the IRA. The demo had culminated with a rally in Hyde Park. Claire and Nigel had even spoken from the platform, although they'd been unhappy about their slot which had been early on — while most of the marchers were still chanting their way noisily through the West End. The others had come straight back after the rally or had drifted back over the next couple of days. But Andy had gone AWOL and there'd been a rumour that he might have packed in the protest for good — but they needn't have worried, he was soon back amongst them.

Andy was a hard-case, one of the protest's official rough diamonds. He'd turned up out of the blue just like I did — a casual-job young drifter hitching through the area and brought back for the night by Claire in her green MG. It was a habit she'd cultivated, I realised soon enough. But while most recipients of her generosity cleared off the next day — or the day after that — Andy, like myself, stayed on. I never found out exactly where he came from — *I'm from all over, mate,* he used to say — and his accent was hard to pin down. Northern, guttural, maybe even Scottish — nobody seemed to know for sure. He was a couple of years older than me. Not much in reality — he'd turned twenty-three that autumn — but enough, at the age I was, for him to seem like a man of the world. Experienced, clued-in. Nigel was his champion naturally enough. Nigel stood up for anybody who hadn't been to college, who didn't have much in the way of formal education, who didn't have a comfortable background waiting to welcome them back with open arms anytime they grew tired of direct action against the OCS (the Oppressive Capitalist State in case you've forgotten, Dear Reader).

Andy kipped down in the basement along with his rows of demijohns and wine-making paraphernalia. It was probably Nigel who suggested there was room for me down there too — which, to be fair, there was. Two things really made Andy cool beans to Nigel's way of thinking. First of all he had actual *form*. Burglaries and car theft mainly. But serious enough — or at least sustained enough — that he'd apparently done a couple of stretches in a couple of Borstals (as they were still known back then).

After his last stretch — this was item two in his favour — he'd joined the army, the way a lot of 'bad lads' did in those days, had seen action in the Falklands. Except that the experience had made him anti-war, anti-government. It had politicised him (Nigel's term) and he'd got out, de-enlisted, as soon as he could afterwards. To Nigel, characters like Andy were 'outlaws', natural rebels: all they needed was the finishing school of a little bit of proletarian history (plus a little bit of Trotskyist theory) to turn them into fully-fledged revolutionaries in his own image. To be fair too, I was happy enough down there for a while. I didn't quiz Andy too much about his past and he didn't ask me too much about my own life pre-Myrtle Cottage. I found an old mattress in a storeroom, cleaned it, aired it, used it as a base for my sleeping bag.

The basement was a reasonable size — and with Andy's wine 'laboratory' in the middle of the room and our sleeping quarters staked out on opposite sides, we both had some privacy. Andy had rigged up a couple of light bulbs down there as well and the skylights let in some daylight. If I'd known what was coming for me of course — a couple of decades in prison — I'd never have slept down there for a single night, would have camped in the freedom field instead, slept out in the open under the stars. But you can't know the future, can you? Like I've already said, my friend, if I'd known what was coming, I'd never have set foot in Myrtle Cottage in the first place, never have clambered into Claire's too-inviting passenger seat. Taking sweets from strangers: it turned out my mum was right on that score after all.

Andy showed me the ropes — or his version of them. He went into Crowby with me the day I signed on at the DHSS, briefed me on what to say during the official interview. Quite a few of the protestors out at Myrtle Cottage were drawing the dole and not all of those who bothered to actually needed the money the way that Andy and me did — for some of them it was more a point of principle. Especially for the anarchists. They seriously loved the idea of getting the state to *pay* them to take action against it. It was what they called a *contradiction* — and exposing contradictions, I gradually understood, was something that more or less everybody out at the cottage was keen on. Andy's lady of the moment came in with us too. Hilary. A tall girl with full breasts and broad hips that weren't entirely disguised by her usual outfit of shapeless cardigans and baggy trousers. Hilary was a Sociology student from Crowby Polytechnic who spent most of her time out at the cottage and hardly any of it at the Poly as I found out later (a lot of the cottagers were cagey about who they really were, or what they really did, until they got to know you a bit). When we were eventually through at the DHSS, the three of us

79

sank a few beers in the Market Tavern before we headed back out to the cottage. Hilary was still full of her story about concentration camps that she'd picked up in London after the demo — she'd gone to a NVDA (nonviolent direct action) workshop which was where she'd heard the tale.

'A lot of them are just going to be old army barracks and stuff like that,' she was explaining, 'but apparently some of them are going to be brand-new, purpose-built.'

'You really think they're going to lock folk up just like the Nazis did?' I asked her, when I could get a word in.

Both of them looked at me as if I was a naïve, trusting fool — which is pretty much what I was.

'Believe it, mate,' Andy said. 'Marches and demos are one thing. But the moment it starts to look like our side's winning — if we can get there — that's when the big clampdown will start. And I mean big. They'll be rounding up anybody they think is a ringleader or seriously committed. Internment without trial, mate — just like they did in Belfast.'

Hilary was nodding enthusiastically.

'Thatcher and her paymasters in Washington can't afford to lose control of the situation, Martin. Once they've got the whole population against them, they'll clamp down just like Andy says. They'll do anything to stay in power — even a military coup.'

I drank from my latest beer — an over-chilled Guinness that I'd regretted ordering the minute I'd tasted it — and gaped at them. I was no fan of the government as far as I'd ever thought about it (which wasn't all that far) but I didn't actually know what a military coup was, although it didn't sound like a good thing.

Andy explained the concept to me — a long ramble about Allende, Pinochet and Chile, amongst other examples. Hilary told me about the special police station she claimed 'they' were building near Paddington Station. According to Hilary, it was being designed especially for political prisoners. The big feature would be silent, sound-absorbing cells where you wouldn't be able to hear your own voice or even your own footsteps — where you'd go mad within days unless you cooperated with your interrogators.

'All a bit pointless then, isn't it?' I commented. 'I mean — it looks like you can't win either way, can ya?'

Andy leaned in across the table, lowered his voice conspiratorially.

'The *people* will win, Martin. That's what this is all about. There'll be casualties amongst the vanguard all right — prison for some, probably more than a few deaths — but we gotta make sacrifices if we want to win.'

'You make it sound like a war,' I objected.

Hilary leant forwards too.

'It *is* a war,' she said. 'They're trying to turn the world into a nuclear prison camp, trying to enslave us. If the people can't stop them, they'll end up blowing us all to kingdom come.'

I'll remind you — again — that I was nineteen, right? My life up to that point didn't amount to much. I'd been poor and miserable at

81

home, unhappy at school — and all I'd achieved since I'd buggered off on my own was a couple of years of lonely, aimless drifting. I'd been pretty much a lost soul until, that afternoon in the Market Tavern, I started to see new, entirely unexpected possibilities for myself. Suddenly I had friends — young, bright, both sexes. Suddenly I could have a purpose if I wanted it, a chance to be part of something bigger than myself. Hilary's paranoid conspiracy theories about the government would have put a lot of people off. But, for me, right then, they had the opposite effect. Myrtle Cottage, the way Andy and Hilary told it, was a link in a chain of protest that was stretching around the world, growing bigger and bigger. It wasn't just about the threat of nuclear war either — although that was the biggie, the issue that united everybody in a common cause. No, there was a lot more involved besides. Myrtle Cottage had a transforming vision for all the world's ills — peace, socialism, revolution, call it what you will. And they were inviting *me* to share it with them, inviting *me* to join them, to get involved, to work with them.

Andy, one of Nigel's star pupils as I eventually worked out, was in his element.

'The next twelve months are crucial, mate. The first missiles are due at Greenham next month — and next year we'll probably get a decision on the Sizewell B inquiry.'

I didn't know what the fuck Sizewell B was but I didn't let on, just sipped my botched Guinness and nodded.

'Then there's the coalminers, Martin,' Andy continued, 'ever heard of a guy called Ian McGregor?'

'No,' I replied bluntly.

'A half-Yank bastard, mate. He did a hatchet job on British Steel, chucked thousands on the dole.'

'And now Maggie's brought him in to do the same with the pits,' Hilary cut in, excited again. 'The rumour is he'll go for big closures and the miners won't stand for it. There'll be a national coal strike — and with any luck that could turn into a general strike. Just like back in 1926.'

'*The workers united will never be defeated*, Martin,' Andy said, smiling. 'This time next year who knows what the situation will be?'

A couple of drunk quasi-dossers at the next table muttered something under their breath about effing communists. The Market Tavern in Crowby was never the most salubrious watering hole. Not now, not then. Andy and Hilary had got carried away with their invective, had forgotten about keeping their voices down. Fortunately, it only took Andy to give the two old drunks a quick menacing look for them both to shut it and get back on with their intermittent, chaotic game of cribbage.

Untutored as I was — and keen as I was to be kept on at the cottage — I remember that I still stated a few doubts about what they seemed to be arguing for (as far as I understood it anyway).

'But the government, Andy — I mean, most people support them, don't they? Voted for them and all that.'

Andy shoved his Golden Virginia pouch and his Rizlas across the table, offered me a roll-up. Weird: to this day I can still see that trivial action in nearly every detail. He had big, powerful hands, his fingers tattooed above the knuckles with L-O-V-E and H-A-T-E. He wore a couple of bulky-looking rings too. A coiled snake on one, a skull with ruby eyes on the other. I can still *hear* the moment too. Somebody had forked out for the jukebox — OMD, 'Enola Gay' — and the barman had just turned up the volume.

'They only got elected with forty-three per cent of the vote in seventy-nine, mate,' Andy told me against the din. 'They got even less this year — and nearly one in three didn't vote for anybody at all. That's not what I'd call a mandate, Martin. The trouble with people in the UK is that they're all sleepwalking, like they've been fucking hypnotised or something. That's what the protest movement's all about, waking them up, de-brainwashing them.'

I slid out a cigarette paper, helped myself to Andy's rolling tobacco. Hilary was resting her head on his shoulder now, her hand resting on his forearm. I could move out any time I liked, I reminded myself, I wasn't joining a cult or anything like that. Why not stop on for a bit, see how things turned out? Hilary leaned up, whispered something personal and indecipherable in Andy's ear, something that made him smile with anticipation. Well of course watching them made me think about Claire, about what she'd be like. All of it — all of it from day one — was always about Claire.

11

Two cars drove over to the Crowcross Arms. Jacobson and Kerr following Mick Hume and DC Williams. It was lunchtime now but the place was as quiet as you'd expect an out-of-the-way country pub to be on a Monday afternoon. Mick Hume, going in first while Jacobson made a few more necessary calls on his mobile, had a discreet word with the landlord, set everything up. The pub had a fearsome CCTV system inside and out — the closest one they knew about so far to both crime scenes. The inquiry team would need a copy of the hard disc or the master tapes (depending on the technicalities), would potentially need to examine every frame on the system. But right now, immediately, Jacobson just needed somebody with a trained eye to scan quickly through the last twenty-four hours, with an emphasis on last night and early this morning. He'd earmarked Mick Hume for that task. Ray Williams and DS Kerr, meantime, would talk to the customers, especially if they turned out to be locals. Jacobson himself planned on dealing with the management: *John Colin Ewing*, according to the licensing notice above the main entrance. The Crowcross Arms had three public rooms: a formal restaurant plus two lounges. The evenings-and-weekends-only restaurant was closed and there were no more than a half a dozen drinkers in the biggest lounge plus a solitary barmaid who, pen in hand, seemed to be mainly engrossed in the pages of a puzzle magazine. Jacobson caught up with Ewing in the second, smaller lounge, which was otherwise empty.

Ewing was behind the bar counter. Hume had taken over his backroom to scan the CCTV system and Ewing had evidently re-located himself through here with his accounts and order books. He was a short, stocky figure in a neat green polo shirt that had stretched in the middle to accommodate his beer gut. His thinning brown hair was combed forward unconvincingly over a spreading bald patch. Jacobson made him any age between forty-five and sixty. Beyond forty, he'd come to realise, you couldn't reliably tell a man's age any more just by looking. Exercise, diet, lifestyle, genetic inheritance, wealth, fashion-sense — they all played their part in how old someone looked these days. To guess accurately, you needed access to *data*. If it was at all important, he'd found, it was simpler and quicker just to ask.

Jacobson produced his ID and Ewing nodded, still casual, still kept unaware (on Jacobson's instruction to Hume) of the full reason for the police visitation.

'Something to drink, Inspector?' he asked. 'It's a hot day out there.'

Along with the no-smoking pledge, Jacobson had a new booze rule too: nothing before six o'clock — at least on a working day.

'Thanks. A fizzy water, if you've got one chilled.'

Ewing found a glass, took a squat bottle of Perrier out of the cold cabinet, undid the cap a fraction. Jacobson stuck a two pound coin conspicuously on the counter. It was another rule. But an old one. He never accepted free drinks — hard, soft or otherwise — on licensed premises. Ewing half-filled the glass, placed it and the bottle within Jacobson's easy reach.

'Your detective said this was something serious — I mean the one who's looking at our CCTV.'

'Serious as in murder, old son,' Jacobson replied — then told the publican as much as he thought he needed to know: Martin Grove had been found dead in his home early this morning — and the death was being treated as suspicious.

'*Jesus* — Charlie Gilbert said he'd seen a few police vehicles out that way all right. Though he seemed to think they were heading over to Crowcross Wood.'

'We're looking into an incident over there too. It could be related, we think.'

DCS Greg Salter had called a press conference for three o'clock, according to his latest text message. Before then, Jacobson intended to be as circumspect as he could get away with. He picked up the glass, drank a mouthful of cool water, then drank another deeper one.

'Who's Charlie Gilbert by the way?'

Ewing had found a set of pint tumblers that he'd started to polish with a white dish towel. A classic nervous reaction to unexpected bad news — do something normal, do something mundane and routine. Even so, watching him, seeing

87

how clumsy he was at the chore, Jacobson thought that he didn't look like a man who'd spent all of his working life behind the bar of a country pub.

'Oh, just one of the original locals, Inspector. Colebrook Farm's his place — over near the old airfield? He called in earlier, he does most lunchtimes in fact.'

'And what about Martin Grove? Was he a regular here?'

'I wouldn't call him a regular, no. But he certainly looked in every now and again. He was as fond of decent real ale as the next chap — Black Sheep usually.'

Ewing finally gave up on his displacement activity, put down the towel and the latest tumbler, answered a question that Jacobson hadn't asked yet.

'*Dead*. I just can't believe this. Despite it all, he was always welcome under my roof, Inspector, *always*.'

'Despite it all?'

'Not everybody in the locality was keen on him being here obviously. The old timers still remember the case — you know, the Myrtle Cottage murder. As for the newcomers — well, they've made their pile and moved here for the peace and quiet, haven't they? The country lifestyle? Guilty or not guilty, Martin Grove didn't really fit in. He's not — he wasn't — really typical Aga-set material, if you think about it.'

Jacobson topped up his drink.

'So Grove's had trouble locally?'

'No, I wouldn't go so far as that — not actual trouble. More the cold-shoulder treatment. He'd come into the bar and conversations would stop for a minute or two, that's all. Then they'd start up again. Nobody ever *said* anything to him — or not that I ever heard anyway.'

'How did Grove react?'

'He didn't really. He'd order his drink and find a quiet corner. He nearly always had a book with him if he came in — or a newspaper. He'd drink a couple of pints, read whatever he was reading and then he'd go. He did a lot of walking in the area apparently. Sometimes he'd have a map with him — Ordnance Survey, you know? — and he'd spend his time looking at that.'

Ewing helped himself to a neat whisky from one of his optics, knocked it back in one.

'I don't usually during opening hours,' he said. 'But this — *Jesus*.'

'Was he always on his own when he looked in?' Jacobson asked, recalling what PC Helen Dawson had already told him about Maureen Bright being rarely seen in the locality.

'As far as I'm aware,' Ewing replied. 'His, eh, girlfriend or whatever, is a bit of a mystery woman. You see her drive past in her car from time to time — but that's about it.'

'You live on the premises then, Mr Ewing?'

'Please — the name's John. Yes, I do. Cosy little flat upstairs. My wife and I took the tenancy on three years ago — I used to be a circuit-board designer, got laid off in the first big cull over at Planet A. So we thought sod it — we did the brewery training course, sold up everything and moved in here. It was always her dream life — running a country pub. Only she got ill last year, died at Christmas . . . '

Jacobson felt a rush of sympathy. There didn't seem to be too much that was remarkable about J.C. Ewing. Not at first glance or not on the surface anyway. Just an ordinary, everyday man, a lot of people might have thought. And overweight, unhealthy-looking. But ordinary, everyday men had dreams too — and hopes and plans that got roundly stuffed by fate.

'The last few days, John — you haven't noticed any unusual faces around? Anybody that made you suspicious in any way?'

'Well it's the summer, isn't it? We get a lot of restaurant trade in the evenings. Folk drive out from Crowby for a bit of fresh air. And we even get tourists now and then — Americans, Japanese. But we've not had any kind of trouble if that's what you mean. And not anybody I'd call suspicious. Couples and family parties mainly. They eat, drink, pay up, leave — '

'Fair enough. Though my team might want to speak to your restaurant staff when they clock on, see if they've noticed anyone they think we should know about.'

Jacobson polished off the rest of the Perrier. A strong black espresso would have washed it down perfectly. But the gleaming Gaggia behind Ewing's left shoulder was clearly as out of lunchtime commission as the rest of his deserted second lounge bar. The restaurant must be coining it, he thought, if Ewing was keeping his head above water.

Jacobson handed him one of his cards and then headed along the dark corridor to the tiny office where Hume was scanning the quad-screen CCTV monitor.

'Take a look at this, guv,' Hume said, not bothering to look up. 'Eleven-fifty-two last night according to the time stamp.'

The image was paused and jerky. Jacobson looked. Then he looked again. Then he asked Hume to rewind the sequence and press slow-play.

12

Martin Grove.doc

The first month I spent at Myrtle Cottage coincided with the anti-airbase campaign revving itself up by several notches. As people still said back then, things were about to 'get heavy'.

The reason was the rapid construction, virtually overnight, of a shiny, new perimeter fence all the way around the old airfield. A left-wing MP (there were still a few around back then) asked questions in Parliament and was rewarded — eventually — with a bland official answer: *Although no longer in use, Crowcross Airfield remained MOD property and the fence would prevent any future repetition of the recent acts of vandalism which had occurred there.* The alleged 'vandalism' was understood by everybody concerned to be a reference to the Sunday back in August (near Hiroshima Day) when the cottage had organised a mass sit-down on the moss-blown, crumbling main runway. But there was still no government admission (or government denial) regarding the alleged plan to revive the airbase for the use of NATO's nuclear bombers.

The new fence had a single, entrance point: two broad, tall gates, festooned with warnings not to trespass. Behind the gates, a couple of sturdy portacabins also appeared which func-tioned as the HQ for the small teams of security guards who now started to patrol the area twenty-four hours a day, complete with flashlights, batons and Alsatian dogs.

Everybody at Myrtle Cottage read these developments as a vindication of why they were there. As Claire herself often said, if there was really nothing planned for Crowcross then why the hell had the MOD gone to all that trouble? Especially as — so far — they weren't using their own personnel to guard the base but had gone to the extra expense of hiring a local contractor, CrowbyGuard Security, to conduct the daily patrols. The cottage became even more of a rumour factory than it already was. One big question dominated every discussion: how should the protest respond?

The freedom field backed onto a lonely stretch of the airfield near to the end of one of the smaller runways (it was the proximity of the field that gave the cottage its strategic importance). Swiftly, the top end of the field became an everyday focus for cottage activity. Peace ribbons were tied to the fence, patrolling guards were regaled with impromptu peace concerts or attempts, always unsuccessful, to engage them in conversation. None of it had much effect really — or got any media coverage, which amounted to same the thing. Everybody was soon hacked off about the situation, especially Nigel and Claire. The fence was *symbolic*, Claire told us all again and again. The fence was an assertion of the oppressive power of the state — it needed to be successfully breached to demonstrate that oppressive power could be challenged, that it could even, ultimately, be defeated.

Plans began to be hatched — and personnel to be selected. I was heavily involved in the flyposting 'squad' by then — had instantly seen it as a job I could especially help out at (and impress with). Flyposting usually happened late on Thursday nights, so that our posters always had a good chance of being seen over the weekend when Crowby was at its busiest. Nowhere was safe from our efforts. Advertising hoardings, bus shelters, shop windows. Anywhere a poster could be seen, have an impact, get the message out to the public. The police probably viewed the poster campaign as not much more than a low-level nuisance, probably had far bigger crimes to worry about. But they were still definitely on the look-out for us, especially as they were coming under pressure from the Town Hall on the issue. The squad had been caught out a couple of times and a few protestors had been hauled up before the magistrates' courts and fined. Then I came on the scene — with my 'expert' local knowledge of rat runs, back streets, short-cuts and myriad devious ways in and out of the town that I'd grown up in. The first result was that more of our posters got posted and nobody posting them got busted. The second result was that, at a Monday Evening Planning Meeting, I was duly proposed by Nigel, duly seconded by Claire, and voted onto the newly created Perimeter Fence Action Sub-Committee. It was only the second time in my life that I'd ever experienced the warm glow of peer approval. I wasn't to know, of course, that it would also be one of the last times.

The Fence Com, as it quickly became known, took itself very seriously. The level of day-to-day paranoia in Myrtle Cottage was more-or-less average for any anti-government protest in 1980s Britain — in other words, it was just generally *assumed* that there were informers amongst us, naming names and relaying regular reports of what we were up to back to the relevant authorities. So the Fence Com always met down in the basement, well out of general earshot. The location also made sense in that Andy and me were both Fence Com members anyway — as was Hilary. Plus, inevitably, Claire and Nigel.

The Fence Com brought me closer to both of them. Another unwary step on the road to hell. But I couldn't foresee that then.

The Fence Com's real job was to plan illegal action. Everybody knew that. But I also found out that they weren't above considering auxiliary bureaucratic measures — or boring old crap, as I regarded it at the time. Claire, for instance, reckoned the fence had been built without proper local planning consultation. She raised the issue at the first meeting. (She was wrong as it turned out — the MOD didn't need anybody else's permission to fence in their own land.)

'As the owner of an adjacent property, I could try and lodge an appeal with the county council,' she told us, summing up her argument.

As the owner. Even now, years later, I can still hear her uttering those three astonishing words. Naïvely (as ever), I'd thought until that moment that we were *squatting*. I'd no concept that we were actually there legally at the owner's invitation — or that Claire was the lawful owner of Myrtle Cottage and the land that came with it. I'd wondered about the fact that we had an electricity supply and a working telephone connection and that the DHSS hadn't made too much of a fuss about the address I'd given them. But I'd never put two and two together. I was young and stupid basically. Unlike now, when I'm nearly old and uselessly wise when it's far too late for wisdom.

My amazement must have been written all over my face.

Claire smiled at me.

'Oh, sorry, Martin — I just assumed you knew like everyone else,' she said gently.

She'd tied her hair back for some reason (maybe because the shower head in the decrepit bathroom was broken again). I thought the look suited her. It emphasised her fine, even features — and her blue eyes, the colour of warm, untroubled skies. Not that the way Claire looked was ever the most important thing about her. Not to me, not to anybody else. Not even remotely. Claire grabbed at life, that was what made her special. She made you want to grab at it too — grab at it *with* her.

'Claire's a spoilt little rich girl, Martin,' Nigel said. 'A class enemy who's changed sides.'

'Better than a class enemy who hasn't,' somebody else commented — probably Andy.

Everybody laughed.

When the meeting broke up (nothing much

got decided that first day), Claire and Nigel said they were going to take a walk over in Crowcross Wood, clear their heads with some fresh air. They invited me — and only me — to come with them.

'Yeah, sure,' I said, or something monosyllabic to that effect.

The Fence Com always liked to lubricate its debates with Andy's strong rice wine. Nigel grabbed a bottle that was still two-thirds full, wedged the cork back into its mouth, and we set off.

I was disappointed that we couldn't use Claire's MG. Since it was a classic two-seater, there was no way that Nigel and me could both fit in as passengers. We took Nigel's battered, grey minivan instead. You could walk to the wood from the cottage (if you didn't mind walking along past the airfield) but Claire had letters she wanted to post at the pillar box in Crowcross so we drove there first, then parked up near the wood on the way back.

It was a windless, late autumn day. Fallen leaves turning golden under our feet. Squirrels frantic in the high branches. The occasional caw of a distant crow. We passed the bottle back and forth as we walked and they told me more about themselves than I'd ever heard before.

Claire's upbringing was what she called 'solid'. Her father was a merchant banker (third generation) and before she'd gone to Oxford (where she'd met Nigel) she'd been educated at Roedean. When I looked blank at that piece of information, Nigel explained that it was the top girls' public school, the female equivalent of Eton. Claire, it seemed, had used a modest slice of one of her (several) private allowances to buy up the Myrtle Cottage property when the story about the airbase had been leaked to the press.

Nigel's background, though, wasn't all that different from mine. Midlands council estate, nth-generation working class. With the major exceptions that Nigel's dad still lived with his mum and Nigel had gone to school more days than he'd stayed away — sailing through his eleven-plus and, later on, his A levels (it was Claire, on another occasion, who added the details that he'd also been good at sports and sickeningly popular, especially with the girls when he'd reached the sixth form). He'd studied at the LSE — BSc Econ — before he'd gone to one of the Oxford colleges as a postgrad. Somewhere on his journey from the bottom of the shit-heap, he'd evidently traded up his original accent for something glib and classless. Claire, although I never considered the fact at the time, had probably made a similar trade *down*. But how Nigel spoke — or what he said — was never really as important or impressive as his confident air of total self-belief.

We were in the deepest part of the wood now. The trees standing black against the fading afternoon light. I had only one question and I asked it straight out: *why*? One of them was already rich. The other one easily had it in him to become rich. So why were they roughing it in the middle of nowhere, risking arrest, sticking their necks out?

They looked at each other, maybe working out who should answer.

'Martin, mate,' Nigel said after a moment — and smiling (always he had that confident smile on his face when he wanted to convince you of something), 'wealth's just a smoke-screen, a big, fat diversion. No matter how much you have, someone else always has more. And all of it comes from somebody else being exploited, somebody else losing out. If the human race can't get its act together, can't learn to share what it's got instead of fighting over it like a pack of animals, then we're all fucked — doomed. Once you wake up to that fact, you're stuck with it, you can't *unlearn* it — you've got to *act* on it.'

He passed me the bottle and I took another slug of rice wine. All that week, Andy (and occasionally Hilary) had been tutoring me in the basics of revolutionary theory — and especially on the point that, for a revolutionary, there was no such thing as single-issue politics. Getting rid of nuclear weapons was all well and good — so were gay rights, black rights, women's rights, so was Troops Out of Ireland. Some of these goals could be won in the short term, some of them probably couldn't. But what was far more important, they kept telling me, was that these were all entry routes by which people, and especially young people, could be brought to *real* politics — could be brought to the knowledge that, underlying everything else, the fundamental problem (and enemy) was the capitalist system itself.

'So you'd give up everything — the easy life

— for this?' I asked again.

The revolution sounded great in theory. Top. But even a gormless kid from the streets could see practical snags.

'It's nothing like as much to give up as you think, Martin,' Claire answered. 'There's only two kinds of rich people, believe me. The dull, boring ones and the dull, boring, obnoxious ones. I'd rather be here with comrades who're doing something useful with their lives.'

She asked me for the wine bottle and I handed it to her. She drank from it, passed it on to Nigel, and then performed an elegant hop, skip and jump over a felled tree trunk.

That was so Claire. Deadly serious one minute, falling about with frivolity the next.

'Sides, Martin,' she said, catching her breath, 'my family haven't cut me off — yet. And I've kept hold of the MG, haven't I? I couldn't let my little speed-baby go. I'm still a party-fun girl at heart.'

13

There were three easily visible external CCTV cameras in the centre of Crowcross.

One was on the forecourt of the garage/shop. The other two were focused on the car park of the Crowcross Arms. According to John Ewing, the publican, the parish council had funded a camera unit on the village green the previous year (and another one at the public car park which fronted the long-disused jetty down on the riverside). But there had been arguments about privacy and about expense and they'd been dismantled again in the spring. Jacobson's stroke of luck was that one of the two pub cameras had been temporarily misaligned. Instead of monitoring one half of the car park, it was recording movements out in the street — sweeping along Crowcross's single main thoroughfare in a steady arc.

If the driver in question had kept deliberately away from the pub then he'd screwed up. Ewing's system was hi-spec, newish. At maximum resolution, the registration plate was one hundred per cent legible. Hume was already calling in the letters and digits to the control room. They'd know shortly if they were right: if the white van (not as scruffy in appearance as they'd seen it in the past) was as familiar as they thought it was. Ditto for the blurred face behind the wheel, baseball cap pulled down tight. It could just be a coincidence, plain and simple. Jacobson could no more see this particular fool-to-himself as the killer than he could Maureen Bright. But it was a bloody unusual one if it was. And it wanted looking into. Urgently.

He became aware of DS Kerr, the man most likely to know, sticking his head around the door, DC Williams lurking in the gloomy corridor behind him.

'Take a look at this, old son,' he advised, ushering Kerr towards the image on the screen.

'What the fuck?' Kerr exclaimed — succinctly confirming Jacobson's hypothesis.

Hume's mobile rang a second or two later in any case: the vehicle registration tallied on the PNC/DVLA computer link.

Jacobson decided that Kerr should chase it up on his own immediately. The rest of them, himself included, were still needed here.

★　★　★

Kerr took the quickest route he knew back to Crowby — but that still meant twisting, narrow B roads all the way to Wynarth. He phoned his wife, Cathy, as soon as he was out of Crowcross. He was on early shifts this week — or he would have been without the major disruption of a double shooting. He'd planned on catching at least the second half of Sam's after-school football match and now he'd miss it — again. Everybody on the designated murder squad suffered for their art. Taking regular 'holidays' from your routine CID caseload was a definite upside. But the big downside was that murder investigations didn't keep fixed hours. You came off normal shifts and your personal life went right out the window.

Cathy, who only worked part-time, said she'd still be there to see their son play anyway. Her voice was calm, level, no hint of anger. But Kerr knew she couldn't be happy about it. Worse than that, the lad would be really disappointed. To the rest of the world it was a junior kick-about for the under-nines. To Sam it was the Premier League and the World Cup rolled into one. He was eight now and well started into the phase where his mum always played second fiddle to his dad in importance. Cathy, who'd been reading books on child development for the psychology minor on her Open University course, had explained some of the experts' theories the other night. Apparently the growing male ego needed to differentiate itself from the mother. *It's a natural healthy stage*, she'd said — *so long as there's a positive male role model around*. He told her he'd be home whenever he could, ended the call, promised himself that he'd think of a way to make it up to the boy. But how did you ever make up for not being there? He slowed down on another tight bend then switched on the in-car for distraction. Shuffle mode: go on, surprise me.

It was maybe three months since he'd last clapped eyes on George McCulloch, the Glaswegian, ex-junkie, ex-burglar who he'd used (discreetly) for years now as an unregistered, unofficial grass. Jacobson, Mick Hume and one or two others knew about the arrangement, but there was no official CID record — and no official CID handler. McCulloch cleaned windows for a living these days and had more or less gone straight. As far as Kerr knew anyway. But he still lived out on the crime-ridden Woodlands estate, was still a handy, local pair of eyes and ears when required. Right now, of course, the issue was what he'd been up to at midnight last night — and why he'd been up to it in Crowcross, of all places.

Lucinda Williams, 'Everything is Wrong'. Alabama 3, 'Woke up This Morning'. Ali Farka Toure, 'Savane'. Kerr loved that track. He pulled into a lay-by just outside Wynarth, waited until it finished before he tried the latest mobile number he had for McCulloch.

He answered straightaway. He sounded as cagey as ever, didn't acknowledge Kerr by name.

'I need a word urgently,' Kerr told him. 'This afternoon — it's important and it can't wait.'

McCulloch said he was working over on the Bartons estate. They could meet in the pub over there, the Catchpenny, if that suited.

'OK. Fine,' Kerr said, relieved. 'I should get there inside twenty.'

Informers, official or unofficial, constantly feared exposure. So it was a piece of luck that McCulloch was cleaning windows out at the Bartons, a solidly middle-class enclave where he would feel relatively safe and secure.

The pub was busier than the Crowcross Arms had been. Especially out on the patio under the sun umbrellas. McCulloch had got there first, had found a table as far out of earshot as possible. Kerr brought two beers out from the bar. Plus a packet of salted peanuts he'd bought as an afterthought. He quenched his thirst with a couple of deep mouthfuls and then got straight to the point.

'You could be in serious crap, Geordie. I need to know what you were doing last night — and don't lie or bullshit me. You're caught on camera. Crowcross village at midnight. *Why?*'

McCulloch drew on his inevitable roll-up before he spoke. He was as smart in appearance as Kerr had ever seen him. He was in working clothes — jeans and a T-shirt, but both new-looking, clean and pressed. He might even have shaved sometime since Easter. No baseball cap though — probably to avoid putting off his Bartons customers.

'Ah just went for a drive, Mr Kerr. That's allowed, isn't it?'

'I said don't fuck about. I mean it. I'm trying to help you out here.'

McCulloch was staring at him, trying to read him.

'It's Maxine. She's doing my head in — we row a lot recently. Sometimes ah just need tae get out of the place.'

'Out of the place at midnight? Out on to the North Crowby bypass, then out to Wynarth, then all the way out to Crowcross?'

'I just like tae drive sometimes, get my head straight.'

Kerr took another sip of beer.

'So you're saying you had an argument with Maxine. And you went for a late-night drive to cool off?'

'Aye, that's it in a nutshell. You can ask her if you like,' McCulloch said, offering his mobile for the purpose.

Kerr had never met the famous Maxine, though he knew that she was deeply implicated in McCulloch's successful breakout from heroin and from the small-time crimes that paid for a habit. McCulloch's previous long-term woman, Sylvie (actually his wife), had died from bad gear — which had been another significant moment on his road to Damascus.

'It's worse than that, Geordie. She'll have to give us a formal statement — when you left *and* when she saw you after that.'

McCulloch looked panicked.

'We'll send a uniformed round, obviously,' Kerr added quickly.

McCulloch's neighbours wouldn't bat an eyelid at a patrol car calling by. Anybody from CID would be a different matter, could put McCulloch under unwelcome local scrutiny and suspicion.

'Whit's this actually about, Mr Kerr?' McCulloch asked.

Kerr ignored the question.

'I need to know everything about this drive of yours, Geordie. I need *details*.'

McCulloch told him: when he'd left, how long he'd taken, his precise route in both directions. He claimed that Crowcross was as far as he'd got. He'd driven down to the old jetty, only he'd felt weary by the time he'd got there, exhausted by arguing and tired out by his working day. He'd dozed off in the driver's seat, smoked a roll-up when he woke up, then driven back home.

'And the row with Maxine?' Kerr asked.

The pub camera had clocked his van twice, headed into the village just before twelve and then headed out again an hour later. McCulloch's tale was unoriginal — but not totally unbelievable.

'She wants me tae start college, learn about computers an' that. Thinks we should be going upmarket, mibbe even get off the estate.'

'I've heard worse ideas.'

'Mibbe so. But I'm happy enough cleaning windaes. I'm not the ambitious type.'

Kerr smiled — despite the circumstances. McCulloch was a pretty useless specimen by conventional standards. But Kerr liked him, even admired him. It was easy enough to get into what he'd been into. It was harder, and rarer, to climb back out.

McCulloch turned his attention to his beer at last, sank half of it in a couple of quick mouthfuls. Deliberately, Kerr still hadn't told him the real story about last night.

'The name Martin Grove mean anything to you?' he asked him, as if out the blue.

'I don't think so, Mr Kerr. Should it?'

'So you've never visited Martin Grove's property — just the other side of Crowcross?'

'No, why would I? Unless ah've driven past some time without realising it, of course.'

'And your drive last night didn't take you past Crowcross Wood?'

'No again. The wrong direction, isn't it?'

'Did you notice any other vehicles out and about while you were over there?'

McCulloch shook his head.

'Nothing past Wynarth that I can recall. That's the attraction out that way — somewhere nice and quiet.'

He extinguished his spent roll-up, immediately set about constructing a replacement.

Kerr sipped more beer. He could take McCulloch at his word or he could play it safe. He decided on safe. It was too risky otherwise — for both of them.

'OK. Here's the deal. We'll stay put for the moment. I'll get somebody from duty CID to come out. They'll take a formal statement, ask you what I've already asked you. Meantime, I'll get the plod over to your place, take Maxine's statement. Your van's in the car park here, yes?'

McCulloch nodded. But not looking happy.

'It's going to need to stay there — and you need to stay out of it — until I can get some SOCOs out here. You wearing the same clothes as last night?'

McCulloch looked really worried now.

'Ah changed this morning, stuck yesterday's in the washing pile. Maxine likes tae see me turned out neat these days. Whit's going on, Mr Kerr?'

Kerr finally gave him the minimalist version.

'Suspected double murder, that's what. This guy Grove plus A.N. Other. Both out Crowcross way.'

'Now hang oan a minute — '

Kerr interrupted him.

'It's nothing to you, Geordie — if you're not involved. But your record's longer than your arm. I want you eliminated, that's all. I want you kept well out of it.'

McCulloch grasped the point quicker than he would have done once.

'Oh right, ah see. There'll be time for another pint mibbe then — while we're waiting, like?'

★ ★ ★

Jacobson needed to get back to Crowby in time for the press conference which DCS Greg Salter had called for three o'clock. But he wanted to visit Charlie Gilbert before he left the vicinity. Gilbert was the farmer John Ewing had mentioned earlier. His farm wasn't more than a mile or so from Crowcross Wood and not much more distance from Martin Grove's place. He was an obvious-enough potential witness. With Kerr already gone, he asked DC Williams to drive him over there. A motorcycle cop intercepted them in the Crowcross Arms car park just as they were leaving. Steve Horton, the civilian computer officer, had faxed enhanced facial images of the second shooting victim — the unknown female — to the Mobile Incident Unit. Jacobson glanced at them, kept one, instructed the bike cop to deliver the rest to Mick Hume. Hume was still checking the pub's CCTV system.

'Tell him to show these to John Ewing — and

tell him I said he's to be discreet. Has Ewing ever seen her? Does he know who she is? That's all he's to ask for now.'

En route, he quizzed Williams about the lunchtime customers he'd spoken to.

'Nothing doing, guv. Nearly all non-locals for one thing — out in the countryside for the day. The barmaid said she knew Grove by sight. According to her, he always comes in on his own. She reckons it's a couple of weeks at least since he's last been on the premises.'

Williams took a couple of wrong turns before they found the right farm — and then they had to make their way along the private road which led up to the main set of buildings. The road ran between two fields, flowering rape in both, day-glo, unreal yellow against the blue afternoon sky. They parked in a yard near the farmhouse. Maybe fifty yards away to the right, there was a massive long, low wooden construction, from which emanated a lavatorial stench (even before Jacobson opened the passenger door and clambered out).

'That'll be the fresh country air, I suppose,' he commented maliciously.

'Battery chickens or something like that,' Williams explained. 'Poultry of some kind anyhow.'

Jacobson smirked.

'Remind me to go vegan, old son — and urgently.'

There was a mud-caked Toyota 4×4 in front of the house and the sound of dogs barking somewhere not too distant. They walked towards the porch but didn't get far before they were interrupted. Neither of them noticed exactly where Charlie Gilbert sprang from (one of the side barns, Jacobson decided later). But suddenly there he was beside them on the path, telling them precisely who he was.

'Charlie Gilbert. Can I help you?'

A posh voice — or maybe trying to sound posher than it was really comfortable with. Jacobson made him younger than fifty, older than forty — but tall, lean, fit.

'DC Williams, Crowby CID,' Williams said, shoving his ID near Gilbert's face. 'This is DCI Jacobson.'

Jacobson outlined the same minimalist version of events he'd told John Ewing, scanning Gilbert's tan-red, weather-beaten face for his reaction.

There wasn't much. Maybe he tightened his lips. Maybe he was quieter, less cocksure, when he next spoke. But Jacobson had learned that there were a thousand and one reactions to the news of murder. More people than you might think took it in their stride. Especially if they'd no close connection to the victim.

Gilbert ushered them into his farmhouse (ditching his workboots at the door). Jacobson was surprised by the decent coffee Gilbert swiftly engineered in his modish-looking kitchen (not an Aga in sight). 'You live alone out here?' he'd asked him by then. 'Good God, no,' Gilbert had told him: his wife was a schoolteacher in Wynarth and his youngest son, the one who still lived at home, was out at his day-job, IT support

111

for a firm over at the Science and Business Park. If you wanted to stay on the land these days, he'd added, you had to *diversify*, had to establish as many different income streams as you could.

'I saw a lot of your people parked up in Crowcross Wood, Inspector,' he was saying now. 'I thought to myself — that looks serious.'

Jacobson didn't answer the implied question.

'Let's deal with Martin Grove first. You knew him, I take it?'

Jacobson and Gilbert were sitting at Gilbert's onyx kitchen table. Williams, who'd declined coffee, was standing near the window, occasionally taking a look out at Gilbert's Alsatians, quiet now, in their caged run behind the house.

'I know most people out this way, Inspector. I've lived here most of my life. I'm my father's eldest, you see. The farm came to me when he died.'

'And Martin Grove?'

'I can't say I was delighted when he moved into the area. Bloody odd too. Why the hell would he want to come back here?'

'But you had contact with him?' Jacobson persisted.

'Live and let live and all that. There's a right of way across my land. He seemed to spend a lot of time out walking.'

'And you'd pass the time of day with him?'

'If our paths crossed, yes. Nothing very profound though. The weather mainly.'

'I've heard he liked a pint in the Crowcross Arms,' Jacobson observed.

'Much the same thing. I'd nod hello if I saw

112

him at the bar. But I'm usually in company when I call in there.'

It wasn't the story Jacobson had heard from John Ewing — or maybe it was the same story with a little bit of spin attached.

'So the last time you saw Martin Grove was when exactly?'

'I'm not really sure. Maybe one day last week. Definitely not yesterday, definitely not over the weekend.'

'And you've never been on his property at any time whatsoever?'

Gilbert looked hard at him. There was something rheumy about his eyes, Jacobson noticed. Conjunctivitis maybe.

'No, absolutely not. Never. Why would I do that?'

Jacobson sipped at the coffee, the best he'd had all day, before he spoke again. He felt more grateful for it than Gilbert would ever know.

'You must have been here back in the Eighties then? At the time of the peace camp — and Claire Oldham?'

Gilbert drank his coffee too, took his time answering.

'Well, yes and no. I was barely in my twenties then. Still off at university most of the time. Keele.'

'But, even so, you would have stayed in touch with the farm, visited here on holidays and weekends?'

Gilbert's red face reddened. The question had riled him — all too easily, Jacobson thought.

'Yes, obviously. But I kept well away from all

113

those smelly hippies. Everybody local did. Anyway, what's all that got to do with — '

'Just idle curiosity,' Jacobson lied, 'people's lives interest me. A perk of the job, if you like. You tried uni — but you still came back into farming?'

Gilbert managed an unconvincing smile.

'I went in for engineering — but it wasn't really for me. This place runs too deep in my blood, I suppose. I met my wife there though — so something good came of it.'

Jacobson drained his cup and stood up, evidently ready to leave.

'You still haven't said what your people are doing over in the wood,' Gilbert commented.

'I'd tune into the TV or the radio about four o'clock, Mr Gilbert. They'll probably have the full story by then. But you can look at this for now.'

Jacobson dug into his pocket, pulled out Steve Horton's digitally-enhanced image. Gilbert studied it closely.

'Seen her before?' Jacobson asked.

'No, I'm sorry. I haven't,' Gilbert replied, 'never.'

Jacobson decided to believe him — at least until a better option came along.

14

Nigel Copeland found himself in the ample back-seat of his Lexus cruising smoothly along Mill Street. There was bad traffic congestion out at the motorway junction and Nigel's driver had re-calibrated the sat nav, was planning on taking an A-road route north, theoretically avoiding the worst current tailbacks. Nigel had thought about paying a nostalgic visit to the Mill Street area when he'd gone walkabout last night. He'd rejected the idea as being too depressing, maybe even, from what he'd heard, too dangerous. But now, with Hayle Close itself coming into view, he realised he couldn't resist the impulse.

He asked his driver to park and wait with the vehicle. The driver pulled up near the Bricklayer's Arms. He didn't make any comment but Nigel knew he'd be wondering what the hell Nigel was up to. *And so am I*, he thought. The driver wouldn't be happy about the area either, not even in daylight. Nigel knew that he was big on self-protection — *what with the way things are nowadays* — always drove with the car doors securely locked. Nigel knew he kept a knife under the dash. He'd even broached the idea of a handgun one time, said he could get hold of one easily enough. Nigel had told him no — definitely, absolutely no — not if he wanted to go on working for him. Nigel stepped out onto the pavement and then crossed the street quickly when a reversing delivery vehicle outside the deep-shuttered Londis store brought the stream of cars and vans to a temporary halt.

Hudson's scrapyard, which had stood on the corner, was long gone. A mess of rusting corrugated iron and jagged barbed wire was pretty much all that remained. In the early years of the Hayle Close Free State, the activists and squatters had regularly tapped into the scrapyard's power supply and diverted substantial quantities of liberated electricity for revolutionary and socially-useful purposes. Nigel didn't know — or couldn't remember — when the Hayle Close commune had got going except that it had already been in full swing when he and Claire had set up the Myrtle Cottage protest. It had outlived Myrtle Cottage too, had embraced the anti-poll tax movement in the late Eighties, its last, radical gasp, before it had fallen into terminal decline.

Nigel walked carefully, stepping around the potholes in his way and the dusty mounds of uncollected rubbish. Every now and then, his nostrils picked up the stench of human shit and urine from behind the low walls of what had been well-tended front gardens, once upon a time. In Hayle Close's late Victorian heyday, there had been forty or so neat terraced homes here, occupied by temperate, church-going labourers' families — and the 1980s squat had kept the place in reasonable order too. It had only been later, when the drug addicts and winos had taken over completely, that filth and squalor had moved in beside them.

Loud music — rap or hip hop or whatever (it

was years since Nigel had taken the remotest interest in that kind of thing) — was seeping through the upstairs window of the nearest house. A window without glass obviously. And the property, like all the others, elaborately boarded up at ground level. Myrtle Cottage had always had an uneasy alliance with the squatters at best. Even back then the features that would ultimately destroy the Hayle Close squat had been conspicuous to anybody prepared to think about the situation properly. Too many post-punks and hippies in residence, content to draw the dole and moan about 'the system' so long as they didn't have to lift too much of a finger against it, so long as they were left alone to do drugs and infect each other with STDs in the vague name of freedom. When the cheap 1990s heroin had flooded in (with state connivance, Nigel still believed that), driving out the 'mind-expanding' psychedelics, they'd been a pushover, had tumbled numbly into addict-hood like an easily felled deck of cards.

On the fringes, Myrtle Cottage had attracted its own share of problematic, apolitical elements too. The difference was that the cottage protest had been disciplined and organised at its heart. The freeloaders came and went but they never stayed long enough to have any serious impact. *Too heavy, man,* they'd say after a day or a week — and then fuck off in search of easier 'fun' elsewhere.

Nigel walked right to the end of Hayle Close, stopped outside the remains of number thirty-two — where the squatters had held their 'official' meetings back in the old days. He'd driven over here with Claire a lot more than once, coordinating for support whenever there was a big action on the horizon. Beyond the end wall was the wide scrubland — parched grass, dog turds and needles — that stretched out, void-like, towards the inner ring road. Even back in the Eighties, Hayle Close had been under a demolition order. But somehow it had clung on, a refuge for the desperate, conveniently out of the way of the respectable classes. He listened to the sound of hot, snarled-up afternoon traffic in the distance, honking and hooting, then he turned on his heel and started to walk back towards Mill Street and the air-conditioned interior of the Lexus.

Hopes turned into dust. That was all Nigel could find here now. The dreary smell of defeat. It had been a mistake to stop, a mistake to even glance out the car window. And he wasn't that Nigel anymore anyway. The one who'd believed in stuff, believed in wild, impossible change. He believed in absolutely nothing now — beyond the animal instinct of self-preservation that acquiring his wealth, and hanging on to it, had made possible. Nothing at all.

A young guy clattered out of the house where Nigel had heard the music before, re-positioning the pile of lean-to doors behind him which shored up the entrance way. He was junk-thin and nervy, was wearing a cheap zip-up jacket despite the heat. He walked out of the 'garden' and, noticing Nigel, stayed where he was, blocking what was left of the disintegrating pavement. Hayle Close was empty otherwise, everybody else indoors, still passed out from last night or already scored enough fresh oblivion to get them through another day.

'Spare us some spare coins, mate,' the young guy said.

Nigel, keeping his distance, pulled out a couple of two pound coins, held them out towards the youth, palm open.

'Four quid? Four quid's no good to me, mate.'

He still took them, then started to fumble in his jacket, head down, as if he was looking for something.

Nigel breathed slowly, saw the knife handle well before its owner did. There hardly seemed any need to hurt him more than his fucked-up life had already done. But he closed in anyway, gave him a slap across the head to get his attention and then kicked his legs away from under him. The kid landed heavily on his arse and sat there rubbing it in front of the low, crumbling wall.

Nigel took out his wallet, found a crisp, clean twenty, let it drop through the hot, calm air.

'Here, son,' he said, watching the note fall, 'score one on Trotsky.'

★ ★ ★

Jacobson made it to the biggest meeting room on the third floor of the Divisional building with only minutes to spare before Greg Salter's press conference got underway. The murder of Martin Grove was guaranteed to become national news

119

— even without the bonus of a second, probably related shooting. Not, or not mainly, because of continuing interest in Grove himself but because the killing of Claire Oldham had been one of those rare cases which had entered the public imagination on a long-term basis, not just for a few weeks or a few months. There had been docudramas and exposés over the years (most of them still circulating on the satellite TV channels) plus true-crime books and endless newspaper and magazine articles. The force's press officer, Caroline Little, had been busy since breakfast time, negotiating initial non-reporting agreements in return for a seat at the press conference. As soon as the event ended, the press would lift their self-imposed embargo and run with the story. Jacobson could have lived happily without media attention for a few more hours but the discovery of the second, unknown body meant that was impossible. The quickest way to identify her was to go public — and wait for the calls to pour in. Ninety-nine per cent of them would be worthless — or worse. But all Jacobson needed was the one call that wouldn't be.

He slid onto the third seat on the podium, poured himself out a glass of water from the big jug on the table. Salter was in the middle seat, resplendent in his best Paul Smith suit. Over on Salter's right, Caroline Little was doing the final sound check. *One Two. One Two. How's that?*

As the media had trooped in they'd been handed printed copies of Salter's prepared statement. But now Salter read it out aloud for

120

the benefit of the cameras and microphones. Jacobson listened, his face deadpan. If you couldn't look good on TV then at least you could avoid looking stupid. Smoothie Greg, the master of phoney gravitas and pregnant pauses, was in his element. *The body of a man, believed to Martin James Grove, has been found dead at a property outside Crowcross Village. Officers attending the scene have confirmed that Mr Grove had been shot and a murder inquiry led by Chief Inspector Frank Jacobson is now underway . . .*

To his credit, Salter, assisted by the press department, was sticking to the agreed minimum. The facts you held back were always more important than the facts you let out. Especially early on. When it came to the woman in the woods of course there wasn't much to keep back (apart from the tongue mutilation) because, so far, they knew practically nothing. Caroline Little was holding some kind of electronic gizmo (it reminded Jacobson of a TV remote control) that meant she could bring up Steve Horton's images on the screen behind them while Salter was speaking.

It was a tough call — and, also to his credit, Salter had pretty much let Jacobson call it. Everybody, or just about everybody, had somebody who cared about them. Somebody who didn't want to find out they'd been murdered by glancing at a TV screen or the front page of a newspaper. It was a lot less than ideal. Yet the alternative was worse. Nobody they'd encountered out at Crowcross so far could identify her and Emma Smith's trawl through the misper files hadn't led anywhere very promising. Smith, plus the duty CID she'd co-opted, had extended the trawl beyond the local files to the national database. There were a few long-shots on there, scattered around the country, that would take hours, even days, to check out. But Jacobson wanted to know who the woman was right now — before any trails went cold.

Caroline Little fielded the questions after Greg Salter finished. Most of them Salter (politely) and Jacobson (curtly) declined to answer on 'operational grounds'. As usual, Jacobson's meet-the-press strategy was to keep his mouth shut as far as possible. Then a joker from Sky News raised the issue of whether a locally based CID team was best-placed to carry out the investigation.

'Martin Grove spent twenty years in jail for a crime he didn't commit — and now the police who charged him have been given the job of investigating his murder. The public might wonder whether — '

Jacobson saw red, very nearly shook with anger. He didn't wait to see if Greg Salter had a bland answer ready.

'The public can wonder what it likes,' he snapped, impressed with himself that — under provocation — he wasn't effing and blinding on camera. 'Now, if you'll excuse me, I have a murder inquiry to run — to the highest, possible modern standards.'

Jacobson detached the mouthpiece from his lapel (and discarded the little transmitter which the TV people had slipped onto the belt of his trousers). Before the Sky reporter had unsmacked his gob, Jacobson had exited the room the same way he'd entered — via the side door, leaving Salter and Caroline Little to pick up the pieces of police-media relations.

He kept going. Straight down the broad main stairs (too impatient to wait for the lift) and straight out into the afternoon sunshine via the revolving doors at the main entrance. Five minutes later, he was in the beer garden of the Brewer's Rest, still fuming. But at least he hadn't reneged on his health régime, hadn't resumed his old, daytime drinking habits. Instead, on the chrome table, he'd slammed down a pint glass filled with fresh orange juice mixed with spring water. He drummed his fingers, irritably, incessantly. He cut corners where he could, of course he did. He was a sneaky bastard too. Voice-recording Maureen Bright this morning was a very minor case in point. But he worked hard not to be blinded by prejudice or so-called gut instinct. There was a big, big difference between gathering all the available facts in a case (by whatever means) and only logging those that *fit* a particular hypothesis. And there was an even bigger difference between facts you genuinely discovered and facts that got conveniently manufactured. *Fit* was the word. As in *fit* up. He'd just never done it. Not once. He wasn't that kind of copper. He'd never dished out a beating to find something out either, had never sanctioned one. And now here was a child (the Sky reporter had looked practically under-age to

123

Jacobson's weary eyes) tarring him with the same brush as DCI Hunter and all the other corrupt, bigoted dinosaurs who'd been pensioned off years ago.

Jacobson drank his concoction at last, left off drumming the table. There was no such thing as true, absolute human knowledge (as his hero, Kant, had famously explained to the world) but, as far as was humanly possible, Jacobson had ultimately played it straight with every suspect he'd ever encountered. It was a good record, he thought. Enviable. And there was no point crying crocodile tears for Martin Grove now he was dead. The time to do something would have been years ago — when Hunter had him in his clutches, had bullied a confession out of him. Jacobson had his excuses of course. He'd been young, junior, scarcely involved in the case. Besides, no important, official bugger would have taken the slightest notice of him anyway in those days, except maybe to brand him as a troublemaker, find a way to get him off the force pronto. Plus, Grove had looked guilty, even to him — and it had been years before the science could prove otherwise.

All the same, the reporter had touched a nerve. A man's life had been stolen from him and Jacobson had sat on the sidelines, done sod all, nothing. It felt raw, bleeding and painful. There were other cures — booze, philosophy, ancient history — but the most effective remedy Jacobson knew was work. He switched his mobile back on, checked in with DS Kerr and the rest of his team. Work and more work.

124

15

Martin Grove.doc

I told you about my dad before, didn't I? Left when I was eight, moved away, took up with a younger woman, had no time to spare after that for his only son. My mother tried her best but she was up against it. I grew up on the Woodlands council estate, not as bad an area then as it's become since. Bad enough though, certainly not good. We were stuck at the top of one of the first high-rises as well. Banged up, more or less. Alexander Pope House. Years later, when I found out who Alexander Pope actually was, I laughed my socks off about that. Imagine Pope of all the poets, the snobbish little runt, risking the lift (with *The Dunciad* tucked under his arm) or dragging his deformed body all the way up the stairs to the twelfth floor. I've still got pictures of my mother as a young woman, dark-haired, attractive. But that's not how I remember her, nothing like. She was thin when I was a kid, tired-out, scrawny, already looked older than her age. She worked domestic cleaning jobs mainly, never cared to sign on. Always up at the crack of dawn, taking the first bus into town and then catching another one out to somewhere posh — the Bartons, maybe, or the big houses out on the Wynarth Road. I like to imagine that she would've enjoyed her work, at least sometimes. There would have been hours, wouldn't there, when she'd have had those nice, big places all to herself? Maybe whole mornings or afternoons when she'd have fixed herself a nice cup of tea in a nice kitchen, stuck the radio on, put her feet up. I hope so. I bloody hope so.

I'd get myself off to school easily enough. When I got older, secondary school days, I started to please myself, go in or not bother. But she loved me my mum did, proved it a thousand times. I wasn't the kind of kid who got into mischief anyway. Not usually. I didn't roam the streets looking for trouble when I bunked off. I just used to like to stay at home, snug, daydreaming or watching the telly. Not that there was much on then daytime. Only three channels, Dear Reader, one, two, three, count 'em. What my mum lived for in those years was the weekends, I suppose. She had two friends, Carole and Diane. Saturday nights the three of them would take a taxi into Crowby, always in their best clothes. Out on the town, gone till late. I always had baby-sitters till I was old enough though, don't worry about that. Older girls from the building. Sometimes they'd sneak their boyfriends in once they thought I was tucked up in bed, safely asleep.

I don't remember too many men around either. Not like some of the kids I knew then. The ones who always seemed to have new 'uncles' to get used to. Maybe she'd just had it with blokes once my father moved out. There was one guy I remember though. Tom. That's all. If I ever knew his second name, I can't recall it now. He was a lorry driver. Long distance. A big, friendly man with a big laugh. He took us to Blackpool one September. A long weekend to see the Illuminations. We stayed in a proper hotel as well, not a shabby B & B, and I had my own room. At least I've got that one unqualified happy memory in my brain, squirrelled safely away. Dostoevsky declares in *Karamazov* that one good memory from childhood can keep a man from evil. I got into Dostoevsky in prison. A lot of lifers do. For one thing, the great Russian knew about being locked up and locked down. He ran foul of the Tsar's secret police when he was young, was sentenced to hard labour in a Siberian prison camp for his trouble (and you thought the communists invented the gulags — think again, my friend).

It wasn't so much that *I* was happy — what ten-year-old wouldn't be, munching on a hot dog, queuing for the Big Dipper on the Pleasure Beach? No, the memory I'm on about is about her, my mum. She was lit up that weekend. Laughing, warm, alive, carefree. Tom didn't stay around for long of course. He'd visit less and less and then he didn't visit at all. I crept in on her one weekend morning when she wasn't working. I'd made her tea. Not very good tea — childishly constructed, not nearly hot enough, far too weak. She was already up, which surprised me, sitting in her dressing gown in front of her bedroom mirror. Tears streaming down her face. The creased pages of a letter in her hand, clumsy sentences written out on cheap blue notebook paper.

She took it badly when I left as well. How

badly I only found out later. At the time I just knew there was nothing in the Woodlands for me, nothing in Crowby. I went for the first time when I was sixteen, a couple of months after my birthday. That was helpful for her at any rate. I was a quasi-adult in the eyes of the law by then, no obligation anymore to turn up at school. So there was no problem with the social department breathing down her neck. School failed me of course, that's the truth of it. I realised that later, *proved* it even. I'm not a stupid man, even if I was a naïve, stupid kid. I picked up *two* honours degrees in prison, even got started on an MA thesis for a while. But the North Crowby Comp didn't see anything in me, didn't even seem to particularly care that my attendance was, well, frugal. I wasn't a troublemaker for one thing, so why bother? Days I did attend, I'd sit at the back of the class and doze with my eyes open. Quiet, invisible.

That first time didn't work out too well. I hitched to Anglesey, a destination I chose more or less at random. I looked at a road map and just thought the name sounded interesting. I got kitchen work in a hotel but the wages were shit and the digs that went with the job suited the rats and the cockroaches just fine. Alexander Pope House was a palace by comparison. So I legged it back home, mooched on the dole for a while. I remember I even tried to join the army at one point. I don't really recall why. Maybe I thought I'd get some proper mates at last that way. Don't get me wrong, I wasn't some totally weird no-friends kid that everybody laughed at or picked on. I just never found a niche where I could comfortably fit in. Unlike Andy, the army didn't need me as it turned out. I was rejected on health grounds as an asthmatic, which was news to me — maybe it was just a diplomatic way of saying my face didn't fit there either. Eventually though, the call of the wild grew louder — and I left again, managed to stay away this time. I casual-jobbed it around the country. Everywhere. North, south, east, west. Until — this is where you came in, Dear Reader — eventually I fetched up at Myrtle Cottage.

The reason I mention all this now is to remind you that I was *local*. I was practically the only full-time protestor who was. And I was definitely the only full-time protestor whose last fixed abode was care of the salubrious Woodlands estate.

My mum was glad I was back in the area of course. I'd call over and see her now and again. Usually on a Sunday, the one day I knew when she definitely never worked. I even took Claire to see her that one time. We sat in the front room drinking Mum's cups of tea, eating the biscuits she'd have bought at the Happy Shopper, and everything felt real to me. Get me? Real the way I wanted it to be. As if we were a real couple, the girl brought home to meet the lad's parents. *Such a pretty girl*, my mum kept saying, *such a pretty girl*. She hadn't a clue about the protest and so we didn't talk about it very much with her. No point, as I'd already explained in advance to Claire. Day-to-day life was enough of a struggle for my mum. She'd no time or energy or hope left over to change the world.

For a long time now I've realised that the afternoon I took Claire to my mum's and the weekend Tom took Mum and me to Blackpool exist side by side in my memory as perfect times, perfect interludes. Life as it should be. I'm running ahead of my story of course. But I did tell you, straight off, that I'd be cutting things up, mixing them and matching them. You can't say that you weren't warned.

Mum hugged us both when we were leaving. We took the stairs down instead of the manky lift. Jumping steps, holding hands, even singing the words from a song we both liked (The Beat, 'Stand Down Margaret'). A bunch of little kids scarpered when we came out of the front entrance. In my memory of it later, we didn't even care when we clocked that they'd coin-scratched the MG's paintwork all along one side. *Arise Ye Criminals of Want*, Claire shouted after them. Then she looked up for my mum, trying to pick out the right window so that she could wave to her.

16

Jacobson commandeered a patrol car to get out to the hospital in case there was a need to move quickly through heavy traffic. Robinson, the pathologist, had managed to schedule Martin Grove's post-mortem for four o'clock. The timing was fortuitous. It meant that, if he needed one, Jacobson had an official *reason* why he'd had to break short his involvement in the press conference. His impromptu walkout was the kind of incident Greg Salter was capable of blowing up into a disciplinary issue if he put his small, petty mind to it (or if the ever-scheming Mrs Salter put his mind to it for him). Except that getting to a post-mortem on time was *solid*, professional, overriding. Paper could sometimes wrap stone. But scissors always cut paper.

Robinson had his own assistant these days. A woman doctor, as Jacobson couldn't help but think of her. Candice Black. It looked like Dr Black was mainly watching and learning on this occasion however. She was sitting next to the Coroner's Officer behind the glass screen in the observation area when Jacobson reached the theatre. One of the senior Scene of Crime officers was there too, deputising for Jim Webster. Occasionally at a victim's autopsy you'd find a few permitted proto-doctors present — interns or postgraduates or whatever they were called (even after all these years, Jacobson still had only the vaguest idea of medical hierarchies). Today, though, Jacobson brought Robinson's audience up to a total of four.

The mortuary technician had already wheeled in Martin Grove. His body was still fully clothed, his hands still inside the paper bags which had been put on them at the crime scene. As with all gunshot victims, Grove's hands and clothes were prime sources for trace evidence, propellant grains and blood splatter, so Robinson 'processed' them first (after the X rays) to minimise loss and contamination. When the clothes were finally removed, he moved on to the actual wounds and then to the rest of the body. Jacobson blanked as much as he could blank. Nobody, least of all him, wanted to see the skull beneath the skin (or the heart or the kidneys) and a lot of pathologists themselves worked by techniques of advanced mental dissociation. It was the only way they could do their job and not find themselves puking up in a busy street amongst all the other walking bundles of blood and guts.

Robinson's investigation of the perforating entrance wound and the (larger) exit wound confirmed the scenario they were already working with. A single, fatal bullet discharged at near-contact range. In the matter of Martin Grove's tongue, Robinson pronounced that the partial amputation had, mercifully, been carried out after the shooting and not before. When he was through, he offered Jacobson the option of an informal chat about his findings — in plain English. Candice Black stayed behind in the mortuary, delegated to put Grove's body parts back in (approximate) position and to sew up the incisions.

Robinson's office *felt* like Robinson's office at last. The walls had been re-painted in bright colours and the fading film posters belonging to his deceased predecessor, Professor Merchant, had finally been removed. In their place, Robinson had put up some kind of travel calendar (the Taj Mahal at sunset was the June selection) and a montage of family snaps: mainly his wife and his two-year old, as Jacobson calculated Robinson's son must be by now.

Jacobson wanted to know how he could be so sure about the tongue.

'The main thing's the absence of any kind of *restraining* bruises or marks. Even with a gun stuck to your head, you'd still put up some kind of a fight if somebody tried to cut your tongue out of your mouth, don't you think, Frank? Your body would react even if your brain tried to stop it.'

Jacobson nodded, trying to keep a grip on the familiar sick feeling in his stomach: post-autopsy nausea.

'I'd have expected to see strong indentation marks around the neck or the shoulders or maybe on the arms or the wrists,' Robinson added. 'But there's nothing. Hardly any bruising at all in fact, apart from at locations which are consistent with him hitting the floor when he's been shot.'

'You said it had been cut out, old son, not ripped or torn in some way. Do you think whoever did it had some kind of medical training?'

'It's possible, I suppose. The cut's neat too when you take a close-up look — straight across the *dorsum*. But you'd get pretty much the same result without any training so long as you had a steady hand and a sharp cutting blade — it wouldn't even need to be a surgical blade so long as you could manoeuvre it effectively inside the mouth.'

'There were indentations around the mouth itself though?'

'Definitely. The mouth had to be forced open — and then held open. But you'd wear gloves if you weren't a complete idiot. Maybe even more protection than that.'

Jacobson glanced at the view from Robinson's office window: a ventilation duct emerging from a grey concrete wall. Robinson had removed a fair amount of biological materials from Groves' clothes and body for analysis by the FSS — the Forensic Science Service — over in Birmingham. But any useful, preliminary results from the FSS labs were days away at the very earliest.

'And it could have involved two people?'

'A damn sight easier with two, in my view. One to hold the mouth open, one to do the cutting. Especially as there's no sign the mouth was clamped into position or anything like that — which also argues against somebody with any kind of medical training or experience by the way.'

Robinson paused, scratched the side of his nose.

'One person could have done it though, if they were determined enough.'

Jacobson asked after the pathologist's wife and toddler before he left. He'd been pleased — and relieved — when Robinson had succeeded Merchant in the post. Everybody knew that appointment boards existed primarily to reward toadying, 'connections' and arse-licking. But even they were only human. Occasionally they fucked up and inadvertently gave the job to the very best candidate.

★ ★ ★

Kerr detoured to the school playing fields en route from the Bartons. He only stayed quarter of an hour. But at least Sam saw him there alongside Cathy, standing in the huddle of parents and cheering him on. Sam's twin sister, Susie, was there too, dragooned along and sulking. Jacobson was waiting for Kerr in the hospital car park as pre-arranged. He clambered in and they headed back out to Crowcross via the North Crowby bypass and the Wynarth Road.

Kerr mentioned to Jacobson that George McCulloch was probably telling the truth about last night. His girlfriend had backed up his story and she hadn't kicked up a fuss when the uniformeds had conducted an informal, off-warrant search of McCulloch's house on Wordsworth Avenue. No sign of obvious stolen goods or burglary tools. No drugs either (except for an innocuous eighth of low-quality hash in the bedroom which they'd pretended they hadn't seen). McCulloch's van, likewise, had contained nothing but window cleaning equipment.

'Even so, he has a knack of being in the wrong place at the wrong time, old son,' Jacobson commented.

Kerr let it go. The SOCOs had given McCulloch's vehicle the full forensic treatment. The van had been clean by Geordie's standards — but evidently hadn't been washed in the last twenty-four hours. Plus McCulloch's DNA and fingerprints were filed on every biometric database the state possessed, the secret ones included. If there *was* anything to link him to the crime scene, it would show up in the laboratory sooner or later.

They drove straight to Grove's place, parked up at the foot of the tarmac driveway. The line of police vehicles stretched towards the house. The SOCOs had completed their initial sweep and Jim Webster, in his role as the Crime Scene Manager, had signed off Jacobson's request for a non-forensic physical search. There was a small group of officers ready and waiting outside the porch entrance. CID and uniformeds in roughly equal proportions. The sign-off came with binding conditions of course. Every searcher was to be suited up and Grove's kitchen was still strictly out of bounds.

Jacobson reminded them precisely what they were looking for: *data* — potentially a copy of whatever files had been present on Martin Grove's missing computer.

'A CD, a data stick, an old-fashioned floppy disk. If there's *anything* in here that can be used to store data then I want it grabbing, bagging and identifying. Absolutely anything at all.'

Jacobson and Kerr put themselves to work in Grove's main lounge. They pulled up the carpets, poked in and around every item of furniture, checked for loose floorboards. Jacobson had no specific reason to believe that Grove had made any kind of copy of his computer files other than the fact that it was a common enough practice for computer users, especially if they were using their computer for any kind of important, personal project. The property didn't look like it had been ransacked — but that didn't mean that it hadn't been carefully and professionally searched. Even so there could still be a copy somewhere in the vicinity that the killer or killers hadn't noticed. Jacobson was reasonably certain that the tongue amputation and the missing computer were *linkcd* — sending a message that Grove had been sticking his nose in where it definitely wasn't wanted.

There was a shelf near the TV system with a few DVDs and music CDs. Jacobson and Kerr examined them one by one. Kerr bagged any that looked as if they were home-produced: recordings of TV shows or music downloads from the internet. Home users, himself included, were promiscuous about data storage. You'd easily stick a movie next to a Word file (or overwrite one with the other) if you were in a hurry. Kerr wasn't over-impressed with the selection, audio or visual. The big, popular sellers from the last couple of years mainly. For some reason, maybe unjustified, he saw the choices as Maureen Bright's rather than Grove's.

When they were finally through in the lounge they checked on the progress of the rest of the search team. A few CDs had been found in the back of a drawer in Grove's study. Software installation discs by the looks of it. Even so, Jacobson, clutching at straws by now, gave instructions to bag them as well.

'It's worth a try. Steve Horton can easily zap through them sector by sector anyway, even re-frag them if necessary,' Kerr commented, talking up his limited, inaccurate grasp of the technicalities as per usual.

Otherwise there was nothing doing — apart from the busted iPod which the SOCOs had already found in the kitchen and which had already been transferred to the Mobile Incident Unit for intermediate storage.

Jacobson still hadn't ruled out electronic and infra-red sweeps to deal with the possibility that Grove had made serious efforts to conceal data copies — or anything else. But it was something to think about later, wasn't a justifiable current priority. There was no reason right now to believe that Grove had hidden anything. After all, he hadn't hidden himself. He'd come back to live within a mile of where Claire Oldham had been murdered, hadn't been put off by local hostility. He'd drank in the local pub, had wandered the local countryside, openly and in daylight. He'd lived reclusively but not secretly — and he hadn't made it remotely hard for his killer (or killers) to find him. He decided that what he wanted to do next was to talk to

Maureen Bright again, maybe push her a bit harder this time.

They called in at the Crowcross Arms on the way back towards Wynarth and Crowby. Mick Hume, still in Ewing's cramped back office, had scanned and logged the last twenty-fours hours of CCTV. Now he was transferring a full copy of the last month's footage onto an official police hard-drive. It was unlikely that the camera had been misaligned all that time but the data from the car park might be useful in its own right.

Jacobson asked him for the highlights back to eight thirty last night when Bright claimed she'd driven off to visit Jane Ebdon, leaving Martin Grove home alone.

'That much checks out, guv,' Hume replied. 'The camera picks her up passing the pub about twenty to nine. One of those new-style Minis, registered to her at Grove's address. There's no sign of her coming back on this system though — but that doesn't *prove* that she didn't. The way the camera arcs means that it has several blind spots. It's not a complete record — and you don't *have* to go through the village to get to Grove's place anyway.'

'Fair enough, old son. What else?'

Hume looked down at his scribbled notes. There was an empty teacup at the side of the monitor screen and a blue willow pattern plate covered in crumbs from biscuits or pub sandwiches.

'I logged fourteen separate number plates to one AM. The last one being George McCulloch's. Then it all goes dead till you get the morning off-to-work rush. I've filed them all with the

139

incident room. Somebody over there is compiling two lists — local registrations and visitors. They're prioritising the visitors obviously.'

'Good work, Mick,' Jacobson told him, exiting.

They made good time. It was pushing seven now, most drivers heading out of Crowby, not towards it. Plus Kerr knew a clever route to Jane Ebdon's estate that avoided the Waitrose traffic. Jacobson took an update call from DC Williams: there was nothing apparently useful from the Crowcross area door-to-door so far but they'd identified those commuter properties, empty during the day, which should have someone home soon.

Kerr left the sunroof open a cooling half-inch when he parked up. Somebody in Jane Ebdon's street was getting a barbecue going in a back garden. The warm, woodsmoke smell of charcoal carried in the air alongside a hubble of outdoor voices mixed in with Goldfrapp. He followed Jacobson up the path, tuning down in his mind the knowledge that Cathy and his son and his daughter would be at home now, enjoying a summer's evening without him.

Jacobson had been meaning to call Alison, sort out something for later in the week (a trip to a country pub for instance). He tried to fix it in his memory, lodge it in some reliable synapse where it wouldn't be neglected or forgotten.

Maureen Bright was on her own. They'd seen her checking them out through the lounge window before she'd come to the door and let them in. Jane/Mandy had gone to pick up a Chinese takeaway, she told them, was insisting

140

that she try to eat something. They followed her back into the lounge. Jacobson got straight to the point, asked what she knew about the computer in Grove's study and what he'd been doing with it. For instance, did she know what *kind* of computer it was? She looked at him blankly, probably well into the bottle of Stoli that was sitting near her on a little drinks table.

He repeated the question, finally got an answer.

'I've no idea of the make if that's what you mean. A laptop thingy, you know, portable.'

'It seems to have gone missing, maybe taken by whoever killed Martin,' Jacobson explained, deliberately using Grove's first name only.

'He was working in there last night, tapping away right up till I left,' she said, her eyes still blank.

Jacobson asked her again what he'd been working on.

'His life story, what else? Before prison, in prison, after prison. *I want to set the record straight* — if I've heard him say that once, I've heard him say it a thousand times.'

She was drinking the vodka from a big, orbicular wine glass. It looked neat, undiluted.

'Do you know if he was keeping copies anywhere? Backups?'

She shook her head. Getting pissed was only one side of it, Jacobson thought. She'd washed and changed since she'd come over here. Her eyes were less red and she'd discarded the Scene of Crime jog suit for a loose summer dress. A rich yellow colour that more than suited her.

'If he was, he wouldn't have talked about it to

me. No point really — the TV remote's about as technical as I ever get.'

Jacobson asked her if Grove had mentioned anything about visitors before she'd left.

She shot him a look. Less blank but not less hostile.

'You don't understand anything, do you? Do you think you spend half your life in prison for what somebody else has done — got away with — and then sit around having *visitors*? Marty liked his privacy, his space, liked spending time with me — he didn't have a lot of time left over for the rest of the human race.'

Jacobson mentioned that Alan Slingsby seemed to have kept in contact with him.

'Alan Slingsby's an exception. He stuck by Marty when nobody else wanted to know. Without Alan Slingsby the chances are he'd still be banged up, rotting in a prison cell.'

Jacobson felt like an irritating dog sometimes, a terrier that got its teeth into your trouser leg and wouldn't let go.

'So you're saying that the last time you saw Martin he was working on his laptop in his study and he wasn't expecting any callers.'

Maureen Bright gave a one-word answer.

'Yes.'

She found her Dunhill packet, took one out and lit it up.

Kerr asked a question at last.

'When was the last time Martin — or you — had a caller or visitor at the house? I don't mean to read the meter or anything like that.'

She inhaled, exhaled, looked him up and down.

'Barry Vine called by last month. He and Marty went off on a walk for the afternoon then I cooked them dinner. He's another exception.'

'Barry Vine?' Kerr repeated.

'A prison officer at Boland — or he was when Marty was there anyway. Marty always said he was one of the decent ones, said he owed him a lot.'

Kerr nearly asked for Vine's details, then thought better of it. If they wanted them, they'd be able to get them direct from the Prison Service in any case. As far as he knew, it was only prisoners' records that they had a tendency to lose or mis-file.

Jacobson stood up, ready to leave.

She asked him again about seeing the body. He fished in his wallet, found one of the cards which listed the Victim Support numbers. Helen Dawson should have dealt with it earlier. Maybe she had, of course, and Maureen Bright just hadn't taken the information in.

'Give them a call — or ask your friend Jane to,' he said, handing it to her, 'they'll help you sort it out.'

Robinson had prioritised the post-mortem but everything else would be slotted in to the mortuary's normal workload. The technicians 'tidied up' the bodies for the benefit of friends and relatives. But they were unlikely to get around to Martin Grove much before tomorrow afternoon now, Jacobson thought. Outside of the murder squad, or a rotting pile of medieval plague victims, there was rarely any sense of official urgency about the dead.

143

17

Jane's place was in a cul-de-sac. Maureen watched the detectives' car drive up to the turning circle, reverse and then head off. She stayed at the window until she felt convinced, certain, that they'd really gone. They treated you like their personal property, the police did, if you started to figure in something that interested them. Liberty-takers in every sense. They'd harass you wherever or whenever, kick your front door down in the middle of the night if it suited them. And these two were clever — or thought they were. No shouting, patient — but still making sure they got their answers, got whatever it was that they thought they wanted. A far cry from the foot-soldiers in uniform, the non-entities she'd had to deal with when she'd been on the street. But still from the same army, still do you as soon as look at you. The women were the worst ones back then, she'd always thought. Snooty cows making catty, patronising remarks about the way you dressed. As if it was a choice to hang around in next to nothing on a winter's night so that some foul old git might condescend to pick you out, paw at you for twenty quid, shove his rubbish, rancid cock up you and expect you to smile at him, pretend you were pleased about it. *Go on darling. Nice to be nice, eh?*

She moved away from the window, carried the remains of her latest vodka into Jane's kitchen, found some cranberry juice in her fridge and mixed it in, filling the glass back up to the top. Jane was right, she did need to eat. Marty was dead. Dead. But she felt hungry, couldn't help it. One of them had been on the TV news earlier. The older one, Jacobson. Ticking off some reporter who'd pointed out how they'd framed Marty years ago. All different now, that was this Jacobson's line. All the bad apples were in the past — croaked it by now or retired. Yeah right. He needed to come down to Clarence Square late some night, watch some of the pay-offs that got discreetly doled out to certain patrol cars — cash, charlie, freebie quickies. Not to mention the healthy trade in stitch-ups and tip-offs — setting the police on your enemies before they set them on you.

She shuddered at the memory of it all. A total fucking nightmare. Yet, amazingly, she'd sur-vived, come through. It wasn't just down to Marty, she knew that. Nobody else could get you out of that life. Only you. Exactly the same was true with gear. It smashed your head right up against the wall, held it there, until the day you reached inside yourself, found the places it couldn't get to, the addresses it couldn't reach you at. Marty had been part of it though, had given her an extra reason to try. She thought about the afternoon she'd met him, the very first moment she'd set eyes on him. A summer's day, maybe even hotter than this one, in the Memorial Park.

Everybody, even Jane, had the story of it wrong, had added two and two together and come up with six. Yes, Marty had been using street whores when they met — and yes, she'd certainly been a street whore then. Very definitely, an abject three-quid-a-wank whore. *But that wasn't how they'd met.* It just wasn't.

She'd taken the bus out to the park from the town centre, had just wanted an hour to herself in the fresh air. It was nice over there, the Riverside area, and the entire park was safe — in daylight anyway. Dogwalkers, strollers and joggers everywhere. Mums with babies and toddlers in the play zone. Older kids rowing out on the boating lake. He'd asked her the time, that was all, nothing clever. She couldn't tell him of course, never wore a watch in those days. *Might be later than you think in that case,* he'd said and then he'd smiled at her — a vague, very nearly shy smile.

They'd sat on a park bench and just talked — about everything and nothing. No details that first day. Nothing about who either of them really were (or who the rest of the world said they were anyway). She was *already* getting herself sorted by then. That was what people didn't understand about it. She was on a methadone script and more or less sticking to it. She was ready to move on, ready to be somewhere new. Marty had come along at the exact, right moment, as if her guardian angel had guided his footsteps towards her. Not that she believed in that stuff, not exactly. Yet something might have been looking out for her in those years, mightn't it? A lot of girls hadn't survived that life — and yet she had.

She walked into Jane's conservatory, opened up all the windows and the door against the heat. She couldn't go out into the garden of course. It was too small and overlooked by neighbours on either side. The last thing in the world she wanted to do was to have some trivial conversation with a stranger over Jane's garden fence. But in here she felt safe, still secluded. She sat down on a blue wicker chair, nursing her glass. She shouldn't really drink, shouldn't really touch anything beyond tea or coffee. She had an addictive personality, they'd told her in rehab, something she'd have to watch for the rest of her life. They'd convinced her, she didn't doubt them. But right now she was cutting herself some slack, knew she needed to numb her brain one way or another, knew it as an issue of survival.

Numb it good too. Numb it so that whatever she tried to think of — that first day they'd met, other special times — her mind didn't keep reeling back to this morning, didn't keep reeling back to the fact that Marty was gone, no longer alive, no longer here, totally and utterly *absent*. Numb it so she didn't run out into the street screaming and tearing at her hair — or, worse, just quietly, calmly, walk back into Jane's kitchen, find Jane's sharpest bread knife and slash her wrist veins wide. Wide to heaven.

★   ★   ★

Nigel's driver had finally joined the motorway system at a point well north of Crowby and the clogged-up Birmingham conurbation. Although heavy, the traffic had at least been *moving* — until twenty minutes ago. Now all three lanes had ground to a halt, interspersed with the occasional thirty seconds of stop-start crawling. The driver picked up the explanation on one of the local radio channels: a jack-knifed lorry in collision with a Mondeo towing a caravan two exits ahead. No serious injuries, the radio had reported, but big, inevitable delays. Nigel told him not to worry, he had work he could get on with while they waited. He asked him to switch the radio back off though if he didn't mind. The driver told him he didn't, he could listen on his mobile anyway if he wanted, just plug in his earpiece.

Nigel checked a batch of email, made a few urgentish telephone calls. He wound the window down after that, even considered getting out, stretching his legs at the side of the car, the way a lot of drivers and passengers seemed to be doing. The Lexus was in the middle lane, some kind of haulage truck immediately in front, a battered Ford Transit pulled up behind. Traffic jams were a kind of imperfect, transient democracy, the result of overcrowded roads, accidents, breakdowns and the ancient laws of pure chance. Rich men, poor men, the young, the old, juxtaposed and proximate. He used a private plane now and again when the mood took him, had considered acquiring a helicopter for medium-length UK journeys like this one but had never fully committed to the idea. There was some residual notion in his head, maybe, of not

148

completely losing touch with how 'ordinary' people lived — where he'd come from, the things he'd once believed in.

Finally, bored now, he adjusted the comfortable recline of his seat and switched on the TV screen, an action so rare it took him a minute or two to figure out how to search through the channels. He opted for the news bulletin on News 24. All the news channels were peddlers of unreliable, ideologically motivated bullshit (and the occasional, outright lie) but he'd always found it easier to read the subtexts, distortions and implied omissions on the BBC versions for some reason. They'd just got to the end of the world news segment, were moving on to the latest British headlines. Headshots accompanied the list of upcoming stories: the Prime Minister, the Leader of the Opposition, a football manager (who Nigel had got drunk with last year), a teenager who'd been stabbed to death on a London night bus. Nigel was still fiddling with the volume slider when Claire's image filled the screen, the famous photograph that had become synonymous with the media coverage of her murder. Claire smiling about something, looking clear-eyed and beautiful. Martin followed next, and just as well-known: the black-and-white mugshot where he stared out at you malevolently, like he hated and despised the entire world and everything in it. Nigel maxed the volume, gave the screen his full attention. Something about 'early this morning'. Something about 'found shot dead.' An aerial shot of a property now. But not Myrtle Cottage, which,

149

unconsciously, he might have been expecting. He stared at it, not really taking in what the news-reader was saying. All the same, he recognised it. The longish drive, the neat contours of the back garden, the gazebo on the front lawn. It was Martin's place all right. Apart from the police vehicles and equipment, it looked much the way he'd seen it with his very own eyes — only last night.

* * *

Jacobson ate a solitary meal in the police canteen. Egg and chips with a tomato salad on the side which he overdrenched in Thousand Island dressing. All of his core officers were out at Crowcross now. Kerr liaising with the two, split-off SOCO teams. Emma Smith, Mick Hume and DC Williams taking a lead in the local door-to-door work. First thing tomorrow morning, they'd need to review and cross-reference every single witness statement. So it would give them a head-start if some of the interview data was their own. The hope, as always, was that facts or observations which looked trivial or unimportant, when taken in isolation, would turn out to be significant when his team pieced together the bigger picture.

He'd take the lift down to the incident room when he'd eaten, he decided, sign all the forms that Brian Phelps needed signing. More usefully, he intended to find out how the various trawls and requests for background information were proceeding. He wanted to check that the

Records Office had actually sent on the original Claire Oldham files as promised. Then there was the inventory of Boland prison rioters which the Assistant Governor down there was supposed to be organising for Kerr.

He sipped at the glass of fresh orange juice he'd bought to wash down the coffee he'd bought to wash down the egg and chips. His second dose of the stuff today. Another sop to Alison's drive to get him to eat more healthily, to stop him bloody pegging out early, as she'd put it bluntly the other week. Murder investigations didn't obey the normal rules of time, he was thinking. The hours and minutes sped past, broke all the steady, regular rhythms of a normal day. Already a full twelve hours had vanished for ever since he'd first pulled on a protective suit and taken a close-up look at Martin Grove's limp body and his lolling, bullet-holed head. It was only when you paused, drew breath, that you realised how long you'd been working, plodding, banging your head against as many brick walls as you could find for the purpose.

His mobile rang just as he was putting his knife, fork and plate back on to the red plastic serving tray: the incident room, some duty CID voice he didn't instantly recognise.

'DC Phillips here, sir,' the voice said cautiously, maybe a little too politely. 'We've just received a credible phone call regarding the identity of the female victim at Crowcross Wood. Full name, age and address, sir — and, eh, occupation as well.'

Wednesday

18

Martin Grove.doc

Day and night, the kitchen was a focal point in Myrtle Cottage. It was always warm from the stove and any night that you couldn't sleep, or felt like staying up late, you could wander in there, hopefully find something going on. Usually, there'd be two or three other people around at least, sharing a joint, maybe, and chatting, arguing, debating. If Andy was one of them — and he frequently was, with or without Hilary — there'd be plenty of his strong rice wine on the go too. As things turned out, I was there the one night (as far as I know) that he ever really talked about the Falklands, what he'd done there, what he'd seen.

Generally, it was something he never spoke about other than to say it had been a pile of shit, a waste of young lives. We all knew not to ask him about it, knew it was something he wanted to put behind him. But everybody talks about everything sooner or later. That's a truth you learn in prison. A man will go years even before you find out the thing that's eating him up, the particular lump of iron in his soul. Then one day, out of the blue, he'll corner you, buttonhole you, insist on telling you the secrets he's never told anyone before, not his wife, not his family, not his lawyer. Hilary was there as well that night, sitting beside him. Oliver was there too. Plus

Steve and Liz. Claire and Nigel weren't of course, always famously went up to bed early — and noisily.

Steve and Liz were classic protestors. I don't think I ever knew their second names. Polite, middle-class students who'd packed in college to join the protest. Eco, vegan, pacifist. 'No real politics' in Claire's and Nigel's view of things, definitely not part of the inner circle. They street-sold some kind of anarchist mag around Crowby and Wynarth, had just come back from hawking the latest edition around the pubs. The cover was a page-length spoof of an army recruitment ad. *Barmy — it's a real soldier's job.* At the bottom there was a spoof coupon to fill out. *Name. Address. Age. Coffin Size.*

Andy picked up a copy, studied it for a few minutes, then decided, who knows why, not to see the funny side.

'Nearly a thousand killed, Stevie,' he said, dropping the magazine back onto the table. 'Nearly twice that wounded or fucking crippled. You think that's a laugh do you? Something to be clever-clever about?'

Steve and Liz were a little bit stoned maybe. Slow to react, fuddled.

'Course not, man,' Steve replied after a minute, 'that's the whole point we're making, isn't it? Try and show kids it's not a cool thing to do — getting themselves killed so the politicians can look good.'

Andy opened a fresh bottle of rice wine from the several he'd lugged up from the basement. But he didn't pass it round, just started swigging it, necking it down.

'Tumbledown,' he said, glaring at Steve, as if there was no one else in the room. 'Heard of that, *man*? Mount Tumbledown? Or fucking Goose Green?'

Maybe Steve tried smiling at him. I can't recall that detail. But I know that he didn't answer, didn't speak. Nobody else was speaking now.

Only Andy.

'All you want to do is survive. Shoot anything that moves and survive. I've no idea how many I shot, how many I hit. Get that? No fucking idea. Ever spent all night in a hole, Stevie? All night under fire in a hole. Do you even know what a hole is?'

Maybe Steve shook his head. I don't know, I was watching Andy. Swigging down wine and not in the room. Wherever he was, not in the room.

'A hole is an enemy position that they've abandoned and you've taken. You dig yourself in, you *hole up*, understand?'

He stood up then, paced to the sink, leaned on it, facing us all.

'There was one Argie still in that hole. Dead — but just his body. His head was long gone. Blown off. Exploded. His arms had dropped off an' all.'

He lunged then, pulling Steve right out of his chair, pinning him up against the kitchen notice board, pressing his head against the washing-up rota list. He moved quickly. Lightning fast. Nobody saw it coming.

'We found the head at daylight, Stevie, when

157

we moved out. What was left of it anyway. We had a quick game of football with it. Three a side. Then a quick round of keepie-uppie. I won at that, no question. I won at kicking a dead Argie's head. Now that is funny, *man*, that is a fucking laugh, isn't it? That's what *I* call barmy.'

I thought maybe he'd been tripping or something — there was a lot of acid around the place at that time — or just over-bevvied. Oliver and me tried to pull him away but he was too strong even for the two of us combined. It was Hilary and Liz that managed it in the end, cajoling him to let go. He slapped Hilary for her trouble. Just once — but hard. He swore at her too, called her a smug bitch.

He broke down crying afterwards. I heard that as well. Hilary and him climbing down the stairs to the basement after everyone else had called it a night — and Andy sobbing like a baby, telling her he was sorry. He apologised — publicly — to Steve and Liz the next day. They were gracious about it, told him it was OK. But they left Myrtle Cottage not long after and we never saw them again.

I forgot about them quickly enough to be honest. I was too busy for one thing, too involved with the Fence Com and the issue of the airfield's new perimeter defences. We finally selected the last Sunday in November as the date for the big push.

Weekends were always the best time to stage any high-profile action that required a big attendance. Supporters could travel in more easily from outside the area and you maximised your chances of a nice big turnout. According to Che Guevara or Mao Tse Tung or Lenin — or according to somebody like that anyway (I can't remember exactly who and it doesn't really matter anymore) — the revolutionary 'fish' swims safely in the 'sea' of the 'people', provided that the people have woken up to their world-historical, revolutionary role. On the Fence Com, we viewed the planned November action in a pretty similar light. While the enemy would be kept distracted by the peaceful mass protest, the revolutionary élite intended to kick their reactionary arses the length and breadth of the main runway — and back again.

Nigel and Claire took off for a week or so in the run-up. They'd forged good national contacts at the London demo and had organised a speaking tour which took them all over the country to university campuses and public meetings, building support for November 27th. Back in Crowby, the flyposting squad went into overdrive. NO TO THE BOMBERS — JOIN THE RING OF PEACE was our big slogan of the moment. Half a dozen of the squad got arrested on the Friday night, trying to poster over the main doors of the Town Hall. A mad, breakaway action, doomed to fail. I'd warned them about it but they hadn't paid attention. Recently, the entire area flanked by the Town Hall, the cop shop and the Arndale Centre had been pedestrianised. You couldn't get a vehicle near, unless it was a police car or a taxi. They were sitting ducks. The coppers had most probably finished their cups of tea at their leisure and just strolled across the square to lift them. We were successful otherwise though. The flyposters who *had* listened to me had all got themselves in and out of the town centre unmolested, had even managed to poster up most of the windows of the loathed and hated Conservative Club.

There was a bit of a party atmosphere when we drifted back in our little groups to Myrtle Cottage in the early hours. Andy's rice wine was in high demand and there were the usual joints passing cheerfully back and forth. A kind of privacy issue had developed by then between me and Andy and Hilary. It wasn't supposed to — it certainly didn't fit with Myrtle Cottage's official anti-bourgeois ideology — but it had all the same. They didn't like having sex down in the basement with me overhearing from the other side of the room. I didn't like it either but I still needed somewhere to kip. From time to time, they'd disappear for a day or two over to the room Hilary had kept on at one of the Polytechnic's halls of residence. Although they couldn't do that all the time and still remain part of the protest's hard core. The two of them were sitting in the kitchen — again — when I decided to call it a night. Hilary arguing the toss with an anarchist who was criticising Trotsky's incorrect line on the Spanish Civil War. *I'm going to sleep out tonight*, I told them, *take my sleeping bag up to the freedom field*. It was a cold night — nearly the end of November, after all — but it was dry and clear, not freezing anyway. I'd put up with worse from time to time when I'd been hitching around the country. I'd be fine if I kept enough layers on. Andy just nodded and Hilary just smiled. That was OK though. I knew they appreciated the gesture and just didn't want to make a big deal about it in front of everyone else.

I was as good as my word. I knew where there was an abandoned tent in a corner of the field anyway, planned on crawling in there, making myself nice and snug. I took a mug of rice wine with me too, was soon settled down out there with my nightcap. I kept the tent flaps open, stretched out and watched the sky for any signs of ET or the starman Bowie had promised would show up soon and fix the world's mess for it. That had been a decade before — and we were all still waiting. I'd loved Bowie when I'd been a little kid though, used to play him loud when my mum was out. Something larger than life about him. Larger than my life anyway.

Nigel and Claire got back Saturday lunchtime and over the next twenty-four hours the weekend demonstrators started to arrive. Claire and Nigel were in a different situation from Andy and Hilary, or most of the other shifting couples around the place. Claire had her own fixed room in the cottage which Nigel seemed to occupy as well most of the time. It was the only room there which had a lock fitted. I don't recall anyone ever questioning the fact — or certainly not publicly, at a Monday Night Meeting or anything like that. It would have seemed like rudeness basically — these were *English* protestors after all — and you only had to be around Myrtle

Cottage a week or so to appreciate the extent of Claire's and Nigel's commitment. Other people came and went but nobody doubted that either of them would see the protest through right to the very end.

I slept out in the freedom field on the Saturday night as well — or tried to. The field was full of tents now and rival campfires, each with a circle of protestors gathered around it. I remember two girls up from London, sisters actually, sitting at the fire nearest me. They sang 'Redemption Song' unaccompanied (don't tell me you don't know that one, Dear Reader). I thought it was the most beautiful singing I'd ever heard. I still think that pretty much. It was the night before battle after all. The proper time for a sacred vigil. The calm before the storm.

19

They left Kerr's car in the Edgbaston Street car park, where there'd still been spaces, and made the rest of their journey on foot. Mott Legal Investigations' offices were in a modern building in Colmore Row, up on the tenth floor, high enough, probably, to take in the nearby spire of St Philip's Cathedral and the bulbous expanse of the Bullring, Birmingham's best-known landmark, only a few streets away. Two black-suited doormen greeted them and then an over-perfumed, over-manicured receptionist. An intended double barrier against visitors who didn't check out but no barrier at all against the magic of police ID.

Jacobson helped himself to a mint from the big jar on the reception desk and then they took the fast lift upwards. Mott shared the tenth floor with a firm of architects and a PR company. It was an impressive front that spoke of generously financed clients — the kind who ran up big bills and settled them more or less on time.

Jacobson had finally got the basic dope on Michael Mott via a phone call from DS Barber last night. According to Barber, Mott was Birmingham-born but had spent most of his police career in the Met. He'd reached the rank of DI before he'd taken early retirement and gone private. In an 'industry' known for low standards and sailing close to the wind, Mott was apparently as near to straight as it got. He'd specialised exclusively in legal defence work, burrowing into the evidence and the witnesses officially disclosed by the Crown Prosecution Service. Mott earned his fee by identifying areas of doubt and uncertainty that defence barristers could exploit to their advantage in court. He'd done well over the years, employed his own full-time team of licensed private detectives. Half a dozen or so, Barber had told him. *Minus one now, old son*, Jacobson had commented with trademark bad taste.

Mott was waiting for them in his outer office, waved them through to his private den (the view from the tall, broad window was as impressive as Jacobson had anticipated). Mott was about Jacobson's own age but irritatingly square-jawed and handsome in a too-obvious, near-enough American kind of way. He was wearing a crisp, blue shirt and the suit jacket hanging from his walnut coat rack easily matched or exceeded Greg Salter standards. For all that, Mott looked terrible. Red-eyed, ill-shaven, drawn. Jacobson's best guess was that he'd driven back home from the mortuary last night and proceeded to drink himself senseless.

'Her mother's taking a train up,' he told them, indicating comfy leather chairs, 'apparently she's in no state to use her car. I'm going to meet her when she gets here, see she's looked after.'

'Bedfordshire, isn't it?' Jacobson asked neutrally.

'Luton — or somewhere in the vicinity.'

Karen Holt's relatives were almost certainly irrelevant. But, more or less automatically,

Jacobson's mind ran through what he knew about her background so far. An only child. Mother and father divorced. A steady boyfriend but not live-in. Plus the father and the boyfriend currently out of the country in any case. The (remarried) father on holiday in Greece. The IT contractor boyfriend working in Luxembourg until the end of the month.

'You said last night she'd only been working for you for a couple of years?'

'Twenty-six months and sixteen days, that's what the computer says,' Mott answered. 'The first time I've taken on anybody who's not been ex-job.'

'Do you think that could be relevant?' Kerr asked.

It was the first time he'd clapped eyes on Mott. He'd spent most of last night out at Crowcross, had only heard about the identification of the body from Jacobson at second hand. Mott had tried to contact Karen Holt several times yesterday because she hadn't shown for work. Then, finally, he'd seen her image on Channel 4 News, had called the incident room's public number and had driven straight over to Crowby.

'Well, it might be, mightn't it? Like I say, whatever she was up to was nothing to do with MLI, *nothing*. I've had no involvement in the Martin Grove case since Alan Slingsby used me when they were going for the third appeal. That's got to be eleven years ago at least — the computer's got all the details on that too.'

Jacobson pressed the back of his head against the cool leather.

'So your staff don't usually go moonlighting, then?'

'It's totally against their contracts — totally not allowed. I wouldn't expect them to have the time anyway. I work them hard and I work hard myself.'

'Why did you take her on without a CID background?'

'She persuaded me at interview, that's all. She'd done journalism as you know — came with a range of contacts that were new for me, that looked like they could be useful to my set-up. Plus I'd just lost two women to maternity leave back then. I was definitely looking to hire a female — I need a good gender balance in my line of work. Same as yourself, I expect.'

True enough, Jacobson thought, but didn't comment. It was far too early yet to know whether he trusted Mott or not — or whether, despite his chiselled, manly mush and flash suite of expensive offices, he was prepared to like him. The I-Me-I-Me motif wasn't hugely encouraging.

'We're going to need to see her phone records, her appointments diary, everything,' he said.

'Of course, of course,' Mott replied, trying out an affable smile that didn't quite sit with his bleary eyes. 'I run a clean operation. Totally nothing to hide.'

Totally. That was another word he was over-doing, Jacobson noticed.

'What was she currently working on *officially*?' he asked.

He should have asked last night but he'd

forgotten. It had been gone nine by the time Mott had identified the body and there had been half a dozen other tasks foremost in his mind. Maybe, he'd thought recently, he was getting too old (or too jaded) for his line of work. What got you down in the end was the relentlessness of it. You solved one case, put one sick bastard or bastards away — and then your phone rang again: another day, another victim.

Mott yawned involuntarily and tapped his hand to his forehead. He probably had a hangover banging on it like a bailiff on a Woodlands door, Jacobson thought.

'The Gerry Quigg case,' he answered after a moment. 'We all are — myself and my entire team. It's going to take up my entire capacity until it comes to court.'

Jacobson looked hard into Mott's bloodshot blue eyes.

'I thought you said you ran a clean operation, Mike.'

Mott tried the affable smile again.

'I meant it. Even Quigg deserves a fair trial, wouldn't you say? Always judge a society by how it treats its worst elements, yes?'

'I couldn't have put it better myself. But Concrete Gerry? Whatever the CPS is throwing at him is an effing fraction of what he's got away with over the years.'

'Agreed too — but what his defence needs to check is that the *specific* stuff they're throwing is kosher.'

'The CPS will be using their top retards, old son. I'd expect the case for the Crown to be kosher, halal, non-sexist, non-ageist — and probably carbon neutral and bio-degradable into the bargain.'

'And that's pretty much what it looks like so far. But I'm working under a totally legitimate contract for Quigg's solicitors — it's what I do. It's what I've a *right* to do under the law.'

Jacobson half-smiled, held up his arms, palms open.

'Let's debate legal ethics another time. What — specifically — was Karen Holt's involvement?'

Mott glanced at the computer screen on his desk, maybe trying to create the impression that he hadn't already checked and double-checked her caseload.

'Pretty low-level really,' he said, looking up again. 'She's — she was — my least experienced guy. Forensic liaison mainly — which basically means identifying key forensic elements in the CPS case and getting second opinions from independent experts. You'll find it all in her notes — though it's all strictly confidential of course. You do know that I could apply for a court order against your warrant, I take it?'

'Gerry Quigg isn't my business,' Jacobson commented. 'It's not Birmingham CID business either. I just need to know *where* Karen Holt has been and *who* she's been talking to. I don't give a stuff what about — unless it involves Martin Grove in some way.'

Mott nodded, seemed to accept Jacobson's line of argument. Something chimed melodiously on his desk. Then his door opened and his secretary — a blonde clone of the ground-floor receptionist — ushered in three males. Jacobson and Kerr knew one of them — DS Barber, City of Birmingham CID (*DC* Barber, Crowby CID as was). They assumed, correctly, that the other two were the Birmingham SOCOs they'd been waiting for.

'Barber, old son, can't get away from us,' Jacobson said.

'Who'd want to, guv? DI Coleman sends his regards by the way.'

Oh yes, Coleman, Jacobson thought, another big city egotist. Alison kept telling him he was too negative about his colleagues, too negative about the human race in general. He hoped she was right — about the human race anyway. But history and the news bulletins kept on stacking up the evidence against her.

Barber showed Mott the duly-signed warrant. Mott waved it away with another 'of course, of course'. The arrangement was for the SOCOs, overseen by Barber, to bag and secure everything from Karen Holt's work area that was likely to be of interest. Jacobson wanted a full copy of the hard drive on her computer and anything on paper that looked remotely interesting. He also needed a full list of everybody who worked for Mott, addresses, NI numbers, dates of birth. Barber would talk informally to anybody who was in the office right now. But in the course of the day, Jacobson's plan was that each of them should be properly interviewed. Even if Mott was telling the truth — and he didn't know about his employee's extracurricular activity — that didn't prove that she'd kept quiet about it to her colleagues.

Jacobson was suddenly eager to leave. Barber and the SOCOs could deal with everything here. It was a relief that the Birmingham force had earmarked Barber as the liaison officer on the case rather than some unknown quantity. Mott's detective had been murdered on Jacobson's patch — no argument — but the Birmingham force could be more or less helpful about the facilities they extended to his investigation. Strictly speaking, Jacobson couldn't make a move inside the city without their prior approval.

Mott walked out with Jacobson and Kerr all the way to the lift. He offered Jacobson a firm handshake, his grip predictably manly and over-vigorous. Jacobson extricated his fingers as soon as he could. He half-smiled again as he did so, knowing he'd saved his trick-shot to the end.

'You've said you've had nothing to do with the Martin Grove case for more than a decade, Mike — but we've heard that Grove himself has been in touch with you since he got out of prison.'

If Mott was surprised, he hid it well.

'Well that's true — but it's not exactly the same thing, is it?'

Jacobson didn't reply — just waited.

The lift arrived. Kerr identified the position of the sensor, cupped his hand over it to keep the doors open.

Mott tapped his headache again.

'There was a period about eighteen months ago when he kept calling me up, said he wanted to talk to me about his case, said he was writing about it for a book. I told him that everything I

170

had I'd passed on to Alan Slingsby at the time of the appeal — which is completely true by the way. I actually met him once — bought him lunch at the Ikon, just to get rid. He phoned a few times after that but I never took his calls or returned them. He gave up eventually, I suppose.'

Jacobson stepped into the lift.

'He told you he was writing about the case. He didn't say anything about *solving* it, did he?'

Mott tried his smile again, relieved maybe that Jacobson and Kerr seemed to be going at last.

'Not in so many words. But it was easy enough to see that was part of what was in his mind. I remember he trotted out all the old conspiracy theories about an MI5 fixer, wanted to know what I thought about that stuff. I told him there wasn't a shred of evidence — which there wasn't.'

Kerr got into the lift too, his hand still covering the beam.

'So who *did* kill Claire Oldham — in your view?' he asked.

Mott shrugged, shook his head.

'To be honest, I always thought Grove looked likely for it — I thought Slingsby was flying a kite trying to clear his name. Then along comes modern science and *proves* he didn't do it — which shows how wrong you can be. Thank fuck we're a civilised country and we don't have the death penalty anymore.'

'I'm with you on that, old son,' Jacobson answered, just as Kerr took his hand away and the lift doors started to close.

Kerr had to use the sat nav, which he detested, to find Karen Holt's home address: a Victorian rectory on the south side of the city which had been converted into 'character' apartments. The rectory grounds had a curved gravelled driveway with a separate entrance and exit linked by a low stone wall and freshly painted black railings. Kerr drove in and parked next to the Birmingham SOCO van.

'Gerry Quigg, Frank, we didn't see that coming,' he commented — again.

'No we didn't, old son — we didn't see it at all,' Jacobson replied, still mulling the news over.

Karen Holt had lived on the attic floor — her flat was tiny and felt cramped but Jacobson liked the way you could see a slice of the Worcester and Birmingham Canal from the windows. The forensic visitation was low-key and routine-only at this stage. Mainly a case of knowing what was there should any of it merit a second closer look later on. The place might have been done over of course. Neatly and professionally. Her executioner or executioners could have used her keys, gained easy access without the need for any messy breaking and entering. If Karen Holt had a laptop of her own in addition to her terminal in the MLI offices it wasn't here. Maybe the same was true for incriminating letters, scraps of paper, diaries or notebooks. To the untrained eye, it looked like nothing had been disturbed. But it was possible that the SOCO team might find evidence to the contrary.

Entrance hall, bedroom, bathroom, kitchen, lounge. Jacobson and Kerr kept to the stepping boards, tried not to get in the way of the SOCOs. The base set for Karen Holt's landline was located in a little alcove in the hall. Jacobson asked a SOCO to press the play button for the answer system. There were five messages, all of them left the day before. Four were from Michael Mott wanting to know why she hadn't showed for work, asking her (with increasing ferocity) to get in touch. The fifth — timed at six minutes past eleven last night — was from her boyfriend. He sounded puzzled that she wasn't answering but not especially worried. *OK. I'll try again tomorrow night, babes. Miss you.* Whatever he got up to in Luxembourg in his free time, Jacobson thought, evidently didn't include watching British television via cable or satellite — or not last night anyway. It was a pretty safe bet that if someone had done the place over, they'd have wiped any more interesting messages from the system (there'd been no messages left undeleted on Martin Grove's phone at all). The incident room had requested her call records from British Telecom as a matter of course, which might turn up something — especially when they were collated with the records for Martin Grove's number. Both sets, Brian Phelps had promised in the last hour, should be available later this morning. They'd requested Grove's phone data yesterday but BT had pleaded some kind of technical difficulty in retrieving them (as BT frequently did).

Grove, unusually, didn't own a mobile phone. According to Maureen Bright, he was 'weird' about them, didn't like the fact that your whereabouts became traceable anytime you switched your phone on. Karen Holt did have a mobile of course: but it didn't appear to be in her flat or the MLI office — and it hadn't turned up in the search of Crowcross Wood. Jacobson had asked Barber to get her number from Michael Mott — and then to request her records from the mobile phone company.

He wandered back into the kitchen, watched a SOCO dusting for prints near the electric hob. Ransacker/s, if there'd been any, would've been gloved up for sure — but somebody else who was connected to the killing in some way might have been on the premises on some other occasion and might have been more careless. Ninety per cent of detective work was about covering as many of the possibilities as you could — exploring them, comparing them, confirming them, rejecting them, narrowing them down — and most of the other ten per cent was about lying awake in the middle of the night, worrying about the possibilities you'd forgotten to cover or, worse still, hadn't even considered.

Karen Holt's door buzzer buzzed: the two Birmingham duty DCs who would trace the rest of the apartment-dwellers and interview them. There was CCTV downstairs too, focused on the shared, public entrance. That was Birmingham's gig as well: contacting the caretaker again, taking a copy, eliminating everybody legitimate from the last thirty-six hours or so, ideally coming up with a useful image or two. It was a big task to delegate to officers he didn't know but the strict, inter-force protocols didn't give Jacobson any choice in the matter. He talked to them on the landing outside the flat, confirmed that they'd been accurately briefed about their tasks. He caught up with Kerr in Karen Holt's lounge after that. He was still snooping though her CD collection — a marginally callous activity which seemed to be an important perk of the job as far as Kerr was concerned.

'You should make one of those TV list shows,' Jacobson told him, '*Victims of Murder: Their Hundred Top Tunes.*'

Kerr didn't even look embarrassed, just kept thumbing along the shelves.

Jacobson wanted to get going, had seen all he needed to see. *If* the killer or killers — or their emissary — had already been here, then they had already removed anything that would interest him. He didn't need to know anymore about Karen Holt than that she'd been a private detective for the firm that had once worked on Martin Grove's third appeal. That was why she was dead, that was the connection he needed to unpack. Who she was otherwise didn't really figure.

Plus he didn't like looking at the Creamfields festival poster that took up most of one wall in here. It was a personal touch too close for comfort, the exact same one he'd seen in his daughter's place the last time he'd visited her. Sally was living down in Bristol now, near the university, had moved out of London at least. But she was still unsettled, still changing jobs every two minutes, still hadn't found 'it', whatever the thing was in her life that she was searching for. Which might have been Karen Holt's problem too — was maybe why she'd swapped journalism for private detective work, was maybe why she'd moonlighted on top of her assignments for Michel Mott. A sexist pig, which Jacobson wasn't, might have drawn a smug, repellent conclusion from yesterday's discovery of her stone dead, tongue-mutilated body.

20

Martin Grove.doc

We surrounded the base at three o'clock on Sunday afternoon. The turn-out was brilliant. We found out later that the police had been stopping vehicles on the motorways, especially hired coaches, turning them back at the county borders or just detaining them and delaying them on a variety of pretexts until they were too late to take part in the action. There'd been a similar operation at the railway station in Crowby. Weapons searches, drug searches — anything they could get away with under the still-current sus laws. But even so we were more than two thousand strong — nearly enough bodies to form a solid, human chain around most of the perimeter fence.

By the time everything was ready, the police riot vans were drawn up across from the main entrance gates — and there was a second contingent of pigs, also kitted out in full riot gear, already positioned inside the base. They weren't in formation though, were mainly just standing around near the CrowbyGuard porta-cabins and chatting idly to each other. The BBC had sent a full crew — cameramen, sound, reporters — which was really encouraging. They'd turned up an hour or so before, had already filmed interviews with Claire and Nigel about the purpose of the protest. The police had kept them well away from the main approaches to the base but there was sod all they could do to prevent them accepting Claire's invitation to set up their equipment at the top of the freedom field, which, after all, was lawfully her property.

The plan to circle the fence (*embrace the base* as our posters yelled) fell into a grey area, legally. Other stretches of land — owned by hostile, unsympathetic farmers — backed onto the base in the same way that the freedom field did. And even where the perimeter fence intersected with the public road, there were 'safety' issues that could be invoked against the proposed action. The police could have banned it outright but their attitude on the day seemed to be to let the thing go ahead so long as it remained purely peaceful, so long as it didn't last too long — and so long as there was absolutely no damage to property.

Bang on three o'clock, we got underway. In a long line, we filed out of the freedom field and headed towards the main gates where we separated, some going left, some going right. To the pigs it probably looked fairly random. But the Fence Com had applied mathematics to the task, had divided the circumference of the fence by the number of available bodies. Every protestor knew in advance which way they were headed — and the 'action squad' pre-selected by the Fence Com even knew the approximate interval of regular protestors they had to place between each other for maximum effect. By three thirty, the base was encircled by noisy, enthusiastic protestors, chanting JOBS NOT

BOMBS and NO TO THE AIRBASE, NO TO THE BOMBERS. There was a helicopter overhead — maybe the police, maybe the media, nobody seemed to be really sure. In the hopes that it was the latter, we kept our hand mirrors in our pockets (if you think you might ever need to keep a fascist helicopter off your back, Dear Reader, always carry a mirror — you can reflect dazzling light into the pilot's eyes, stop him from getting too close to you).

I was with Andy and Hilary, over on the far side of the base, looking out towards Crowcross Wood. There were about thirty of us all told in the action squad, scattered in cells of two or three all the way around the perimeter fence: tooled up and ready. The theory was that if we tried all at once from different directions, some of us at least would get through. Hilary was our cell timekeeper. When her watch reached three forty-four, she started the countdown. But softly, quietly, so that only Andy and myself were aware of it. *Fifty-nine. Fifty-eight. Fifty-seven.* I started taking deep breaths, willing myself not to bottle it. *Thirty-two. Thirty-one.* I checked and re-checked my grip on the bolt cutters, loosened my jacket, got ready to pull them out. I'd been practising all week, was determined not to fuck up. *Four. Three. Two. One.* Finally. This was it: *go.*

They cut like a dream, like a piece of absolute piss. And then we were through the fence, all three of us, running free as the wind. Our ultimate objective was the portacabins. Every now and then since the fence had gone up, there'd been sightings of vehicles and visitors to the base who'd looked nothing like humble security guards. Guys in suits, guys with briefcases. Engineers or architects, it was rumoured, measuring the site up for the nuclear bombers. We wanted to get inside, check for plans, evidence. And even if we didn't get that far — or there was nothing there to find — we'd still have scored a victory just by being there, just by breaching OCS security.

We were on the old runway now, heavy going on the cracked concrete. All around the perimeter, echoing cheers egged us on — and a lot of the ordinary protestors started piling on to the base as well, unrehearsed but spontaneously abandoning the human chain and following our example. Scores of them sat down — or lay down — in defiance of the riot police.

We kept going. Hilary lagging behind, but urging us not to worry, not to slow down. The riot pigs were caught on the hop. This was before the Miners' Strike, don't forget, before Orgreave. For a lot of them, it was probably their first real taste of action. With hindsight, what they should have done was obvious: build a tight formation around the portacabins and the main gates — and *only then* send out snatch squads to clear the protestors off the runways. Instead they panicked, tried — and failed — to do everything at once. In the distance, we started to make out the other action squad cells. It wasn't all that difficult. The police and the regular protestors were running around like clueless monkeys — but here and there you could make out two or three purposeful figures, moving swiftly and steadily, converging on a goal.

We were maybe fifty yards away from the cabins, when the first cops reached us. Two of them. Biggish bastards with their visors down — and no sign of a numbered lapel on their shoulders (they'd mastered that part of their training at any rate). I ran one way around them and Andy and Hilary tried the other. In the context, their shields and batons only slowed them down — and we easily got past them. They came after us though, one of them screaming blue fucking murder.

We were gaining distance on them, putting them behind us, when Hilary tripped, hit the concrete hard. She told us, gasping for air, just to leave her, to keep going. Andy hesitated and so did I. Then one of the cops — the screamer — reached her. I expected him just to wait there for his mate to catch up. Then, I imagined, they'd carry her off the base the way I'd seen other coppers do — via the TV news — at other sit-down demos and protests. I've told you before how naïve I was in those days. The cop put his shield neatly to one side on the ground and then he leaned over her. Even then, I probably thought he was checking that she wasn't hurt.

Thud. Thud. Thud. The bastard truncheoned her three times. Once on her thighs, once on her kidneys, once — madly — on the side of her head. Screaming abuse the whole time too. *Whore. Slag. Commie Bastard.* Andy went for him, somehow levering his forearm around his throat, pulling him away from her.

181

'Look out,' I shouted.

But too late. The other cop had reached us. He clubbed Andy from behind — had to hit him four times before he went down. I couldn't take on two of them (I probably couldn't have taken on one of them — not if I expected to win). All I could think of was to get them away from Andy and Hilary, to stop them hurting them anymore. I picked up the screamer-cop's discarded shield and hurled it at him. It bounced harmlessly off his baton — but it was enough to distract both of them. I started to run again, checking over my shoulder that they were both in pursuit.

I ran until it felt that my lungs would burst. Soon I'd outrun the screamer and his mate (or they'd found other prey), had ducked and dived around half-a-dozen other coppers. There was mini-carnage everywhere by then. It seemed as if the coppers had no real strategy other than to club anybody they could catch. Later, of course, I realised that a lot of them had just completely lost it, had gone out of control. I swear to God I saw one of them truncheon a heavily pregnant woman while she sat peacefully on the grass, not even trying to get as far as one of the runways. The BBC caught a lot of it on camera but mysteriously the worst footage never made it onto the news bulletins — there was even a rumour later that it had never made it out of the freedom field, that the coppers had intercepted the film crew on their way out, had destroyed most of their film canisters on the spot.

Still I kept going, kept running. I was less than ten yards from the nearest cabin — I could even see Nigel and a handful of others unveiling their banners from the main cabin's rooftop — when I noticed Claire up ahead, suddenly felled by a rugby-style tackle. Two big coppers pulled her to her feet. One of them held her from behind, pinning her arms tightly to her sides, while the other one (I swear this to God too) pulled at her clothes, got his piggy hands all over her — everywhere. I ran straight for him. I tried to do what I'd seen Andy do before. But I couldn't get my arm around under his helmet and visor. He knocked me backwards off my feet like I was no more than a buzzing fly — and then the two of them set on me.

'On you go,' I managed to shout to Claire before I felt a baton cracking on the side of my head.

I don't think I ever completely lost consciousness. But there's a phase where my memories are jagged, episodic — like a digital TV signal cracking up. I came to in the 'medical' area that the pigs put together later: rows of injured protestors waiting for first-aid attention. The whole thing was surreal. Eventually an ambulance guy (or a doctor if you were really lucky) checked you out and pronounced whether you needed hospital treatment or not. Then you joined 'exit queue one' or 'exit queue two'. Either you were headed for the hospital — and the police would do you afterwards — or you were arrested and processed on the spot, i.e. you were kept waiting for a couple of hours with nothing to eat or drink (and no toilet facilities) until you could be bussed into whatever local nick still had a few overnight vacancies available.

21

Jacobson left a message on the telephone extension of Ted Nelson, his only personal contact inside SOCA, the Serious Organised Crime Agency — or his only personal contact there who wouldn't either ignore his call or phone back solely for the pleasure of telling him to fuck right off (networking wasn't Jacobson's greatest social skill). Thereafter, he sat in silence while Kerr drove them out of Birmingham and back towards Crowby. Kerr was silent too, didn't even shove on any of his music. Jacobson knew why. Like him, Kerr would be trawling his mind for everything he knew about Gerald Donovan Quigg.

To say that Quigg was a drug dealer was like suggesting the Queen owned the odd property portfolio or two. Quigg was top-end, theoretically untouchable. The Midlands was pretty much his fiefdom — and his cartel even had its fingers in a few, disputed pies up in the north-west and down in London. Quigg's empire was old school, a classic mafia-inspired, pyramid selling set-up. Under-dogs, dogs, bigger dogs and top dogs — with Quigg as the biggest dog of all. Quigg touched nothing, knew nothing — but profited from everything. Even Quigg's under-dogs were at the top of their own personal trees, engaged in back-office supply and distribution only. Once you were fully a member of Quigg's organisation, your days of actually doling out product to end-users were strictly over. You left all the street-level business to your drones, had much bigger and much more profitable fish to fry. Quigg had started a long time ago and worked his own way up. He'd started right at the absolute bottom too: quid deals and microdots in student pubs back in the 1970s. If he'd gone in for selling computers or washing machines, he might have been a captain of industry by now, invited onto government think-tanks and giving inspirational guest lectures on MBA courses. Instead, his business being what it was, not too many people who weren't police or career criminals had even heard of him. Until recently anyway.

SOCA was only a couple of years old, was intended to be the latest 'supercop' initiative, organised nationally and tackling complex cases which were defined as exceeding the capabilities of local and regional police forces. Except it had run into its full share of problems and fuck-ups. Not the least of its troubles was that it wasn't purely a police set-up, and included elements from customs and immigration too. All three had different working styles but now, suddenly, they had to find a way to rub along together. So the SOCA operation against Gerry Quigg was being talked up as potentially the new agency's first indisputable major success story.

Quigg had built and then run his empire by the usual, crude carrot and stick methods. Loyalty and hard work were positively rewarded. Disloyalty and error earned you anything from a punishment kicking to a punishment death — and all stops and stations of the cross in between. In his early years, Quigg was rumoured to have taken out up to a dozen enemies personally. Even now, there were CID diehards keen to dig up particular sections of the M6 where, it was believed, the skeletal remains of some of his victims were still waiting to be found. But, bodies or no bodies, for years no police unit of any kind had ever got hold of enough definite evidence to implicate Concrete Gerry in anything more serious than a speeding offence — until last year.

Jacobson didn't know the details. Nobody outside SOCA did — and they weren't saying. It was unlikely, probably impossible, that there wasn't an insider in the mix somewhere. An acolyte close enough to Quigg to bury him up to his neck in solid proofs of his misdeeds in return for immunity from prosecution — and brave or mad enough to believe that the witness protection programme would keep him alive for more than ten minutes after Quigg got sent down.

The motorways were clear after yesterday's marathon hold-ups — Kerr exited at the North Crowby junction and they reached the hospital with quarter of an hour to kill. They headed straight for the visitors' café and took their drinks outside. The patio — cheap decking that creaked under your feet, nondescript shrubs in squat concrete cubes — only opened on warm, summer days like this one.

'They'll never let us talk to him, Frank, if it

comes to it,' Kerr said, stirring the sugar into his tea.

'We'll see, old son. We'll see. We need to know exactly who Karen Holt has been in touch with recently. Whether she's talked to them by phone or in person, it doesn't matter — but anybody in that category, we've an absolute right to interview. And that includes Quigg in my book — or any of his front men.'

Kerr couldn't help but smile at the thought of it. Driving up to Quigg's security gates, flashing your ID at his toerag bodyguards, putting him on the spot.

'Mott said her involvement was pretty low-level, though, Frank. Her phone records are probably just a list of forensic freelancers and the like.'

'I know, Ian, I know. But even a provincial DCI can dream — and don't forget forensics are central to the SOCA case, they've let that much slip to the media. Even if Holt didn't need to speak to Quigg, Quigg might have wanted to speak to her, might have wanted to know MLI were doing a proper job for him.'

Kerr nodded, conceding the point.

'I'm going to move the briefing forward to eleven thirty. If I'm not there on time, you can start it off without me,' Jacobson said, taking out his mobile and then calling the incident room to pass on the message.

They lapsed into more silence after that, concentrated on their drinks. There were a few rose bushes bordering the edge of the patio. Pale pink, desultory, not in the best of nick. But roses just the same. Jacobson sipped at his coffee, watched a bee glide lazily from stamen to stamen.

* * *

Kerr headed back out on the by-pass and then diverted onto the old Wynarth Road. With no Jacobson in the passenger seat, he hit the in-car: New Order, 'Blue Monday', and then Captain Beefheart, 'Safe As Milk' — just the unlikely kind of mash-up that MP3 had been invented for. It wasn't a market day so he found a space easily enough right in the centre of the square next to the war memorial. It was the first time in a while that police business had brought him into the centre of Wynarth — and he'd stopped going there, as much as was possible, on any other kind. Cathy had wanted to trawl the antique and bric-à-brac shops a couple of Saturday afternoons ago (something to do with finding a leaving present for one of the bosses in her office) and he'd driven over with her, hadn't been able to think quickly enough of a plausible reason not to. The whole time he'd been on edge. She'd wanted a drink in the wine bar at one point (he'd talked her into a cup of organic, fair trade coffee in one of the veggie cafés instead) and then she'd hit on the idea of visiting the Looking East Gallery. The departing boss was keen on photography apparently and she'd thought maybe there'd be a framed print there that would suit. There was — but the price tag was beyond the amount of cash that had been collected in the kitty. Kerr had joked, agreed with possible selections, disagreed, looked interested, all on autopilot. The whole time he was thinking that he was here — on Thomas Holt street itself — only a couple of doors away from where Rachel's flat had used to be.

He'd run into one of her friends, Kate, earlier in the year, one of the few who didn't seem to hate him, didn't seem to think that Rachel was well shot of him. He'd bumped into her in CD Heaven of all places, the second-hand record shop over in Longtown. Kate had given him the bad news straight. Rachel had put her flat on the market, had moved in full-time with Tony Scruton, the lover who'd pre-dated Kerr — and now, Kate had finally confirmed, had post-dated him too. Kerr had still been stalking the streets of Wynarth back then, visiting old haunts, thinking that by chance one of those days — or nights — he'd run into her, at last get the chance to explain about the time he'd dangled Scruton up against the Looking East Gallery window, had only just kept his hands from throttling the little bastard's neck.

Well fuck her, he'd thought, *fuck them*. From now on, he'd sworn, it would just be him and Cathy — and the kids. Cathy complained from time to time about not seeing him enough, about how he put his work before everything else — but she didn't sneer at him for what he did, didn't act like she was slumming it every time she let him fuck her, didn't sit up in bed and read clever little articles out of the *Guardian* to him about police corruption, police scandals and police incompetence.

He'd never been so glad to get out of a place in his life. Rachel had even worked there on occasions — when her paintings weren't selling or she'd no clients for her feng shui consultancy. Every step back to the car, he'd feared running in to her. Not that she'd say something, drop him in it, just that that she'd read the situation wrongly, assume that Kerr had dragged his wife over to Wynarth, not the other way around, assume that he was still obsessed with her, even just with the chance of seeing her.

Well fuck that, he thought again now, *fuck that*, fuck *that*. He got out, stared glumly at the base of the war memorial. Rows of names who'd never lived long enough to have a wife, never mind cheat on one. So what if she saw him, so what if they saw him, her and Scruton, hand in hand — let them think what they liked. He found the address he needed easily enough. It was just off the market square, although in the opposite direction to Thomas Holt Street. The property was mid-terrace. Neat, well-preserved stonework, Midlands red brick, like all the rest. The tiny front garden had been gravelled over, was barren apart from a set of wind chimes, hot June silent, which had been mounted on a stumpy wooden post. Kerr rang the bell and waited.

No answer. He waited some more and then stepped onto the gravel, peered in through the front window. Nobody home, or so it appeared. He tried the bell again — and then bent down, took a look through the letter box. What he saw

190

made him instantly put his shoulder to the door as hard as he could. When that didn't work, he stepped back, started to kick at the lock. The door was solid enough and he nearly abandoned the task as hopeless — but on the fourth kick he thought he felt something give. A couple of neighbours, both women, had turned up to see what was going on by then. Breathless, he'd fished in his pocket, shown them his ID. He used his shoulder again, fell into the hallway more than shoved the door open. The neighbours peered in behind him. One of them carried on gaping but the other one turned away, shocked, close to fainting, at the site of Ann Ledbury, Martin Grove's nearly-wife, dangling from a make-shift noose over the bottom step of her stripped-pine stairs.

22

Martin Grove.doc

Everybody who'd been arrested out at the airbase spent at least one night in the cells. On the Monday afternoon, I pleaded guilty to affray at the magistrates' court, got fined twenty-five quid and got a lift back out to the cottage from a pro-CND vicar. The local CND also paid my fine for me out of donations, did the same for quite a few others. The Crowby Radical Law Collective had advised the 'plead guilty' strategy for most of us who'd been arrested. It was a plea bargain in all but name. You said nothing about the police riot, made no complaints, and you walked swiftly away with a minor conviction and a low-level fine. Word got to us, too, that this was also what Claire and Nigel wanted to happen. Apparently their thinking was that we were more use to the protest out on the streets than banged up on remand.

Claire hadn't been arrested herself, had got clear of the airbase after I'd 'rescued' her. Nigel had though. Six of the action squad, him included, had made it onto the roof of the main portacabin (they hadn't, to everyone's regret, been able to get inside), had spent nearly an hour up there, waving banners and making political speeches for the benefit of the TV news — which the TV news had neglected to broadcast (or maybe that footage had disappeared too). They were facing more

192

serious charges to do with damage to MOD property. The plan was for all of them to plead not guilty and to use the court case as a publicity vehicle. Three got bail but three — very soon known as the Crowcross Three — were remanded. Nigel, 'a known agitator' according to the magistrate, was one of them.

The atmosphere at the Monday Night Meeting was hard to define. Muted might be the best adjective to describe it. Claire seemed to think the action had been a success. Even though the extent of the police violence had been covered up in the mainstream media, she argued, at least some of it had got reported, would surely make some people sit up and think about what was happening in our country. Plus the Law Collective were saying that the trial of Nigel and his co-defendants could be months away, plenty of time, according to Red Claire, to build support and spread the word. Her view was always pure Trotsky (though I probably didn't understand that so well at the time): *worse is better* — since the capitalist state is also a fascist state, the more it bares its claws, the more the people can see it for what it is.

Not everybody agreed. Especially a lot of the local opponents of the airbase from Crowby and Wynarth. They were angry about the action squad's invasion of the base and especially about the fact that it had been planned in secret and without any consultation. The way they saw it, what should have been a peaceful demonstration had been hijacked. A lot of them were so pissed off about it that we never saw them out at the

193

cottage again. The plead guilty line came in for criticism too and quite a few had ignored it anyway. Mostly they'd achieved bail but there were some that hadn't, including protestors who'd turned up at the base with no idea of invading it. *They'll be spending Christmas in the nick, thanks to you, Claire,* one guy from Crowby CND pointed out.

Andy and Hilary remained staunch of course. Andy milked the stitches in his head for all they were worth, said he'd do it all again, do it as many times as it took. My friend Alan Slingsby, who you'll meet later, says he was there that night too, though I don't remember him. He says he was there on behalf of the Law Collective, says he made a little speech of his own. My mind might have wandered by then of course. It often did. To me, nineteen and thick, the day before had just been exciting, something different, a laugh as much as anything. Or it had been in the beginning. I could have done without the beating and the conviction for affray (which would come back to haunt me later) — and I hadn't liked being locked up overnight, I hadn't enjoyed that part at all. There'd been four of us, all protestors, held in a cell at the old Wynarth police station (long since closed down). Even though I wasn't on my own, it freaked me out, I mean really freaked me out. A hundred and one fears, that I'd never known I had, bubbled up, kept me from any idea of sleeping. The place could burn down and we'd be trapped inside — or (this was the one that really creeped me) the police could be lying to us and they'd just keep us locked up there for ever, maybe even let us starve to death. It looks daft, idiotic, when you write it down but it doesn't feel that way in the middle of the night when you're firmly locked in behind a door that only unlocks from the other side. I never even hesitated in the morning when the Law Collective solicitor told me that if I pleaded guilty I'd be released that day, wouldn't be locked up again that night. I'd never worried about going to prison much before then but now I knew — or thought I knew — that I was the type who definitely couldn't handle it, the type who'd go mental inside, completely and utterly mental.

So with all that running through my head, I might well have missed Alan's contribution to the meeting, might have been far too busy, as usual, with my own stupid thoughts. Uppermost of which, beyond even running rings around the coppers and then getting banged up for it, was the thrilling conceit that while Nigel was away . . .

23

Jacobson's second post-mortem inside twenty-four hours had been no more fun to watch than the first one. Candice Black did most of the work this time, closely supervised by Robinson. Only three results mattered from the police point of view (although Jacobson found a moment to speculate whether the evidence of her recent abortion would be news to her boyfriend and her mother). Two of them were pretty much as anticipated: Karen Holt had died as a consequence of the bullet which had lodged in her brain — and her tongue, like Martin Grove's, had been mutilated after she was dead. Retrieving the bullet had been a forensic bonus of course, would make life easier for the FSS ballistics expert. The bullet that had killed Grove had entered *and* exited his skull — inconveniently, it had then been removed from the scene by whoever had shot him.

The third result, though, was a great, big, fat surprise. Opening up Karen Holt's stomach had revealed that she'd eaten her last meal only a couple of hours before she'd been killed. Amongst the partially-digested contents had been pasta, chorizo and vegetables — potentially the very same pasta, chorizo and vegetables which had been found, in a slightly-less digested state, inside Martin Grove. The strong possibility was therefore that Grove and Holt had dined together before they'd been murdered — presumably *chez* Grove, since there was no evidence so far to suggest that Grove had left his home after Maureen Bright had driven off (to visit Jane Ebdon) at nine o'clock. Robinson, like all pathologists, hated to be pinned down on the matter of precise times of death. But he'd conceded that the scenario which put Grove shot dead around midnight and Karen Holt maybe an hour later wasn't an impossible working hypothesis.

They were back in Robinson's office again. Like yesterday, Dr Black had been left behind to sew up the body on her own while Jacobson and Robinson unpacked the results into standard English.

'So Karen Holt's called in sometime after his girlfriend's gone out, Grove's cooked her a bit of supper,' Jacobson said, extrapolating. 'Unfortunately, their evening's nose-dived a little bit after that.'

Robinson smiled but didn't comment. He wasn't a rude, unhelpful bastard like his predecessor, Merchant — but he had his own politer ways of hinting that he had other work of his own to be getting on with.

Jacobson stood up, taking the hint. There was only one more thing he wanted to check again.

'And you still reckon that she was killed exactly where her body was found?'

Robinson stood up too, seized the chance to open his office door wide to the silent corridor. Hospitals bustled — but mortuaries were uncanny oases of quietude.

'There's nothing to suggest otherwise, Frank. It's true that if you move a body within the first six hours, the patterns of lividity will shift with it — which can give a killer a nice bit of leeway. But against that, you've got compelling crime scene evidence in Crowcross Wood. Blood traces in the vicinity, consistent with the general position of the body — and especially consistent with the angle of the head wound.'

Jacobson heard the news about Ann Ledbury while a patrol car ferried him from the hospital towards the Divisional building in the centre of Crowby. If he'd stayed there another ten minutes he might have seen — or heard — the ambulance rushing her into Emergency. According to the control room, all the hospital was saying so far was that she was unconscious and receiving treatment. According to Kerr, she'd only just been breathing when he'd cut her down. Her neck was a mess not just from the noose, Kerr told him, but also from the deep gouges her fingers had clawed into it, her body instinctively fighting for its life, clinging on to every possible second. She could only just have done it, Kerr had reckoned, even another minute or so and it would have been too late: *Course it still might be, Frank, or she could be brain damaged if she does pull through, totally doolally.*

Jacobson took the lift up to the fourth floor. The day was too hot for the stairs and he was in too much of a rush. Faintly, in the distance, he heard the Town Hall clock chiming out the half-hour. He was on time — just. Kerr, still out

198

at Wynarth, would be missing but that couldn't be helped — he wasn't about to postpone the event a second time. When he reached the incident room, crowded with co-opted duty CID and uniformeds as well as the murder squad regulars, he eased off his jacket and helped himself to a plastic cup of tasteless, one hundred per cent purified water from the cooler. Oxygen and hydrogen molecules in perfect balance and nothing else — certainly not flavour at any rate. It occurred to him that this was maybe the first major incident briefing that he'd ever fronted without the nerve-soothing crutch of a freshly lit B&H between his fingers.

He stood in front of the whiteboard and gave them the big picture as he currently saw it.

'Martin Grove's been out of prison for five years. For the last three he's been living quietly out at Crowcross with Maureen Bright and not seeming to cause anybody any trouble. Except that all this while he's been writing his life story — with an emphasis on his involvement in the Claire Oldham case and very likely with a view to finding out who really killed her. Karen Holt visited him out there last night and both of them ended up shot dead, probably with the same weapon and by the same third party or parties. There's a good chance Holt was helping Grove rake over the coals regarding Claire Oldham. For instance, it's possible that her home computer's gone the same way as Grove's — and then you've the fact that she's been dragged over to Crowcross Wood to be killed when it would have been a lot easier to shoot her in Grove's kitchen along with Grove himself.'

He paused for a moment, scrawled the three names he'd mentioned onto the board with a red marker pen, then drew clumsy arrows to connect them.

'That's not all. Here's two more nice big kites that might or might not fly. One: Grove was banged up in HMP Boland during the riots there in the mid-Nineties and he gave evidence against the ringleaders afterwards. Two: Karen Holt's most recent day job was helping Gerry Quigg's solicitors put together his very expensive defence for his forthcoming trial.'

He added 'Boland' and 'Gerry Quigg' to his whiteboard list, scrawled a few more criss-crossing arrows.

'The Boland and Quigg angles might lead nowhere of course, might just be coincidental. We need to know that either way.'

He fidgeted with the marker pen, then put it down, discarding it as an inadequate substitute for a lit cigarette.

'Usually I don't feel the need to spell this out but I'm making an exception for Martin Grove. It could be that what I've outlined is well off the mark. It's far too early to say. Any fact that seems to fit, I want it flagged up — but I don't want anyone disregarding evidence because it points in the wrong direction. There is no wrong direction — there's only finding out what happened. We follow up every line of inquiry with an open mind. Understood?'

He scanned every face. He wasn't a mind-reader, couldn't know if every one of them did understand. But at least they all looked as if they'd been listening properly — except for maybe Mick Hume, who was sitting behind a computer terminal and kept glancing at the screen.

'Message received, guv,' DC Williams said. 'So, for instance, a purely *local* angle isn't completely off the cards yet?'

'Not completely, Ray, definitely not that. But why now? He's been there three whole years without any kind of incident. They put up with him in the local pub, don't forget — even if they don't talk to him if they can help it. Or has something come in from the door-to-door that I don't know about?'

Williams shook his head.

'No, there hasn't. Those that know who he is — or was — all say the same: he didn't bother them and they didn't bother him.'

'That's pretty much it,' Emma Smith commented. 'And nobody admits to having seen him in the last couple of days. Maureen Bright filled up her Mini at the petrol station on Monday afternoon apparently — but Grove wasn't with her.'

'When was the last confirmed sighting locally?' Jacobson asked.

He was pleased to see Williams and Smith backing each other up, cooperating. Maybe the sex-based animosity between them had finally receded into ancient history.

Smith looked at her notes.

'Saturday lunchtime — he was seen walking in Crowcross Woods. On his own.'

'Who by?'

'Eh, one Liam Gilbert, guv. DC Phillips spoke to him in the Crowcross Arms last night.'

'That's right,' DC Phillips, one of the duty CID co-opts, said, from the back of the room, 'Gilbert's a young guy, was out walking with his girlfriend. According to him, Grove acknowledged them, gave a nod, but that was about it.'

'Any relation to Charlie Gilbert, by any chance?'

'He's his son,' Phillips replied.

He was a youngster himself, Jacobson noticed. Tall, thin, something nearly diffident about the way he spoke.

'And nobody local remembers seeing Karen Holt anytime or anywhere?'

'No, guv,' Ray Williams said, 'not according to any of the statements we've taken or cross-referenced so far.'

Jacobson picked up the marker pen again, wrote the word 'LOCAL' on the whiteboard, and put a score through it. Then he wrote up two more words: 'VEHICLES' and 'CCTV'.

'Any news on Karen Holt's car? For those who don't know, it's not parked at her home address, it's not parked anywhere obvious near her workplace and it's not anywhere in the immediate vicinity of Crowcross.'

'Not so far,' Brian Phelps, the civilian incident room manager answered, 'but her reg number's gone out to the traffic divisions regionally as of eight AM this morning.'

'Fine, Brian,' Jacobson commented, always glad of an opportunity to keep the King of the

Paper Clips happy in his work.

He noticed that Mick Hume seemed to be giving him his full attention at last.

'There's no trace on the Crowcross Arms CCTV,' Hume announced. 'But we've now got full negative confirmation re the mystery Range Rover. Just this minute.'

Since last night, a team of duty CID had been working their way through Hume's list of the vehicle registrations that the pub cameras had picked up on Monday night. The appearance of this particular vehicle, a Mk 3 Range Rover, jet black, had instantly conflicted with the associated data entry on the PNC/DVLA link.

'Cloned plates then, Mick?' Jacobson asked.

Hume stood up to make sure he could be heard in all corners of the crowded room.

'And how, guv. The genuine vehicle's a Volvo estate, belongs to a retired headmaster up in the Lake District — Keswick. The local CID sent somebody around to his place in person — he checks out cleaner than a very clean whistle.'

Jacobson's mouth nearly impersonated a smile.

'Which means that the Range Rover definitely isn't. When was it clocked again?'

'Ten past eleven — and fourteen seconds,' Hume answered. 'It's not seen again after that — but if a vehicle drove over to Grove's place and then on to Crowcross Wood it could easily get out to the Wynarth road without going back through the village.'

Jacobson nodded.

'It's something to go on, all right. We can

action a wider trawl through the traffic camera systems for one thing. If we can plot a route in and out that could give us a further lead. No luck with the image enhancement though?'

Hume deferred to Steve Horton, the civilian computer officer, who was sitting nearby.

'I'll keep trying,' Horton said, 'but the windows are seriously tinted — more or less blacked out.'

Jacobson moved on to the low-level practicalities, indicated who would do what or, at least, who would have overall responsibility in each area. The searches out at Grove's place and at Crowcross Wood were still incomplete. There were locals who still hadn't been interviewed. There were phone records to compare and analyse (available at last, according to Brian Phelps). There were still vehicles outstanding from Hume's original list. Most of it was spadework, hardly glamorous. Yet in Jacobson's experience, solid, honest plodding was usually the key to solid, honest results. If honest results were what mattered to you anyway. He didn't kid himself that every single bad apple had retired years ago along with DCI Hunter and his unpleasant sergeant, DS Irvine. But there were human cesspools in every walk of life. All you could do was fight your own corner, occupy your own territory — and keep your own hands clean, maybe encourage a few others to do the same.

24

Steve Horton, the anti-geek, caught up with Jacobson in the corridor after the briefing. To be more precise, Horton had rushed out of the incident room after him. Horton was the anti-geek (in Jacobson's mental universe) because he was tanned, muscular and blandly handsome. An inverted stereotype if ever there was one. And especially so when he was wearing his neatly-pressed white T shirt on a bright summer's day.

'I wanted a word about Grove's missing computer, Mr Jacobson. I've got an idea about it that you might not have considered.'

Jacobson stopped in his tracks. He'd learned over the course of several serious investigations that Horton's ideas were usually worth listening to.

'Go ahead, old son.'

Horton kept it as non-technical as he could: Jacobson had assumed that they either had to find the missing computer or locate some kind of *physical* data back-up — but it was possible that Grove had used *virtual* storage instead, had uploaded data copies to a digital storage facility.

'Digital storage?' Jacobson asked.

'That's right. You upload a copy of anything you don't want to lose if your computer crashes — or gets nicked — to your personal virtual storage area. A lot of the big broadband providers offer it as a customer service, guarantee to keep a copy of your data safe in their central servers.'

'So if Grove's used a service like that, you could trace it? And the same goes for Karen Holt?'

'If the inquiry team can find out who their ISPs are anyway. It's basically a needle and a haystack situation otherwise. But if they *have* used vaults — recently, anyway — there should be a clear trace in the ISP usage logs.'

Jacobson felt mildly pleased with himself that he'd followed Horton's argument so far. Apart from one point.

'If the *inquiry team* can find out, Steve? Find out how exactly?'

'If they've used internet providers, then they'll have paid for the privilege like everybody else. So there's probably going to be an entry on a bank statement or a credit card bill that shows *who* they've been paying.'

'Fair enough, lad — speak to Brian Phelps. He can pass the message on to the search teams. And if we can't find a paper bill, we can try going to the banks directly.'

'Great,' Horton said, flashing his whitest smile.

Jacobson watched him disappear back along the corridor in the direction of the incident room with all the boundless, optimistic energy of youth. It made him feel tired-out, weary, even just to look.

★ ★ ★

DC Jason Phillips studied the next registration number on his list and then typed it into the computer. He checked that he'd typed every letter and number accurately and then he hit send. He'd been fifteen months in CID now — and this was the second occasion he'd worked on a high-profile case headed up by DCI Jacobson. A minor role both times — but still in on the action. He glanced discreetly around the room while he waited for the PNC/DVLA link to process its response. It wasn't the quickest computer system he'd ever used (or the most accurate, according to popular CID belief). His eyes found what they were looking for easily enough: Emma Smith, over in the corner, reading something off a terminal screen and talking into her mobile simultaneously.

He considered the fact that she'd remembered his name, had used it in the briefing. But then why wouldn't she? They'd both been out at Crowcross last night, had both been door-to-door in the same area. She hadn't remembered him then — which was probably far more significant — hadn't remembered that they'd worked together (briefly) on last year's Art Gang case. Most probably he just wasn't her type. Even if he was, the fact that he was a new recruit, a nobody, would weigh against him. Jacobson's A-Team were an informal élite, several cuts above the ordinary CID rank and file. It was a matter of basic organisational sociology. Why shag down for no good reason? There was the fact that he was younger than her too. Not by much, but enough maybe to have him dismissed as a kid, a mere lad, not somebody to take seriously. Worst of all was his status as a graduate entrant. The lowest of the absolute low. An object of general contempt and suspicion, practically guaranteed (more popular CID belief) to fuck up and screw up any task requiring the slightest iota of common sense.

He enjoyed watching her for a few more seconds and then he turned his attention back to the computer screen. The details were all there now. Make. Model. Year. Vehicle Identification Number. Registered Owner. Registered Owner's Address. Cheshire, he noticed, one of the well-known 'rich towns' up there that increasingly out-rivalled and upstaged the traditional southern hang-outs of the rich and famous. He'd read an article all about it in one of the Sunday papers a while back. Not that wealth interested him personally. How could it when he'd signed up for a police career?

He copied the first line of the address and the postcode into a second window, ran it against the on-line telephone directories. No result. He tried again in case he'd made a mistake. Still nothing. Must be ex-directory in that case, he thought. That wasn't a problem though since he knew the procedure by now. You called BT on a special, dedicated phone line and a live operator disclosed the number to you — provided you could quote the relevant, up-to-date police code. Jason already knew it by heart, had an excellent memory for things like that. He looked around the busy room again, wondered if he had the balls to pretend he didn't know it, to get up out of his chair — and just walk over and ask her.

★   ★   ★

Even in the circumstances, Nigel had seen no need to alter his morning routine. It was useful of course, less *complicado*, that Saskia, his current quasi live-in girlfriend wasn't here, had taken herself off at the weekend for a shopping trip to New York, had phoned him last night to say there'd been a change of plan and she was staying on there until the end of the week. There was a gallery opening or a theatre premiere — something like that anyway — that she wanted to take in. Her and her sister, Rula, who'd gone with her. Maybe it was true, maybe it wasn't. Maybe they just liked swanning around Manhattan on his money and fancied a few more days of it. Nigel didn't really care — unless they did something that got them into the gossip columns (or any other kind of public attention) and he figured Saskia, at least, as far too bright, far too committed to her personal well-being and preferred lifestyle, to do anything that stupid. So he'd risen before seven, as he often did, and had woken himself up with a brisk length or two in the pool and then a gym session. He'd taken it easy though — no point expending all your energy before breakfast. He'd lifted a few weights, played around on the cross-trainer and then pounded the treadmill on an easy incline. He'd taken his coffee and granola out to a table on one of the terraces, one with a nice, sweeping view down to the lake. 'His' lake — an idea that could still, on rare occasions, take him by bemused surprise, caught off guard by the way his life had turned out. The air had felt fresh, still cool, although definitely not cold. He'd sat there for a while, more or less entranced, only letting nature impinge on his thoughts, nothing else. Plump little dots that were probably moorhens emerging from the reeds in the distance; a cooing wood pigeon over in the conifers.

After that he'd packed some clothes, barely more than a couple of shirts, and checked (via his housekeeper) that the security company he used had been updated about his departure and would upscale their patrols and surveillance. The housekeeper lived on site and there were gardeners and cleaners around on a daily basis but he saw no reason to take unnecessary chances. Nigel always travelled light, no matter where he was going or how long for. Anything he wanted at the other end, he bought there — and often left there. Apart from the practical convenience, he liked the small irony inherent in this habit of his, the way it parodied the bogus trickle-down effect which he still caught hack, imbecilic bourgeois economists trotting out in the media from time to time.

He'd peeled and eaten an orange, a breakfast afterthought, while his Lexus cruised through Alderley Edge and Wilmslow and then on the few short miles towards Manchester Airport. His driver had insisted on stopping the car and opening the door for him when they reached the terminal building. Nigel hadn't really argued, knew by now that he was happier, for whatever reason, providing the full, over-the-top service. They'd arranged to meet up in the executive lounge after the driver had parked the Lexus in the long-stay and they were both checked-in for the flight.

Nigel had decided on Zurich for more than one reason. There were a number of useful, if non-urgent, business tasks he could pursue there. Plus it never did the investment banks he dealt with any harm to be visited unexpectedly from time to time and to find out exactly what they were up to with his personal, non-company cash. When it came to those who earned their money from his money, Nigel liked to keep them right up on their toes like nervous, first night ballerinas. The main consideration of course was that Switzerland was in Europe but, constitutionally, independent of it. If it came to anything worryingly *legal*, Swiss law would protect his interests in a way that the UK courts couldn't — not even with the best UK lawyers money could buy in his back pocket.

It wasn't that he'd done anything wrong on Monday night — not directly, not personally. They'd talked to him for an hour, maybe, had been leaving just as the woman had been arriving. The new Martin had been impressive on many levels, despite his bullshit theories about Claire's murder. Nigel had done what he could on that score, had told him he was wasting his life, his second chance at freedom, raking over the past; why not just forget it? Too much of the conversation had been an exercise in

211

nostalgia. Do you remember when we did this? Do you remember when we did that? *Well, of course I remember, Martin,* he'd said at one point, *but what tangible use are memories? You can't touch them, smell them, eat them — you can't live off them.*

He sank deep into the lounge chair, mildly irritated by the artificial trickle of water in the artificial water feature. The police would trace him of course at some point, most probably. Unless they were still as bent and useless as they'd been twenty-odd years ago, which he was prepared to believe, but not prepared to bet on. To an extent, he'd be happy enough to talk to them: by telephone if they'd buy that — or maybe some hard-up cop could fly over, enjoy a little freebie in Zurich at the taxpayers' expense. After all, it wasn't completely *Nineteen Eighty-Four* yet — there wasn't a government chip installed in his brain and nobody could *prove* whether he'd heard about the shootings from the TV or the newspapers or not. The thing that really worried him, that had really decided him on his temporary, precautionary exit from the country, was the issue of media coverage, the potential for bad associative publicity. The market had extreme jitters; there were even idiots talking about a 1930s-style depression, a world collapse. Client confidence and current reputation were central to his business model. He could live quite happily without the press camped out on his doorstep, asking questions and demanding interviews about his connection to a high-profile, double-murder. Well, now, they'd have to find him first.

As for what had happened at Myrtle Cottage, the past was the past. Over, dead, gone. People banged on too much about closure these days, a banal, meaningless, bankrupt concept if ever there was one — all those hypocritical, sanctimonious politicians standing up in public to apologise for the holocaust or for slavery or for some other historical evil that had nothing to do with them personally. Just what good would come for anybody if the truth about Claire's murder was finally revealed after all these years? Just what good had come to Martin for meddling in it?

His driver sat down opposite him. He looked tired. As if, unlike himself, he hadn't slept well.

'Cheer up, Andy,' Nigel said, watching him, trying to assess his mental state, 'the flight's on time, no delays. We're nearly out of here.'

25

Martin Grove.doc

Christmas came and went. In January, the numbers of protestors living out at Myrtle Cottage shrank to their lowest ebb. The November battle with the police had deterred a lot of those whose commitment had never been all that high, who'd liked the idea of playing at rebellion for a little while — so long as things never got seriously uncomfortable for them. One by one, they drifted back to their university courses or their careers, if they had any. The cold winter weather didn't help much either, put a dampener on the volume of weekend sympathisers and supporters. You could walk into the freedom field on a Saturday morning and see nothing there but icicles on the hedges and white-green frost-covered grass. The cottage was warm enough in the kitchen and in the lounge, where the wood fire was always kept going. But everywhere else, the wind whistled around draughty beams or rattled against ancient, inadequate windows. Claire could easily have afforded all the necessary improvements, I know that for a fact. But for all of us, even me, there would have been something unromantic, something non-revolutionary, about fitting double-glazing and calling in a central heating firm.

The police riot had caused other trouble for us too. The locals had never been keen on us

— ranked us alongside travellers and gypsies as an unwelcome presence in 'their' countryside — but before that Sunday in November, they'd shown their distaste mainly by cold-shouldering us. There'd be an uneasy silence if anybody from the protest ventured into the pub or the village shop (there still was a shop back then, separate and distinct from the filling station) — but they'd still serve us, still take our money. Now their attitudes hardened. It was as if the police action had given them the green light to unload all of their pent-up prejudice. 'No protestors' signs appeared in the windows of the shop and the pub and two nights in a row, just after New Year, we'd been woken up in the cottage by the sound of smashing glass. When we got outside, we found broken windscreens and slashed tyres on some of our vehicles and we heard the noise of running footsteps fading in the distance.

There wasn't anything we could do about it by normal channels. We had suspicions, but no proof, about who might be involved. And, practically speaking, we were in no position to go to the police. The last thing we wanted were the pigs crawling all over Claire's property, looking for 'evidence' — and that's assuming that they wouldn't just have laughed in our faces at any complaints we made in the first place. What we did (always the Myrtle Cottage way) was to elect a safety committee. The committee's chief recommendation, swiftly implemented for once, was to organise a nightly safety patrol — a minimum of four bodies per night, working on a rota. We kitted ourselves up against the cold, armed with powerful torches (which we had to go into Crowby to purchase) and stout wooden sticks which we carved ourselves, sharpening the ends into points. I remember that Andy always preferred to call them staves, evidently relished the old-fashioned resonances of the word. He'd been reading *The World Turned Upside Down*, the book Nigel had lent him about the English Civil War, and his head was full of stories about the Diggers, the Ranters and the Levellers. The way Andy — and quite a few others — saw it, the peace camps that had sprung up around the country were in a proud tradition of radical dissent that stretched back for ever. A couple of centuries after Gerrard Winstanley you got the Chartists, a couple of centuries before him you got the Peasants' Revolt. *And now it's our turn mate*, he said one time, bottling a fresh batch of rice wine, *here's to Maggie's head on the end of a pikestaff — cheers.*

We took everything so seriously at Myrtle Cottage. Although maybe, as things turned out, not seriously enough. We varied the times of the nightly patrol in case somebody, unseen, was taking notes — and we created a new house rule: no one was to go into Crowcross village on their own. Not that there was a huge need. We vastly preferred our own company to the dreary, snooty locals in the pub and it was far cheaper to drive over to Crowby and do our shopping — our consuming — in the supermarkets there. Practically the only reason to go into the village was to use the postbox (no email and no texting back then, Dear Reader) and not everybody was happy with that arrangement anyway. Everybody 'knew' that letters got intercepted by the state and there was a view that we should always post from different, randomly-selected postboxes to make life as difficult as possible for the snoopers. The same went for telephone calls. The Myrtle Cottage line was used purely for trivial personal calls. The favoured number for anything more serious was the payphone in the jukeboxnoisy lounge of the Wynarth Arms (where anybody from the protest wasn't just tolerated but was positively welcomed).

While Nigel was on remand, Claire liked to drive over there most evenings so that he could call her and speak to her. I was always more than happy to ride shotgun in the MG if she asked me. The Wynarth Arms was a young people's pub, often had a band playing in the back room (still is, still does, decent ale too). Sometimes we'd stay on after she'd taken the call, have a couple of drinks, chat. That was when I first really got to know her, I guess. I think I must have been easy to talk to because I understood practically nothing, didn't have much of an agenda of my own beyond hanging around (especially hanging around her) and seeing how things turned out.

Claire herself wasn't serious all the time — I was one of the few people who saw that, understood it instantly. The cottage was big on old-style feminism and most of the women out at the cottage (Hilary was a prime example) were into dungarees and no make-up like it was a compulsory uniform. Claire hated all that, sexed up her look whenever she damn well wanted to. She'd typed out a poem and stuck it on the wall in her room above her writing desk. The old D.H. Lawrence thing, if you know it, about making a revolution for fun, pleasure:

don't make it in ghastly seriousness,
don't do it in deadly earnest,
do it for fun.

I remember she had the Clash blaring on the kitchen tape deck one time, uber loud ('(White Man) in Hammersmith Palais' I think it was). Some old guy from Wynarth CND popped his head around the door, asked her to turn the volume down because he was trying to compose a press release in the lounge about the Crowcross Three.

'If I can't dance, it's not my revolution,' she told him, treating him to her best impish smile and turning the volume up even higher.

I was in there peeling potatoes with her at the time, couldn't work out why the guy just backed off when she said that, practically apologised. It was years later (in the prison library of HMP Boland) that I discovered that she'd quoted a saying of the legendary anarchist Emma Goldman at him — had appealed, effectively, to a higher anti-authority.

Claire spoke on the phone to Nigel nearly every night and I didn't get the chance to go with her every time — but I took every opportunity I got. I never once reminded her that I'd taken a truncheoning on her behalf on the day of the airfield invasion, just hoped that she'd noticed it, appreciated it. I was over in the Wynarth Arms with her one night when she had a big falling out with Nigel on the phone. I wasn't sure what about exactly — whether it was something personal or something to do with the campaign. Nigel was a good-looking bastard but their relationship was based as much on their mutual political commitments as on anything else (even I understood that much) so it was hard to tell. *Intransigent, arrogant sod*, she'd said when she came off the phone — that and, *Let's get plastered, Martin.*

There was a Two Tone ska-punk band over from Coventry playing in the back room that night. The place was packed and they'd brought quite a crowd of their fans with them, all sharp jackets and pork pie hats. We stayed till the place closed, drinking, dancing, not bothering to talk too much over the maxed-up amps. We'd started on beer but soon moved on to beer and spirits, then just spirits. It was madness afterwards really, Claire driving back to Myrtle Cottage pissed like that — and far too fast. It was misty as well, very nearly foggy, the moon an occasional pale glimmer. But we made it somehow without killing ourselves or hitting anything, not even the safety patrol who were heading out along the lane when we reached it. We parked behind Nigel's battered minivan. The cottage looked quiet, unusually subdued. All the lights were out. Even in the kitchen it seemed. Everybody was probably asleep, we realised, apart from those on the safety rota.

Claire carried on with the rant she'd started as we'd driven out of Wynarth. *The world is so beautiful and so fucked up*, she'd kept saying. *They'll really blow it up, Martin, if we let them, really do it*, she was telling me now, *destroy everything rather than lose their power, their empires.* We all believed that then — and by all I don't just mean left-wing protestors like Claire. Everybody was frightened, although only some of us were angry as well. You sensed it on the streets, casual conversations that you overheard, gallows humour everywhere. Everybody thought we were on the brink of Armageddon. I didn't really say much back to her as usual, just listened to her, just watched her. She'd been laughing in the pub and now she seemed close to tears.

'Fucking Nigel,' she said, her voice soft with anger, 'he can't just agree stuff like that. Agree stuff all on his own.'

'What stuff?' I asked her.

'Believe me, Martin, you don't want to know. Internal party stuff — our views on policy decisions.'

She smiled at me then, brushed a strand of hair from her forehead like she was brushing away a bad thought: 'C'mon, let's go inside.'

In the front garden, I took the front door key from its hiding place in the uncared-for rockery, opened the door quietly then replaced the key. Since we'd got out of the car neither of us had said a word. There was a light switch just inside the hall but neither of us reached for it when we stepped inside. I shut the door with what felt like infinite slowness. We stood there on the doormat, just looking at each other — I mean really looking.

'Your place or mine?' she whispered — and then very nearly giggled.

'I — I — ' I know that I stammered, I think I probably blushed scarlet too. But she might not have seen that in the semi-dark.

She put her hand around my neck, reached up and kissed me on the mouth. Deep whisky kisses.

'Mine I think, Martin. Definitely mine.'

26

Kerr had time to take a good look around Ann Ledbury's terraced house in Wynarth before any of Jim Webster's team reached the scene. In the end only two of them turned up, all that could be spared from the ongoing efforts out at Crowcross. Their presence was pretty much a formality, Kerr thought, a case of going through the motions. She hadn't left a note anywhere obvious — anywhere he could risk looking in advance of the forensic tests — but he was clear in his own mind that what he'd disturbed had been a suicide attempt that didn't involve any extra parties. The noose had been clumsy, amateurish, and she hadn't figured out a way to restrain her hands, to keep herself from struggling instinctively with the rope once she'd kicked away the little stool which Kerr had found near the bottom of the stairs, only a few inches from her flailing, dangling legs.

He'd been as careful as he could of course, had pulled on fresh, unused crime scene gloves. Habitually, he carried a pair around with him, just like the sharp, unauthorised knife he'd used to free her. The place had been neat, tidy, and decorated in the classic Wynarth style. *Beaucoup de* ethnic rugs and wall hangings. A poster of smiling Tibetan monks in the hall and bits and pieces of Buddhist paraphernalia in the front room. Courtesy of his stolen hours with Rachel, he knew a mani, the hand-held variety of a prayer wheel, when he saw one. Likewise the big framed mandala on the wall behind the sofa. He'd resisted the temptation to give the mani a spin or two and build up some badly needed extra merit for his next life, just in case there was something in the idea of reincarnation after all. He didn't even want to think about what a copper might come back as. There were some pictures of Ann Ledbury herself in the kitchen. He thought it was her anyway — her face had been a distorted, purple mess when he'd cut her down and phoned for an ambulance. One of them was a group photograph. Trekkers it looked like, taken somewhere Himalayan, their kit (and their Sherpas) just visible in the background. No sign of anything to do with Martin Grove though — other than this morning's *Independent*, lying open at page five on the kitchen table. He'd glanced at the headline — *Miscarriage of Justice Victim Shot Dead in Double Murder* — and the first paragraph, hadn't bothered to read any of the rest. The other items prominent on the table were an empty glass and a near-empty bottle of Bombay Sapphire gin.

He left as soon as the SOCOs turned up. CSIs — Crime Scene Investigators — was their official job title these days but nobody (except maybe the odd, proud mother) ever called them that. A duty CID guy, who Kerr only knew by sight, turned up too. It would be his task to talk to the neighbours, dig further into the background. Also, if possible, he'd need to come up with some next of kin or close friend, somebody whose day was going to be spoiled by bad news. Kerr took the Wynarth Road back to the North Crowby by-pass and then he joined the motorway system, headed directly south.

He vaguely remembered Ann Ledbury from the press coverage when Grove had won his appeal at the High Court, even thought he might have seen her interviewed on television one time. It was a weird modern phenomenon: women, often lonely, unhappy ones, who befriended murderers and other categories of serious offenders. They'd start off by writing to them. Then visiting. Then the next thing you knew they were petitioning the Home Office to marry their new soulmate and life partner. Ann Ledbury wasn't the most extreme kind of case. After all, for at least half the two decades Martin Grove had spent in prison, he'd had plenty of completely sane supporters on the outside who'd believed that he was an innocent man, wrongly accused and convicted. Far stranger still were the groupies who wrote love letters to unapologetic serial killers, psychopaths and rapists, who claimed to find something redeemable deep inside their twisted souls.

The Ledbury-Grove connection, as far as Kerr recalled, had come about when it had been reported in the media that Grove had become interested in Buddhism in prison, had taken to meditating long hours in his cell. Ann Ledbury, a committed believer, had written to him, sent him books and study material and it had gone on from there. Except that, as Jacobson had found out from Alan Slingsby yesterday, Grove had shunned her when he'd been released, had refused to move in with her as planned, had eventually taken up with Maureen Bright instead. It sounded like a sad enough little story but Kerr read it as probably irrelevant to the investigation. She would be worth talking to of course — if she regained consciousness, if she hadn't already passed on to the bardo, the intermediate plane between death and the next rebirth. Rachel knew about all that stuff. But fuck her, he thought again, *fuck her*.

The drive took him an hour and he managed to find the location all on his own — without the assistance of bloody sat nav. Oakfield Open Prison. Low security. Modern. From the distance it could have been a call centre or a warehouse facility. The kind of set-up (TV in every cell, computers, flash gyms) the tabloids liked to come down on like a ton of bricks from time to time when they rolled out their too-bloody-soft-on-'em story on a quiet news day. He pulled in at the check-point and got out of his car, wasn't surprised when the jobsworth screw checked inside the interior, even took a quick look in the boot.

'No offence,' he'd said dourly, scanning Kerr's ID on both sides and then handing it back to him.

Kerr could see his name on the visitors' list, knew that Brian Phelps had phoned ahead for him in any case.

'Put me down as just visiting,' he told him.

It wasn't much of a joke — but Kerr sensed that this was the kind of screw who wouldn't laugh even if it was a professional stand-up telling them. He got back behind the wheel and drove slowly towards the main building, parked precisely where the screw had said that he should. He could hear shouting from the direction of the playing fields when he got out again — the mid-morning rehabilitational football game in progress.

Barry Vine had his own office so they talked in there. Vine had been a regular grade prison officer when he'd worked at HMP Boland but he'd studied, gained extra qualifications, a series of promotions and now, here at Oakfield, he was in charge of the education department. He was a small man with quick, darting eyes.

'Poor old Martin,' he was saying, 'everything he went through — and then it ends like this.'

'Maureen Bright told us you visited him last month.'

Vine nodded.

'That's right. I've seen him at least once a year, let's say, since he got out. He'd phone me up, tell me I needed a day in the fresh air, promise me one of Maureen's slap-up meals. The appeal court fully quashed his conviction, don't forget, so I wasn't overstepping any official mark.'

'No, I'm sure you weren't,' Kerr said, 'but still unusual though?'

'I'd say so. There's always a few prisoners you develop respect for over time, even something close to friendship. But usually as soon as they're out of the big doors, that's it.'

'She also reckoned you were one of the

226

privileged few he had any time for.'

'I did what I could for him in Boland. I suppose he appreciated that.'

'What did you do exactly?'

'By the time I got to know him, Martin had already done a dozen years inside, protesting his innocence the whole way. He'd already done his share of jail rebel stuff elsewhere. Dirty protests — smearing excrement on the walls of his cell — a hunger strike, more than a few violent run-ins. By the time he got moved to Boland, he'd developed a new strategy. He was pretty much the model prisoner in every single way by then, apart from still denying any guilt.'

'Which cost him parole?'

'More than once. The parole board *never* looks beyond the sentence. That's totally fundamental to how they operate. To them, you're guilty as charged. Unless you admit it, you're automatically defined as denying your offender behaviour pattern and you've sod all chance of early release.'

'But you believed him?'

'Not necessarily — I had an open mind on that, at least in the beginning. But I didn't like the way the system was denying him other opportunities because he wouldn't hold his hands up to the crime. It happens a lot even still. You want to do an Open University course or something like that and you're stuck at the back of the queue unless you play ball about your convictions — a case of the deserving versus the undeserving from the official point of view. That's the main practical way I helped him out

— eventually I got his study registrations stamped and approved.'

Vine's desk phone rang but he ignored it, pressed a button to silence the ringing. There was a giant year planner on the wall behind his desk, the days and weeks a blur of marker-penned meetings and appointments. Kerr had never fancied the prison service as a career, not for a single minute. The screws went home in the evenings (if they weren't on late shifts) and they had weekends and holidays away. But most of the rest of the time they spent on prison premises, cogs in the prison routines. Kerr couldn't see how the gloom and the despair and the general negativity wouldn't rub off, wouldn't turn you into some kind of prisoner yourself.

'Did you ever run into Ann Ledbury,' he asked, 'the Buddhist woman who wanted to marry him?'

He didn't mention her suicide attempt.

'Not in person. But Martin talked about her a lot at one time. I think he was keen enough on her for a while — and then something changed.'

'Any idea what?'

Vine shrugged.

'Who really knows? I don't think he liked it that she talked to the press about her visits. Maybe he got the notion that her motives were more about solving her own problems than helping him with his. He told me once that she'd got into meditation in the first place after she'd had a messy divorce or something.'

'This Buddhist kick was serious then? For Grove I mean.'

'It seemed so to me. He had a real monk visiting him as well for a while. Red robes, shaved head, the lot.'

Vine's phone rang again — and he ignored it again.

'The main thing about it, the most convincing thing, was that Martin had a real serenity about him by then. A presence. Even the hard cases left him alone — like he was special, above the fray.'

'Even during the riots?' Kerr asked at last, cutting to the chase.

'I was lucky, mate. I'd switched shifts with a bloke who wanted the day off to visit his sick mother, otherwise I might have been the officer they snatched. I was meant to be on the late shift that evening — *and* I worked the wing where all the action kicked off.'

Which wasn't exactly what I asked you, Kerr thought. He stretched back in his chair, settled in, sensed that Vine would get there in his own way.

'And that was the wing where Grove was too?'

'Precisely. Cut Throat Alley, it was known as. All lifers, all killers. Quite a few professionals — gang-land hitmen, career heavies, all that. Anyway, they grabbed the senior officer from that shift as a hostage and then, using his keys and codes, they managed to nab a couple of sex offenders as extra collateral. The rest, unfortunately, is history. They beat both the nonces to death and the prison officer likewise — *he* got his head kicked in trying to protect them.'

Vine coughed, cleared his throat.

'None of it should have happened of course.

229

This was the mid-Nineties, don't forget. Several years after the big riot at Strangeways and the venerable Lord Wolfe's report. Elsewhere in the country, prison conditions had been overhauled. The trouble was that the powers-that-be in Boland dragged their feet, let problems and grievances simmer and boil over instead of easing the pressure.'

Kerr didn't really need the history of penal reform lecture — but he saw no option except to let it run on to its conclusion.

'The stand-off lasted until they couldn't bring the officer to the phone. The riot police went in then, literally smoked them out — and cracked heads. I'm regarded as a liberal around here — but I don't mind saying I'd happily have strung them up on the spot and bugger the courts.'

'But not Martin Grove?' Kerr asked, seeing a possible way back to the ostensible subject of the interview.

'Martin's conduct throughout was exemplary. He even spoke up for the nonce hostages to the rioters, stuck his neck out, said to just leave them alone.'

'But he was a sex offender himself, wasn't he? Rape as well as murder?'

'Jails are a little world all of their own, Sergeant — with their own peculiar moral logic. Not every sex offender is regarded as such. Kiddie fiddlers are automatically — they're the very lowest of the low. But other cases are decided on their merits, if you'll forgive the term. Martin was convicted of murdering a woman he'd been in a relationship with, who was giving him grief, according to the prosecution. To some eyes on the lifer wings, I'm afraid, that's seen as more or less a form of normal behaviour. So, no, he wasn't generally regarded as a nonce himself.'

'They didn't listen to him though? I mean as in take any notice.'

'No, they didn't do that.'

'And he gave evidence against the ringleaders?'

'Yes, he did. He didn't testify about the actual beatings though, claimed he'd barricaded himself in his cell by then, claimed he hadn't seen it.'

'Do you think that was true?'

'Only he knows that — or knew that, I suppose now — him plus the rioters who dished out the punishment. Nobody was ever brought to book for the actual killings — none of the inmates who turned Queen's evidence admitted to having seen it. The proverbial wall of silence. They didn't have that much of a death wish, I guess.'

'But if somebody came forward now?'

Vine stretched his arms behind his head then lowered them again, seemed to consider the point before he answered.

'Depending on who they pointed the finger at, they could still be taking their life in their hands, especially if they mentioned something that could definitely get the cases reopened. By all accounts, the bodies were dragged into the showers and thoroughly washed down after they'd been killed. Plus all their clothes were burned and probably some inmates' clothing was too. The forensics were inconclusive, didn't lead to any chargeable suspects.'

Kerr was still waiting for the list Boland's present-day Assistant Governor had promised him. 'This afternoon, definitely' was the most recent word he'd had from that quarter. He'd hoped that, in the meantime, speaking to Vine would fill in some of the background.

'You ever talk to Martin about this stuff since he's been out?'

'No, not really. Books, music, art — that's what I liked to encourage him to talk about. Positives, you know? Not negatives. He started work for a thesis once he was out but then he packed it in, decided to write his bloody life story instead.'

'You didn't think that was a good idea then?'

Vine shook his head.

'I thought it was a terrible idea, mate. He was what, forty, when he got out? That's hardly old these days. The whole world was his oyster — and there he was, wasting his time stuck in Crowcross, re-living all the crap in his past, day after day.'

His desk phone rang again. This time he picked it up and answered it, as if he was eager by now to have something else to think about other than Martin Grove. Anything else maybe. Even the mundane news, as far as Kerr was able to follow the telephone conversation, about a visiting education tutor whose car had broken down and who was going to be late for his class. Grove had been one of Vine's success stories more or less, probably one of a small handful over the years. Except now he'd gone and got himself killed, had spoiled Vine's job-well-done tally. Until the next meditating, thesis-writing innocent man came along anyway.

27

Jacobson had time alone with the Claire Oldham files at last. Not much time, most probably, and not the entire set of boxes that had turned up in the incident room either. But at least it was a start, a step in the right direction. He'd grabbed the investigating officer's final report from the main boxfile after the briefing, had decided to start with that, and retreated up here to his office on the fifth floor. He'd spread the report out on his desk, loosened his collar and eased off the knot on his tie. The images flooded back as he read. The pounding rain, the noise their feet made squelching on the wet ground, the way her dead eyes had seemed to be watching him — just him — especially him — when he'd shone the torch on her body for DCI Hunter's benefit.

Hunter had been in the pub, he suddenly remembered. Not seriously pissed or anything like that but there had been beer on his breath — and whisky. Hunter, DS Irvine and their 'in-crowd', as Hunter liked to call his hangers-on, were in the habit of repairing to the Brewer's Rest most work-day evenings in life. Except Fridays funnily enough. One of Hunter's maxims was that he didn't like to be hungover on a Saturday morning when, as was usual in those days, a DCI wouldn't ordinarily turn up for duty. *Hangovers are for company time, lad,* he'd told Jacobson on one occasion, *nobody wants a bad head on a lieu day.*

This had been a Thursday evening though, not a Friday. Jacobson had been on his way home, had nearly been out the door of the Duty CID room, when the call had come in from the Wynarth sub-station: a dead body, female, over in Crowcross Wood, very likely a murder victim. He'd phoned Janice at lunchtime and she'd told him that she'd arranged a baby sitter for Sally, that they could have a proper night out on the town for once. She'd mentioned a film, *Chariots of Fire*, that was re-showing at the Odeon and that she wouldn't mind seeing. 'Wouldn't mind' had been Janice-speak in those years for something that she really wanted to do. That was another strange thing to be thinking about now — about how happy he and Janice, his long-since ex-wife, had once been together. Close, sharing the ups and downs of parenting a toddler, still planning for a long future together. It sometimes felt that two Janices existed side by side in his mind. The one from those early years. Warm, companionable, always on his side, always taking his part. The one he could still feel pangs of longing and regret for. And the later model: the one who'd hurt him to his core, cut him to the quick.

The discovery of the body had meant that Janice never got to see her film — or not that evening anyway. Jacobson's orders had been to pick up a pool car and then drive Hunter and Irvine from the pub out to the crime scene; pretty much a standard task for a new, green recruit. Hunter and Irvine conversed loudly in the back seat en route. Jacobson, new as he was, already had enough nous not to offer any unsolicited contributions of his own. The message from Wynarth had indicated that the victim was probably one of the airfield protestors. Jacobson remembered how he'd kept his eye conspicuously on the traffic while Hunter bellowed to Irvine about how pissed off that particular item of information had made him.

'I've said that lot would be nothing but trouble, right from the start. The ones that aren't fucking communists are fucking layabout hippies. The uniformeds should have turfed them out fucking months ago.'

Hunter had been a heavy consumer of cigarettes, more or less a chain smoker. Jacobson found he could still recall the way he'd halted mid-tirade, jettisoned a dead Embassy and immediately taken out and lit up a replacement.

'That didn't happen of course, so now *we've* got to clean up the shit and the mess.'

DS Irvine had nodded vigorously in agreement, had lit up a fresh cigarette of his own. Neither of them had offered one to Jacobson.

According to Hunter's report, they'd reached the scene at ten minutes past eight. In Jacobson's memory, he would have put the time as later. Probably, he thought now, because it had been such a filthy night, jet-black dark when they'd got there, the rain falling in sheets between the trees. They'd stopped in the car until the pathologist turned up. Burroughs was his name, according to Hunter's notes, but it was a fact Jacobson couldn't verify from what he remembered. He thought that maybe he'd only run into him that one time. There'd been something toffish and old-fashioned about him perhaps. Had he been wearing a dinner jacket and black tie underneath his raincoat? Maybe. Maybe not. A fair few pathologists had come and gone back in that era before Professor Alasdair Merchant had descended from on high and, with supreme condescension, made the job his own for a couple of decades.

One of the Wynarth uniformeds had led the way when they were ready. Golf umbrellas had been miraculously found from somewhere for Hunter and the pathologist. Everybody else had just had to put up with rain dripping down their necks and seeping into their clothes. In his torch beam, he'd picked out black muddy puddles between the trees.

Hunter had been untypically kind when Jacobson had turned away from the sight of the body splayed out under the willow tree and puked up the current contents of his stomach. He'd handed him the handkerchief he'd used to clean himself up and told him that it happened to everybody sooner or later. *Better out than in, lad. You'll be fine now, next time.* When Hunter and Irvine had done everything they'd wanted to do at the scene, Hunter told Jacobson to drive them over to the sub-station in Wynarth. Jacobson had been glad of the steering wheel between his hands, something to hold on to, something material and solid, something that was nothing remotely like human flesh, alive — and beautiful — one minute, stone dead and useless the next.

The Wynarth cop shop was a poky little set-up, even in its prime. The civilian had been shunted into a side-room, given a cup of tea, told to wait. Hunter had glanced in on him, closed the door again and then, out of his earshot, had asked the Wynarth desk sergeant for the entire story as far as he knew it. Jacobson hadn't been given any marching orders to do anything else, so he'd stood there, next to Irvine, and had listened in. When the sergeant had finished, Hunter lit up another Embassy, took a deep drag before he spoke. Jacobson remembered the action distinctly because he'd wanted a cigarette himself but didn't want to risk it. It would have steadied his nerves, sure, but it might have set his stomach off again too.

'So he says he was worried about her when she didn't come back — and he's gone off wandering the area in the pissing rain looking for her?'

The sergeant had nodded gravely, probably hadn't wanted to contradict Hunter unless it became absolutely necessary.

'Then when he's found her and realised she's dead, he's run all the way into Crowcross, covered in blood, to dial nine nine fucking nine?'

Another grave nod.

'That's his story, sir.'

'And he admits that he's one of these protest monkeys, admits he lives out at crazy cottage?'

'So it appears, sir. Says his mother lives in Crowby though, over on the Woodlands estate.'

Jacobson thought Hunter had snorted at the mention of the Woodlands but he knew he couldn't be certain about that. Memories, he understood, were all too easily embellished and distorted. You thought you had an indelible record of your life tucked away in your head. But you didn't. What you really had was an unfinished film, a work in progress, that was constantly being re-edited and re-shot, every new version overwriting and deleting what was there before until, eventually, you could no longer access the original raw footage. The way Jacobson recalled it now, there had been silence next for a long interval. Except for the old station clock ticking steadily away — and except for the regular rhythm of DCI Hunter's (still muddy) shoes pacing up and down while he smoked his cigarette and looked thoughtful.

'OK,' he'd said finally, 'no more cups of tea for sonny boy. Arrange a patrol car to get him over to the Divisional building — and if he's cheeky enough to ask about a lawyer, pretend you didn't hear it — or give him a slap. I don't much care which.'

DS Irvine laughed loudly but, as Jacobson recalled it, the desk sergeant didn't.

'You think you've got enough to charge him, sir?' the sergeant even found it inside himself to ask.

'I will have before very long, pal. You can count on it,' Hunter barked, stubbing out his cigarette with the heel of his mud-caked shoe.

Jacobson's desk phone rang, interrupting his reverie. It was all so long ago, he thought, picking up, difficult to be certain about any of it anymore. There was some of it he'd swear to though, swear to on his own life or even on

239

his daughter's: Hunter saying 'pal', Hunter dropping his fag-end on the police station floor, Hunter telling the desk sergeant he was welcome to 'slap' Martin Grove if he felt so inclined.

28

The call was from the incident room. Young DC Phillips again, passing on to Jacobson the news that the searchers out at Crowcross Wood had discovered the remains of the severed slice of Karen Holt's tongue. Remains was probably the right word, Jacobson thought, after he'd listened to Phillips' second-hand account. The emerging theory was that the tongue had been mutilated in situ immediately after she'd been shot. Then, like Martin Grove's, it had been unceremoniously dumped inside a plastic carrier bag. Except that, this being woodland, it had been carried off later by an animal or animals. What had been left had been found a mile or so away and in the vicinity of a fox hole. Apparently there wasn't much left but probably there was enough, Phillips had told him, for the forensic laboratory to confirm the identity.

He replaced the handset in its cradle, his mind still focused on the past. Hunter had made a couple of telephone calls from the Wynarth station and then he'd told Jacobson to drive him and Irvine back into Crowby. It was likely that the patrol car Hunter had ordered for Martin Grove would have passed them on the way, heading in the opposite direction. But Jacobson found he had no memory of it. Hunter and Irvine had gone off to use the lavatory before they'd left the sub-station — 'taking a slash'

Hunter had called it — and the desk sergeant had gone back to his paperwork.

Gingerly, Jacobson had opened the door to the side-room a fraction, glanced quickly inside and rapidly closed the door again. Martin Grove hadn't had time to notice him, he didn't think, and he hadn't got much of a look at him himself. A scrawny youth in scruffy jeans and a worn-looking plaid shirt, dark green in Jacobson's memory of it. His hair had looked straggly, unkempt, and Jacobson didn't know whether he'd really had a glazed, puzzled look on his face or whether his mind had added that significant detail later. In those days, they didn't instantly bag everything you were wearing for forensic analysis but, on this occasion, someone had at least had the presence of mind to have already taken his Levi's denim jacket away from him. Earlier on, en route between Crowcross and Wynarth, Jacobson had noticed the uniformed PC guarding the phone box on the village green while a SOCO was at work inside, taking samples.

Hunter had dismissed him once they were back at the Divi. *Off you go, lad. Give her one for me*, he'd said, or something else patronising and mildly offensive along those lines. *Me an' all*, Irvine had added, leering unpleasantly. More than once in those days, Jacobson had thought about knocking the job on the head and doing something else — anything else — for a living. But each time he was on the brink, he'd think about all the Hunters and all the Irvines up and down the land, bullying little kings in their

242

personal fiefdoms, and would swear to himself that he'd stay put, find a way to do things differently.

He thumbed through Hunter's report to the appendices at the back. There was a photograph of the faded blue jacket in Appendix C. It had been well-taken. Jacobson stared at it, studied the badges pinned to the top pockets, two on either side. CND, the Anti-Nazi League, Troops Out Of Ireland. Jacobson thought the fourth one had probably been the most effective. *Protest and Survive* it said, a pun on the civil defence booklet, *Protect and Survive*, that the government had mailed to every household in the country back then. Jacobson half-smiled to himself. From what he remembered of the contents, bend down and kiss your arse goodbye would have been a more helpful, accurate and honest piece of advice.

Martin Grove's jacket had become famous — or notorious — later on when the prosecution barrister had introduced it with a flourish at his trial. Jacobson hadn't been in the courtroom, hadn't actually heard what had been said. But it wasn't too difficult to imagine the kind of thing. *Soaked in blood as you can see, members of the jury, despite the heavy rain that evening.* He'd have made that point, wouldn't he? *The blood is type 'AB', m'lud — Claire Oldham's highly distinctive blood group.* And that point too — the point about the blood group — he'd have made that point for certain.

★ ★ ★

243

Nigel liked Zurich for its blatancy, its total lack of shame. This was the absolute belly of the beast, the world centre of the banking system, the official gatekeeper of accumulated capital. Marx had long ago defined wealth as the surplus value appropriated from every sweating, dangerous act of toil and labour. Zurich was where all that wild, reckless profit came to be ordered and tamed, to sit securely in the bank vaults and grow and prosper more sedately. Their quick, smooth flight had landed on time and he'd checked into his room in the Baur Au Lac without a hitch. He'd considered using its rival, the Hotel Widder, up in the old town, but had rejected the idea, had decided he wanted a more open, natural vista to gaze out at. There had been no grand suites available at immediate short notice — or not to Nigel, via his PA, anyway. Money and power are always relative. Nigel had acquired enough of both for his own needs and purposes but in the strict hierarchical orbit of Zurich's business élite he was a medium-level player only, not a drop-everything high-roller. The room was an excellent room, however, spacious, opulent — and the view from his balcony was the essential, coveted one: the lapping waters of Lake Zurich.

He'd dined in the main restaurant, Le Pavillon. A deliberately modest meal. A steak dauphin and a simple glass of beer to wash it down. Now he was walking along Bahnhofstrasse, amongst the expensive stores and the window-shopping tourists. His PA had set up the handful of meetings he'd asked her to arrange but none of them were scheduled before tomorrow. When he'd walked his food off he planned on working wirelessly from his hotel room for an hour or two and then he'd do nothing very much for a while. Visit the hotel's gym, maybe, or take another stroll, probably down by the lakeside next time. He needed to think — and Zurich was a world-class venue for thinking. Einstein, James Joyce, bananas Carl Gustav Jung, to name only a few, were all associated with the place. Even Lenin had thought (and written) here, though he hadn't kipped in the Baur Au Lac, had descended, cheerfully enough, into humble lodgings in the city's 'lower depths'. To keep the trip as ordinarily professional-seeming as possible, he'd billeted Andy in the Moevenpick Hotel, out at the airport. Ostensibly, his driver had the day off, apart from sorting out a hire car should one prove necessary. He'd find a café in a little while, sit down and call or text him, make sure they were mutually up to speed.

Damage limitation. He said the words under his breath, almost audibly, forcing the idea to the forefront of his thoughts. There would be unavoidable damage. Get used to it. The question was how much — and how serious. Copeland Insight's business model was fundamentally straightforward, non-complex. Buy into struggling enterprises, turn them around and then reap a share of the profits or sell upwards and onwards if the price was right. It was a model predicated on good business and market intelligence — and, above all, on Nigel's flawless personal record of shrewd decision-making. Even before the internet and all the other tools of modern investigative journalism, a few news sources over the years had made the connection between Nigel Copeland, bit player in the Claire Oldham murder case, and the business guru of the same name. Nigel had still been securely on remand when Claire had been murdered but his relationship with her had figured in the prosecution case at Martin's trial. He'd had to give a witness statement even though he'd never been called to give evidence personally. That connection wasn't the problem that worried him though.

Nigel wasn't the only subsequently rich, successful man who'd worked for revolution in his youth. Far from it. No, the business pages and the shareholders wouldn't give too much of a stuff to be reminded again about all of that. Myrtle Cottage's ancient history wasn't the problem — Monday night's recent history *was*. He might even become a suspect. That would really give the Copeland brand name a boost in the worst financial climate for decades. Monday night, as far as Nigel could see, was purely a matter of bad luck, of bad timing. But it would *look* to the world and his rivals like a bad judgement call. And without his rep for sound, reliable good judgement, Nigel was naked in the market place, a stall-holder with nothing to sell.

He changed direction, took a side street that (as far as he recalled) would bring him out near the Fraumünster church where there was a little

Italian-run place he liked. He'd have his coffee there, contact Andy over at the Moevenpick. He'd phone him, he decided. Under the circumstances, it might be foolish to rely just on a text.

29

Martin Grove.doc

Claire kept a kettle in her room, I discovered the next morning. And teabags. And a fresh carton of milk. I'd woken up before her, amazed to be watching her sleeping, amazed to be lying next to her, listening to her breathing, even feeling the warmth of her breath on my face when she'd turned sleepily towards me. We'd made love again in the dawn half-light. Twice. I was young and clumsy — but eager as hell. Maybe it was the eagerness that Claire liked. I was a kind of puppy dog, really, uncomplicated, so easy to please. We sat up under her duvet, drinking tea after I'd made it in two mugs, one teabag, extravagantly, in each, and told each other little snippets about our lives growing up. It was a conversation we'd been having for weeks by then, backwards and forwards. Me on the Woodlands estate, Crowby, Claire down in Sussex, then at boarding school, then at university. She'd studied something called Greats at Oxford, she told me, then had to explain what that meant: philosophy, politics, economics, 'the ultimate bullshit primer in bourgeois ideology, Martin.' I never understood half of what she said back then, but I soaked it all up, unpacked it at my 'leisure' in prison later on. Years later, when I was studying properly on my own, I'd pick up a text — Plato or Hegel or whatever — and remember something Claire had said back then, finally see what the hell she'd been getting at. Whenever that happened, in an uncanny way it was like having her with me again, making some kind of weird re-connection with her even though she was dead, utterly gone, no longer present on the earthly plane.

It was a strange, unsettled time at the cottage. The Crowcross Three on remand, the casual supporters drifting away — and splits, ructions, animosities developing amongst everybody who'd stayed on. The Claire-and-me thing didn't help. I didn't sleep with her every night and neither of us made a big, public deal about it. But we didn't hide it either, weren't ashamed of it, and so, gradually, more or less everybody got the message. Some of them didn't like it. Sexual freedom, the rejection of conventional morality, was meant to be part of the Myrtle Cottage package but, nonetheless, some people were really pissed off, really got up on their high horse, about Claire-and-Martin. Andy more or less stopped speaking to me unless it was objectively necessary to get some practical task accomplished — although Hilary didn't, was one of those who stuck up for us, declared that it was nobody else's bloody business, that they should all keep their bloody noses out. The issue was Nigel really, of course. He'd gone to prison for the cause and Claire became regarded in certain quarters as betraying him behind his back. Some of them were sarcastic about the age-difference too (Claire died a few days before her twenty-fourth birthday). I overheard Hilary one time telling Oliver, a guy

I'd never gotten on with, not to be so fucking sexist. His own girlfriend was several years younger than he was, so why was there a problem in reverse?

Claire was conflicted about telling Nigel, I know that for a fact. There'd always been honesty between them — but there was the complication of telling him while he was banged up. Nigel was a tough nut but he wasn't unbreakable. Especially since he was apparently a lot more serious about Claire than Claire had been about him. As it turned out, she never got the chance. Somebody else — I never found out who — clued him in. Claire carried on phoning him most nights of course, even still visited him. But she gave the impression (to me anyway) that, from then on, their contact was always purely business, solely about the protest campaign.

The airfield itself stayed quiet, inactive, through those cold winter months. The security guards and their dogs and their portacabins were still there and the guards and the dogs were still making their regular patrols of the perimeter fence. Their numbers had been increased, we thought, after the action in November but otherwise there didn't seem to be any new developments. The Myrtle Cottage rumour mill filled the vacuum of course. The chief rumour in circulation was that the MOD were simply biding their time, waiting for spring: as soon as the weather improved and the days lengthened the contractors would definitely be going in, would definitely be starting construction work on the 'death base'.

As far as I was concerned, none of it really mattered much more than as a backdrop. Not Nigel and the others banged up, not the airbase, not the wider politics (a national miners' strike was finally looming — exactly as Andy and Hilary had predicted that time in the Market Tavern). Not even, if I'm completely honest, the imminent danger of the entire human race being blown to kingdom come. That's new, self-obsessed young love for you, Dear Reader, as you know yourself — and, if you don't, I pity you from the bottom of my heart.

Claire and me liked to go walking in Crowcross Wood a lot, to get out into the fresh, clean air, away from the increasingly claustro-phobic, closed-in, hermetic world of Myrtle Cottage. We'd trespass quite a bit too, take shortcuts across the farms, leave the occasional gate deliberately wide open. Well why not? They were all against us — and some of them, we guessed, were behind the car-window smashing and tyre slashings. Occasionally, we'd get out of the countryside altogether. We were getting more and more into the Two Tone thing and we started to drive over to Coventry on a regular basis, caught a lot of the big-name acts. We got talking to some of The Selecter in a pub over there one night. Claire sold them on the idea of a Crowcross Three benefit gig — but it fell through, like so many plans, when she fetched up murdered.

A few times I went down to London with her. I'd no licence, and not much experience, but she'd even let me drive the MG on the M1 leg of the journey, foot down (no speed cameras to worry about back then, my friend) and the radio or the tape deck blaring. 'Going to London' meant attending the closed meetings of the central committee of the RCV — the Revolutionary Communist Vanguard — the tiny, secretive ultra-left organisation that both Nigel and Claire belonged to. The RCV saw themselves as a true Trotskyist cadre. You couldn't just join the RCV because you felt like it — clipping out the coupon on the back page of a party newspaper the way you could for the Socialist Workers Party for instance. Instead the RCV chose its recruits by careful invitation only: on the basis of an existing and proven high degree of activism and advanced political understanding. *That's what a fucking vanguard is, mate,* Andy had told me more than once over a bottle or two of rice wine, *people who know what they're doing, people who can give a lead — not a bunch of newcomers who've only just worked out that capitalism fucking stinks.* Andy wasn't an RCV member but it was clear that he had aspirations in that direction. He'd packed in his oath to Queen and country, Claire said about him one time, but he was still a soldier at heart, wanting a cause to fight for, to stay loyal to. I never found out the truth about how influential the RCV actually was. A fraction of a fraction inside a fraction most probably. But that didn't mean they had no influence at all. The way Nigel and Claire had set up the Myrtle Cottage protest was a classic example of RCV tactics — building a broad alliance in defence of a popular cause and using the situation to teach the need for a wider revolution. From the RCV point of view, nuclear disarmament was a textbook 'transitional demand': a good, obvious idea to a significant slice of the population but totally impossible to achieve under the existing, oppressive, profit-driven system.

I wasn't invited to Claire's RCV meetings obviously, usually didn't even know precisely where they took place. I got the impression that the venues changed frequently — and often at the last minute, motivated, I'd say now, by the usual left-wing paranoia about snoops and infiltrators. They'd use a room hired in a student union one time, the back room of some obscure pub the next. I didn't mind being left out. I'd wander the West End for the day, maybe go and see a film or mooch around Soho or Covent Garden, sinking a few beers and trying to spot the famous yuppies that were meant to be London's big new thing back then. We'd stay on for a day or so when we went down there, longer than was strictly necessary for RCV purposes. Claire liked to book us in to what she called a decent hotel and what to me, naïvely, looked like palaces. The one I remember best was the Hyde Park Hilton. Claire liked to gaze out at the park and tell me how many demonstrations, near-riots and actual riots there'd been there over the centuries. Even the railings had been pulled up more than once, she'd say, and turned into handy, makeshift spears. I commented one time that she wasn't very peace-loving for a so-called peace protestor. She looked at me in deadly earnest and said that there would be time enough for peace after the last banker had strangled the last arms dealer with the last copy of *The Wall Street Journal* — and then she burst out laughing and kissed me. Did she believe it all? Or was it just a game, a phase, a delayed adolescent over-reaction against her own privileged family? I only wish she'd lived long enough for me to have found out. I only wish she'd lived full stop.

I never discovered (because she wouldn't say) whether the posh hotel thing was something she'd also done with Nigel when they'd both come down to the meetings or whether it was a special treat just for me. The nights were the best of course — pure bliss, magic. We'd take in all the happening clubs and venues wherever they were located. Camden, Brixton, all over — anywhere and everywhere. I remember one time we ended up, don't ask me how, partying on a Thames cruise boat into the early hours. I did a line of coke (Claire declined) with some guy she'd known at uni. Later on, laughing her head off at me, she told me that he was a researcher at Smith Square, meaning (as she had to further explain) that he was working for Mrs Thatcher's Tories. What it might have been was that she just liked the freedom of it, the fun of it, the hell of it, moving at will between different, conflicting worlds.

Our last visit to London together wasn't very long before she died. We didn't go out very much that time. Mainly we stayed in our hotel room in our big, comfortable bed. I was an expert on

Claire's body by then but no less keen. There was a thing she did when she came, a unique kind of little shudder that ran through her, that I remember as much as I remember her voice or her eyes or her smile. It was still daylight, driving back the next day, when we reached the lane outside Myrtle Cottage. We could see at once that there was fresh trouble in store. Two of the upstairs windows looked cracked, broken, and the front door had been scrawled over, ungrammatically, in blue paint. *Hippie Scum Get out. This a warning.*

30

Jacobson grabbed a coffee takeout from the canteen and took the lift down to the incident room on the fourth floor. Emma Smith had just phoned him to say that already there were some significant results from the analysis of Martin Grove's and Karen Holt's telephone data. Almost reluctantly, he'd closed up Hunter's investigating officer's report and told her he was on his way. To make everything easier to follow, Smith had written three neat lists of numbers up on the whiteboard and then drawn connecting arrows between some of them, together with dates and times. So far, she'd told him, they'd only been tracing calls as far back as Friday of last week. The phone companies had supplied data for the last month — so there was still a lot more data for them to wade through.

Jacobson studied the three lists and sipped his coffee. It still wasn't what you'd call great — but it was more or less drinkable, had certainly improved during the last few months since a specialised franchise had been allowed in to the Divisional building. Britain no longer had an empire, reliable trains or honourable, selfless politicians — but at least the catering arrangements had got a little better. List A was Martin Grove's landline. Lists B and C were Karen Holt's mobile and landline respectively (Grove, as they already knew, hadn't owned a mobile).

'Go ahead, lass,' he said simply.

DC Phillips — Jacobson recognised him now — was hovering in the vicinity, presumably for a good reason. As far as Jacobson recollected from the briefing, Phillips was primarily supposed to be working on Mick Hume's vehicle registration list now, acting as today's incident room link for that line of inquiry.

Emma Smith started by stating the obvious: Karen Holt had made and received a lot more calls than the reclusive Martin Grove had. Grove's phone had rung only twice during the whole of Friday and Saturday. Both times the caller had been Maureen Bright using her mobile. On the Friday evening she might have been over at Jane Ebdon's again (easily checked) and on the Saturday afternoon she could have gone off shopping or something equally mundane (and again easily checked).

'This is the stuff that's more interesting, guv,' Smith commented, pointing to another sequence of connected marker-pen lines and numbers. 'Karen Holt's phoned Grove twice on Sunday and then twice again on Monday. She's used her home landline both times on Sunday and then she's used her mobile the next day. The second time was just after seven thirty PM — maybe her confirming that she was driving over to see him that night?'

Jacobson nodded.

'Sounds likely enough.'

'The only other callers Grove gets over the last two days of his life are from these two numbers here.'

He looked where she was pointing. A mobile number (with the distinctive 07 start digits) and a landline number with an area code he didn't recognise. Emma Smith was smart, was maybe his best basic-grade detective, and he knew from the twinkle in her coal-black eyes that she thought she was onto something.

'The subscriber details on both numbers are identical — a name and an address up in Cheshire. The landline's ex-directory incidentally.'

Smith coughed, paused. For effect, Jacobson thought, definitely for effect.

'The thing is that these details were already logged into the inquiry system,' she said finally, patting the nearest computer screen. 'The registered owner of one of the vehicles picked up by the Crowcross Arms CCTV.'

Phillips did the honours, brought the details up on the screen.

'The Lexus LS 600h L, sir — the brand new model,' he said, maybe unaware of Jacobson's famous lack of interest in motor vehicles for their own sake.

Jacobson tried to get the sequence clear in his head.

'So this character's phoned Grove from Cheshire on Sunday evening and then used his mobile to call him a couple of times on Monday as well — *and* we can place his vehicle in Crowcross on Monday night?'

'Clocked driving past the pub at three minutes to nine,' Phillips answered, 'no trace thereafter though, so we don't know when it left the area.'

The young DC brought another window up

on the screen: an entry from the database of company directors held at Companies House.

Jacobson lodged the name in his memory. Nigel Alexander Copeland.

'Do we know owt about him?'

'We've only started looking, guv,' Emma Smith said, 'we've only just made the correlation. He's a big-shot though, runs some kind of international business investment set-up. He's got quite a few hits under his belt on the *Financial Times* site.'

'OK, make him an immediate priority. Find out everything you can. I'll get on to the local side up there. We need a car in the vicinity of the address straightaway. Discreet surveillance until we're ready to make a move.'

He took another sip of his coffee. Then:

'Anything else?'

'We've still got a lot of Karen Holt's numbers to work through,' Emma Smith said. 'Most of them are probably going to be irrelevant: her work colleagues, her mum, her boyfriend.'

Make sure you check out every single one, Jacobson nearly said but stopped himself just in time. It would have been a needless, demoralising comment. He knew full well that Smith was every bit as thorough a workaholic as he was himself. Instead he pointed to a specific number on the list of calls that Martin Grove had received (somehow it hadn't surprised him that Grove didn't seem to have made any outgoing calls himself).

'You said this one was Maureen Bright's mobile?' he asked.

DC Smith nodded.

'OK. Get back on to the phone company when you get a minute. We may as well take a look at who else Maureen's been calling recently while we're at it.'

'You think she's looking suspicious then, guv — because she's never mentioned any of these phone calls to Grove?'

'Just a fraction, lass. She's conveniently driven off the premises a couple of hours before Grove gets shot. She's denied that he was expecting any visitors that night — and now it seems that, when she's home, she never hears his phone ring, never asks him who was he was talking to or what they were talking about.'

* * *

Kerr pulled into the Crowby motorway services, decided he'd better grab a sandwich or something before he drove back into town towards the Divisional building. Even the police canteen beat this place hands down but on a murder case you dined when the opportunity presented itself, couldn't take the risk of waiting for something better to come along later. He phoned Cathy in her office after he'd eaten (a BLT, a bag of crisps and an over-chilled, over-waxed apple), checked that there was nothing special or important happening for either his son or his daughter after school today. She told him that there wasn't — *just their general, unreasonable demand to spend time with both their parents*. Kerr ignored the

260

sarcasm, mild by Cathy's standards, promised her he'd get home the very first second he could — but he didn't concede any specifics, such as which particular hour the second was likely to occur in.

He treated himself to ten minutes in the WH Smith outlet, browsed the latest music and computer magazines. When he went back outside, he saw a traffic patrol vehicle in the middle of the car park, its blue lights flashing ineffectually in the bright afternoon sunshine. It wasn't too far, he thought, from where he'd left his own car. He strolled off in that direction, still vaguely regretting not having bought the magazine with the file organiser software on the free CD. His music downloads at home were all over the place, badly needed to be put into some kind of order — if he ever got the chance. After Cathy, the kids and not-missing-Rachel, non-essential hobbies claimed a very poor fourth position in his list of strapped-for-time priorities.

The patrol car had parked across the front of a dark green old-style Mondeo, deliberately blocking it in, unless the car in the row behind suddenly vacated its space. Two youngsters climbed out of the jammed-in vehicle. A youth and a girl. Kerr, drawing closer, made them sixteen or maybe seventeen, not much more than that. The lad's baseball cap had a long, white peak. The girl looked furious with him, punched his arm hard before one of the traffic cops warned her to stop it. The other cop seemed to recognise Kerr (it wasn't mutual), waved him over.

'Joyriders, bless 'em — doing a hundred in a speed-check area then thought they'd call in here for burgers and fries,' he told Kerr.

'I didn't even know it was stolen,' the girl said. 'He told me it was his frigging sister's. The lying little toad. The little f — '

The traffic cop told her to cool it again, turned his attention back to Kerr.

'The blue Renault Clio, Sergeant,' he said, 'word's just come in on the radio.'

Kerr looked at him blankly, his mind maybe not still fully back on duty. The joyriders were in a Mondeo, why was he being told about a Clio? What did any of it have to do with him anyway?

The traffic cop finally explained it, finally started to make sense.

'One of the vehicles on Inspector Jacobson's look-out list? The number plate definitely matches anyway. This Martin Grove business?'

Kerr caught on — at last. A blue Renault Clio. *Karen Holt's missing vehicle.*

The cop explained that another traffic patrol had just located it — on a cab firm forecourt, over near the railway station. Bridge Cars. Kerr knew them, decided to amend his journey, make a detour in that direction. He tried both of Jacobson's numbers en route, didn't get a reply. So he left a message for him on his mobile — and updated the incident room (in the form of Brian Phelps) for good measure. The patrol car was still there when he reached the place: carrying out guard duty on the Clio until the SOCOs turned up. Kerr took a tentative look into the (locked) interior. A couple of road atlases, a discarded Red Bull can, a disconnected sat nav. The patrol guys explained that they'd just been answering a routine call. The Clio had been sitting on the forecourt since Monday night, the owner hadn't come back for it — and the taxi company had eventually reported it to the traffic division.

Kerr talked to the co-proprietor in the cluttered portacabin office. Ramesh Mishra. Kerr had first known Mishra when he'd been a waiter at the Viceroy Tandoori in Wynarth and Kerr had been dealing with race-hate incidents over there. Mid-twenties, hard-working, straight up. Kerr unpacked the story as quickly as he could. Karen Holt's sat nav had packed in on her drive over from Birmingham. Not knowing the area, she hadn't fancied trying to locate Grove's rural retreat on her own. So she'd found a taxi firm — this one — and taken a cab instead. The arrangement was she'd book a cab back later and pick her own car up then — except that Bridge Cars had never heard from her again.

'You just let it sit here for two nights, Ramesh?'

'Customers aren't always reliable, Sergeant. So we thought — wait and see for a day or so.'

Karen Holt's car details hadn't been made public, Kerr knew, but that still left the question of the TV and newspaper appeals concerning the private detective herself. Hadn't anybody here recognised her?

To his credit, Bridge Cars' co-owner didn't pretend that he didn't know what Kerr was talking about.

'No, it's strange isn't it? I wasn't here Monday night though — I didn't see her anyway.'

'What about the driver — surely he must've put two and two together? Don't you log destinations?'

'The driver is my third cousin, he's not been here too long. He comes over here to marry, really. But then there's some problem concerning the girl's family . . . '

Kerr got the picture. An unlucky cabbie crapping himself about his immigration status, wanting to come forward, not wanting to come forward.

'Just give me his details, Ramesh. *I* don't need to see his passport — that's not my department — *I* just need to know about Monday night. When exactly he dropped her off, whether she talked about why she was visiting Martin Grove. You've got CCTV here, I suppose?'

Kerr had already noticed a sleek looking laptop on the desk, next to the stack of invoices. Mishra, maybe looking relieved, turned the screen in Kerr's direction: four live camera feeds

'Neat, yeah?' Mishra explained. 'It's a totally wireless set-up.'

'Nifty,' Kerr agreed, mixing in an impatient PR smile.

Ramesh Mishra moved his cursor, made a couple of clicks and selections. He minimised three screens, maximised the fourth: Karen Holt walking into the cab office, carrying what looked like an *A to Z* in her left hand. Ignoring the seconds and fractions of seconds, the time on the screen read Monday night, nine twenty-one.

Kerr studied the photograph on Mishra's wall calendar — a street market in Jaipur — while Mishra printed out his cousin's contact details. He'd probably be at home now, Mishra said. He wasn't booked in for his next shift until six o'clock.

Kerr finally managed to raise Jacobson's mobile just as his car became stuck in the lengthy mid-afternoon queue approaching the Flowers Street junction. He told him about the Clio and the cab firm. Jacobson told him about the Nigel Copeland development, ended the call. Kerr edged his car ahead. When the lights changed again, he calculated, he'd probably make it through. He switched on the radio — Crowby FM — and then swiftly switched it back off again. Norah Jones: Rachel's night-in-with-a-bottle-of-wine favourite not so very long ago. Fuck her. Fuck her. *Fuck her.*

The address was in Longtown. A cramped bedsit above an Asian grocer's. Ramesh Mishra's cousin, Prakash, was a highly nervous inter-viewee but in the end Kerr was satisfied with his story. He'd driven Karen Holt out to Martin Grove's place on Monday night, had reached it just around ten, he thought. He'd insisted on dropping her off at the top of the driveway, had even waited until he'd seen the front door opening and watched her go inside. He hadn't liked to leave her on her own in the countryside otherwise, he'd told Kerr. He'd noticed another car parked there, confirmed that it was a Lexus: the new LS 600. He was a lot happier talking about cars than about Karen Holt but, according to his story, she'd sat quietly in the back seat, had been looking at something on her laptop for most of the journey.

Kerr double-checked the detail.

'A laptop, you're sure about that?'

'Sure, a white MacBook. It looked nice.'

Kerr noted carefully what he said he'd done next. A fare from the Wynarth Arms down into Crowby and then another one out to the Beech Park estate. It was all readily checkable — and if it did check out, Ramesh Mishra's cousin was in the clear. There were bastards on the force who'd flag him up to the immigration service just for the hell of it — or (maybe even worse) because it was 'procedure'. But Kerr wasn't one of them, was still his father's son to that extent at least.

31

Martin Grove.doc

You spend a lot of time watching the jury when you're accused and standing trial. You make up little stories about each of them, make guesses about them based on their age and appearance, other little details. Do they look kind or unsympathetic? Intelligent or stupid? Are they rich or poor? Happy or unhappy? What do they eat for breakfast? What TV programmes do they watch? Who *are* they in the rest of their lives? The foreman of my jury was a bluff old character. Red faced, white-haired, usually wore a dark double-breasted jacket. I had him pegged down as a reactionary (another word I'd learned from Claire), a comfortably-off retired type, the last jury member in the world who'd be willing to believe in those days that the British police would coerce a confession from a suspect or that I was anything other than a young, savage, murderous tearaway. This was years before the Birmingham Six and the Guildford Four were cleared don't forget. There were still millions of people in the country then convinced that British justice was the very best in the world, well-nigh infallible. To be fair, there were some young people in the jury box also. Youngish anyway. But none of them looked like me or like anybody else out at Myrtle Cottage. There was a woman, attractive enough, who dressed like a secretary and a bloke in a neat suit who might have been a car salesman. I've no prejudice against ordinary, everyday people, Dear Reader, I'd like to make that very clear. Yet nobody on that jury looked to me like they'd ever been on a protest march or, even less, been on the receiving end of a police baton charge. I didn't see anybody sitting there that I thought would have a clue about me or the way I'd been living.

My confession was the big, gargantuan obstacle I faced during the trial — and during the long prison years that followed it. Alan Slingsby, my defence solicitor, made that clear to me the first time we met. I was charged and on remand by then and the police investigation, as far as it went, was over, done and dusted. Without the confession, they'd nothing, he reckoned. Or next to nothing anyway — circumstantial evidence at best. He'd brought a copy of my statement with him, dated and signed by me on the last page. I told him how it had all come about, how I'd ended up signing my name to that total, utter pack of lies. I always remember that he looked sympathetic, something that meant a lot more to me at the time than he probably realised. But he didn't have good news for me. *I believe you, Martin*, he explained, *the trouble is that the jury may not — and the judge is going to take against you, direct them against you. Retracting a confession, claiming you signed under duress — judges don't like any of that, don't like any suggestion that the police and the legal system are anything other than squeaky clean.*

Alan Slingsby was correct, of course. The judge didn't like it one little bit, constantly reminded the jury that my only defence was retraction — and that, in order to believe me, they would have to take the word of a young, unreliable, uneducated man ('in his own words, a drop-out and a drifter, ladies and gentlemen of the jury') against that of serving police officers with unblemished records of achievement ('dedicated public servants, who enjoy the high esteem of their own peers and colleagues'). The day I exercised my right to give evidence on my own behalf, he fumed and fidgeted and coughed his way through my testimony, allowed every single technical challenge by the prosecution. The contrast to the reception he gave to DCI Hunter could hardly have been greater. Hunter was virtually welcomed into the witness box like an old, honoured friend. Hunter didn't disappoint his host either. Where I was tongue-tied, nervous, sometimes inaudible, Hunter exuded clarity and confidence, spoke in full, deep measured tones. Did he reject the defence suggestion that the accused had been improperly treated while in police custody? The prosecution barrister liked that question so much he asked it a lot more than once. Hunter gave the same answer each time: *I do (m'lud, ladies and gentlemen of the jury), I do reject it — I reject it one hundred per cent.*

I trod a Buddhist path for a while when I was in my last years in prison. Or I tried to anyway. Maybe I'm still some kind of a believer, who knows? The Buddha taught that the world of everyday perception is illusion, impermanence, maya. That if you could just see properly, the so-called real world would fall away to nothing. It's a liberating idea when you're stuck behind bars. I'd sit in my cell sometimes and imagine the walls dissolving, melting down into non-existence. The same, liberating idea applies in the courtroom. Ultimately, in Buddhism, we are all one — all the saints, all the sinners. Every seemingly distinct, discrete personality is no more than a shell, a temporary mirage. The outside edge of your skin doesn't truly separate you from anyone else, Dear Reader. Not from me, not from anyone. Neither does the incessant chit-chat in your head, persuading you that you're unique, special, cut off from the rest of creation.

I got respect for my beliefs inside — or a fair bit of friendly curiosity anyway. I got to know a lot of killers when I was banged up — real killers, truly guilty men. Some of them (certainly not all of them, I wouldn't claim that) thought a lot about life and death, whether there's a purpose or a meaning to any of it. Especially about what might happen next. Hell can loom large in your thoughts if you've committed the ultimate sin. I'd tell them that — as far my limited understanding of it went — the Buddhist concept of Hell had similarities to the old Christian idea of purgatory. You paid off your debts of bad karma in the 'Hell realms' and then you might get another chance on the wheel of life. It made sense to some of them anyway.

I was still engaging with the Buddhist path

when I got caught up in the riot at HMP Boland. Those two nonces were foul, little shits. Neither one of them denied the despicable things they'd done and it was really hard, in the normal run of things, the normal way of thinking about things, to feel the tiniest shred of sympathy for them. But I spoke up for them — or, at least, for leaving them alone anyway. I knew that if I didn't, nobody else would. The mood had turned ugly by then. The Boland Governor was a lying piece of scum (even the Prison Service found a reason to 'retire' him a year or so later) — and the rioters knew they couldn't believe or trust a word he said. Those two were the victims of defeat as much as anything else. Everybody knew the riot was going nowhere. Eventually — running out of food and essentials — there would be no choice but to back down, give up, surrender and generally eat whatever crap the Governor and the screws decided to dole out. The two of them were put on 'trial' in the TV room. They were stood up, shitting themselves, on chairs, so that everybody could see them. The way it got reported later, it was made to sound like a beating that had got out of hand or gone too far. That had a grain of truth so far as the prison officer went. If he hadn't tried to intervene at the last minute, he probably wouldn't have been kicked — fatally — in the head. But it was clear straight off that they planned to kill those two, intended — deliberately — to beat and pummel them to death. *Make them suffer*, somebody shouted from the crowd at one point, to loud, general applause.

I felt guilty in the aftermath for speaking out, weirdly enough. As if I'd helped to make the process legitimate in some way by taking part. *Martin Grove even spoke for them, don't forget — they got a fair, fucking trial*: that was an argument it was easy enough to hear around the wing in the days and weeks afterwards. That guilt soon fell away though. I'd done what I could and no man can expect himself to do more than that.

The 'execution' place was the shower block. They were frogmarched in that direction by the designated execution squad. Like Pilate, I'd washed my hands by then, had gone back to my cell, was taking the precaution of constructing what barricade I could behind my door from my limited jail possessions. I had respect, I knew that. Most of the blokes on my wing believed by then that I was innocent, understood the long hard road I was walking to clear my name. But I was still inside a dangerous, volatile situation that day. I'd stuck up for the hated scapegoats — I certainly wasn't immune from the risk of maybe being next.

I was struggling with a pile of books when the execution procession went past, right outside my cell. I could have looked conspicuously away (it would have been a sensible, easy move). But who looks away from a car crash? So I saw all of them — the killers and the condemned — walking straight past my door. At my own official, lawful, state-approved trial, the particular screws who'd looked after me, who'd brought me up into court from the holding cell and taken me back down again, hadn't been bad to me. Court escort seemed to be a bit of a jolly really, a screw's day out — so they were often in jovial mood. But something changed on the last day. After the verdict. After the judge wholeheartedly accepted the jury's unanimous decision that I was guilty on all charges, every single count. An indefinable distance crept in then between them and me. The universal distance, maybe, between those with hope in their lives and those with none.

I read distance this time too, except distilled even further: right down to the elemental difference between the living and the soon-to-be-dead. They'd tied their hands behind them, strung makeshift cardboard placards around their necks: *peedo bastard* and *kill me*. Their deaths were going to be brutal, collective, primitive. I knew the men who would do the killing, recognised them, knew all of them by name. But, when it came to it later, I refused to name them, claimed — lied — that I hadn't seen them. That guilt hasn't gone away though. It won't ever go away, Dear Reader. Not unless I name them here — name them soon and damn the consequences.

32

Jacobson knew he had to push Maureen Bright again. This time about Grove's telephone conversations with Karen Holt and Nigel Copeland. If he gave anyone else the job, he'd have to take them away from something else that needed doing. So he allocated the task to himself, even took his own car. He'd nothing more urgent to do anyway — until he heard from the Cheshire police regarding Copeland.

Jane Ebdon let him in, resolutely followed him through to the kitchen where Maureen Bright was sitting hunched over the table, still hugging herself tightly against the world. She looked more or less sober and she wasn't smoking. Not right now anyway — but there was a crowded ashtray in front of her and a nice big rack of wine bottles over in the corner. Ready and waiting.

'According to your statement, you were at home with Martin all of Sunday and most of Monday,' Jacobson said, pulling out a chair for himself, entirely uninvited.

She barely glanced at him.

'So?'

He sat down, put it to her directly. Seven calls over two days from two apparent strangers. She must have been aware of them, might even have answered the phone herself.

'A male caller by the name of Copeland,' he added. 'Plus Karen Holt — the private detective

274

who visited Martin after you drove over here on Monday night — the one who turned up dead in Crowcross Wood.'

He studied her reactions while he spoke — but if she had something to hide, she was hiding it well, burying it deep under her blank, weary expression.

'It's news to me,' she said. 'I told you yesterday I'd never seen the woman before and I've never heard of anybody called Copeland. As for the phone, it can ring anytime, can't it? I could have been out in the garden, I could have been taking a shower — '

'Maureen doesn't know anything,' Jane Ebdon cut in. 'Why can't you just believe that and leave her alone? Or maybe old habits die hard in Crowby CID?'

Jacobson ignored the slur, kept his eyes fixed on Maureen Bright's bleary expression.

'Suppose I believe you never actually met Karen Holt — you must have known Martin had called in a private 'tec all the same. To help him rake over the coals about Claire Oldham. You were his support, his *soulmate* — he told you everything he was doing, didn't he?'

He saw instantly that soulmate had been the right word to pick. Cruel, apposite. It hurt her, cut through her defences. He watched her fight salty tears. She looked away from him, not wanting him to see.

'No, he didn't,' she answered, still not looking at him. 'You're wrong. He didn't tell me everything. Not even me. He swore blind he wasn't raking it all up again — not in the way you mean anyway. Not detectives and all that. If I'd known, I might've managed to talk him out of it.'

Then, maybe — she didn't add the words, didn't say them, but they hung in the air like a bad, futile smell. She would cry in a minute, he could see that. Dissolve into tears as soon as he was gone.

'Satisfied?' Jane Ebdon asked him, not bothering to show him to the door when he stood up to leave.

He still wanted DC Smith to go ahead with the phone checks on Maureen Bright's mobile — anything else would be sloppy, non-thorough — but she *hadn't* known, he decided, *hadn't* passed the information on elsewhere. Or she'd known Grove's arrangement and not been able to stop him, had even stormed off in anger because Karen Holt was on her way over. Either way, it didn't really matter. He'd eliminated a possibility, Jacobson thought — but that was all. He couldn't actually call it progress, couldn't actually call it getting anywhere.

His desk phone rang two seconds after he got back to his office in the Divisional building. He picked up the handset and carried it over to the window, stared down into the pedestrian precinct while he took the call. It was from Ted Nelson, his one and only personal contact inside the new, tri-agency supercop set-up, SOCA.

Nelson had been a DCI in Coventry right up until the beginning of the year. Off and on, Jacobson had known him for a long time, had worked with him on more than one major

276

investigation, last year's video gang case being the most recent. He hadn't given Nelson's transfer a huge amount of conscious thought but it had surprised him all the same. Before he'd heard the unexpected news, he'd had Nelson down as a like mind. A solid copper who'd preferred to stay put as far as possible, who'd resisted the restless gypsy lifestyle of the manic promotion-junkies who moved desperately around the country from one force to another, a year here, two years there, chasing advancement. Nelson, like Jacobson, had tried to understand the world and the people in it by drilling down deep in one place. Except now Nelson had upped sticks and taken the SOCA shilling.

Jacobson got straight to the point: Gerry Quigg's name had come up on the periphery of the Martin Grove-stroke-Karen Holt case and he needed to know as much about the SOCA operation against Quigg as Nelson could risk telling him.

'I have to be very careful what I say about that, Frank,' Nelson said, 'you know how it is.'

'That's understood, old son. But I'm guessing you are on the team?'

'Yep, I'm on it. Quigg's empire is still primarily Midlands based, so a lot of the team are guys with a substantial Midlands background.'

'And you think you've really got something that can be made to stick this time?'

Jacobson sensed a pause: Nelson weighing up what he could divulge — and what he couldn't.

'So long as the CPS don't blow it, we've got him. Permitting premises to be used for the illegal manufacture of a controlled substance. That's pretty much a definite — and worth a few years away in Quigg's case. If we're very lucky, we might have him for accomplice to murder as well.'

Too much to hope that Quigg would ever carry the can for actual murder, Jacobson thought — but kept it to himself. He cradled the handset and watched the shoppers down in the square while Nelson told him the (edited) story.

A cannabis factory had been located and raided over in Herefordshire. Small beer in itself — just a rural smallholding with a polytunnel or two of skunk hidden about the property. Except that when SOCA's forensic accountants looked into the issue of ownership they'd found an untypically careless audit trail which led all the way to one of Quigg's personal holding companies.

'Some minion fucked up, Frank. On this occasion, the normal layers of legal separation between friend Quigg and the action just weren't there.'

'That is careless. But even so, it's not much in isolation is it? I assume he at least had nominal tenants on the books — and I assume you still need to *prove* knowledge on the part of a landlord to charge them with *permitting*?'

'That's the beauty of it. Quigg was there on the day of the raid — in person. A skunk factory's bog-all compared to his heroin and cocaine networks — but it's the fact that he was actually there on the premises. Bloody amazing.'

'Do we know why?' Jacobson asked.

'It seems discipline was getting slack down on the ground in a few areas. Stuff getting sold off on the QT beyond acceptable rake-off levels. It also seems that Quigg was undertaking a personal tour of suspect sources and outlets — restoring the fear of God where necessary.'

'A high-risk strategy for him, wasn't it?'

'Very, as it's turned out. But also highly effective — even just the idea that Concrete Gerry might be calling by would make most sane toerags think twice about any personal initiatives with the company product. We reckon he's only actually risked it a couple of times — more than enough *pour encourager les autres.*'

'So you had a tip-off about this particular visit of his?'

Nelson told him no, they didn't in fact. It had been a case of pure luck. The raid had been a local drugs squad initiative, nothing at all to do with SOCA initially.

'We didn't even know where he was that week, Frank. Other than not being at home. He'd given our surveillance teams the slip for several days in a row at that point.'

'So how did — '

'Fortunately, the local DI on the day clocked him straight off. The fucker tried to do a runner, out across the fields. Seems he's not as quick on his pins these days as he was once.'

'Who is, old son? You said something about accomplice to murder though?'

Nelson paused again. More careful pre-editing, Jacobson thought.

'The short version is that somebody might

have been murdered on the same premises. Not necessarily that day but very recently. Before they had time to clean up properly anyway. The forensics point that way at least — and they also point to Quigg himself being in or near the vicinity of the killing, if there was one.'

'Karen Holt's main job re Quigg for Mott Legal Investigations was setting up a forensic defence team,' Jacobson commented.

'Doesn't surprise me, Frank. If the decision-makers do decide to put murder into the mix, it'll be a forensic bun-fight in court under the disclosure rules.'

Something about the way Nelson used the term 'decision-makers' communicated to Jacobson that his old colleague was less than impressed with the quality of his new bosses. No change there, he thought.

'Am I allowed to know who the murderee might be?'

'I don't know that myself, Frank. Honestly. Everything's need-to-know around here. Somebody mid-level in the organisation who'd seriously pissed Quigg off, that's all I've heard.'

'Quigg must have been exceptionally pissed off to go hands-on, surely?'

'I get the impression it was personal in some way — not just business. Topped on site and then the body disposed of elsewhere, that's the theory. Completely off the record, unless a body *is* found, the accomplice charge is going nowhere.'

'Why 'accomplice' anyway?'

'Two of Quigg's personal protection guys were

arrested with him. If a body does turn up, Quigg will persuade or coerce one or both of them to put their hand up for it.'

'So Gerry Quigg might go down for a bit of cannabis. It's like Al Capone and income tax, old son.'

'Or Saddam and the dodgy dossier. Doesn't matter what we do him for, as long as we do him — with the difference that the evidence against Quigg happens to be real.'

Jacobson watched the crowds out in the sunshine. Nothing to worry about, many of them, except shopping, idling or returning a book to the public library. All right for some, he thought — and then forced his mind back on track. SOCA (and the Home Secretary) would have a PR field day if they did manage to cause Quigg serious grief. But drugs-based organised crime was a hydra. You pulled off one head and ten new uglier heads filled the vacancy.

'It's a remote possibility at this stage, Ted. But just suppose I need to speak to Gerry Quigg — '

The phone went dead in his hand. A few seconds later it rang again: Nelson on a different (presumably more secure) number — and virtually whispering.

'Not a chance officially. He's locked down as SOCA property. You find out anything, or you need anything, you flag it up and leave it to us. That's the official line. Even the DI who nabbed him down on the farm was lucky he wasn't reprimanded. If you want to risk something *unofficial*, that's up to you.'

'As if I would, old son.'

'Be careful if you do, Frank. I mean that in every sense of the word.'

The phone died again. Jacobson replaced the handset and sat down at his desk. He scribbled a few notes based on what Nelson had said. Nelson had been predictably vague in places but Jacobson concluded that he'd only told him one outright, officially-mandated lie: the far-fetched claim that there'd been no tip-off. The raid might well have been ostensibly local but Jacobson wasn't buying the idea that SOCA hadn't pre-approved it at one level or another — or that Quigg's convenient presence on the day had been a total, out-of-the-blue surprise. There was a SOCA informant inside Quigg's organisation. He'd bet his pension on that. He'd bet Nelson's pension on it too — especially with its generous SOCA enhancement added on.

He got as far as re-finding his place in Hunter's yellowing investigating officer's report before the next, distracting call came in: DC Emma Smith. She told him that she'd just found out something unexpected about Nigel Copeland. Something that she thought he'd want to know about straightaway.

* * *

Ann Ledbury had been unlucky, the doctor — Stockton — was saying. The overall 'success' rate for self-hanging attempts was high, above eighty per cent on most estimates. Even if you got quick, unexpected help the way she had and reached a hospital alive, you still had a good one-in-three chance of not pulling through.

'So she's going to make it?' Kerr asked.

Stockton was the junior consultant on the case. A short, stocky customer in his late twenties with unruly hair and a bad complexion. But his manner was pleasant enough, well below the accepted norms of medical condescension.

'The signs are promising although she's still comatose right now. You must have got to her inside the first five minutes or thereabouts. It looks like she hadn't a clue what she was doing with the ligature of course — the knot could have been a lot tighter and that's definitely helped. But even so, she'd done enough to fatally asphyxiate herself if you hadn't happened along at the crucial moment.'

Stockton paused to take another sip of the tea he'd been drinking when Kerr had walked in on him. The two of them were sitting in a cramped, windowless office near the intensive care unit. Kerr had been on his way back to the Divisional building when the call from the duty DC who'd been digging into Ann Ledbury's background had changed his mind for him. He'd used a route out to the hospital that Mick Hume had told him about recently. A detour through the Bartons estate that had knocked ten clear minutes off the journey.

'So why unlucky, Doctor?' Kerr asked, puzzled.

Stockton hadn't struck him as the sarcastic type.

'Two aspects really,' Stockton said. 'One is that if she meant to kill herself then that's her right, basically, in my opinion. But the main thing is that there's a big possibility of brain damage. A very big possibility. Despite your intervention, I'm afraid she's probably suffered an interval of total anoxia.'

Kerr looked blank at the term, although he'd known (from the paramedics) that brain damage was on the cards.

'Interruption to heart and blood circulation — and no oxygen going in. Even three or four minutes in that state is enough to knacker the brain permanently,' Stockton explained, translating the science elegantly into layman's terms. 'If she does survive, she might be what we're not supposed to call a vegetable anymore.'

Kerr thanked him for his gloomy summary and left him to his cup of tea. He walked the short distance back along the corridor, pressed the switch outside the intensive care unit, but didn't venture inside when the doors slid open. He hadn't driven out here to learn Ann Ledbury's medical prognosis. Not primarily anyway. The object of his visit was somewhere inside the ICU, probably hunched in a chair at her bedside. He waved to the nurse at the nursing station, hand-mimed what it was that he wanted. He could live quite well, he'd decided, without the sight of Ann Ledbury wired up to the machines that had stopped her from dying and that now threatened to return her to the world as a witless, helpless moron.

The duty DC had done a good job, had discovered — which nobody else had — that Martin Grove had obtained a legal restraining order against Ann Ledbury eighteen months ago.

She'd moved to Wynarth in the first place, it transpired, purely because it put her in Grove's vicinity. Prior to the order, she'd turned into his stalker essentially; driving by his place at all times of the day and night, bombarding him with unwanted letters and phone calls. The DC had also dug up a concerned ex-husband who was still living at one of her previous addresses: Moseley, over in Birmingham.

The nurse brought him to the sliding doors. Kerr said who he was, suggested they talk down in the visitors' café. The ex-husband looked reluctant but the nurse promised that they'd come and find him if there was any change, any change at all. The café was busy but they managed to find an empty table.

'It was good of you to come over,' Kerr said blandly, tentatively. 'A lot of exes don't want to know when something like this happens.'

Mark Ledbury looked straight at him, trying, fairly obviously, to weigh him up.

'Ann and me,' he said quietly, 'it was always going to be a life sentence. But I never thought she'd do something as fucking stupid as this.'

Ann Ledbury was thirty-seven, according to the duty DC. Kerr made her ex-husband about the same age. A sad-looking man in cargo pants and a yellow NO2ID T-shirt. Or sad-looking today anyway. He was some kind of artist apparently. So's Tony Fucking Scruton, Kerr had thought when he'd heard the news, his usual reaction when he encountered anybody in that line — and then he'd reminded himself sharply that it was no decent reason to hold the profession against somebody else.

He sipped at his tea and wondered where to start.

Ledbury saved him the trouble.

'We met at art college. Years ago. Went out together, broke up, went out again, broke up again. Eventually her best mate, Evelyn, just packed all her stuff up and moved it into my place.'

He half-smiled at the memory, looked less sad for an instant.

'We were together for near enough twelve years, married for five of them. I put up with it the first couple of times she ran off — she always came back full of apologies and 'never agains' — but it really gets you down eventually. Like it's you who's at fault?'

Kerr didn't think Ledbury actually wanted a reply so he didn't give one.

'I divorced her in the end. She didn't contest it.'

'This was before Ann got involved with Martin Grove?'

'Yeah, it was. Only just though. I think she first started to write to him later in the same year.'

'The divorce wasn't a total split, then? You were still in touch with her afterwards?'

Ledbury half-smiled again.

'Just call me muggins, mate. I could never see past that woman. I still can't. Anytime she gets in trouble — money, landlords, whatever — I stump up, fight her corner.'

'She's an art teacher, isn't she?' Kerr asked, recalling the basic facts he'd picked up from the duty DC.

'She has been — off and on anyway. Off again since Martin Grove got his restraining order, the LEA dropped her like a hot potato. Even before that, she had problems holding on to posts. Drink, basically, that was the difficulty. We all used to get hammered at college. It's only later on you realise that some people were getting a lot more hammered than everybody else. She got into Buddhism that way — some rehab centre where they had a meditation teacher. It worked great for a while, really seemed to sort her out. Even the Martin Grove thing seemed fine at first. She threw herself into the campaign for his release. It seemed to give her a real focus, you know?'

Kerr nodded, sipped his tea. People with nothing to hide, incidental witnesses, told you all sorts. Their whole, true life stories — the stuff they kept hidden from everybody else. They knew they'd never see you again, knew you couldn't just blab whatever you liked back to their friends and families.

'But then Grove didn't want to know when he got out?'

Mark Ledbury's half-smile vanished.

'I expect you know the rest. All the obsessive stuff. Though she seemed to be getting over it recently. She was off the booze again anyway. Even went trekking last year. Nepal.'

'At your expense, Mark?' Kerr guessed.

'It's only money, mate. What's the point of it if you can't look after people you care about. You haven't heard of me, have you?'

'Should I?'

'Not so much if you're not into painting. But I've had my share of success. Brit Art, the Saatchi Gallery, all that toss.'

Kerr thought about the name. Ledbury, Ledbury. Maybe Rachel had mentioned it sometime but he couldn't remember it if she did. The truth was he'd switch off listening half the time she banged on about art. And then he wondered why she'd — no fuck that, *fuck that*.

'When did you last see Ann, Mark?'

Ledbury shot him a look.

'No, I don't mean it like that,' Kerr said. 'There's no suspicion that — '

'Only checking, mate. But it has to be at least a couple of months ago. I had a show on at the Ikon and she came to the opening night. Beautiful as ever and not touching a drop. And now this — she's really fucking done it this time, hasn't she?'

Kerr didn't answer again, knew his silence was the very same thing as saying yes.

'There's people like that. That's the truth of it. Ann was one of them. There's just something empty inside them, something you just can't fucking reach. She couldn't have kids, you know? Went through a phase of blaming everything on that. But no kids wasn't the problem. It wasn't anything so fucking simple. Even Martin Grove — it wasn't his fault either, the poor bastard. He had enough on his plate to deal with without picking up all of Ann's garbage as well.'

'You really think she'd stopped hassling him recently?'

'Well, I can't be certain. But, like I say, I think

so. Him being murdered — I guess that's just come out of the blue and finally pushed her over the edge.'

'Did you ever meet Martin Grove yourself, Mark?'

'No, never. And before you ask I was in London on Monday night. A preview at the Serpentine and then dinner with my agent. Tons of witnesses all called Rupert or Nemone.'

Kerr had no more questions. Mark Ledbury had nothing else to get off his chest. They sat there awkwardly for a few more minutes, finishing their drinks. He seemed a likeable-enough guy, Kerr thought. Successful but down to earth. A combination that was all too rare. He'd even let a woman screw his life up for him. It didn't get more ordinary, more everyday, than that.

33

Greg Salter insisted on a smart-looking patrol car and a uniformed driver to transport the two of them over to County HQ, out near the motorway. Jacobson and Salter both sat in the back, conspicuously as far apart as possible. Salter made a busy-busy show of reading and answering emails on his PDA. Jacobson eased off the knot in his tie and slouched a little, created a deliberate impression of idling, even of slightly dozing. In reality, his mind was running through the latest developments.

Nigel Copeland's name hadn't rung any bells — and wouldn't have done until he'd managed to read further into Hunter's report. So it was just as well that Emma Smith's meticulous searching had uncovered an old magazine interview from the mid-Nineties that somebody in the USA had uploaded onto an investment advice website. In the interview, Copeland had commented briefly about his connection to the Claire Oldham murder case (*Tragedy stays with you, Copeland tells me. There's an uneasy silence and then he adds that, nevertheless, life has to go on*). The interviewer had tried to contrast Copeland's time at Myrtle Cottage with his later business career but Copeland had brushed the contrast aside (*Copeland smiles at my question and slightly mis-quotes Clemenceau — a man who isn't a socialist at twenty, he tells me, has no heart*). Anything outside the country was always a headache of course. Greg Salter always insisted on getting involved and so did the Chief Constable's office. Phone calls and faxes flew all over the shop. Scotland Yard. The Home Office. Interpol. Jacobson checked his watch just as the driver pulled up at the security barrier: five PM on the dot. Not bad as this kind of thing went actually: barely two hours to liaise with London, Cheshire and Zurich and to get the show on the road.

The video link suite was in the main building. Kerr was already there when Jacobson and Salter walked in, drinking tea (inevitably) and talking to the technician. They used the twenty minutes until the scheduled transmission time to discuss the interview strategy. Salter, to his credit, didn't intervene too much or make too many unwelcome suggestions. The technician ran them through the operational basics and then arranged the seating, positioning each of them optimally for the camera. Behind them on the wall was a big blue backdrop with the force's crest and insignia as its centrepiece.

The Swiss made their introductions first. Two detectives and the two criminal lawyers that Copeland's Swiss business lawyer had speedily hired for him. Copeland sat between his lawyers, bulwarked against whatever was going to be thrown at him. There was a translator present in Zurich too, although the Swiss all seemed to be fluent in English and it appeared unlikely that her services would be needed.

Salter set out the ground rules and the Swiss

lawyers confirmed that it was a reasonable basis to proceed on. All that would be happening right now, Salter announced, would be a 'conversation' which Mr Copeland had voluntarily agreed to participate in. The aim was to clarify anything he might know about events at Martin Grove's residence in Crowcross on Monday evening. Full copies of the recording would be kept by the Swiss police and by the Crowby police. A full copy would also be made available to Mr Copeland and his legal representatives. The recording would safeguard the interests of everyone involved.

While Salter sorted out the bullshit, Jacobson poured out a glass of water and studied Nigel Copeland's image on the big screen opposite. He looked tanned, fit, healthy — and a good ten years younger than his date of birth suggested. Jacobson knew that Copeland wasn't all that much younger than he was from his official details but he conceded to himself that he'd never have guessed the fact from looking. The only slight consolation was that, between the two of them, the rich handsome bastard was the one who might just possibly be in the frame for double murder.

Jacobson summarised out loud what he knew. Nigel Copeland had phoned Martin Grove on Sunday and then twice on Monday. Not only that but Copeland's Lexus was caught on camera, driving through Crowcross village just before nine o'clock on Monday evening.

'Can I assume that you visited Martin Grove at home on Monday night, Mr Copeland?' he asked when he was done.

Copeland glanced at both his lawyers but neither of them said anything.

'I also know that a quarter of a century ago, you were involved in the peace protest at Myrtle Cottage,' Jacobson added. 'You were Claire Oldham's lover in those days — before she was murdered.'

Copeland coughed, cleared his throat, before he answered.

'OK. Yes. I visited Martin on Monday evening. I had business in the Crowby area the following day so I thought I'd look him up.'

'For old times' sake, Mr Copeland? The man who raped and killed Claire — or so the legal system believed for twenty years. A man you must have hated all that time?'

'That's true enough. I did hate him. Even when the doubts about the conviction started to surface, even when he was cleared, I went on hating him. It's taken me a long time to adjust to the fact that Martin didn't do it, that whoever did do it has never been caught. But eventually I got to that point. That's why I wanted to see him, to let him finally know that.'

'So this was the first time you'd contacted him since he was released from prison.'

'Yes it was, definitely. When I spoke to him on Sunday, it was the first time I'd done so since before Claire was killed.'

Jacobson hadn't used the video link before, hadn't realised just how much he valued the intimacy of a traditional interview. Physical closeness told its own revealing stories. The way someone sat, whether they were breathing fast or slow, whether they smelled like truth or lies. This was nothing like that: half the cues he relied on weren't available.

'How did you get his number after all these years?' he asked. 'It's not in the book, we've checked that out. He went ex-directory to avoid nuisance calls.'

Copeland glanced at his lawyers again — and the lawyers said nothing again. It was a simple enough question but maybe it was one he hadn't anticipated.

'Hilary Watson — she's an old friend who's kept in touch from those days. Another protestor back then. I knew she was also in touch with Martin — so I just phoned her and asked. You can check that with her if you like.'

'I do like. Thanks. Do you have her details on you?'

Copeland bristled a little, Jacobson thought, though it was hard to tell when you weren't right in his face — weren't in the same room, weren't at the same table. The rich never liked to be told what to do, no matter how trivial the instruction. He watched him fishing his Blackberry out of his jacket pocket, watched him scrolling down the screen. When Copeland read out the details, Jacobson wrote them down with deliberate, cumbersome slowness, got him to repeat part of them a couple of times. A London address, he noticed. NW1.

'And how did this meeting go exactly, Mr Copeland?'

'OK, I guess. A bit awkward at first. But I

think he knew I was being sincere, that I believed he hadn't done it, that I was pleased he'd cleared his name, made a new start. We talked a little about the things that had been good back then, the things we've all lost — the hope, the idealism.'

'But it never occurred to you to come forward, to contact us? We put out an appeal on national TV last night — asking for anyone who knew anything about Martin Grove's whereabouts in the last few days.'

Copeland looked directly at the camera. This was a question he had anticipated, Jacobson thought. That much was written all over his face, even at this distance.

'I never saw it. Simple as that. I didn't know about what's happened until the police here came to see me at my hotel. I would've got in touch otherwise, obviously.'

'Who exactly was present when you visited Martin Grove's house?' Kerr asked, as if he'd suddenly woken up.

They'd agreed that Jacobson would drive the interview — but it was always useful to have the occasional question thrown in unexpectedly from the sidelines. *The Rough Guide to Subtle Intimidation*, page one.

'Myself and Martin,' Copeland answered. 'That was it. He talked about his girlfriend — Maureen? But he told me I'd missed her, said that she'd driven into Crowby to see a friend.'

Jacobson ran with the ball.

'You didn't meet Karen Holt either then?'

Copeland coughed again, rubbed his fingers

against the side of his head, just above the ear.

'I think I did actually. She arrived just as I was about to leave. But Martin didn't introduce us for some reason and I didn't press him. To be honest, I thought maybe she was another girlfriend. You know — sneaking around while the other one was elsewhere? She wasn't of course. I realise that now.'

'And you left when?'

'About ten o'clock. I couldn't say for certain.'

'And Martin Grove's mood — did he seem nervous, agitated, anything like that?'

'I didn't think so. He struck me as very calm, if anything. Hard for me to know of course. I'd not seen him since he was nineteen. And he'd certainly changed a lot since then. He'd got degrees in prison, educated himself — but maybe you already know that.'

Kerr lobbed another side-shot.

'You familiar with firearms, Nigel? Handguns, pistols?'

The older, taller Swiss lawyer queried the relevance of the question.

'Mr Copeland says he met with Martin Grove in Martin Grove's home on Monday evening. Literally, their first meeting in decades,' Jacobson commented. 'An hour or two later, somebody shot Grove dead on the premises. Frankly, I think the relevance is self-evident.'

Copeland rubbed the side of his head again.

'No, I don't,' he said. 'I don't know the first thing about them. I've never fired a gun in my life — except maybe at a fairground when I was a kid.'

Kerr changed tack slightly.

'Where exactly did you go inside Martin Grove's house?'

'*Where?*' Copeland queried, either not understanding the question or pretending not to.

'That's right — *where?*' Kerr persisted. 'I mean which rooms. Did you use his bathroom for instance?'

Copeland may have scowled — but it was difficult to be certain via the video screen.

'No, I didn't,' he said. 'I was in his lounge. I think that was it.'

'Were you in his kitchen at any time?' Jacobson asked, taking over again.

Copeland shook his head.

'No, I'm sure I wasn't. Martin fetched a couple of bottles of beer — I assume from the kitchen. But I was in his lounge the whole time. I'm certain about that actually — now you've asked me.'

'Tell me about later,' Jacobson said, 'after you left Martin Grove's place.'

'I went back to my hotel — the Riverside in Crowby. I expect the receptionist there might remember — I had some couriered documents to pick up. Yesterday I was in business meetings and then last night I was back home.'

'Your PA tells us you only asked her to book you onto a flight to Zurich last night — you called her while you were still on the M6, she says. Short notice, isn't it?'

'There's nothing unusual in that. Short notice trips go with the territory when you're involved in international finance,' Copeland answered.

Jacobson thought he detected a hint of smugness in the reply, a hint of you-wouldn't-know-obviously. With deliberate over-politeness, he told Copeland that his officers would check with the Riverside Hotel and attempt to confirm exactly when he'd got back there on Monday night.

He drank a slow mouthful of water and then formally raised his request for fingerprints and for a DNA sample. There was no legal obligation for Copeland to assent to the request (certainly not immediately anyway) or for the Zurich police to assist Jacobson with processing it. Behind the scenes, the Swiss lawyers had probably already discussed the issue with Copeland. If he was confident that he'd absolutely nothing to do with either killing, they would've advised, then there was no reason not to cooperate. It would speed up establishing his innocence and it would also put him in a good light with the Swiss authorities.

Copeland looked straight to the camera again.

'I don't like the way you guys hold onto innocent people's DNA beyond the strict purpose. But if it helps catch whoever's done this then yes — OK.'

Another pre-rehearsed answer, Jacobson thought. He wondered whether there was the slightest hint of sweat on Copeland's forehead — or just a few faulty pixels on the screen at that particular point.

★ ★ ★

The Swiss police kept Nigel kicking his heels for another half-hour before they took his prints and his DNA swab. He'd been fingerprinted before, when he'd been arrested on demonstrations back in the Eighties. Though probably too far back (or too unimportant) for his prints to have been archived onto the police's modern computer-based systems. Not that it mattered either way. The DNA swab, on the other hand, was something new. It felt weirdly humiliating and invasive — as if his innermost core was about to be processed, logged, classified and taken away from him. He grabbed a cab back to the Baur Au Lac as soon as they were through. According to his lawyers, there was no question of any restrictions on his movements, although it would be 'polite', one of them had said, to let the police know when he was leaving Switzerland or, before then, if he planned on changing hotels. They'd even returned his passport. For all that, Nigel decided to act on the assumption that his movements locally were likely to be monitored, at least for the next few days.

He went straight up to his room, showered, changed, and then poured himself a Johnnie Walker's from the minibar. He drank it down in one and then immediately poured out another. He decided to nurse the second shot. What he needed to do urgently, he knew, was to review his conversation with the police, think through every single implication, ramification and possibility. He stepped out onto his balcony, barely noticing the warm, early evening air or the yachts idling out on the calm lake.

He ran through the sequence of events in detail, considered every angle. He'd acted appropriately surprised when the Swiss detectives had knocked on his door at the Baur Au Lac. He'd gone with them voluntarily (once he'd established that he could call his lawyer first), had played the responsible international citizen to the best of his ability.

He hadn't mentioned Andy at any point, but then nobody had specifically asked about him. Julia, his PA, might have referred to booking two tickets, one for Nigel and one for his driver, although it was just as likely that she hadn't. Andy's existence might come up when the Crowby police snooped around at the Riverside Hotel of course. In which case, he'd just claim that his driver had waited outside with the car while he'd spoken to Martin. Why the hell wouldn't he? He may as well keep Andy out of it if he could, avoid an unnecessary complication that would entail more explaining, more delving into the past, more involvement with the police investigation. That was what the pigs liked after all, anything that made you appear unusual, non-standard and, therefore, generically under suspicion. *The pigs*. Weird. Even all these years later, that was what he still thought of them as in his mind, he realised. The pigs. The filth. The goon squad of the Oppressive Capitalist State.

34

Jacobson eluded Salter after the video conference, hitched a lift back to the Divisional building with Kerr. Salter would probably hang on at County HQ anyway, find a pretext to grab a word with the Chief Constable or, failing that, one of the Assistant Chiefs. The pretext could be Jacobson's sharp, televised exit from yesterday's press conference of course (Salter, typically, hadn't said a word to his face about it). But, if so, Jacobson would worry about any consequences if and when he had to.

His first port of call was Jim Webster, the Crime Scene Manager. Webster's one item of news wasn't encouraging. The FSS ballistics expert had taken a preliminary look at the bullet removed from Karen Holt's brain and had just faxed over his summary.

'The main point, Frank, seems to be that the bullet has less-than-average reproducible characteristics,' Webster said, fidgeting with one of the pens from his famous collection.

The legend was that he kept them in serried rows on his desk, neatly ordered for size and colour. Jacobson, one of the select few to be tolerated inside Webster's cubicle-sized fourth floor office (partitioned-off from the second Scene of Crime lab), knew that the truth was more prosaic. Webster kept them, like anybody else, stuffed into a handleless china mug. But, in fairness to myth, the mug did look very clean — and there were a *lot* of pens stuffed into it.

'Too badly deformed, old son?'

'That's what it looks like — so it's going to be difficult to establish clear striation patterns.'

Jacobson had only a basic understanding of firearms which he was always meaning to improve. The trouble was that the topic bored him. He'd pick up the manual, then put it down again after a few pages. But he knew enough to understand what Webster was getting at: the usual test-firing techniques might not be able to definitively link the recovered bullet to a suspect gun — if one was ever found.

'Not good, Jim. A Walther's still in the frame though?'

'Or something very similar. Something nine mill anyway.'

The nine millimetre Walther was the UK's most popular illegal handgun. Widely available and cheap.

'That narrows the field down to an elite handful of master criminals,' Jacobson commented gloomily.

Webster confirmed that the Crowcross weapons search was virtually complete (without finding anything). The house search likewise.

'No hidden data storage then?'

'No, Frank, nothing.'

'What about prints, DNA?'

'We're processing everything we've found. But, so far, the only matches in the police systems are Martin Grove's and Maureen Bright's. There might be fibre links across the two crime scenes that don't originate with Karen Holt — it'll take FSS to confirm that obviously.'

But no help to us until there's a suspect or two in custody, Jacobson thought.

He walked along the two corridors which separated the Scene of Crime labs from the incident room. Somebody needed to check out Nigel Copeland's claim that he'd left Martin Grove's place around ten o'clock and returned to his room in the Riverside Hotel. His A-team already had their hands full with the tasks they'd already been allocated so — who? Duty CID were flotsam and jetsam unless you happened to know them from previous cases, had already formed a view of their usefulness or otherwise. DC Phillips was tap-tapping on a nearby computer terminal when Jacobson entered the room, completing his shift report on the list of vehicles thrown up by the Crowcross Arms CCTV. OK, him then, Jacobson thought. He seemed young and keen enough — plus it would give him a break from following Emma Smith around like a puppy dog. Not that Smith seemed to mind, Jacobson had noticed — or thought he had anyway. None of my business, he reminded himself. Lonely hearts advice wasn't in his job description the last time he'd looked, which was probably just as well. He hadn't even managed to phone Alison yet, he realised, keep his own attachments on track. And now the call would have to wait another hour or two — until Phillips had dealt with the Nigel Copeland issue. Alison was the Riverside's manager so Jacobson was always ultra-scrupulous whenever Crowby's self-styled best hotel cropped up in his investigations (especially as that was how he'd met her in the first place). It was another way the force had changed since the days of DCI Hunter and his ilk. Hunter had regarded every personal contact as an exploitable resource, had never made the slightest attempt to separate duty from pleasure.

He checked the vehicle situation with Phillips before he despatched him over to the hotel. Apart from Copeland's Lexus and the mystery Range Rover with the phoney, cloned plates, Phillips told him, the only other out-of-area vehicle which the pub CCTV had picked up was a hired Suzuki which had been traced to its latest location, Stratford Upon Avon. The hirers were middle-aged Japanese tourists who'd been Monday-night diners in the pub's restaurant. Everything else was local: Crowcross, Wynarth or Crowby. None of them had shown up on the PNC or on the localised intelligence database.

'In all probability, sir, the ones who don't live in Crowcross were probably just out at the pub for the evening — having drinks or meals.'

Jacobson nodded. The way he'd set it up, Phillips had run the incident-room-based checks, while a couple of other duty DCs were out and about visiting each registered, local owner in person.

'Never mind, lad,' he said. 'It's still worth us talking to all of them. One of them might have seen something worth seeing — and we can't rule out yet that one of them *isn't* connected in some way to Martin Grove.'

Emma Smith herself was still progressing through the telephone data. Nothing more to flag up, she told Jacobson when he asked. But she was still plodding on and there was still data to come in that hadn't reached them so far. Maureen Bright's mobile fell into that category (mobile records still took significantly longer to access than landline records). So did Jacobson's latest request: all the numbers they could uncover for Nigel Copeland. DC Smith produced the requisition forms for the latter, shoved them under his nose for counter-signing. He mooched around the incident room for maybe another ten minutes after that, checked there was nothing else he should be knowing about that he didn't know about, maybe got a tad under everybody's feet. He phoned Ray Williams out at Crowcross but there was no significant news from the second day of door-to-door spadework either. He was thinking he might go and seek out Steve Horton if he hadn't clocked off yet. Horton was in the new computer lab apparently, working on enhancing the Range Rover images, although it was his virtual storage theory about Martin Grove's missing computer files that Jacobson chiefly wanted to ask him about. But then a call came in for him on the incident room's main number: Mick Hume, over in the Town Hall.

Jacobson enjoyed the stroll across the pedestrianised square, enjoyed, as ever, the sight of the white 1930s Town Hall prefaced by the sturdy row of oak trees outside its main entrance. A mild breeze rustled the broad green leaves as the perfect summer evening replaced the too-hot June afternoon. The square was surrounded by buildings on all four sides: the Town Hall, the Divisional building, the public library stroke NCP multi-storey, the arse end of the Crowby Arndale Centre. The Town Hall with its Art Deco flourishes was the only one of the four that Jacobson thought he would bother to put a fire out in (although as a responsible public servant he'd want to get any humans and other living creatures out of the other three before he cheerfully fanned the flames). Hume was down in the Town Hall basement where the CCTV OCS — Operational Control Suite — lived. Jacobson followed the evening security guard down the cool marble stairs and then into the windowless, air-conditioned rooms where Crowby's official snoopers scanned and monitored their fellow citizens on the sunny streets above.

Hume was waiting for him, as promised, in the dedicated police viewing room.

'Progress then, Mick?' he asked, grabbing a vacant chair next to Hume in front of a bank of monitors.

As a matter of routine, Hume had plotted the possible routes between Crowcross and Crowby and had been searching Monday night's camera footage for any traces of the vehicles which were now officially of interest in the murder inquiry. His priority task was to confirm the route and timings of Nigel Copeland's Lexus out from the Riverside Hotel and back — but now he'd also picked up intown images of the cloned-plate Range Rover.

'I'd say so, guv. Dribs and drabs anyway.'

Hume lined up the relevant sequences and then talked Jacobson through them.

'He hits the camera system from the Wynarth direction, which is exactly what you'd expect if he started out in Crowcross. One nineteen AM according to the timestamp, which means, potentially, he's spent a good couple of hours out in the Crowcross vicinity.'

Jacobson nodded. The Crowcross Arms camera had picked up the Range Rover about ten past eleven as far as he recalled.

The best results came from the traffic cameras at the Flowers Street Junction: the vehicle turning into Flowers Street, its cloned plates clearly visible. Hume rewound, froze the nearest screen on what he said was the clearest interior image. He stretched it, magnified it, cropped it, generally played around with it. The street lighting in Flowers Street was a lot more powerful, a lot more penetrating, than anything out at Crowcross. The blurry upshot was a solo driver (probably), a baseball cap pulled tightly down over the face, a dark, high-collared jacket zipped all the way up to meet it.

'Yeah, I know — its pretty crap in itself,' Hume commented. 'His own mother wouldn't know him — assuming it *is* a bloke.'

'Doesn't matter, Mick,' Jacobson said. 'Whizz-kid Horton might be able to do something with it. But what's more significant at the moment is the timing and the sequence. Can we plot the route any further?'

'That's what I'm trying to do now. I've sent an

alert to Regional Traffic by the way — in case anything shows on the motorway systems. But they haven't got back to me yet.'

'I'll flag it up with Smoothie Greg — he should be able to raise the priority level for us, he has to be good for something, after all.'

He left Hume to it. It was good, painstaking work and he didn't want to throw a discouraging spanner at it. So he kept to himself the obvious downsides. The driver could be anywhere by now and the Range Rover could be in any kind of state. It could be right out of the country or it could be burned down to nothing on some waste ground. Camera evidence was all very well (if it wasn't blurred and useless) — but it functioned solely in the past tense, never stopped anybody in the act. Note to hack politicians, he thought, video surveillance does NOT deter. He blanked Jeremy Bentham, the sleazy OCS supremo, on his way out. The way the job had gone in recent years you had no choice except to work with the camera Stasi when necessary. But there was no rule — yet — that said you had to smile at them or shake their damp, sweaty, self-righteous palms.

⋆ ⋆ ⋆

Kerr sat behind his desk in his shared office, engrossed. His room-mate, DS Tyler, was working days this week, had probably gone home hours ago. They were rarely both in the room at the same time for very long. Which was just as well, given its cramped size and hemmed-in, claustrophobic atmosphere. Kerr's and Tyler's office was on the fifth floor, same as Jacobson's, but on the inner spur. Instead of the world outside, the only view was into other Divisional building offices much like their own. The effect was like staring back at yourself. But at least it was quiet up here in the evenings. Somewhere (unlike the incident room) you could hear yourself think.

The Assistant Governor at HMP Boland had finally faxed through the paperwork he'd been promising him since yesterday morning: an inventory of the prisoners who'd been convicted of offences during the Boland prison riot. Kerr made quick notes of his own as he read through. It looked like a meticulous set of data as far as he was able to judge — so maybe it had been worth waiting for. Prisoner numbers. Original sentence details. Additional sentence details. Subsequent prison transfers. The Assistant Guv had even highlighted the really important data with a bright yellow marker: the names of the four rioters whose final release dates had already elapsed.

Kerr took each name in turn. He studied the HMP Boland summary, fed the name into the PNC and then ran it, as an extra check, against the two other computer resources he used on a regular basis — Google and the BBC news site. In all, around sixty prisoners had been additionally convicted in the wake of the riots but, if the data was accurate, only these four had so far been released. It wasn't all that surprising, Kerr thought. Most of them had already been banged up on lengthy terms for serious Cat A offences and would probably still be inside even if they hadn't participated in the riots. Nobody knew of course who had killed the prison officer and the two sex offenders except the prisoners — and all of them, including Martin Grove, had maintained a wall of silence on that topic ever since. The ringleaders had been identified at the time (all of them were still in prison) but another big unknown was whether they'd merely doled out the orders for the killings (which they'd denied) or whether they'd also acted as the killers.

The first of the four names fell at the first hurdle. A convicted murderer, Lee Derek Stephens, had been paroled a couple of years back. The PNC had picked up his confirmed release date but, unlike the BBC, hadn't yet recorded the fact that he was currently on remand again, accused of attempted armed robbery last month against a Securicor depot in south London. John Michael Anderson, name number two, was even less of a candidate for any kind of retaliation against Martin Grove. He'd been released under licence six months ago on compassionate grounds, having been diagnosed with advanced bowel cancer. A few phone calls were sufficient to establish that his condition had been terminal: he'd died in April at a hospice up in Northumberland.

Kerr took a break, clicked on his illicit kettle and made a cup of Earl Grey. In the absence of fresh milk (ideally, he preferred it with a very precise dash of semi-skimmed), he decided he'd drink it black. The next possibility was a Bulgarian who'd been doing time for a botched kidnap-for-ransom attempt. According to the information the Assistant Governor had sent on, he'd been deported back to his country of origin on release. Kerr knew he couldn't just take that at face value, spent the next half-hour telephone-chasing the Home Office night desk and the Bulgarian Embassy before he was finally persuaded that the ex-inmate was definitely out of the country — what clinched it was the email he received from a jail outside Sofia confirming what the embassy official had told him: the guy had been immediately re-arrested on arrival for equally-serious local offences.

He called home but nobody answered. He tried Cathy on her mobile. She'd taken the kids over to visit his dad, she told him. He was pleased about that — he worried about Kerr Senior spending too much time on his own these days — but he also felt guilty. Cathy had time to check on *his* dad and he hadn't. He told her he'd be back as soon as he could and ended the call before he got more embroiled. They were the people he was meant to care about but he was too busy to spend time with them — even at a distance via the telephone.

One to go. He finished off the last (cold) dregs of tea and studied the details. Colin Edward Dobell. Age forty-two when he'd been released in January this year. His latest known address was in the Lozells area, over in Birmingham. Dobell's manslaughter sentence had been for killing his girlfriend of the time. Kerr googled the case and discovered (in the *Daily Mirror* archives) that he'd strangled her to death with her underwear when he'd come home and found her in bed with her personal trainer (he'd also put the personal trainer in intensive care). He pulled Dobell's full record from the PNC and printed out a hard copy. Dobell had form back to his teens — burglaries, extortion, illegal possession of a firearm, GBH. Taken in isolation, the manslaughter rap (for an unpremeditated killing) might have been technically correct. But in Dobell's case, it neglected the full, waste-of-space context: a career low-life who kicked and punched anything that moved.

He dialled down to the incident room, asked Brian Phelps for DS Barber's contact details. Phelps gave him two numbers, desk phone and mobile. Kerr tried the mobile first. Barber answered on the third ring. Loud conversation and louder music in the background — the Arctic Monkeys, 'Teddy Picker' — but Barber came through clearly enough.

'I'm in Broad Street, mate. Nice little wine bar. I've just been chatting with some of her, eh, work colleagues.'

Kerr understood that 'her' meant Karen Holt — and also that Barber was in a situation where he had to watch what he was saying. Kerr told him the essentials: Dobell's address needed checking out, Dobell needed talking to urgently.

'And I wouldn't call round on your own,' he added. 'This is a nasty piece of excrement — whether he's got sod all to do with Martin Grove or not.'

He ended the call, shut down his computer, re-concealed the officially-prohibited kettle in the filing cabinet drawer marked 'confidential — do not open.' He needed to find Jacobson next, update him. It remained to be seen whether Dobell was relevant or not. But he fitted Jacobson's prison-related theory all right. A violent career criminal with firearms offences on his sheet — and an extra eight years in jail thanks to Martin Grove's notionally anonymous testimony. He was worth checking out — even if (irritatingly) it had to be done at second-hand, via the City of Birmingham force.

35

Martin Grove.doc

The graffiti on the front door and the broken upstairs windows marked an escalation point in the local hostility towards us. (I've gone back to the Myrtle Cottage days again, if you're wondering what I'm on about. I told you at the beginning I'd be jumping backwards and forwards all over the place — I did warn you about that.) We were down to less than a dozen full-time protestors by then and maybe we were starting to look like an easy, isolated, vulnerable target. We held a meeting of everyone who was left the next morning. The big decision we made then was to stand down the nightly safety patrols. Taking four of our number away from the cottage after dark was no longer as sensible an idea as it had been. It just meant there were fewer people around in the cottage itself. And it was even possible, as Hilary (I think) pointed out, that somebody had been observing the patrol and had learned how to avoid it. We'd always varied its timings and movements but they weren't completely unpredictable. The new rule was for a 'night watch' instead (from *inside* the cottage) and for an arrangement of bells, pots and pans which could be used to rouse everybody quickly in the event of an emergency. Andy and Oliver spent the next couple of days checking and replacing worn locks, repairing and securing windows and rigging up a system of spotlights to cover the front and back approaches to the cottage. With personnel in short supply, they even condescended to let me work alongside them. Nobody was to sleep out in the freedom field anymore, that was the other significant new decision that was reached at that time.

It was late March by now. The Crowcross Three trial was still a few weeks away and the anti-Cruise protests around the country were being upstaged by the newest show in town, the Miners' Strike. Activists from all over headed up to Yorkshire, where the heart of the action was, along with a major media circus and bus-loads of heavy duty pigs on truncheon-a-striker bonuses. Thatcher addressed the nation on the telly every night (or so it seemed), denouncing 'the enemy within' and setting herself up for a political battle she couldn't afford to lose. At the cottage, we did what we could. Miners Support Groups sprung to life everywhere and we got involved with the local group in Crowby. Claire spoke at pro-strike rallies whenever she could, always stressing the argument that to be anti-nuclear was necessarily to be pro-coal and vice versa. Coal was a safe, trusted energy source — and, unlike nuclear energy, it had no 'weapons grade' capability to melt babies and destroy the human race.

Nonetheless, outside interest in the Crowcross protest was waning. Apart from the fence and the civilian security guards, there'd been no developments at the airfield for months now. A few women came up from Greenham Common one weekend and passed on a rumour that Crowcross was actually one of a series of MOD 'phoney sites'. According to their story, Crowcross, and half a dozen other similar locations, were never intended to be used as nuclear bases. *They're decoys, basically,* they told us — set up deliberately to attract the attention of protestors while the real, serious preparations went on elsewhere, mainly hidden deep inside existing, well-guarded military installations. Years later, I still don't know the truth of it. Nothing ever got built at Crowcross that's for sure. But, after Claire's murder, a second wave of protests exploded there — grew to be even bigger than Greenham for a time. So whether we won — or whether we were dupes and stooges, tilting at windmills — is something that history will need to judge, once all the secret archives for the period finally get declassified: and always assuming that the relevant files aren't conveniently 'weeded', 'lost' and shredded in the meantime.

Claire, of course, the revolution's true daughter, was predictably brilliant in her response. It didn't matter a toss, she argued, whether they were actually going to use Crowcross — or anywhere else — or not. The point was that the planes and the missiles were here, in the UK, wherever they were stationed. The government didn't deny that much, even crowed about it. The point of the protest, the point of all protests, was to wake people up to what was happening before it was too late.

Her argument carried the day, especially with the Crowcross Three due in court shortly. In some ways that weekend, when those Greenham women visited us, was the last 'proper' weekend we ever had at Myrtle Cottage. That's how I remember it anyway. We had other weekend visitors too, as we still frequently did. A priest from Christian CND who was also an anti-apartheid activist showed up along with some of the actors from a Soweto theatre group who were touring the country and getting board and lodgings en route from local radicals in the areas they were visiting. Whenever you see the Eighties depicted on TV these days, it's all power-dressing and manic cockney wide-boys making a killing on the newly deregulated Stock Exchange. Not surprising really — history mainly gets written by the victors — but that wasn't the Eighties that millions of others lived through. A time of struggle and resistance and hopes for a saner future. All of that was present that weekend, especially on the Saturday night. The real, genuine Myrtle Cottage spirit in party mode. The Africans taught us ANC songs and Oliver (who was a talented musician as well as a bit of a prat) returned the favour with Woody Guthrie, Dylan, Elvis Costello. Around about midnight we all trooped out into the freedom field under a full moon, dancing, singing, laughing as we went. A couple of the pagans who were still around wanted to cast a new cleansing spell on the base, had invited us all to watch, even, ecumenically, the CND priest. There was a solitary security man patrolling on the other side of the stretch of perimeter fence that backed onto Claire's property. A muzzled Alsatian on a

317

leash padded along beside him. Both of them were illuminated not by the moon but by the fierce perimeter lighting that had been installed along with the fence.

'Come and join us, mate,' Andy shouted at him, waving his latest bottle of rice wine.

We knew that the guards were under strict orders not to talk to us or have any kind of human contact with us — but a few others repeated the invitation, gave him a friendly wave. The guard stopped in his tracks for a moment, turned and looked at us all before he moved on, walked away. He was a young bloke, early twenties, not too much older than I was at the time. He didn't utter a single word but Claire and me both caught the look on his face. Wistful. Regretful. Maybe even ashamed. As if somewhere deep inside, he knew he'd made the wrong choice, knew he was on the wrong side of a lot more than just the MOD's big, ugly fence.

We stayed in bed blissfully late the next morning. Up in Claire's room. Making love and then drinking tea, swapping more of our life stories. Claire often talked a lot about being sent away to school when she'd been young. The loneliness of it — and the diamond-hardness you had to manufacture inside yourself to survive. The schools I went to could hardly have been more different from hers on the surface. But underneath, it had all been the same old crap: the cliques, the bullies, the scapegoats. I think that was the morning I told her about my brief career as a hero, aged thirteen.

I'd blagged off afternoon lessons and taken a

bus down into Crowby. It had been a hot summer's day and I still had some birthday money burning a hole in my pocket (I was a June baby, if you're interested to know, born under Gemini). I walked all the way out to the Memorial Park, thought I might have a go on the pitch and putt or something like that. They've done up the boating area over there now, 'regenerated' it in the jargon, but back then, the original Victorian lake was still on its last, dismal legs, weed-infested, dank-brown, long past its glory days. It was a matter of seconds only, minutes at most. Two little lads, brothers, were fooling around on a rowing boat (nowadays they'd be too young to take one out on their own) and the littlest one fell in. Neither of them could swim. It was just pure luck that I was walking past at the very nearest point. I wasn't all that much of a swimmer myself but I was good enough to reach him without getting caught up in the weeds — and before anybody else had so much as set foot in the muddy water. Even so, the lad was in a bad way when I got him out. He needed a first-aider to give him the kiss of life and then he needed an ambulance. I dreamed about him recently funnily enough. A nightmare really — like I'd been too late and he'd really drowned, grabbing at me, clinging, trying to pull me down with him. The local paper ran it as a story — and featured the brothers and me eating 'celebratory' ice creams on the front page a few days later. I got a spontaneous round of applause at the school assembly when the news got round — I also got called to the headmaster's study and was caned for 'flagrant absenteeism' (they could still do that then, by the way, torture and intimidate kids with full state approval). That wasn't the thing that screwed me up about it though. In a way, given the rules, the caning was fair enough. It was the way he led up to it — a sarcastic little performance intended to fool me at first that I was about to be given another reward for bravery. That was the day that turned me off school — and the society that lay behind it — for good. My mum went to see him when she found out, tore as much a strip off him as she could. The newspaper backed her up, even eventually extracted a written apology from the board of governors. But it was too late, the damage was already done. I could tell all that stuff to Claire, trust her with stuff I'd never tell another living soul. And she told me stuff too, trusted me too. I can hear your thoughts, Dear Reader. I know you think our relationship wouldn't have lasted, that there were too many ways in which we were different, that Claire would have gone back to Nigel (or somebody like him) sooner or later. But, with respect, *you* weren't there, you never kissed her, you never held her — and I was, I did.

That shitty little headteacher taught me a valuable lesson about power and hierarchy and petty tyranny though. I saw hundreds like him inside, hiding behind their prison service uniforms, only able to feel important, or even alive, at someone else's expense. And I met another shit like him the day I ran into Detective Inspector Hunter. But I'm not going to write about him yet. I'm not ready to face that yet. Nearly but not quite. I'd rather linger warmly in Claire's room for a while, watching her wake up again, watching her yawn, watching her smile. Watching it all in my memory, over and over and over. And editing out the bad bits. Like when, finally, we ventured downstairs into the kitchen, hand in hand, wanting lunch or breakfast, and Hilary told us about the cottage cat. A short-haired bruiser, not far off feral, that had just appeared one day and stayed on, tolerated by some, fussed over by others. Except that was the Sunday morning when Andy and Hilary found him lying dead in the back garden — under the wall and just beyond the range of the new spotlights. His throat had been slit wide open. A neat, clean, deliberate cut.

36

Jacobson took the lift straight up to the fifth floor when he got back from the Town Hall. He needed to be in his own office, needed to spend more time with Hunter's report. He read on more quickly than he would have liked, making notes and cross-referencing them as he did so. One of the report's appendices was Nigel Copeland's deposition, which Copeland had given to Hunter's second-in-command, DS Irvine, while he'd been on remand for offences connected with the Crowcross anti-airbase protest. Jacobson had glanced at Copeland's statement earlier, when he'd been preparing for the video link interview, but now he looked at it in more detail.

According to Copeland, Claire had visited him at his remand prison (over in Wolverhampton) on the afternoon of the day she'd been killed. They'd talked about his upcoming trial and, also, Copeland claimed, about their own future together when he got out of jail, whether that was to be sooner or later. *I told her it was likely to be sooner. If I'm found guilty, my lawyer says I'll get three to six months. I could be out in weeks if that happens since the time I've spent on remand will be deducted. I knew all about her and Martin Grove. Claire told me she was going to finish it. She said it had been a mistake, a fling that had got out of hand.*

Jacobson's desk phone rang: DC Phillips. Nigel Copeland's modern story was checking out so far anyway. The receptionist on duty was the same one as on Monday night and she'd told Phillips that she remembered Copeland. He'd come in some time after ten and had signed for a Fed Ex delivery. Him and his driver. Copeland had been booked into a suite, his driver into an ordinary executive room.

'Better get the driver's details as well,' Jacobson interrupted, 'just in case.'

'I'm already on it, sir. I'm going to look at the CCTV next, the lobby and the car park, try and get a fix on exactly when Copeland's come back — and when he's left again.'

'Good work, lad. Keep at it.'

Jacobson turned his attention back to Hunter's report. Parts of Copeland's statement would have been inadmissible as evidence. Since there was no third party verification, the precise words he'd put in Claire Oldham's mouth would have been completely ruled out for example. But any half-decent barrister for the Crown would have found a way to get the central message across to the jury: Claire had come back from visiting Nigel Copeland in prison, had told Martin Grove their affair was over — and Martin Grove had killed her for it, had killed her in 'a drug-fuelled frenzy' according to an ancient newspaper headline which had just leaped, unprompted, into Jacobson's memory. A nice, simple crime-of-passion motive that any dunderhead jury member could easily grasp without over-stretching their limited mental capacity.

Plus, which, of course, it was substantially the admission made by Martin Grove in his own signed confession. Grove had been given to daily outbursts in court, retracting every word of the confession and insisting he'd been tricked and coerced into signing it. But — unanimously — the jury hadn't believed him.

Jacobson read on. The limited forensic evidence available at the time had been ambiguous at best. Grove's denim jacket had been covered in blood which matched Claire Oldham's blood group. But, as the defence would have pointed out, the blood-stained jacket was consistent with Grove finding her in the woods as she lay dead or dying and holding her, desperately, in his arms. Plus they'd been lovers, spending entire days and nights together. It would have been more surprising if strands from his hair and fibre traces from his clothes *hadn't* been lifted from her corpse. The other hole in the prosecution case was the missing murder weapon. She'd been literally battered to death with the proverbial blunt instrument, had mainly died as a result of savage head wounds. The Crown expert had suggested that something like a standard DIY hammer might have been the kind of weapon responsible. But extensive searches in the woodland (and back at Myrtle Cottage) had drawn a complete blank. There had been a small collection of household tools in the cottage but none of them had borne any traces of violent use when examined. According to his notes, Hunter had considered the possibility for a while that one of the wooden staves found in the cottage might have been implicated but every expert he'd consulted told him no, that wasn't possible. Hunter had been entirely undeterred in his certainty that Grove was responsible however: *The accused possesses a good knowledge of the local countryside and may have concealed the weapon in such a way that it has been subsequently impossible to retrieve it.* In Grove's 'confession', he'd claimed he couldn't remember what he'd hit her with or where he'd hidden the weapon afterwards. It was another entire layer of uncertainty in the prosecution case. But, to judge by the verdict, it hadn't bothered the original trial jury in the slightest. Grove had signed his name to his confession, whatever he'd claimed later, and DCI Hunter had smiled pleasantly at the assembled courtroom and stated in his clear, practised baritone that, personally, he had no doubt that Martin Grove was the 'actual, and only possible killer' of Claire Oldham.

It was gone nine when Jacobson had read enough to refresh his memory about the key elements of the case. After he'd driven Hunter and Irvine back to the Divisional building on the Thursday night that Martin Grove had phoned from the call box in Crowcross and reported the murder, he'd had no further personal involvement. But, like everybody else who'd been in Crowby CID at the time, he'd followed events as closely as he could. Hunter had kept Grove in custody overnight and on the Friday afternoon had charged him with possession (a modest selection of then-popular recreational drugs had

325

been conveniently found in a kitchen drawer when Hunter's team had warrant-searched Myrtle Cottage on the Friday morning: cannabis, speed, acid). It was unlikely that the charge could have been made to stick personally against Grove but that hadn't been its purpose. Hunter had successfully opposed bail when he'd hauled Grove before a well-disposed magistrate on the Saturday morning — and then some unforeseen administrative 'difficulty' had prevented finding him an immediate space in a remand prison. The result was that Grove remained shut up in a Crowby police cell over the weekend. By Monday morning, his confession had been signed and dated and officially filed.

* * *

Kerr drove home after he'd updated Jacobson about Colin Edward Dobell. Jacobson had been ensconced in his office, reading, was more than capable of poring over the Claire Oldham records late into the night. Jacobson had just grunted at him in that abrupt way he had when he was absorbed in some self-selected pressing task — *fine, see you tomorrow, old son.* The rest of the world often mistook Jacobson for an everyday rude bastard. You had to work with him, get to know him, to realise it was a little bit more complicated than that. Kerr kept his mobile switched on until he was signalling left, approaching the entrance to the Bovis estate, when he killed it. If anything urgent came in overnight, he'd get a call on his home number in any case. He didn't think that was too likely. Even assuming Dobell was relevant in some way, it was for DS Barber over in Birmingham to a) locate him, b) talk to him, c) detain him if necessary. None of it, he reminded himself, was his immediate, personal responsibility. He squeezed his car onto the short, narrow driveway in front of Cathy's Yaris. There was room for both vehicles — but only just. Cathy's car, as she'd pointed out the other day, wasn't that old but it was starting to give problems, had maybe been a 'Friday afternoon' model.

He kicked off his shoes, grabbed a stumpy bottle of continental lager from the kitchen, twisted the cap off, found his wife in the front room. She had the TV on a low volume (one of those buying a house abroad programmes) and half a dozen books related to her Open University course beside her on the sofa. One of them was folded open on her lap. He'd missed the twins' bathtime and bedtime again, he realised. He missed it far too often. He'd missed the evening meal too. She asked him if he was hungry. He said he was but that he'd fix himself something in a while, once he'd unwound a bit, relaxed.

'You need to eat properly, take more care of your diet,' she said, 'you don't want to end up looking like Frank Jacobson.'

She moved some of her books out of his way and he sat down next to her, stretched his legs out. A couple of them, he knew, had been borrowed from Jacobson who'd done a similar course when he'd been an OU student. He also knew that she liked Jacobson or at least found him interesting. Unfathomably, some women did.

'Jacobson was probably born looking the way he does. Plus he smoked like a trooper for years — and drank like a fish at one time.'

'Even so,' Cathy said, closing her main OU textbook, A207: *From Enlightenment to Romanticism.*

'Sides,' Kerr said, stretching out again, 'his lack of boyish charm hasn't deterred the lovely Alison. How's my dad by the way?'

'Fortunately, women, being superior, are grown-up enough to see beyond looks. He seems OK. Wanting to see you, I think. Not that he'd ever say.'

They sat there for a while, catching up idly on the day. Kerr fetched himself a second beer, brought her a glass of red. He'd thought — hoped — she might have still been out in the garden. But the streetlamps had been on when he'd been driving back and now, outside, it was finally turning dark. She told him what the kids had been doing and he told her a little about the case, editing out, as usual, the gory details. You weren't supposed to talk about your work to your partner or your family — but he didn't know any police who stuck one hundred per cent to that impossible rule.

Cathy switched the TV off and Kerr stuck on a CD: Martha Wainwright, his wife's latest enthusiasm. Kerr didn't care for her, thought she was hyped way beyond her talent but Cathy liked her — right now that was the important thing. He loved coming home like this, he'd realised lately (although not the aspect of being too late for dinner and his children). Nights when Cathy didn't remonstrate about him not being there, just seemed pleased to see him. A chill ran through him when he thought how many times she could have found out about Rachel, about how all of this real, solid life would have collapsed, ruined, on his head — and yet she hadn't, as if some dark, twisted angel of cheating and deceit had been looking out for him.

She mentioned her car again. Apparently the clutch was playing up now. They'd maybe save money long term, he told her, if they went out soon and replaced it. They talked about money in general after that, how tight things were. Not as bad as some, they agreed, nothing to lose any sleep over. But still.

He made himself a cheese and pickle sandwich, didn't bother with another beer. The cat appeared via the recently installed cat flap and he treated her to some fresh milk. Jacobson was probably still in the Divisional building, he thought, was probably still reading about the ancient murder of Claire Oldham. The man was obsessed, as both his fans and his critics inside the force agreed — and drew their different conclusions from. But, when you thought about the bottom line (and you had to sometimes), at least Jacobson had made DCI, had been able to come up through the ranks in a different era. Kerr had already passed on two promotion boards because he knew that if he accepted promotion there was a high likelihood he'd have to give up CID work — and certainly the murder squad — at least for a few years. That was how it worked now if you wanted to get ahead. It was stupid, retrograde, in Kerr's opinion, but there it was. *A desirable breadth of experience*, they called it in the promotion board literature. He'd have to decide soon, he remembered, if he wanted to put his name forward for this year's board.

Cathy stuck her blonde head around the kitchen door, announced she was going up to bed. He looked at her sometimes recently and couldn't work out why he'd ever wanted to spend a second away from her. When he was here, home, Rachel didn't exist. Never had done really.

'You won't be long will you?' she asked him — in a certain way.

No, he told her, definitely not. He ate his sandwich, listened to the news headlines on Crowby FM. *No new developments tonight in the Martin Grove murder investigation.*

There were all kinds of nine-to-five regular hours desk jobs that came with the rank of inspector. More time to spend with his family — and more cash to spend on them too. Somebody had to clear up the really bad stuff. OK, agreed. But did it have to be him, year after year after year? It had been a kind of madness, maybe, he'd been suffering from. A delusion of self-importance combined with a fear of boredom, of one working day being too predictably like the next. Or a contagious disease from Jacobson, who still had it, who would always have it, right up until the day he retired. Probably to the very last hour and minute of that day. He rinsed up the few kitchen items he'd used, filled the kettle ready for switching on in the morning. It was like the thing with Rachel, was maybe even the same thing. You thought you couldn't give something up, thought you couldn't ever live without it. And then one day, suddenly, you glimpsed the possibility that you could.

★ ★ ★

Jacobson broke off to fetch more boxfile documents from the incident room. There was an email waiting for him when he got back to his office: from Steve Horton, who he'd failed to raise by telephone earlier. No progress on the images from the cloned-plate Range Rover. Limited progress on the possibility that Martin Grove and/or Karen Holt had backed-up their computer data onto virtual storage. Horton had traced the internet service providers they'd been using and had therefore been able to check on something he referred to as their recent FTP activity. It seemed that neither of them had used any of the obvious, well-known digital vaults (such as BT's) but there were scores of smaller outfits that he still had to check out. Both Grove's and Holt's ISPs provided their customers with 'static IP addresses', according to the boy wonder. Jacobson hadn't the slightest idea what the hell Horton's gobbledegook meant.

331

And cared even less. But he inferred from the wording of the email that it was a good thing in terms of carrying on the search for the missing data: *assuming it's out there to be found*, as Horton had added in a plain-English PS.

Jacobson kept reading until he felt he'd mastered all the fundamentals: Hunter's Investigating Officer's Report, the original forensic summaries, the statements given by Martin Grove himself and by the other inhabitants of Myrtle Cottage who'd been interviewed by Hunter's team. It was getting on for eleven o'clock when he decided his powers of concentration were fighting a losing battle against the fatigue of a long day. He re-checked into the incident room on his way out of the building. A couple of duty DCs were typing out their shift reports but mainly the room was late-night empty and nothing new had come in on the phone lines. He sat in his car for a couple of minutes when he got into it down in the police car park. Typically these days he drove in to work in the morning and drove home again in the evenings. Between times, he used his DCI prerogative to be ferried most places that he needed to be. He toyed with his mobile for a minute or two, wondered if Alison would be pleased to hear from him at this hour. *Maybe*, he decided, if it was about making definite arrangements for meeting up soon (the Grove investigation permitting).

She answered on the fifth ring, told him she'd just been thinking about him. She must have caught the tiredness in his voice, or the unconscious, unexpressed need.

'Come over now, if you like,' she told him. 'I've a meeting in Leamington tomorrow and I'm going straight there instead of calling into the hotel first — so I don't need to be up especially early.'

Jacobson did need to be up early. But he didn't feel that the fact amounted to any kind of convincing counter-argument. She had the Glenmorangies waiting when he got to her place. His with ice, hers without. Alison lived on Riverside Crescent, an old Victorian mansion that had transmuted into modern apartments. Alison's was on the top floor plus what had once been the attic level. There was a wide skylight in her bedroom that filled with stars on a cloudless, summer night.

'You could always pack it in,' she said later, maybe wanting to make the point before Jacobson drifted off to sleep.

Sometimes they talked for hours. Sometimes Jacobson told her far more than he should about whatever case he was working on. Tonight though he'd said practically nothing. It had been enough to be here with her — and to put the sorry life and death of Martin Grove temporarily on hold.

'I mean it, Frank. You could take early retirement — cash in that cushy public sector pension of yours.'

Jacobson was still sipping the last of the whisky he'd taken up to bed with him.

'Yeah — and what would I do all day?'

'Well, there's all those history and philosophy books you bury your nose in for one thing.

You're always saying you wished you'd got into all that properly when you were younger. You could do a postgraduate course, even go fulltime — an MA or something.'

He put his whisky down on the bedside table. There was one star twinkling brighter than all the rest. Or maybe it was a planet. That was one area of knowledge he hadn't explored, wasn't even sure how to identify the Pole Star or the major constellations. It was an idea he'd thought about more than once. Changing the guard: just walk away, spend his days in a decent, quiet library somewhere. He'd never mentioned it to Alison before though. He could almost resent the way she read his mind so easily, the way he could never dupe her, never mask his feelings. It hadn't been one of Janice's skills — or maybe she just hadn't bothered to exercise it in his case.

'I might never have been a copper if I had done — who knows?'

'And that would have been a bad thing because?'

'I'd never have met you then, would I?'

He loved the closeness of lying beside her, after years of going to sleep on his own.

'What — you'd never have wandered into the Riverside for a drink or a meal? Or any of a thousand other coincidences?'

He didn't reply, kissed her one more time instead. He was too sleepy, finally, to dredge up a convincing answer. Not about meeting her but to her original question. Why shouldn't he pack it in? Pack it in — and let somebody else worry about the uncaught killers and the miscarriages of blind, inadequate, fucked-up justice.

Thursday

37

Martin Grove.doc

A dead cat possibly doesn't amount to much in the grand scheme of things. Yet to the hard-core, still living out at Myrtle Cottage, killing 'our' cat felt like the last straw. We had no absolute proof as to who was actually behind the incident — or any of the previous incidents. But we had very strong, well-grounded suspicions, all of them centred on Colebrook Farm, whose land was the nearest to us. *[note: Charlie Gilbert still alive and almost certainly litigious. Insert pseudonyms, change identifying details etc., pre final public draft]* The family who owned the farm and lived there were the Gilberts. The eldest son, Charlie, was our chief suspect.

He was an obnoxious piece of work. A tall, lumbering oaf in his early twenties. He was supposed to be an engineering student or something, off at university, but he seemed to spend a lot of his time back on the farm. He was around Crowcross most weekends and occasionally midweek as well. He'd tear around the country lanes in his dad's new Jaguar (British farmers are great at the old sob stories, aren't they? But has anybody ever actually *met* a poor one?) — or hang around the Crowcross Arms with his braying, Hooray Henry mates. In the days before the pub banned anybody from the protest (and refused to serve anybody they thought looked like a protestor), there'd been more than one altercation and near-fight in the vicinity around closing time. Gilbert thought it was a really funny joke to sniff the air like he'd noticed a bad smell anytime a protestor passed near him in the throng at the bar — provided he had sufficient numbers of his mates close to hand in case the situation kicked off. Earlier on, official Myrtle Cottage policy was simply to ignore him and his cronies. As Nigel used to remind us at the Monday Night Meetings, we had bigger fish to fry — and more important tasks on our hands than crossing swords with a handful of reactionary country bumpkins.

Gilbert had even attempted, fairly pathetically by all accounts, to chat up some of the Myrtle Cottage women. He'd chance his arm if he saw one of them in the village shop or using the phone box on the village green. Any excuse or occasion really. None of them had felt intimidated (as if) but a lot of them said that he really gave them the creeps. *The sort that gapes at you like you're some piece of meat on a rack*, I remember Hilary saying one time.

We didn't go into the village anymore of course by then unless we had to — and certainly none of us went in on our own. Gilbert still found a way to get his message to us though. A couple of days after the cat incident, Claire was driving back from Crowby in the MG and got stuck behind a tractor not far from the main gates of the airfield. Gilbert, she told us later, had roared past in his Jaguar, swerving out into the other lane, not remotely content to wait his turn. He'd slowed down enough though, according to Claire, to lower his passenger window and smirk at her: *Meow, meow, that's what the kulak pig shouted at me, I swear it.* (The kulaks, Dear Reader, were the class of 'rich' peasant farmers foolish enough to resist Comrade Stalin's programmes of agricultural collectivisation.) We all sat in the kitchen that night and decided unanimously that Nigel's do-nothing policy had been superseded by events and that now there was only one possible response: full retaliation.

Andy stepped up to the plate as people (irritatingly and bafflingly) say these days. His army experience plus his background in car thefts and burglaries made him the obvious choice in any case. He drew his plans carefully and then set them in motion.

We knew we had to be careful. There had been no point in us taking our complaints about local harassment to the police — but the same didn't apply in reverse. We knew we had to get in and out unseen and leave as few traces as possible. Deliberately, we left it for a couple of weeks and, even then, we were guided by the weather, picked a dull night with plenty of low cloud cover.

Hilary was the driver, dropping us off and then waiting for us in Nigel's minivan at a point in Crowcross Wood that was easily reached from Colebrook Farm if you knew the best trespassing routes — which we all did by then. Andy, Oliver and me comprised the hit squad. The job of everybody else was just to stay put in the cottage and to swear blind that's where we'd been too if the boys in blue came snooping around at a later date. Andy could probably have done the job on his own but we'd all taken the view that he ought to have back-up with him in case a problem developed and he had to fight his way out. Oliver and me carried our safety-patrol pikestaffs for that reason, Andy had other protection on board. We knew the Gilberts had Alsatians but we weren't sure how many. We were prepared for up to six. More than that we decided we couldn't deal with, would just abort the operation and make a run for it.

It was midnight when we reached the target zone. Creeping single file towards the hit range we needed on the farmhouse. Move. Stop. Check. Move on. We'd set them off barking a couple of times by then. But nothing serious, nothing that we figured would seem too unusual. The nearby woodland crawled with foxes and badgers, even deer. We reckoned — or more precisely we hoped — that the occasional familiar dog bark wouldn't disturb the slumbering Gilberts. It would take all of the Alsatians at once to do that — and the noise would need to be sustained, incessant.

When we finally got in range, Andy used the night-vision binoculars to reconnoitre. Claire had done us proud in the equipment department. She'd gone home to Sussex the previous weekend, had bought or acquired everything that would be needed well out of the local area. *Just four*, Andy whispered to us when he was done, *easy peasy*. I've always remembered that. I can close my eyes right now and I'm back there, hearing it all, seeing it all.

I handed him the sack and he moved into position. He lobbed the steaks into the yard one by one. He didn't miss once — strong, elegant throws. The lead dog pounced on the first steak and the others followed suit. We didn't know how long the poison would take or the deep-basted sleeping-pill marinade. We were prepared for a long wait but in the event it all went off quicker than we'd hoped. The dogs just dropped where they'd been standing, barely managed a few low growls in the process. We gave them another half hour though — just to be on the safe side. And then Andy did his real work, the work nobody else had volunteered for. He worked quickly too. Slitting one dog's throat and moving straight on to the next one. He told me later that the trick was to shove the head down towards the chest before you applied the blade. In films, brigands always pulled the head back to cut the throat but actually, Andy claimed, that made the job of deep-cutting harder, not easier.

It went like a dream. Hilary drove us to a spot down on the Crow after we'd made it back to the minivan. A stretch with deep water. Andy chucked the knife in and then the sack. Then Hilary drove us back to the cottage. We made one other stop on the way: the bus shelter on the outskirts of Crowcross which lay in the Colebrook Farm direction. Nowadays you'd die of starvation or exposure waiting for a bus there — but the Crowby and Wynarth Rural Route was still a going concern back then. Oliver leaped out of the van and did some rapid sign-painting while Hilary kept the engine running. *P-E-A-C-E* in nice big letters with a CND symbol and an appropriate message underneath: *Give Up The Dogs of War*.

It was an added risk obviously — but at the time it seemed worth taking. In any case, the Gilberts never went to the police as far as we ever heard. Maybe Charlie talked his old man out of it — frightened maybe (needlessly in my opinion) that the pigs would've also taken a dim view about his own nocturnal activities if they'd got to hear about them. Or maybe, I remember thinking, he planned to get his counter-revenge some other way.

He still lives out here actually, took over the running of the farm when his father died. I like to wander along the right of way across his land now and again. I reckon it must really wind him up. Childish and against all the teaching of Dharma, I know — but he's the one who still snubs and ignores me all these years later if I call into the Crowcross Arms for a pint of beer, still encourages his weak-willed companions to do the same. I've encountered him face to face on his land more than once. But he never says a word, just keeps out of my way, just watches me with his watery, red, unhappy eyes. I've noticed though, my friend, that he keeps his yard dogs muzzled these days.

38

Jacobson drove back early to his own flat on Wellington Drive, cherishing the image of Alison, still fast asleep under the duvet when he'd crept out. He showered, shaved, changed into fresh clothes. He decided to indulge in the luxury of a cab into town and then wished he hadn't. The cab driver had Radio Four on, the *Today* programme. An interview with the Home Secretary — the usual hyped-up alarmist hysteria about 'the security threat' and how to defend liberties by chucking them away. Under the latest legislation, Jacobson knew that, as a senior cop, he could grab practically any innocent bastard off the street and lose the key for weeks on end. It wasn't knowledge he relished — but the worst thing was knowing that there were plenty of others in his position who did relish it. He took his breakfast in the Portuguese café that had opened recently on Silver Street. Good, strong coffee, eggs, bacon, *tostas*. And no politics on the TV — just sports commentary in a language that, happily, he didn't understand, that didn't impede on his thought processes. When he came out, he didn't bother to buy a *Guardian* at the newsagent on the corner the way he sometimes did. He knew that there was no point. He was in the thick of the investigation now, knew that the day wasn't his own to indulge himself in.

He rendezvoused with Kerr in the police car park and they drove out of town towards the old Wynarth Road. The winding, ambling road between Crowby and Wynarth was a sedate locale of imposing old houses with large, expansive leafy gardens set well back from the traffic. Alan Slingsby lived out this way and so did the Chief Constable, 'Dud' Bentham. Their destination, the expensive, upmarket retirement flats complex, had finally opened with a flourish the summer before last. Landscaped eighteenth century gardens and exteriors combined with hi-spec modern facilities and, apparently, high standards of care for those who needed it. They checked in at the reception and a young Polish woman wearing the corporate tracksuit was summoned to escort them to the right place.

The man who'd once been DCI Hunter of Crowby CID was sitting in a comfortable-looking chair on a pleasant little terrace. A quiet area with café-style marble tables and a would-be continental ambience. There was an Italianate fountain nearby where a couple of sparrows were gingerly making their morning ablutions. What Jacobson and Kerr mainly noticed however was the wheeled-in oxygen cylinder at Hunter's side and the little yellow breathing mask that clung — at the ready — to his neck. He shook Jacobson's hand limply, didn't bother to shake Kerr's even though Kerr held it out to him. He'd been a big man but his big, bony hands were practically the only part of him that still gave that impression.

It comes and goes. That had been the doctor's

non-technical verdict when Jacobson had raised him via his mobile en route: *Good days and bad days — frankly good minutes and bad minutes*. Strokes and dementia plus, recently, emphysema had been his slightly more technical summary. Another young woman in another corporate tracksuit brought drinks out to the table. Coffee for Jacobson, tea for Kerr. Nothing for Hunter who had some kind of pale green medical concoction sitting neglected in front of him. Jacobson had assumed that Hunter had still been living out in Spain and then, last night in the canteen queue, DCI 'Clean' Harry Fields had mentioned he'd been back in the area the last few years. He'd been in some old-style nursing home in Wynarth before the new, posh place had opened. He'd gone ga-ga somewhere out in Valencia, according to Fields, had taken to wandering into the local Plaça Mayor without his trousers on, amongst other problems. His only son (who lived in Australia) had shipped him back to Crowby but hadn't lingered once the job had been done.

'As ye sow, so shall ye reap,' Bible-thumping Fields had commented, typically.

Jacobson said who he was three times, thought he caught a glimmer of recognition on the final iteration.

'Frank Jacobson, DCI,' he repeated again, 'I used to drive for you and DS Irvine.'

'Wanker Irvine,' Hunter said, 'Willie Wanker Irvine.'

His voice was a croak that you had to strain to hear. His faint smile only seemed to work on the right side of his face.

'I've been reading back into the files about Claire Oldham and Martin Grove. Back in the 1980s. The Crowcross anti-airbase protest. You did him for murder.'

Hunter said nothing for long seconds.

'Jacobson. Podgy Jacobson. Fucking wife had great fucking tits — '

His voice rasped to a halt, and he used his mask, gasping in and out.

'He got promotion later. The new breed. No verbals. No fit ups.'

Jacobson drank his coffee, looked inside himself for a source of natural, human sympathy, found it hard to find any.

'Claire Oldham, Martin Grove,' he repeated.

'Thirty years in the job. I felt some collars,' Hunter whispered.

Just speak in an ordinary way, the doctor had advised. Every now and again, he'd told him, something clicked in. There could still be brief interludes of lucidity.

'Only Grove didn't do it — they proved that when low copy DNA came along,' Jacobson said.

'I had that little shit crapping himself. Little Woodlands toerag.'

'You'd no one else in the frame? No one else at all?'

Jacobson waited but Hunter never answered. He looked lost again, dribbled up some green.

A nurse appeared, lifted the cup of bile-o-ade up to his lips. Hunter managed a few sips, then shook his head, a refusenik, maybe mustering every shred of self-determination he had left.

346

The nurse replaced the cup on the table, checked the oxygen cylinder. Jacobson finished his coffee, sensed that the moment — if it had been a moment — was gone, over and out.

★ ★ ★

Nigel had taken a dip in the Baur Au Lac pool when he'd woken up and then he'd enjoyed a leisurely room-service breakfast. The way things were he felt that a low profile was probably the best order of the day. He still had an hour to kill before he set off for his first business meeting. He phoned his PA, Julie, back in the UK, established, in a discreet, round-about kind of way, that she hadn't passed on to the police the news that he hadn't travelled alone to Zurich. That done, he idled his time with the newspapers. He'd asked for a tabloid as well as his usual English selection, wanted to see the kind of lurid coverage Martin's murder had attracted. The hotel had brought him the *Express*. If their coverage was typical — and why wouldn't it be? — Monday night's shooting had mainly been used as a tag to hang the usual sex-and-drugs Myrtle Cottage story on. All the usual old photographs of photogenic Claire looking beautiful and all the usual old nonsense about the 'free love' anti-establishment commune. They'd even put together a page on some of the old conspiracy theories (*Did MI5 order Claire's death? — see Page Five*). He phoned Andy at the Moevenpick to check that he'd be ready on time. A couple of his scheduled meetings were out in peripheral areas which conveniently justified Andy's chauffeuring presence should anybody official become interested in Nigel's arrangements at that level of detail. The other reason was that he needed to hear Andy's voice, needed to listen to every vowel and intonation, needed to know that he was fully, one hundred per cent sober.

Satisfied, he ended the call. He took a whisky out of the mini-bar, decided there was nothing to stop him calming his own nerves that way, ease himself into the day. No reason whatsoever. He wasn't Andy after all, knew he could completely trust himself to take it or leave it.

Sometimes only a cliché could render the truth of things, Nigel had often thought: his world had fallen apart after Claire had been murdered, had fallen apart in all directions. Unexpectedly, all three of the Crowcross Three had got twelve months each, not the three to six which their lawyers had glibly predicted. In court, they'd run up unluckily against the worst possible kind of judge in a case like theirs: a rancid old fascist who'd forged senility and the politics of Attila the Hun into one, wrinkled, malevolent, sarcastic package. Nigel had served his full year too. He'd got into a couple of rucks in prison, had lost every possible scrap of remission from his sentence. Earlier on, he'd applied for permission to attend Claire's funeral but her family had indicated that they didn't want him there and so his application had been turned down. That day in July (the body had been kept in the mortuary for weeks on end before it had been finally released) was probably the lowest low point of all. Banged up inside while Claire's family subjected her earthly remains to a C of E funeral he knew she would have detested as a convinced atheist. Her family had also succeeded in keeping anybody from the RCV or Myrtle Cottage away from the church. But they hadn't been able to prevent hundreds of CND supporters lining the route to the cemetery or laying hundreds of floral tributes at her graveside. That had been the start of the second wave of the Crowcross protest. Thousands from all over the country came every weekend for the rest of the year and joined hands around the base, many of them carrying posters featuring Claire's most famous photograph.

Myrtle Cottage itself was finished though. Everybody who'd been there at the end melted away in the days and weeks after the murder. Claire's family would probably have served eviction notices on them if it had come to it anyway — but everybody left and saved them the trouble. They all lost contact with each other too. Almost as if the murder had turned the protest into a guilty secret, a shameful history they needed to put behind them. Andy and Hilary had kept on visiting him in prison far longer than most. But then they'd split up and Andy stopped coming. By the time he was finally released, Hilary was the only person from the cottage that he still had any contact with.

The world Nigel came out to was different as well. The IRA attack on the Grand Hotel, Brighton, had hugely strengthened the moral authority of the government, had made them more or less invincible. The Miners' Strike had been totally defeated, more or less starved into the ground, while the general strike that the RCV had hoped for had spectacularly failed to materialise. The first weekend he was out of prison he bought *The Observer* and read about the so-called Battle of the Beanfield, a vicious police assault on New Age travellers that sounded like a re-run of the police riot at Crowcross. Everywhere that Nigel looked, his dreams were as dust. The 'people' were queuing up to buy their council houses and their British Gas shares. The revolution, it was clear, would not be occurring any time soon.

And worst of all he missed Claire and hated Martin. Neither of them had ever worried about fidelity, had viewed it, at least in principle, as a purely bourgeois virtue. He'd slept around a few times and was more or less certain she had too. But the Martin thing — incredibly — had felt different, like she really preferred that scrawny, semi-literate urchin to him. He hadn't believed it when she'd told him it was just a fling, not serious. But that's what she'd said anyway (maybe wanting to sugar the pill while he was in prison) and so that's what he'd told the CID pig when he'd asked. He'd known it would go against Martin in court. But at the time that's what he'd wanted to happen. Everything he'd read, everything that anybody told him, pointed to that skinny bag of bones bad-tripping and battering all of the lovely, beautiful life out of her.

Nigel had just gone back home for a couple of months when he'd first been released, back to his mum and dad's neat, grey council semi, had needed to draw breath, make plans. And another blow had fallen. His dad had woken up one morning, screaming in pain and clutching his guts. Appendicitis, the ambulance driver had told his mum, the hospital would soon get him sorted out. Like hell — it was cancer of course, advanced pancreatic cancer. Nigel had watched his dad die in the local, shitty underfunded NHS hospital. He'd only even had a (dingy) room to himself right at the end. There was no internet then but Nigel had trudged over to the university library in Birmingham a few times, had waded through the international medical journals, picked up news about tests, new drugs, advanced techniques. None of it was available in the UK — and certainly not if you weren't paying.

He knew he'd disappointed his dad in those days, knew as well that his dad had kept his disappointment to himself, had gone on believing in him. His dad (and his mum) had been old-school working class, had believed that 'getting an education' was the way out for their kids, the key to a better future.

'Just let me have your old Bentleys, son,' his dad had liked to joke when he'd come home from a hard day's toil and catch Nigel doing his homework, poring over his schoolbooks.

Nigel would smile at him and carry on studying. It had been a joke that was also meant as serious. Nigel would do well and then his son would do even better than him. That had been his dad's well-intentioned, simple philosophy. Except that Nigel had fucked it up, had caught the revolution bug at university and had ended up strapped without a penny or a future. A no-hope unemployed graduate who'd blown his personal opportunities on behalf of the people: that's how he'd been fixed when his dad was dying. For which sacrifice the people had said thanks but no thanks (hadn't really even said that much).

He'd never turned his back on Marx, never would. The ex-Hegelian had stood the world the right way up, at least in theory. His analysis had been deep and pure, would endure as long as capitalism itself. Where Marx had failed was in his naive nineteenth century optimism that human beings, as presently constructed, were equal to the practical tasks he'd set them. They weren't — not even remotely, were quite often worse (and horrifically so) when they tried than when they didn't bother.

He freshened his breath with mouthwash when he'd finished the whisky and then poured himself some orange juice. Alcohol was fine at the end of a meeting, when you'd sealed the deal, had something to celebrate. But it was bad practice to go in smelling of it. He wandered out onto his balcony, forced himself to actually notice the yachts out on the lake this time — and to feel the warm sun on his skin, smell the fresh air in his nostrils.

He'd made friendships at university that he could still use however. Other young idealists who'd subsequently become less so. Eventually, one of them had helped him into his first professional slot with a minor investment broker. His BSc Econ and his postgraduate experience had looked good on his CV and he'd just lied and disambiguated about everything else. Either he'd lied cleverly enough or his early bosses hadn't given a stuff about who he'd been when they saw what he could do now. This was the wild Eighties after all and Nigel demonstrated a sure, instant golden touch, out-earning his keep from day one. It took him ten years — the rest of the decade and into the Nineties — to reach the very top. Success at that level brought a little journalistic interest but by then his conviction was spent (couldn't be reported) and his radical youth added a bit of colour to any business magazine feature.

He'd maybe thought — back in the heat of grief — that he'd make good, posthumously, on his dad's dream. Marriage. A family. Wealth that would get passed on. But the more she became a memory, the more Claire became an impossible, impeccable rival to any living woman he ever met. He became one of those rich men who relegated women to the realm of accumulative pleasure only — like paintings, fine wines, vintage cars. He looked after his mum though, moved her to the Cotswolds, moved her to Mallorca, then moved her back to her old estate when she grew nostalgic for it. He looked after his brothers and his sister too — and their kids. He helped them all. Money. Connections. Whatever it took.

Tony Blair had come to power, Thatcherism

repeating itself as farce, before he met Andy again — on a cold November evening at Moorgate Underground Station. Nigel had been at a meeting with a Japanese bank around the corner in Finsbury Circus. The meeting had run on late and he'd emerged onto the London streets in the middle of the rush hour. He knew that a cab would take an eternity to get him to his hotel through the snarled-up traffic, even using the bus lanes. So he decided to brave the tube for once. He was buying an *Evening Standard* from the seller at the entrance when he saw an ill-kempt figure staggering in the wrong direction against the tide of humanity sweeping towards the stairs. A drunk or a junkie, some kind of stinking, filthy dosser. He was still struggling precariously when Nigel, newspaper tucked into his briefcase, drew nearer. They were bumping him, jostling him, pushing him out of their way. A piece of inconvenient human garbage. Without really thinking it through, an instinctive action only, Nigel threw out his free arm, pulled him out of harm's way. A drunk — mainly — to judge by the breath. Old manky coat, matted hair and beard. But something familiar nonetheless about the eyes and the face.

He'd got some funny looks from the hotel doormen, had had to fix them with generous, upfront tips. They'd helped him after that, offered use of the service elevator. Nigel had kept him in his suite for the rest of the week, had more or less locked him inside on a couple of occasions. Emergency detox, emergency dry-out. He'd called on professional help too. Doctors, a specialist nurse. A barber, an amenable tailor. That had only been the beginning of course. There'd been a couple of years where Andy's routine was to sober up for a period of weeks or months and then relapse, dive into his next massive bender. Nigel had been persistent though, had approached the problem logically, as if it had been a business challenge. He moved Andy up to Cheshire where he could keep an eye on him, check his progress, eventually he'd invented a job for him. He'd never been sure why he'd gone to all that trouble. Andy was a link with Claire maybe — or he was another one of the charitable projects that somehow kept Nigel right with himself in his own mind, that bridged his past to his present. Like the anonymous donations he'd make from time to time to causes he considered to be sufficiently radical. The Stop the War Coalition, stuff like that. Even, very occasionally, the slumbering embers of the RCV.

39

The call had come in on Jacobson's mobile just as he was clambering into Kerr's passenger seat: DC Ray Williams, out at Crowcross. The Scene of Crime and search teams were packing up there this morning and Williams was acting as CID liaison officer for the final stint.

'It's only a little pond but well-hidden unless you know it's there,' Williams had explained.

But Jacobson had barely been listening by then. He'd asked for the coordinates, repeated them out loud to Kerr and told Williams he was on his way.

Kerr had to use Charlie Gilbert's farm tracks to reach the general area and then, finally, there was no option but to get out and walk. Kerr parked next to the Scene of Crime vans that hadn't been able to navigate the terrain any further either. Gilbert, it turned out, had his own little mini-stretch of woodland on the very edge of his property. Tangled with briar and creepers, not in the best state. A young uniformed PC had been sent out to meet them and they followed him towards the densely packed trees and then towards the area marked off with police tape.

The pond was a natural formation, apparently, fed by underground streams and rivulets that ran down, ultimately, to the lower elevation of the River Crow. Jim Webster was on site, looking pleased with himself.

'I was undecided about trawling this far, Frank. I was going to check with you again,' Webster said. 'But Gilbert was making such a song and dance about whether I had the right or not that I just thought sod him, do it.'

'And do we have the right, old son?'

'Yes, we do. The general authorisations Brian Phelps arranged yesterday cover all outside, open spaces within a three-mile radius of the crime scene — regardless of who owns them.'

Gilbert's mini-wood backed on to Crowcross Wood itself, was separated from it by an ageing rusty stretch of barbed wire and a peeling Keep Out — Private Property sign. Neither of them looked up to the job.

'Tell me we need a diver out here,' Jacobson said, 'that'll screw up Greg Salter's budgets for the month very nicely.'

'No, we don't, I'm afraid, Frank. It's not deep enough for that. You can wade right out, easily enough.'

Jacobson and Kerr watched the search team at work. It looked like fishing really to the untrained eye. They were dredging big nets across from side to side, low in the water. Although there were modern electronics involved too: some kind of submerged motorised camera.

'But you are making this a priority?'

'Of course,' Webster said. 'If these have been chucked here, then there's a possibility the murder weapon's been dumped here too. The team will sift every inch, that's a promise. We'll also look at the possible routes on foot back to the Karen Holt crime scene. There could be fibres, shoe prints, who knows what.'

'These' were the reason Jacobson and Kerr had driven out to take a look. Two laptops, which had been ported carefully into separate evidence bags. Sodden and weed-crusted but otherwise intact. They'd been unearthed by the very first trawl of the pond. One of them was an Apple MacBook, the model that Prakash Mishra had stated Karen Holt had been using in the back of his taxi.

'The route could have been across the farm, though, couldn't it? Instead of coming over from the woodland?' Kerr asked.

'*You're the detective*,' Webster said, his stock automatic-pilot reply. 'But it's definitely the long way round and you'd probably want to drive some of it, which sounds riskier to me. Whereas, via the wood, it's ten minutes on foot from the crime scene if you take the right direction.'

Jacobson moved off to one side, had managed to reach Steve Horton back at the Divisional building. He clamped his phone to his ear. Horton's assessment was different from what he'd been hoping for.

'In the long term, data recovery *could* be possible,' Horton told him. 'Though of what quality is another story. There's no guarantees. If you want to destroy a hard disk, water's very nearly as good as fire. Plus you're looking at sending out to specialised companies, specialised laboratories — and it absolutely won't be quick. The first task is just to dry everything out properly. Even that takes time.'

Jacobson told him to set it up anyway, do

whatever could be done.

They grabbed a word with Charlie Gilbert on their way off the farm. He seemed to have got over the invasion of his property but he denied having seen or heard anything relevant to the discovery.

'We do get stuff dumped in the pond now and then. Even old washing machines occasionally, big stuff like that. Imagine, they must lug them all the way through Crowcross Wood. No offence, but it's always townies — you can bet on it. Eventually I'll get round to electrifying the fence down at that end.'

'None taken,' Jacobson lied.

He'd sent duty CID to take Gilbert's official witness statement yesterday. If Gilbert was in need of an alibi, he hadn't been over-elaborate. He'd been at home all Monday evening with his wife. His son, Liam, had come home around nine o'clock with his girlfriend in tow. All four of them had watched *Shane* on TCM and his son's girlfriend had stayed at the farm overnight. At the moment, Jacobson had no grounds to doubt it — especially as the girlfriend, and the girlfriend's flatmates in Crowby, had confirmed the story. He didn't care for Gilbert — but in the bad old days even Hunter and Irvine had usually had something slightly more convincing than basic dislike to go on when they were sifting their paperwork for suspects.

They headed back to Crowby via Crowcross and Wynarth. The dredging of the pond apart, there'd been no new developments out this way. Precious few developments altogether. It was one of those drives where neither of them said very much, both of them intent on recapping mentally on where exactly the investigation was — and where exactly it needed to be. Jacobson would have wound the passenger window down and lit up a fresh B&H if he'd still been smoking. Instead he made do with winding it down and letting his forearm and fingers dangle in the cool air currents. The weather outside was still hot and sunny, the way it had been all week.

He focused his thoughts on Nigel Copeland. If he could definitely get Copeland out of his mental picture that would be something accomplished, a useful task. DC Phillips had left a message on his desk phone in the middle of the night — well, two AM anyway. He'd sounded dog tired but certain about his results. Phillips had stuck with the Riverside Hotel's CCTV footage until he'd confirmed all the elements of Copeland's version of events. Copeland was caught on camera exiting and returning to the premises on Monday evening just when he'd said he'd done — and his exit and return correlated with his driver taking the Lexus out of the Riverside's parking level and bringing it back later (the hotel had cameras scanning both the entrance and the exit barriers). Copeland was also identifiable as going out and returning earlier in the evening, presumably on foot and alone. The receptionist on duty thought she remembered that too. Copeland had told her he wanted to take a look around the town centre because it had been years since he'd last been here. *Lucky old you*, the receptionist had said she'd told him. Thereafter, the trip to Crowcross apart, nothing — until Copeland checks out Tuesday morning and his driver fetches the Lexus again. Ten forty-two AM according to the camera in the Riverside's main lobby. Pretty much precisely as Copeland had claimed. Phillips had wound up by saying that he was still waiting for Copeland's PA to come back to him with Copeland's driver's details. *I'll chase her again first thing*, he'd said — or words to that effect. The PA had prebooked the hotel rooms so the only information held about the driver in the hotel computer system was minimal. The receptionist hadn't seemed to remember him particularly, according to Phillips. The young DC had done a thorough job though. He'd even found out that Copeland had dined in the restaurant but that the driver had stuck to room service. Phillips had an initial and a name for him as well. A. Smith. *Yes really, sir — A. Smith*, he'd commented at the end of his message.

Jacobson ran his mind across the investigation's extensive series of non-results and pending results. Mick Hume had tracked the cloned-plate Range Rover through the town centre but it had taken a turn somewhere out near Copthorne Road and hadn't surfaced again — and nothing had come in for it so far from Regional Traffic's motorway systems. He'd asked Brian Phelps to ask the uniformeds to get a patrol out to the area, take a closer look around, maybe concentrate their efforts on the old Copthorne Road industrial estate. There were a few private security firms operational over there who might have clocked something overnight — or not, as the case might be. Steve Horton had said he'd work on the new interior images as well as carrying on the search for virtual data storage. *Fine*, Jacobson had told him, trying to sound upbeat. Even just definitively eliminating the latter possibility would be good though, he'd thought — Horton was sounding less and less confident about it so tick it off the sheet and move on.

He needed to check-in with Emma Smith as soon as they got back to base, he reminded himself, find out the latest state of play with the telephone records analysis. Probably that wasn't looking too hopeful either. If something really significant had come to light, he knew that Smith would have flagged it up with him instantly — and she hadn't. DC Smith was 'pro-active' in the jargon — or not a useless, gormless idiot, in unreconstructed Jacobsonese.

★ ★ ★

DS Kerr took the main stairs up to the incident room on the fourth floor, leaving Jacobson behind waiting for the lift. He caught up with him again in the corridor just outside, followed him in. Brian Phelps waved a telephone receiver at Kerr as soon as he caught sight of him. A call had just come in for him on the main incident room number, Phelps explained: Barry Vine, phoning from Oakfield Open Prison.

Kerr found the nearest free handset and

Phelps transferred the call.

'I was thinking about our conversation yesterday,' Vine said, 'I've also got a mate — I won't say who — who's working on your force these days. A Community Service Officer? We just happened to be talking last night.'

'OK, right, I see,' Kerr said, not seeing at all — but assuming Vine was going somewhere with his preamble, hadn't just called a major inquiry line for the sake it.

'My mate's heard a rumour about Martin and the other murder victim — that there was some kind of mutilation as well as the shootings?'

The mutilation aspect had been kept strictly under wraps. It was the classic kind of restricted detail that no sensible investigator ever released to the public, mid-inquiry, without a very good reason to do so. But inside the force itself, restricted details had a way of circulating far beyond the official need-to-know list.

'I can't really comment on that, Barry,' Kerr said evenly.

'Fair enough,' Vine replied. 'I didn't really expect you to. But I was wondering how familiar you are with the all the details about the Boland riot? It was a good few years ago now after all.'

'Three dead — nobody charged for it. I know more since I talked to you yesterday than I remembered before that.'

Kerr fidgeted with a box of ink-jet paper on a nearby empty desk, sensed that Vine was building up to something.

'The thing is this,' Vine said finally. 'One of the two sex offenders was also a long-term grass, according to the rioters. After he was dead, they cut a slice right off his tongue to make that point clear. I just thought you might want to know about that — in case you didn't know about it already.'

40

DS Barber drummed his fingers on his desk while he tried to work out whether it was worth sticking with the call or not. Bridge Street West, the relevant local nick, had put him on hold — for how long was anybody's guess.

Colin Dobell was good for something, he was sure about that much at any rate — if only because since Monday night he'd gone to ground, vanished, vamoosed. His Lozells address had checked out when Barber had called round there last night with a uniformed patrol back-up. A flat near Villa Road. They'd trod warily. Lozells had its other sides, to be fair, but it was indisputably an area of racial tensions, street crime, poverty-inspired scams and aggravation. The woman who said she was Dobell's girlfriend had been off her face. Laughing one minute, hysterical the next. The best sense that Barber had got out of her was that Colin was away on 'business'. What kind of business or where had got the response that she wasn't his keeper. That much had been all too evident. If there was any keeping going on it was all in the other direction. And Dobell's track record made him a very nasty keeper indeed. There'd been a cut above the woman's left eyelid. Bruised, purple, probably of fairly recent origin. Barber had resorted to threatening her with the drug squad but she hadn't given a shit about that, hadn't batted either her bruised eyelid or her other one — was obviously a lot more frightened of the absent Dobell than she'd ever be of the drug police.

He'd called in to the local station next, had studied the local CID intelligence sheet on his target. Known associates, known hangouts, suspected involvements. Given Dobell's PNC entry, it had all seemed surprisingly sparse. Then Barber had disturbed a local DI at home. When the DI had finally stopped whingeing about missing *The Apprentice* he'd given Barber the lowdown. Dobell was still a toerag all right but he'd kept a low profile locally since his release, seemed to have learned something at least inside: the value of not shitting in your own backyard. Barber had tried a few obvious hangouts after that — had been met with the full-on stonewalling he'd anticipated. Then he'd had a spot of luck. The DI had leaned on his sergeant to have a word with a 'source': an unofficial, unregistered local informer the DI had claimed was 'eighty per cent' reliable. The eighty per cent reliable story was that Dobell liked to drink out of the area as well these days, was a regular at a pub over in Aston. 'A real regular' according to the source. As in seven nights a week and a member of the darts team. He'd been there on Sunday night apparently — but he hadn't been seen once since.

Barber decided to stick with the call. He scanned down his computer screen while he waited, spell-checked the Context Report he'd put together on Karen Holt. He was just saving the document when his phone came back to life:

the Lozells DI from the night before.

'Well, it could be Dobell,' the DI said, referring to the Range Rover interior shot from Flowers Street in Crowby, which, as of five minutes ago, had been uploaded onto the National Alert Image System. 'But, to be honest, it could be anybody, couldn't it? It could be you or me once we've zipped up a jacket collar and pulled a baseball cap right down over our face.'

'You're happy he's not on your patch though?' Barber asked.

'I'd be happy if he never came back, mate — but he's not anywhere I'd expect him to be. We've put a team onto it for the rest of the day — a DC and a couple of uniformeds. If he's around at all, they'll find him out.'

The DI had mentioned Gerry Quigg in passing last night. Barber wanted to quiz him on the topic while he had the chance.

'That was years ago, mate. Before my time really. But what I've heard is that friend Dobell was entry-level in Quigg's organisation for a spell. Not for long though. Quigg likes them smart not just violent. Dobell didn't have the right stuff, didn't make the grade.'

Barber mentioned Karen Holt, how Mott Legal Investigations were currently under contract to Quigg's defence solicitors.

'I'd see that as coincidence, plain and simple. Just about anything criminal anywhere in the Midlands and there's going to be some connection to Concrete Gerry, *n'est-ce-pas?* It's your six degrees of separation, mate. From what you're saying, and what they're saying over in

367

Crowby, I'd put Dobell down as on a one-man mission. Grove's fucked him over by testifying about the Boland riot and now that he's finally got out, Dobell's gone looking for his revenge. Supposing Dobell was one of the Boland killers, there could be a shut-Grove's-big-fat-mouth motive as well.'

Barber re-opened the document again, thought it could be worth adding the DI's comments before he sent it.

'You could see Dobell for that? The prison killings?'

'He's mean enough. The only thing I'm not liking here is the vehicle. A Range Rover? That just doesn't smell entirely right. Not for Colin Dobell.'

Barber thanked him, ended the call. He typed a new paragraph at the end of his report then did a quick re-check from page one. The SOCOs had found no evidence that Karen Holt's flat had been done over — and nothing had really been found there that didn't fall under the rubric of irrelevant personal effects and possessions. The neighbours (the ones who knew her anyway) had had nothing suspicious to tell duty CID when they'd called by. The standard heard-nothing, seen-nothing routine. The most useful thing Barber had done personally had been to speak to her co-workers at Mott Legal Investigations. He'd played up his city 'tec credentials while he'd been snooping around the MLI offices, had got himself invited along, easily enough, to an after-work drinks session in Broad Street. Most private investigators were ex-job and most private investigators were keen on cultivating CID contacts and picking up CID gossip. They'd all been in that strange near-party mood where bad, tragic news makes you that little bit reckless, more determined than normal to squeeze every second out of life.

It turned out that they all knew about her moonlighting arrangement with Martin Grove (everybody except their boss, Michael Mott, knew about it apparently). Mott had declined to take Grove on as an official client a while back. But then, earlier this year, Grove had approached a few MLI employees directly and personally. Karen had been the only one interested. Even then they didn't think she'd done all that much for him. Mainly just reviewed Mott's old case records and files on the QT. When she'd visited Grove out at Crowcross on Monday evening, the consensus was that it had probably been for the first time.

Barber re-saved his document, attached it to a brief email and pasted in a destination address and header: CROWBY MAJOR INCIDENT ROOM TWO, FAO DCI JACOBSON / DS KERR. He'd asked the PIs why they thought Karen had taken on the extra, non-contractual work. The best answer he'd got was that she was bored. PI work hadn't lived up to her expectations, had been too much like any tedious attention-to-detail office job than she'd imagined it would be. A woman called Fiona, who seemed to have known her best, told Barber that she thought Karen was planning to leave and go back to her old occupation as a journalist. *If she'd got anywhere with the Martin Grove thing, that could have been a real scoop couldn't it? Maybe put her into the big league.*

He hit send. He'd managed not to make the obvious bad taste remark to her friend that she'd made nearly all the front pages anyway. TV and radio too.

★   ★   ★

Jacobson retreated to his office. Down in the incident room, the chances were that most of the CID present aspired to the role he played, occupied, in major cases like this one. The Senior Investigating Officer. The big cheese. The caller of shots. But there were intervals in any big investigation where Jacobson knew that for a specific stretch of time — ten minutes, an hour, half a day — the SIO was the most expendable member of the team. Once you'd established your lines of inquiry there were interludes where all you could really do was to let the deployed officers get on with their allocated tasks — and hope that you'd deployed them wisely, that they'd come back to you with useful results. Even more so when the current major line of inquiry was no longer local — not even mainly. Colin Dobell had no links or connections into the Crowby area. If he was their man, he'd come here solely to get his business done. He was unlikely to have hung around afterwards. Similarly, there wasn't a sign of him back in his home area. A guy like Dobell, long years inside, would have forged bonds and associations right across the country. There'd be debts he could collect on, favours he

370

could call in. Dobell, basically, could be anywhere. To an extent all Jacobson could do was sit and wait — and hope that somewhere out there a smart copper would see something worth seeing and act on it.

To justify his existence, he dotted a few i's, crossed a few t's. He checked with Brian Phelps that a uniformed patrol was over in the Copthorne Road area, as he'd requested, knocking on doors and looking out for any sign of the cloned-plate Range Rover. Phelps told him that it was, even patched him through to the patrol car. No luck yet, the patrol's non-driver told him, maybe surprised to get a direct call from the DCI in charge. It was a long throw anyway, Jacobson thought. There were devices now you could fit in-car that would plot you minimal camera routes in and out of built-up areas. The Rover could have been using one of those, could have detoured through the Copthorne area just for that simple reason. He found a scrap of A4, jotted down a quick tick-off list.

HILARY ~~WATSON WILLIAMS~~ NO WATSON
   — GIVES GROVE'S PHONE NO TO N COPELAND
   ACCORDING TO N COPELAND
KAREN HOLT CAB DRIVER
KAREN HOLT CLIO

He called Phelps again — found out which duty DC was currently doing what. Every allocated task was logged — eventually — in the Inquiry Management System: process, outcome, summary. But Jacobson liked to chase up the little details when they occurred to him. Sometimes he knew he was just being pernickety. Other times he sensed his subconscious kicking in, trying to tell him something.

Both Nigel Copeland's story about Hilary Watson and the whereabouts of the cab driver, Prakash Mishra, after he'd dropped off Karen Holt, checked out so far. Jacobson raised the DC who'd phoned Hilary Watson last night. She'd confirmed to him that Copeland had rang her a month or so ago, had asked her for Martin Grove's contact details. She was a Senior Social Worker for Highbury and Islington Council these days, according to the DC. Married to a doctor. Mother of two grown-up children.

'Doesn't surprise me, old son,' Jacobson commented, ending the call, 'probably drives a hybrid car into the bargain — and only buys undrinkable organic wine.'

The sarcasm didn't save him from a pang of memory though. Claire Oldham bloody, wet and dead. Sicking up down his shirt front. The rain pounding on the leaves of the trees. Claire might have been a mother now too — or a teacher, an artist, even just a useless rich bitch. But something alive anyway. Something warm to the touch and human.

The Bridge Cars fares log tallied with the times and routes Mishra had itemised to DS Kerr. Duty CID had traced all of his subsequent passengers. Every piece of data correlated the way it should. He checked the Clio situation from two angles. One of Jim Webster's Senior SOCOs confirmed that all the proper forensic tests had been carried out. It was probably only theoretically possible, Jacobson thought, that Karen Holt's killer or killers had had any contact with her car prior to the murders. But you checked everything, took nothing for granted — or you ended up back with DCI Hunter's fatal, indolent mixture of gut-feeling and prejudice. The other angle was the CID one. According to the IMS entry on Jacobson's computer screen, DS Kerr had called in at the vehicle workshop last night, had inspected the contents of the car in case there was anything of relevance, had decided that there wasn't. Kerr must have checked it out before he'd gone home. He hadn't mentioned the fact that Jacobson could recall — probably because it had been a non-result. Somebody (probably not Kerr) had even logged a list of contents and given the list a reference number. Jacobson drew the line at following the audit trail any further than that. If Kerr wasn't reliable, the entire game was up.

He'd brought another boxfile of Claire Oldham paperwork up with him. If the tongue mutilation detail was really as telling as it was now starting to look then maybe he needn't have bothered. But he'd brought all this stuff out of storage. It seemed a pity to send it all back without even taking a peek. He had bog all else to do anyway — until one of his phones went off again and brought him the next, fresh development.

He read into the afternoon, only breaking off at lunchtime to eat an uninspired, lukewarm lasagne in the canteen. Kerr had gone back out to Crowcross, had said that he wanted to take another good look at Martin Grove's property before the police guard out there ended its final shift. Not for any particular reason, Jacobson realised. Like himself, Kerr just needed the illusion that he was doing something useful. Maureen Bright had been told she could move back into her home this evening, assuming she could face it. Victim Support had offered her a personal support worker. Predictably, she'd told them to stuff it.

Hunter's murder investigation, as revealed by the yellowing paperwork, was a dismal classic of bad police work. His chief suspect (effectively, his only suspect) had come straight to him on a plate: wild-eyed and covered in dead blood from the murder scene. AB blood at that, the rarest group for British caucasians. Hunter had barely looked elsewhere. He'd gone through the motions only because he knew that he had to. He'd taken rudimentary statements from everybody else who'd been living out at Myrtle Cottage, had asked them where they'd been all day and what they'd been doing, had pretty much accepted what they'd told his detectives at face value. The same was true of the statements he'd taken from the security guards at the airfield and from the local farmers and villagers.

Jacobson knew that some of the statements had been challenged by Grove's supporters and by his defence team over the years. But they'd never come up with anything that would count as new or significant for the appeal courts and, with every year that had passed, it became more and more difficult to prove or disprove anything. Throughout the Nineties, the defence hope — if hope wasn't too sick a term in the circumstances — lay with an item of Claire Oldham's clothing which had been preserved amongst the original evidence and which bore minute traces of semen from her attacker. The sample had been far too small for the early days of DNA analysis. The defence had to wait for the development of low copy number techniques right at the very end of the decade to achieve the result they needed: a low copy DNA profile which excluded Martin Grove as its possible genetic source.

Jacobson yawned, stretched, thought about strong, black coffee. The profile was lodged in the FSS-maintained database — would force the case to be re-opened if a potential match was ever triggered.

41

Mid-afternoon, his final appointment of the day ended, Nigel took a walk up to the Lindenhof, the leafy square at the heart of the old town with views over the River Limmat. He wanted to clear his head from numbers, share values, profit margins. It was quieter than he'd expected. Just a few chess players and a few camera-snapping tourists.

He sat down on a bench, took stock. Saskia had called him earlier from New York. She'd sounded sleepy but witlessly full of her stories about shopping, restaurants, galleries. Rula (her sister) said this, wanted that. Rula wanted that, said this. He'd listened patiently until the torrent had run its course. Saskia was a nice girl really, had a good heart. In a year or so, she'd move on, find somebody younger, more serious about her, more committed. Nigel didn't think that would trouble him when it happened, even thought it might actually come as some kind of relief.

It had cheered him all the same to hear her voice, her lilting enthusiasm for everything and everybody. He was starting to relax his guard a fraction maybe. He'd heard no more from the police and there'd been no whisper of his name when he'd caught a news item about the story on BBC World. Maybe he'd panicked, over-reacted. But so what? He'd done some useful business earlier — the trip had hardly been wasted. When Andy had been dropping him off, he'd told Nigel that he was going to hit Langstrasse later, meaning that he was heading over to the red light district, was planning on renting a whore for an hour or two.

'Enjoy,' Nigel had told him, more or less meaning it. Andy had been morose all week — maybe a hooker would set him right again. Andy had been stand-up sober for three years now, the longest stretch he'd ever achieved since Nigel had plucked him from the streets. He didn't like the moroseness — knew it had been a bad signal in the past, an indicator. He preferred Andy garrulous, spouting any old bullshit nonsense. The Martin thing had got to him. It must have done. It had got to both of them on some level. To meet up like that and then to hear the very next day that he'd been shot dead.

Martin had been looking good, Nigel had thought. He was older, obviously, forty plus, but there had still been something boyish about him, something spirited and keen. That had surprised him. He'd expected bitterness, or resignation at best, but the new Martin didn't seem to be like that. He was intense, hard work, no question. But instantly you felt you were in the presence of somebody worth knowing, somebody who could teach you something. Martin had journeyed in one of the darkest places imaginable — an innocent man on a life sentence — and he'd survived, come through. He hadn't broken in pieces, hadn't lost his mind. The worst that anybody could say about him, and it wasn't much, was that he'd had a little wild time when he'd first got out of prison. He'd talked to them about that in fact: the women, the drugs, the boozing. He'd called it his 'extra-time youth'. At one point he'd referred to it as his 'tantric phase': *seeking the sacred in the profane*. From Martin's lips, somehow the words didn't sound remotely laughable or pretentious.

They'd talked a lot about the old days, a lot less about his years in prison. He'd told them about HMP Boland though, the riots that happened there. He'd seemed to especially want to talk about that, as if it had been currently on his mind. *I know who did it, I know all of them,* he'd said. He'd said what they'd done too, ghastly details that had never been made public, like cutting a piece of the tongue off one of them. *Jesus, Martin,* Nigel had asked him, *you're not going to name them now surely?*

He'd already mentioned his writing by then, how it was his main daily activity, how he wanted to set the record straight, tell his side of the story.

'I don't know, Nigel. Somebody let me rot inside for the thing that they did, lived with that guilt. What does it make me if I turn a blind eye in the same way?'

It's not the same though, is it? Nigel had argued back. *Nobody else is doing time for it, nobody else is having their life stolen from them.*

Two tourists interrupted him. A couple. Americans, young, smiling. He took the proffered camera phone from the man, snapped them holding hands under a Linden tree. He took three shots so they could select the best one to send home.

Martin had talked a little about his girlfriend. Maureen. That had been good to hear about. Really good. A real connection. Something that had rooted him, kept him solid. He'd been surprised to see Andy of course, that was obvious. He hadn't recognised him at first, had seemed genuinely sorry to hear about how it had all gone wrong for him after the demise of Myrtle Cottage. He'd heard bits from Hilary. But not much, not the whole story. Andy gave it to him: breaking up with Hilary then drifting around again, casual job to casual job. And always, always drinking — more and more and more until he'd hit the proverbial, inevitable rock bottom. *There was nothing after Myrtle, mate, not even rice wine*, Andy had said (profoundly for him), *all the good times were strictly in the past, all the hope too.*

The private detective had turned up just as Nigel and Andy were leaving. Martin had asked them earlier if she could interview them sometime. Separately and individually would be best. Nigel had told him he'd have to think about that and Andy had said something much the same. Nigel had pointed out that he'd been in prison himself at the time anyway, banged up on remand.

'That doesn't matter, Nigel. There might still be some detail you remember that's been overlooked all these years. Something that helps. Karen agrees with me that the police interviews are complete rubbish. She reckons we need to talk to everybody who was living at the cottage again. Somebody saw something or knows something. That's just common sense. The pigs never asked the right questions at the time. They'd no incentive to, Hunter saw to that. And there's DNA now, don't forget, a low copy profile.'

Nigel had asked him why he was bothering. His final question before they'd finally left, finally set off back to their hotel in Crowby. After all, Martin was free now. He had his education, his new life. So why the hell was he wasting his time on the past? He couldn't unravel it, couldn't alter it.

'The truth is all there is, Nigel. Interpreting the world first, changing it second. That's what kept me going — more than study did, more than meditation. Knowing that one day I'd have the truth about who it was that killed Claire and then let me take the blame. The truth of it — simple or complex.'

⋆   ⋆   ⋆

Kerr's phone hadn't gone off in a while, nobody had been chasing him. All the same, he'd probably spent long enough out here. After he'd looked inside Martin Grove's house — and noticed nothing that he hadn't noticed before (or nothing that seemed important anyway) — he'd decided to walk the territory. None of the distances involved were huge, not even on foot. Grove had kept a battered, well-used Ordnance Survey map of the area in his front room — on a shelf where he'd also stacked other walking maps. The Brecon Beacons, the South

380

Coast Way, the Lake District. Opening Grove's map up before he'd set off, Kerr had realised that, if you wanted to, you could impose a loose isosceles triangle on the immediate landscape. There were three apex points: Grove's house, Myrtle Cottage, and the specific point in Crowcross Wood where Claire Oldham and Karen Holt had both been found dead a quarter of a century apart.

He'd tested the theory out, even timed himself. You could stroll from any one of the three points to any of the other two inside an easy ten minutes. He didn't actually try running, didn't see a need. But running would halve the time, roughly, for anybody in reasonable physical shape. From either Grove's place or Myrtle Cottage, you had to reach the wood first if you wanted to get to Crowcross village, the nearest encroachment of civilisation.

He was actually inside the cottage now, poking around, careful where he put his feet, keeping a wary eye on what remained of the roof. It had crumbled and collapsed in one section and an entire chunk of the upstairs had fallen with it. As far as Kerr could work out, the remains of the kitchen must be somewhere under the resulting rubble. He was standing in front of the narrow stairs that led down to the basement. A woodwormed door had fallen off its hinges barring the way. It didn't matter — Kerr had no intention of risking it. If there was ever a good reason for anybody to descend down there, they'd need to be in the company of safety experts who knew exactly what they were doing.

He retraced his steps and came out into what had once been the front garden. Nature had claimed it back a long time ago. Wild flowers, couch grass, tall weeds. He didn't know what he'd been expecting to see here really. Maybe an ancient slice of graffiti or a peace symbol carved somewhere into the stonework. Some lingering trace of Martin Grove or Claire Oldham or their friends from years ago. But he'd found nothing like that. He'd found nothing more recent either. No signs of rough sleepers or kids fooling around with beer cans, condoms, cider bottles. The cottage was too remote maybe — or just too plain dangerous-looking to attract those kinds of attention.

The side of the triangle that got you to Crowcross Wood from the cottage ran past the old airfield for part of the way. When the perimeter fence had been here, you'd have needed to keep to the lane. Nowadays you could cut straight across the disintegrating runways if you felt like it. Absolutely nobody was going to stop you if you did. The land still belonged to the MOD of course. Mick Hume had picked up a local rumour in the Crowcross Arms the other night and had passed it on to Kerr: the MOD were looking to *sell* — if they could sort out the planning issues and get a housing developer interested. The modern locals weren't keen apparently. *Not In My Back Yard* etcetera, Hume had told him.

Still no messages on his phone. For a further, idle moment he watched a rook preening its feathers on the falling-down garden wall. Then he set off again. He'd moved his car off Grove's driveway and parked it on the road outside to avoid any possible complications. The police guard (one bored looking junior PC) was standing down in the next half-hour or so. After that Grove's property would no longer be an active crime scene and, strictly speaking, Kerr would have no more right to park on the drive than any other uninvited member of the public.

He climbed in and turned the ignition. He wanted to get going before Maureen Bright showed up with her overnight bag and her sad, accusing eyes.

42

Jacobson had finally got to *A. Smith*. Somebody in DCI Hunter's team had compiled a Related and Previous Convictions List. They'd taken the names of everybody living out at Myrtle Cottage at the time of the murder and checked whether any of them had form. A painstaking task back in the days before on-line databases and national computer networks. The results were pretty low-key. Affray, mostly in relation to political demonstrations, was the biggest category. Plus a few cannabis busts, traffic offences, minor breaches of the peace. Andrew Smith stood out on the list because he'd done Borstal and because he had more convictions than his nearest rival by a big margin. Burglaries and car thefts mainly. Lucky for him, Jacobson had thought, that Hunter had latched so quickly on to Martin Grove as his suspect, hadn't needed another promising candidate for a stitch-up.

Even then the name had hardly sung out to him. The world was full of *A. Smiths*, absolutely crawling with them. *B. Smiths*, *C. Smiths*, *D. Smiths* likewise. But years of automatically cross-referencing information as a matter of course had imprinted that behaviour on Jacobson's mental circuitry. Especially since, in this case, DC Phillips had emailed him the employer's record of Nigel Copeland's driver within ten minutes of Jacobson scanning the

384

ancient list. That had been the stroke of luck maybe. If Nigel Copeland's PA had forwarded the details to DC Phillips when he'd originally asked for them, *A. Smith* might have been buried in Jacobson's memory by then, shovelled under a pile of subsequent inquiry data. Instead, virtually before his brain knew it, Jacobson's eye had registered the first big coincidence: identical dates of birth. He'd gone to the police-DVLA link after that, using Smith's current home address as the marker, had discovered an identical place of birth too. All he'd done then was make two telephone calls.

He'd phoned Hilary Watson, pulled her out of a social workers' case conference, discovered that her long-ago boyfriend was now Nigel Copeland's recovering-alcoholic protégé. Then he'd phoned Nigel Copeland's PA directly, wanting to know where Andrew Smith was while Copeland was out of the country. The PA had given him the honest answer.

'Prat,' Jacobson had thought out loud when he'd come off the phone, meaning Copeland.

He wasn't an idiot, that much was clear. Yet he'd acted like one by failing to mention who his driver was. Prakash Mishra had statemented that he'd seen a Lexus in Martin Grove's driveway — he'd said bog-all about a cap-doffing chauffeur sitting patiently behind the wheel. Smith had been *inside* the house, sharing his boss's reunion with Martin Grove. Why wouldn't he? That made Smith's DNA and prints essential for forensic elimination: just as essential as Copeland's. The whole thing probably amounted to obstruction if Jacobson decided to push it in that direction.

'Prat,' he thought out loud a second time.

He fumed for five minutes, got it out of his system. Then, nearly calm, he checked in his notebook and dialled the contact he'd been given at Zurich's central police station: Inspector Wilhelm Herzog. He needed Herzog to arrange for Smith's samples to be taken. He also needed him to set up further on-the-record video link sessions. Smith on his own — and then a second interview with Copeland.

Herzog wasn't instantly available but he returned Jacobson's call inside ten minutes, swiftly agreed the requests. Ideally, Jacobson knew he'd sleep easier if Copeland and his faithful retainer were under discreet surveillance for the time being — but he also knew he'd no legal right to ask. Not without the self-defeating prospect of whole days filled with time-consuming paperwork and authorisations. He decided he'd nothing to lose by sounding Herzog out on the matter.

The Swiss listened and then laughed. He told Jacobson that Copeland was being informally watched anyway. On Herzog's orders — and under an appropriate canton statute.

'This is a murder inquiry, no? Always best to know where people are.'

Jacobson said thanks, meaning it, ended the call. He redialled, reached Kerr on his mobile and brought him up to speed. Then he walked downstairs to the incident room.

Emma Smith waved him over to her desk. He

saw something urgent in her expression. She'd been about to put a handset down, end a conversation. But now she was passing it to him, signalling that he definitely needed to speak to whoever was on the line.

He listened intently. A few minutes in, he started making notes. When he was done, he walked to the front of the room where the whiteboard was, made sure he got all their attention by tapping at it with the bottom end of a marker pen — hard.

43

Martin Grove.doc

May the Fifth. A Thursday. That's when Claire was killed. When they drove me into the old police station in Wynarth later that evening, I didn't know that I was about to become a captive of the state, held at its whim, for the next two decades. *[note: maybe too heavy on the melodrama. Never mind, can change later. First importance: set it all down]*

Claire had driven over to Wolverhampton in the afternoon. She'd received a visiting order to see Nigel in his remand prison. There'd been no comeback to our nocturnal adventure over on Colebrook Farm but the general mood remained pretty gloomy. There was uncertainty about the future, a feeling that maybe Myrtle Cottage had run its course as a rallying point. Claire didn't confide the inner workings of the RCV even to me but she'd hinted that the central committee had the protest under review, were maybe less enthusiastic about its value as an agitprop exercise than they'd been at the start. That might have been one of the things she was planning to talk to Nigel about when she saw him.

There were fewer than ten of us in residence by then, all told. Oliver was still strolling across the freedom field with his guitar strapped over his shoulders, lost in composition. Andy was still brewing up copious amounts of his potent rice wine. Hilary was still around too, although she was also spending more and more time back at the Polytechnic in Crowby. The reason she gave was her impending summer examinations. But I can remember thinking that maybe Andy and Hilary weren't quite as tight an item as they'd been in the past. Personally, I was still walking on air. I'd moved into Claire's room by now and taken my stuff, what there was of it, out of the basement. I was worried of course about what would happen if the protest did end. But Claire had told me to remember that the cottage was her home. *Even if the protest does pack up, we don't have to go anywhere else, Martin — unless we want to.*

She gave me a lift into town in the MG on her way over to Wolverhampton. It was my signing-on day. After I'd signed on, I was planning to visit my mum out at the Woodlands estate. She was doing early morning office cleaning at that particular time, was usually at home in the afternoons. Everybody else out at the cottage had already gone into Crowby as far as I knew. There was a pro-miners rally planned outside the Town Hall at lunchtime and they'd gone in to lend support. Leafleting before the event and then fundraising in the afternoon, roaming the town centre with plastic buckets and giving out 'coal not dole' stickers to anybody prepared to take one.

Claire dropped me off on Market Street. She kissed me and I hopped out, watched her go, leaving me. She smiled at me and waved and then nipped smoothly into a gap in the stream of traffic, The Specials blaring on her tape deck: 'A Message To You, Rudy'. At least she was smiling, happy. One final good memory.

I stayed longer than I'd intended at my mum's. She was pleased to see me, the way she always was, and it was always difficult to leave. I was old enough by then to understand that her life was on the lonely side and that she'd learned to bear it. She was brave, my mum — proved that a thousand times later, speaking up for me, petitioning for me, keeping going when others would have faltered, given up.

It was a two-bus ride to get back to the cottage. From the Woodlands back into Crowby and then the rural bus back out to Crowcross via Wynarth. I missed the connection at the bus station, had to wait twenty-five minutes for the next bus. The nearest stop for Myrtle Cottage was the bus shelter near Colebrook Farm, the one we'd graffiti-ed the night we'd settled the score with Charlie Gilbert. I don't actually remember the time I got off the bus but according to the route timetable (yes of course I got hold of a copy later) that particular bus would have dropped me off at around six, which sees me back at Myrtle Cottage no later than a quarter past.

Claire's MG was parked in the lane and so was Nigel's minivan, which some of them had used to get into Crowby for the miners' rally. I wasn't remotely surprised, I was expecting that by then everybody else would be back at the cottage. It must have been a few more minutes after that before I realised that Claire wasn't in her room or anywhere else obvious. Andy, Oliver, a few others, were in the kitchen. I asked them if they'd seen her. Oliver told me she'd gone off for a walk in the wood after she'd got back from Wolverhampton. He told me he didn't reckon that she'd been gone for long. It wasn't until the trial, months later, that I discovered Oliver had passed on second-hand information. The one who'd actually seen Claire head off to the woods was Andy, who'd called off from going into town at the last minute, had spent the day at the cottage mucking around with his demijohns.

The prosecuting barrister wiped the floor with Andy's testimony and with Oliver's. There were others who'd made similar witness statements but who weren't summoned to give evidence. Their statements were trashed too. The prosecution argument was that they were all lying to protect me, lying to introduce an element of uncertainty when really the case was simple. I'd gone with Claire to the wood. She'd told me she was going back to Nigel — and I'd killed her for it. After all that was what my confession stated. Why had I signed it if it wasn't the truth? When the defence raised the issue of the missing murder weapon, the confession had an answer for that too: I couldn't remember what I'd used or where I'd concealed it because I was tripping out on acid at the time. The police forensic experts had 'proved' that from the analysis of the urine sample I'd given (along with a blood sample) when I'd been arrested. I had been tripping that week it was true. I was nineteen, right? Still experimenting with life. But not on the Thursday. The defence had pointed out that the detection period for LSD via urine tests can be up to three days at normal dosages. But nobody was interested in that. Least of all the jury. The damage had been done to the way they saw me. I was an out-of-control drug fiend living in a commune, evidently I was more than capable of rape and murder.

It took me half an hour to find her, I think. Something like that. The place where she'd been killed wasn't far from the road or the cottage. But it wasn't one of our favourite parts of the wood, wasn't where I'd expected her to go walking. The sky had turned an evil grey by the time I discovered her and, in my memory of it anyway, the heavy rain started to belt down almost the moment I clapped eyes on her. I knew she was dead, just knew it, although I'd never seen a dead body before. I held her anyway. Held her in my arms, rocking her back and forth. Then laying my head on her breasts, willing her to breathe, willing her still to be warm.

Hunter and Irvine kept on at me later about why I'd run all the way into Crowcross and used the telephone box on the village green instead of going back and using the phone in the cottage which was much closer to where the body was. They kept on about it like it was an admission of guilt in itself. The truth was that at first when I left her I was running away, running away from what I'd found. The direction didn't matter, I just wanted to run, I just wanted to blank it out. When that feeling passed I'd very nearly reached

Crowcross. They couldn't get that, couldn't see that. I'd phoned as soon as I was able to — and from the nearest phone to hand.

I was nineteen, right? Yes, I know, my friend, it's my boring old mantra, you're hearing it every few pages. But it's true — I was. Hunter and Irvine terrified me. They told me they'd lock me up and throw away the key, told me that the police had secret prisons all over the country, where they could 'disappear' little bastards like me whenever they wanted — and for as long as they wanted. It was just like Pinochet's Chile, they told me — rape and torture cells. It was ludicrous, laughable, absurd. But I was a frightened, terrified kid. I really was. I'd just found the one good thing that had ever happened to me lying dead with her face pummelled out of recognition and her clothes ripped and torn. Hunter was a bastard but he was good at it — he could read what made people tick, what scared them, what frightened them. There was physical stuff too. Of course there was. Slapping, punching, shouting. Long interviews where I'd no chair provided and I had to stand the whole time while they sat lounging (Sounds mild? You try it, my friend.) Sleep deprivation too — all the old tricks. But it was the disappearing thing that got to me, that got under my skin. My only way out was to confess, that's what they made me believe in the end. Hunter turned nice guy at that point. The confession was all they needed, all they wanted. They'd have done their job then and they could both go home. As for me, I didn't need to worry about it either. I could retract it all in court. It didn't mean anything. It was nothing. Look, get the lad a cola or something, Mr Irvine. Relax, Martin, we'll help you with what to put, what to write, then this whole thing will be over.

I was angry about it for years, smashing up cells, smearing my shit on the walls. Then anger turned to shame that I'd been so easily broken, so easily pulled apart and dismantled. Shame was worse than anger. I was a ghost then for a long time. A figure that shuffled in queues, ate, slept — but with no spirit inside, no hope. You can delve deeper than that though if you've nothing better to do during long days and long nights. You can reach the place hidden inside that's pure, inviolable. And when you finally connect to that, you can come to life again, come all the way back.

Karen Holt wants to look at all the Myrtle Cottage testimonies and statements again, thinks that's where the truth lies. Karen Holt is a private investigator who's helping me — I'll tell you more about that later. I'm not so sure though about where she wants to put her focus, her emphasis. The conspiracy theories have taken a battering over the years but I'm not convinced that they've been fully, properly explored. I was watching TV last week. *Newsnight*. An interview with an ex-spook who's written his memoirs. You get a lot of that now. This one was telling Paxman all about some operation he'd been involved in to do with the miners' strike and the NUM. But I didn't really take in what was being said so much. I was too busy looking at him, studying his face. He was older obviously. White-haired in fact. But I'd swear on my mother's grave that he was the guy I snorted coke with that night in London on the Thames cruiser. Remember? The one who'd known Claire at university? Connections like that. That's where we need to be looking in my humble opinion.

[note: good first draft. Maybe revisit later. Mention denial of access to lawyers, the 'accidental' bucket of water. But look at Boland again next. Don't shirk that. At least number Dobell — the worst of them all — the real instigator]

44

'Colin Dobell's probably out of the running, at least as far as we're concerned,' Jacobson announced.

The room was packed and suddenly, unusually, quiet. All of his core team, except for Kerr, who was still on his way back from Crowcross. Most of the duty CID who'd been co-opted onto the case over the last couple of days.

He told them why. The cloned-plate Range Rover had been apprehended an hour ago by West Mercia police — he'd just spoken to one of their DIs — on a farm road near Evesham. A crew of four had been arrested and taken into custody. *A good job and high time*, the DI had said. The crew had been busy over several months, mainly using the same vehicle but changing the plates regularly (though not regularly enough as it had turned out). Warwickshire, Worcestershire, other rural counties. *Horse box theft*: a thriving, profitable black market apparently. You scouted the country roads, noted movements, market days, even snooped around at race meetings, county fairs, watched horses and their owners. You tailed them sometimes, built up intelligence. The favoured MO was to call when the owner wasn't home, hitch a nice, new, expensive box to your towbar and fuck off. They were nasty with it too, prepared to offer violence if anybody got in their way.

The West Mercia DI had said they'd been close to catching them before. There'd been a couple of near misses recently. He reckoned that was why they'd been out Crowcross way: reconnaissance for new business. Except that the big police operation after the shootings on Monday night would have scared them off the area, had probably sent them back to their old haunts.

'The Range Rover's out then for sure,' DC Williams commented. 'But Dobell could still be in the frame, couldn't he? He still has his motive — and there's still the tongue mutilations to think about.'

'I agree he's still got his motive, Ray,' Jacobson replied, 'but we can't place him out there, that's the problem. You can reach Grove's property, as we know, without driving through Crowcross village. In which case, your vehicle avoids being logged on the misaligned pub camera.'

'We've checked every vehicle on the Crowcross Arms footage now,' Mick Hume said. 'The rest of the journeys check out as legitimate, unrelated. The Range Rover was the only dodgy card in the pack.'

'Except for Nigel Copeland's Lexus,' Emma Smith commented. 'I mean, he *visited* Martin Grove.'

'I know, I know,' Jacobson said. 'Except he's tucked up in bed at the Riverside Hotel before the murders, even on Robinson's very earliest time-of-death estimates. The CCTV says it, the hotel employees say it, the Fed Ex receipt of delivery says it. There's nothing says otherwise.'

A phone line buzzed and then, from the back of the room, Brian Phelps interrupted the discussion.

'DS Barber in Birmingham. News about Dobell. He says it's urgent.'

Jacobson took the call, asked Phelps to put it on broadcast so that they could all listen in.

'Dobell's been located, guv. Picked up at New Street Station, coming off the Glasgow train. He says he's been attending a funeral up there. Some old lag he knew from prison years ago who's croaked it from a coronary.'

Too many Mars bars deep-fried in chip fat, Jacobson thought. But he kept it to himself, didn't interrupt Barber's report.

'We suspect there's more to it, maybe meeting up with prospective partners, planning something. But his story's checking out nonetheless. Train times, local witnesses. He's been in the east end of Glasgow when your shootings took place, that's looking clear.'

'There's your answer, Ray,' Jacobson said, when the call ended.

It happened that way sometimes. You built up a theory over a period of days — and then it collapsed on top of your head within a matter of minutes.

Mick Hume asked the pertinent question on behalf of the others.

'So what next, guv?'

Jacobson walked back to the whiteboard. The front of the room — where they could all see him.

'Back to basics, old son. What else? Every

witness statement we've got, every logged camera event, every logged phone number. We need to double-check everything again. First things first — start with your own notebooks. Revisit everything you've done personally since we got going the other morning. Ask yourself: what have I missed, what am I not seeing?'

He found a spare desk with a spare computer terminal. He preferred the solitude of his own office. But there were times when you had to be *seen* to be working.

He thought about the time line again. When Maureen Bright had driven over to Jane Ebdon's, when Copeland and Smith had arrived and left, when Prakash Mishra had deposited Karen Holt on Grove's driveway, when the pathologist estimated the time of the shootings: midnight (Grove), one AM (Holt). He just sat there and thought for a long time. Then he pulled Monday's overnight Current Incident Log from the system, opened it on the screen.

Jacobson had worked with incident sheets, as they'd used to be known, more or less from his first day in CID. The sheets were electronic now but they still performed the same function as of old. They were still compiled once every twelve hours, still listed basic details of every reported incident within the time frame. They were a fundamental resource for any solid detective, told you what else was going on at any point in time that interested you. He'd already read the Monday night sheet as a matter of course. But that had been a couple of days ago — he hadn't looked at it since. He re-read carefully, line by line, highlighted everything between ten o'clock and midnight.

He saw it nearly straightaway. He got up, fetched a plastic cup of water from the cooler, sat back down, looked at it again. A car theft on Riverside Walk, logged at a quarter to twelve — although the actual reported time of the theft was eleven twenty-five. It would have been irrelevant when he'd studied the sheet before. At that stage, the entire focus was on Crowcross and what was going on out there (hapless George McCulloch in his white window-cleaning van for instance.)

He drank the water, copied and pasted the crime number, pieced as much together as he could from the computer system. He called the control room after that, asked to be patched through to the relevant patrol officer. His luck held. The guy was on duty, answered the call instantly, demonstrated a good recall of the incident.

Kerr was back in the room by now. Jacobson talked it out with him once he'd pieced it together, needed to know he wasn't flying a kite.

The Riverside area. Where Alison lived, where his friend Kenneth Grant lived. A stone's throw from the Memorial Park and the Riverside Hotel. The car had been an old-style Fiesta, a dozen years old. A teenage son's runaround vehicle nicked from the driveway outside the family home. Easy to break into, easy to hot wire. The kid had actually seen the tail-end of the theft, had looked out of his bedroom window, had seen his beloved first car disappearing out onto the road. He'd ran out — uselessly

— after it and then he'd dialled 999. The overnight patrols would have kept an eye out. But it was hardly the crime of the century and it hadn't been spotted again until the following morning. That was the strange, standout, odd detail. The Fiesta had been brought back to the area, had been abandoned on Riverside Avenue, virtually around the corner from where it had been stolen. No real damage either. Just a broken bit of fascia and the ignition wires left dangling.

'What do you think?' he asked Kerr simply when he'd talked him through it.

'Yeah, it's possible,' Kerr answered, 'at least it's all testable.'

They did what could be done immediately. Jacobson allocated the CCTV aspect to Hume and Williams. They could start in the Town Hall OCS, see if the Fiesta's route showed up on any of the Crowby camera systems. He sent Emma Smith and DC Phillips over to the hotel. They could talk to the staff again — and liaise with the SOCOs when they turned up to examine the hotel room. Kerr arranged for the Fiesta to be impounded, forensically examined. Jacobson telephoned Inspector Herzog again, impressed on him the new level of urgency.

Everything would hinge, ultimately, on cross-comparison between the samples Jacobson needed Herzog to obtain and the forensic data lifted from the two crime scenes (three crime scenes if you included the low copy DNA profile that had proved Martin Grove's innocence). That plus any crime scene matches that could be made to the Fiesta. Hot wiring a car, driving it

401

around for a couple of hours. There'd be traces all right, Jacobson thought. You could bet on that.

When everything was set up, they went off in search of DCS Greg Salter. Issuing an international arrest warrant was a complex administrative process. If Jacobson was right — and it went as far as that — then the sooner Salter and the force's hierarchy started to prepare the groundwork the better. None of it would be quick. A matter of days as a minimum. Even with everything fast-tracked at the FSS laboratories. But that wasn't necessarily a problem. Jacobson's team would need the time to fill in all the details, check and re-check every element.

Salter's office was on the eighth floor. They used the lift. Kerr followed Jacobson in when it arrived. They were the only passengers.

'The tongue mutilations, though,' Kerr said. 'How do you account for that? That's still a big coincidence.'

'Agreed, old son,' Jacobson replied. 'But only if it *is* a coincidence.'

45

Andy had paid for two hours, still had twenty minutes to go. He lay stretched out on her bed, smoking a cigarette, the ashtray propped comfortably on his stomach. She was East European, the way a lot of them were. Croatian or something. Big dark eyes, nice long legs. She was brushing her hair in front of her dressing table mirror, fussing with it. She wanted him to go now, that was obvious. It was the polite thing to do anyway, a matter of etiquette. For God's sake get dressed and leave, allow her a little interval of peace, a little time to herself. His mobile rang on the bedside table. He picked it up. Nigel: the Zurich police needed Andy to go into the station, the exact same routine that Nigel had been through yesterday. DNA, prints and a video link interview. The Crowby police had obviously put two and two together for themselves, Nigel commented. *It didn't come from me*, he added. *But so what, anyway? All we did was drive out there and talk to him.*

Nigel told him the time when the police were expecting him. He promised he'd be there to meet him along with the Swiss lawyers he'd retained. *It's nothing to worry about really.* Andy said he'd be there. Nigel signed off.

He finished his cigarette without rushing, stubbed it out on the ashtray. Thinking things over. He spoke to the girl again a minute or two later.

'Do me a favour, love. Go out and buy me a bottle of whisky. Make sure it's a decent brand. I'll pay for another hour. I just want to lie here for a while. Enjoy a quiet glass.'

She rolled her eyes, cursed (probably) in her own language. He was upsetting her way of working, he knew that, disturbing her routine. He stood up, found his wallet, took out a ludicrously high amount for the small, extra services he wanted. That did it. She pulled on her jeans and a sweater, took the money, came back with the bottle inside five minutes. That was what he liked about whores, what he'd come to appreciate over the years. You paid your money and you got what you came for. You didn't get short-changed — or abandoned, left behind, suddenly surplus to requirements.

It was like fire going off inside your throat and your belly — or like fireworks exploding in your head. Loud colours. A deep simultaneous rush of well-being and excitement. No matter how long you'd left off, the first sip, the first glass, did it every time. Welcome home. Bienvenue. Willkommen.

He only drank a third of the bottle. That was enough for now, enough to start him up. He left her the rest. She looked at him warily as he was leaving. Glad to see him go, not liking his unpredictability despite the cash. He left the hired Merc where he'd parked it, used a taxi to get across town instead. The driver dropped him on Talstrasse and he walked the rest of the way. He detoured, needlessly, along Bahnhofstrasse for the final stretch. But that was the way he wanted to go.

He reached Bürkliplatz down on the lakeshore just in time for the next sailing. He bought a round trip ticket to Rapperswil, the furthest destination along the lake, and made his way to the embarkation point, joined the queue of passengers boarding the lake boat. Tourists mainly — the sailing at this hour was on one of the historic steamers. There'd be music later, maybe a barbecue on deck.

He went into the restaurant as soon as it opened, secured a table with a good view out over the water. He only wanted the simplest thing to eat. A Wiener schnitzel, a side order of vegetables. But he ordered a good bottle of wine to go with it. A nice Mosel. The wine was the important feature as far as he was concerned. The waiter asked him if he also wanted water. But he didn't. He only wanted the wine.

He'd expected the tongue mutilations to throw them off the scent, send them in the wrong direction. His mind had leaped on that detail from the moment Martin had mentioned it to him and Nigel. He'd underestimated them obviously. Nothing stood still. Just because they were as thick as shit years ago didn't mean that they still were.

Back then they'd scarcely troubled him, scarcely troubled any of them. They had the man, the motive, the confession and that was it as far as they were concerned. Martin was theirs, stuffed, cooked, sliced up and served. You'd think maybe, if you'd no personal experience of it, that you couldn't live with guilt like that. Yet you could. You did. When something's done it's done. You can't undo it, can't apologise for it, can't take it back like an insult you didn't really mean.

You could look at it all and say that at least the drinking had been a consequence of it, a punishment. That it had driven him to it, driven him down into the gutter where he richly belonged. But you could look at it the other way, see that the drinking had been a prime cause or had certainly been a link in the chain. He'd been drunk that day. Of course he had. Pissed as a rat down in the basement, drinking himself pie-eyed while everyone else was out building the revolution. He probably hadn't been noisy either, might even have dozed off drunkenly for a while. Claire wouldn't have known he was there anyway, that he hadn't gone into Crowby with the others. She and Martin had been up in her room all morning. Not having sex for once but reciting poetry to each other, loudly at times. It was a cottage joke by then — Claire educating Martin like he was Eliza Doolittle or something.

He'd heard her on the phone when she'd got back, up in the hall, hadn't believed what he was hearing at first.

He was halfway through the wine before his food arrived. He poured himself out a new glassful, took a deep, full mouthful before he started eating. He wondered if there'd be time for a second bottle.

He'd confronted her, of course he had. The call had gone on. Ten minutes, maybe longer. Certainly long enough for him to form an opinion.

'It's not what you think,' she'd said.

She'd heard him by then, heard his feet creaking on the stairs, had clicked the receiver down instantly, mid-sentence. She was still there when he reached her. Standing next to the telephone, not sure what to do.

'Isn't it?' he'd asked her — then quoted some of it back to her.

She'd been keeping tabs on all of them — since day one by the sound of it. Names, backgrounds, contacts, risk categories, levels of extremism.

'No, you've got it wrong, Andy,' she'd said. 'Entirely wrong — *Jesus*.'

She'd even smiled at him then. Her you'd-like-to-fuck-me-but-you-can't smile. She really shouldn't have done that. Not made him think about her and Martin — or about Nigel banged up for something he actually believed in, putting himself on the line.

'Have I?'

'Yes you have — it's all about *disinformation*, feeding them what we like. Lies, distortion. *Jesus*. If they think they know what's going on that gives us the breathing space we need. It's standard RCV practice, Andy. *Dis*-fucking-information.'

Maybe she'd moved away from him a little by then. A first inkling.

He'd brought his latest bottle of rice wine up with him from the basement. He'd stood there staring at her and taken a long swig. He'd cornered her too — without really thinking about it, without really realising it. He had her against the wall. Shut in. The smile vanished from her face.

'There's not much to report about you anyway. Is there? Drinks like a fish and then falls over. Hilary's had it with you — you realise that, don't you? Had enough drunken fucking fumbles.'

He hit her. Really hit her. She fought back at first, kneeing him, trying to kick his shins. Then all she wanted to do was get away. She squeezed past him somehow and then she was out the front door. Running. He thought she was making for her car but she ran on past it, evidently didn't have the key with her.

He'd have caught her easier or sooner if he hadn't been pissed. And some of it was her own stupid fault. She could have run onto the airfield, thrown herself on the mercy of the piggy guards — or kept to the road, maybe flagged down a vehicle if there'd been one. It takes two to tango after all.

He'd flung her to the ground when he'd caught her. She was no match for his strength even although he was six sheets to the wind.

When it was over, when he'd killed her, he'd just thrown the stone he'd used as far as he could fling it from the spot. He'd no idea why they hadn't found it or where all the courtroom nonsense about a hammer had come from. He'd walked back to the cottage after that. He'd washed, changed his clothes and burned the ones he'd been wearing in the backyard. There was more or less a permanent little fire kept going out there. People liked to sit around it in the evenings, listen to Oliver with his guitar. The embers were rarely completely cool. He'd chucked his bloody, mucky clothes in the middle, got the flames going again. Then he'd gone inside, made himself a coffee, waited for the others to return to the cottage.

He decided against more wine when he'd finished his meal. He wanted schnapps instead — and a good beer to wash it down. He glanced out of the window. The sun had started to set over the lake. Up on deck the tourists would be gawping at the loveliness of it all.

The first days of guilt are the dangerous ones. The ones where you're most likely to crack under the strain. If you can get through the first weeks and months then you can keep on going. They all knew that Martin would plead not guilty — and Andy also possessed the secret, certain knowledge that he wasn't guilty. He had Alan Slingsby on his side after all and later on some bigwig left-wing barrister too. All summer and into the winter, Andy convinced himself he'd get off, walk out of the court a free man. When the trial went against Martin, Andy scarpered, vanished from the area, broke the few contacts he still had with anybody from the protest. The drinking and the guilt combined against him from then on. That was how he saw it now. He'd drank and drank and drank to blank it out. Quite literally to forget. And drinking had brought him low, as low as you could go. Somehow that made it all right. He'd stolen Martin's freedom but he hadn't done anything worth doing with it. He wasn't triumphing at

Martin's expense — he was suffering alongside him. That's why he'd stuck new, fat cat Nigel's patronising, demeaning job too — and why he still had to throw a bender from time to time, still relapse, never, ever, allow himself to be really, properly free.

There would be those who'd think the guilt of it all had finally got to him. That's what they'd say or write later. But they'd be wrong. He'd found a way of living with guilt for decades now, would have gone on living with it if he could. No, it was a question of consistency in the end, of staying true to his own little routines, his own little habits. When your whole existence was founded on getting away with something, that became your first reflex, your primary duty. Always, everywhere. He couldn't bear to be caught, that was all. In a way, getting caught would be even more unfair to Martin. A final insult. His guilt was only about Martin, he'd often reflected. Claire had been gone, finished, from that time in the wood. There was no point to guilt about Claire. No point at all.

He paid his bill in cash, rounded it up to a generous tip. He wandered the decks, got the feel of the layout. He didn't think he looked drunk. He didn't think he stood out. He could always hold it well, he thought, for the first few days of a fresh, new binge.

Martin had let him in, had been a few seconds too late in apprehending the danger. He'd been a hero at the end though. Putting himself between the woman and the gun, even trying to grapple with him, not showing any kind of fear, going

410

out in glory. The woman had taken her chance, had run into the front garden — had kept on running. She'd been fast too, in good shape. She'd reached the wood ahead of him, had tried hiding. But he'd found her easily enough. Everybody who'd lived out at the cottage had known Crowcross Wood like the back of their hand. He'd shot her as soon as he'd found her. No funny business of course. She wasn't Claire, she wasn't anything to him. He'd worked quickly after that. Tongues, computers — and then the weapon thrown into the Crow on the return journey. He'd had his gun for a while now, hadn't heeded Nigel's warning in the slightest. It was easy enough to score a Walther in Manchester. It was virtually a buyer's market, you could even haggle about the price. You couldn't be too careful, that was his view — what with the way things were these days.

He decided on the stern. The easiest point of access to the lake and not too many passengers around. Even then, he lingered for a while, chose a particularly quiet moment. It was dark now and maybe there was some kind of official motor vessel catching up to them, churning up waves. It didn't matter, he'd never know. He heaved himself over the side, surprised at the speed he managed. He surfaced a couple of times, unwanted automatic reflexes kicking in. But he got that under control easily enough. Just hang limp, he told himself. Go with the flow of the water.

APPENDIX:

HISTORICAL TIMELINE

1983
- October 22 Campaign for Nuclear Disarmament Rally, Hyde Park, London
- October 31 Martin Grove hitches a lift from Claire Oldham
- November 14 First Cruise missiles arrive at Greenham Common, Berkshire
- November 27 Police clash with peace demonstrators at Crowcross Airfield, Crowby

1984
- March 12 Arthur Scargill, NUM president, declares national miners' strike
- March 21 Hilda Murrell, anti-nuclear campaigner and rose grower, murdered in Shrewsbury
- May 5 Claire Oldham murdered
- June 18 Police clash with striking miners at Orgreave, Staffordshire
- October 12 IRA bomb attack on Conservative Party Conference at the Grand Hotel, Brighton
- October 15 Trial of Martin Grove begins, Birmingham Crown Court

1985
- March 3 National miners' strike ends
- March 7 Sizewell B enquiry ends, Suffolk
- June 1 The 'Battle of the Beanfield', Wiltshire

We do hope that you have enjoyed reading this large print book.

Did you know that all of our titles are available for purchase?

We publish a wide range of high quality large print books including:
Romances, Mysteries, Classics
General Fiction
Non Fiction and Westerns

Special interest titles available in large print are:
The Little Oxford Dictionary
Music Book
Song Book
Hymn Book
Service Book

Also available from us courtesy of Oxford University Press:
Young Readers' Dictionary
(large print edition)
Young Readers' Thesaurus
(large print edition)

For further information or a free brochure, please contact us at:
Ulverscroft Large Print Books Ltd.,
The Green, Bradgate Road, Anstey,
Leicester, LE7 7FU, England.
Tel: (00 44) 0116 236 4325
Fax: (00 44) 0116 234 0205

Other titles published by
The House of Ulverscroft:

CUT HER DEAD

Iain McDowall

Brady, Annabel, Maria, Adrian. Four bright, sexy, nice-looking twenty-somethings leading the high life at other people's expense. Fighting their perpetual apathy with an interesting hobby: abducting and terrifying young women, burying them alive — and calling it 'art'. Except now they seem to have moved their creative base of operations into Crowby. And unless DCI Frank Jacobson and DS Ian Kerr can crack the case in time — Brady and company may soon be graduating to murder.

LX